JERICHO 3

3 APRIL 2014

ALSO FROM
PAUL McKELLIPS

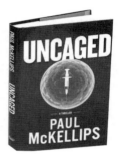

In a thrill a minute read, author Paul McKellips poses a frightening "what if" scenario that will leave the human race on the brink of certain disaster. When a series of attacks on animal researchers leave several people dead, the government—including the President—issues an immediate ban on animal testing. And that's when the real trouble begins…

At the heart of the action are two government agents, the dashing Commander "Camp" Campbell, a man as decorated for his bravery in Iraq as for his own self-professed charm. Lieutenant Colonel Leslie Raines is the more practical of the two, a woman defined by her dedication to rules. Camp has returned to the States, newly reassigned to a government-funded test site. When the ban on animals comes down, Camp pulls a restless act by making off with two hundred rats…and winds up in deep trouble. He is immediately banished for a year, his superiors hoping the ramifications of his stunt will have worn off by then. Raines, uncharacteristically covering for him, finds herself joining him. But where they are headed only increases the risk—both to themselves, to the scientist whose very existence is threatened…and the future of the human race.

Who is really behind the ban on animal testing? And why? Could a deadly, dangerous fanatical group be behind the threat of a new vein of plague sweeping across the country… or worse, could it be someone people have come to trust?

JERICHO 3

BY
PAUL MᶜKELLIPS

FIRST EDITION: July 2012

Published by FBR Press
Foundation for Biomedical Research
818 Connecticut Avenue, NW
Washington, DC 20006

Manufactured in the United States of America
ISBN: 978-0-9853322-0-4

Library of Congress Cataloging-in-Publication data are on file.
0987654321

Cover design by Patrick King, ImagineDesign
Author photo by Liz Hodge

FBR Press

Dedicated to
Rafed, Samir, Mohanned, Raouf and Jawed
in Iraq and Afghanistan

ACRONYMS

AAR	After-Action Report
ABP	Afghan Border Patrol
ANA	Afghan National Army
BUAV	British Union for the Abolition of Vivisection
BSL	Bio Safety Level
BW	Biological Weapons
CAC	Common Access Card
CW	Chemical Weapons
CW2	Chief Warrant Officer, Two and commissioned by the President
DFAC	Dining Facility
FATA	Federally Administered Tribal Area of Pakistan
FOB	Forward Operating Base
HUMINT	Human Intelligence
IRF	Integrated Research Facility
ISAF	International Security Assistance Force Joint Command
ISI	Pakistan's Inter-Services Intelligence
LZ	Landing Zone
MILAIR	Military Air
MWR	Morale, Welfare and Recreation
MRAP	Mine Resistant Ambush Protected
NHP	Non-Human Primates
NIBC	National Interagency Biodefense Center
ODA	Operation Detachment Alpha
PET	Positron Emission Tomography
PETN	Pentaerythritol tetranitrate (military explosive)
SF	Special Forces
SHAC	Stop Huntingdon Animal Cruelty
TMC	Troop Medical Clinic
WMD	Weapons of Mass Destruction

JERICHO 3

PROLOGUE

Forward Operating Base Lightning
Paktya Province, Afghanistan

They left the briefing with the Minnesota National Guard Colonel in the Tactical Operations Center and walked quickly through a row of B-huts on FOB Lightning. The clouds were low and heavy with snow. A light dusting of powdered snow covered the gravel.

"Did you hear him?"

"I heard him, captain. Just let it go."

US Army Captain Henry shook his head in disgust. "That's not how they taught us at the Academy; I can assure you of that."

"Captain, let it go."

"How can you say just 'let it go'? This is freaking tularemia, maybe a bio-weapon, and this idiot who teaches 'lit' in Saint Pete, Minnesota when he's not a weekend warrior tells us not worry to about it…tells us he's not going to elevate it."

"Well, now you're speaking to a weekend warrior from Bucks County, Pennsylvania. Feel any better?" asked Major Dean Banks, United States Army Reserves.

Captain Henry held his tongue. They walked past the dining hall and up the gravel road. Major Banks stopped and turned around.

"Look up there, Henry. Do you see them?"

Major Banks and Captain Henry lifted their eyes to the two hills that rose up from the valley floor. Mountain peaks encircled the valley. Soldiers from the army of Alexander the Great had built massive observation fortresses on each hill. For months they pulled stones and boulders up from the valley floor to build circular sentinel fortresses. No advancing army had any chance of surprising Alexander the Great.

"Battle outposts. Alexander the Great. Not exactly a news flash, sir. They've been here since 323 AD."

"Genghis Khan came. The Russians came. Now the Americans have come. Every one of them had front-line sentinels, scouts whose job it was to sound the alert."

"Roger that, major. But the colonel took your alert and buried it deep within the infinite wisdom of a PhD. No offense, sir, but I don't think he's used to working with a gynecologist."

Banks laughed. "I'm not accustomed to working with professors of literature either. But Uncle Sam is going to get a tour out of all of us, one way or the other. Don't worry, captain. I informed the colonel, but I also sounded the alarm back at Fort Detrick and with Command at ISAF headquarters in Kabul. Battalion surgeons, Reserves or National Guard, have a slightly different chain of command, especially when it comes to infectious diseases."

They walked past the male latrines and the basketball court where some Army Joes were playing four-on-four in the brisk February breeze. The first dusting of snow had just covered the mountain peaks of the Hindu Kush heading over into Pakistan. Pulling the bolt lock back, they walked into the holding pen in front of the checkpoint. Thirty Afghan day-laborers were waiting to move through the turnstiles. They were searched on the way in each morning to make sure they weren't carrying weapons or suicide vests and searched on the way out to make sure they hadn't stolen anything as they cleaned American latrines, emptied American trash and mopped American floors. One path at the checkpoint led down to Terp Village, a small village within FOB Lightning's walls comprised of 10 small B-huts with bunk beds where all of the foreign national interpreters lived. Next to Terp Village were seven Haji shops where the GI's could buy pirated DVDs, batteries, Afghan rugs, or a carton of smokes.

Miriam was sitting on the wood bench, on time and ready for work.

"As-salaamu' alaykum," Banks said as he covered his heart with his hand.

"Sahaar mo pa kheyr," Miriam replied scanning the

morning sky.

"Every day you wear that same cheerful smile, Miriam…and that precious necklace. Is that crystal?" Banks asked.

"I don't know. It was a gift from my husband."

"Miriam is taking a three day leave after work next Thursday, Major Banks," said Captain Henry.

"Great. I'm sure you're anxious to see your son," Banks said as they all walked toward the checkpoint.

Miriam had a pleasant personality and at times, an infectious smile could dash across her face. Like most Afghan interpreters, Miriam wanted the money but she didn't like to work. Even though she was on call every day and every night, she was seldom required to work more than an hour or two each day. Major Banks thought he had found a soft spot in Miriam's personality armor. He always had a kind word and a compliment for Miriam and the major hoped she was warming up to him.

Duty guards from the 101st Airborne Division waived them through as Major Banks and Captain Henry walked past the plain-clothed Gurkha guards from Nepal with Miriam trailing a few steps behind. The Gurkhas were slight of build and not much to look at, but they were ruthless. They made fine mercenaries and their allegiance could be bought for $25 per day, seven days a week, on a six-month contract. They were effective. No one had successfully penetrated Lightning's checkpoint since the suicide bomber detonated at the gate a few years before.

When Major Banks and Captain Henry walked out of the Lightning checkpoint, they walked onto Forward Operating Base Thunder, the sprawling Afghan National Army base and home to the 203rd Corps. The Paktya Regional Hospital was only the length of a football field away from the checkpoint, a short walk along a nicely paved, American taxpayer-funded road on Thunder. A click behind the hospital a Russian Mi-17 lifted up and set its path toward Gardez. The Afghan Army preferred the Russian helicopters for high elevation terrain. Most of the Afghan officers and pilots spoke and read Russian. It was easier for them.

"Never have quite figured that one out," Banks said as he watched the Mi-17 thunder overhead. "The Russians come here, invade, and occupy for 10 years. They were the enemy."

"But they bought loyalty," Captain Henry surmised. "Rubles. A man can smile at you, speak your language, and offer you tea for 10 years or more…as long as you're handing out money."

An Afghan ambulance with lights on, but no siren, passed the three of them and pulled into the hospital parking lot close to the Emergency Room entrance.

"There ya go; a Ford Ranger ambulance brought to you by Detroit and paid for by American taxpayers," Captain Henry started. "American, Russian, Chinese, Pakistani, Iranian…the Afghans don't give a damn who you are or what you think you're going to do with their country. They'll just wait you out and suck all your money until you go home."

Miriam kept her eyes down as Captain Henry finished his rant.

"They teach you all that at West Point?" asked Major Banks.

Captain Henry stopped, turned around, and pointed to the ancient battle outposts perched high atop the valley. "No…your Alexander the Great did. Isn't that right, Miriam? Y'all are just going to wait us out."

Miriam was accustomed to speeches by Captain Henry and every other American officer she had worked under for the previous four years. That's why she hated them, all of them; all of them except Major Banks. At least that's how Banks saw it.

The three walked through the front doors of Paktya Regional Hospital as 10 workers gathered around the front desk stood to greet them. Miriam walked around the entrance wall to her little desk space and sat down. No one had a computer or traditional office equipment. One long row of fluorescent lights lit the corridor between the front desk and the ER. The recovery bay was halfway down the other corridor. It was an open room with 20 beds which was usually filled to capacity.

"Doctor Mahmoud just went down to ER," said Abdul, the front desk manager.

"ANA?" asked Captain Henry.

"No, not Afghan National Army this time. An elder," Abdul answered.

Piping hot green tea was served in the same unwashed cups used every day prior, as Major Banks sipped to be gracious while sorting through patient records.

"How's our isolation ward this morning?" Banks asked to no one in particular.

Abdul tried to answer but quickly gave up and looked over to Miriam and rattled off several phrases in Pashtu.

"All three tularemia patients are resting comfortably. He thinks the room is a bio-containment ward so no one has gone in to see them yet today."

"Have they been fed?" asked Banks, now slightly agitated.

Abdul shook his head. Major Banks and Captain Henry stood quickly as did Miriam. Banks reached for a new set of examination gloves and a sterile face mask. Henry did the same. Miriam pulled her necklace off, unhooked the clasp, and let the solitary glass bead slide off into her hand as she put the bead into the decorative glass vase on her desk. The vase was filled with hundreds of glass beads that supported the stems of her artificial flowers. She removed a tiny metal flask, dabbed a splash of oriental spice perfume on the inside of her wrist and poured the rest of the flask into a plastic iced tea bottle she had taken one day from the DFAC dining facility after a working lunch.

Miriam's flowers were the only colors in a very dreary hospital.

"Abdul, send Doctor Mahmoud down to the isolation ward as soon as he's out of the ER."

"Yes, Dr. Banks."

Two armed guards with the ANA stood outside the door of the isolation ward as Banks, Henry and Miriam entered. The guards followed but stopped just inside the door. Three ragged members of the Taliban were lying in their beds, two heads positioned against one wall, one head against the other. The beds were simple metal twin beds moved over from the Afghan barracks.

"A few days ago we collected some respiratory secretions and blood from each of you," Major Banks said as he paused for Miriam's translation.

"I don't know this word…secretions?" Miriam asked before she translated.

"Fluids."

As Miriam spoke the Taliban patients wouldn't look her in the eyes even though she was wearing the hijab head scarf.

"I got the results back from our hospital lab in Bagram. Each of you has tularemia, or rabbit fever. The lesions you see on your skin are also inside your intestines and in your lungs. That's why you're having trouble breathing. It feels like pneumonia. You run a fever while you experience chills. You feel cold. Your body aches"

Each of the three looked at their own skin ulcers as Miriam spoke.

"One case of tularemia is rare. Three cases could be

an epidemic. I need to ask you some questions. I need to find out where you were and what you were doing when you became sick."

As Miriam translated, the oldest Taliban patient rolled over on his side and faced the back wall away from Major Banks.

Major Banks and Captain Henry noticed the attitude. This was not going to go well.

"I have brought medicines with me. If I give you these medicines, you will live. Now that we know what this is, we no longer need to isolate you. The hospital can use normal biosafety level precautions now. But if you refuse the medicine, then your organs will shut down. You will lose weight. The lesions on your hands will form inside your eyes…then your eyes may burn in their sockets with ulcers that will boil like acid…until you die."

The youngest Taliban patient sat up quickly in bed and spoke directly to Miriam.

"He says that he has a wife and a young son and that he is willing to die but prefers not to die today. He is willing to take the medicines," Miriam said.

Abdul opened the door to the isolation ward and delivered Dr. Mahmoud as instructed. Mahmoud was slight of build and his youth was punctuated with an obnoxious laugh and endless nervous tension. Nothing was calming about Dr. Mahmoud as he walked into the ward, fresh from pronouncing a Zazai tribe elder dead in the ER after a less than urgent ambulance ride.

"Tell them Dr. Mahmoud will give them ciprofloxacin twice daily through an IV for 10 days. After that, they can go home, but they'll need to take more pills," Major Banks said to Miriam as he looked up to see Mahmoud.

Miriam translated as much as she understood as Dr. Mahmoud started visiting with his patients. The oldest Taliban patient rolled over and covered his heart with his hand as the Afghan doctor walked by. Mahmoud touched his shoulder.

"Zar ba yi ter lasa kri, my brother, get well soon."

Then Banks, Henry and Mahmoud left the isolation ward and walked toward the emergency room followed by Miriam.

"What was all that bull about their eyes boiling like acid?" Captain Henry said trying to hold back a laugh.

"Sometimes pictures are worth a thousand of Miriam's words."

"Doctor Banks?"

"Yes, Dr. Mahmoud."

"This tularemia…is it contagious?"

"Francisella tularensis is very infectious. It'll knock your socks off. Less than 10 microbes of the bacteria and you're infected. We haven't seen any proof that it's *contagious,* as in from me to you. But it's still a Category A bioterrorism agent like the plague and anthrax."

"So then it can be transferred from one person to another, Dr. Banks?"

"Not that we know of. There's a difference between

infectious and contagious. It's only on the Cat A list because it could be lethal and widespread if it got into the food or water supply. So far, the bad guys haven't figured out how to make an infectious aerosol for it."

Captain Henry stopped in the hallway. He was not entirely satisfied with the major's reasoning.

"So three Taliban thugs show up in our hospital with rabbit fever, and we're going to chalk it up to random happenstance?"

"To the contrary, I suspect the three of them feasted on some infected and undercooked meat in one of their four-star Hilton caves, captain. But you're probably correct."

"Sir?"

"I'm guessing it was rabbit."

Banks, Henry, Mahmoud and Miriam walked into the ER where Banks removed a box of ciprofloxacin and IV kits that had been flown in from Bagram Air Base.

The radio in the ER crackled to life. Mahmoud answered the call using the handheld microphone as Banks and Henry prepared the medication.

"That was the checkpoint at Thunder," Mahmoud said. "The ambulance is bringing in Colonel Sadik's wife."

"Who's Sadik?" Banks asked as he staged the IVs on a surgical tray.

"He's the head of the ANA Commando unit here on Thunder," Mahmoud said.

"What's her problem?"

"They don't know. The checkpoint guard said she's screaming in pain and holding her stomach. Probably a female issue."

"Probably so," Banks said showing a substantial lack of interest. American doctors were in Afghanistan to take care of American soldiers as well as mentor and train Afghan physicians. They were not deployed to treat Afghan civilians.

"Dr. Banks, you are expert in woman medicine. I am best at colostomy."

Henry laughed. "Damn right! A 13-year-old kid comes in here last month with a sore throat...maybe tonsils. Doc Mahmoud got him all fixed up and sent him out the door with a colostomy!"

"You gave the kid a bag shitter? For a sore throat?" Banks quipped.

"When I studied at Kabul School of Medicine my teachers showed me how to do colostomies. Now I'm expert."

"Well, don't give Colonel Commando's wife a bag, or he's liable to shoot you," Banks said as the IV tray was fully prepped.

"Please, I beg you Dr. Banks; please consult with me on this woman. I need training."

Banks stopped and rolled his eyes at Mahmoud.

"Okay, your English is pretty good. Captain, I'll join Dr. Mahmoud for a 'woman medicine' consult. Can you and Miriam take this stuff down to our 'tularemia trio' and get them hooked up to the juice tree?"

"Roger that, sir."

Captain Henry wheeled the cart down the fluorescent lit corridor followed by Miriam 10 steps behind.

The back doors of the ER flew open as the deep anguished screams of a woman, and lots of Pashtu chatter that made no sense to Banks, echoed throughout the cinder-block ER.

"You get her vitals," Banks directed the Afghan physician, "and ask if she's willing to see an American doctor. Make sure you tell her I'm an American Army gynecologist. I don't want the Afghan colonel's wife going all Jihad Jane on me if I show up unannounced to take a peek at her girl parts, okay?"

Mahmoud nodded and disappeared behind the curtains. He sat down on his rolling stool so that only his well-worn Puma sneakers, dirty pants and the bottom of his lab coat could be seen. Banks could hear Mahmoud talking over the woman's groans. Both ambulance drivers tried to keep her quiet.

The woman stopped groaning after Mahmoud finished speaking. There was a pause.

"Sha!" the woman moaned.

Still seated, Mahmoud pushed his rolling stool across the tiled floor and beyond the curtain's edge.

"Dr. Banks, the woman said okay."

With stethoscope around his neck, Banks walked up and inside the crowded exam room. The ambulance drivers looked at him, covered their hearts, and smiled. The woman was still writhing in pain, though much quieter. Banks practiced the entire Pashtu lexicon he had committed to memory.

"*As salam aleikum. Ze la Amerika.* Doctor Banks."

The drivers put their hands to their hearts again then quickly back to the arms of the patient who needed some restraint.

"*Aya ta pe…po-he-gy Englesi?*" Banks asked.

The woman shook her head no.

Mahmoud stayed seated on his stool while Banks put the stethoscope's acoustic buds into his ears and reached out slowly toward the woman's neck. The stainless steel chest piece had a pink breast cancer bow on the top side as well as pink single-lumen tubing up to the splitter connection.

Banks was watching the woman as she stopped groaning. Her face softened and her eyes fixated on the pink bow, just as violent pain raced through his skull and the major's lights went out.

The Ford Ranger's tire iron crashed against the back of Banks' head as Dr. Mahmoud watched his mentor fall face-first onto the now silent and very healthy woman.

One of the ambulance drivers pulled Banks up so the woman could get off the gurney. Mahmoud pulled out a vial and syringe. He pressed the needle into the vial and pulled the plunger back. A fine mist filled the air before he inserted the hypodermic needle into the bare arm of Major Banks. Mahmoud injected Banks with a full dose of ketamine that he had taken out of the meds cabinet earlier in the morning. Ketamine was the sedation drug of choice in Afghanistan and Mahmoud reasoned the hallucinations from the drug might not be as frightening as the reality Banks would soon face.

The other ambulance attendant wheeled in a second gurney from the Ford Ranger as the now fully-recovered woman and the other driver wheeled Banks out into the waiting ambulance. Mahmoud got into the new bed.

The driver bound Dr. Mahmoud's upper and lower torso with leather restraint straps.

"Zar ba yi ter lasa kri," the driver whispered to Mahmoud as he pulled off a six-inch strip of duct tape.

"I will if you don't cut me too deep," Mahmoud said as he laid back and closed his eyes.

The driver pulled a fresh scalpel out of its sterile surgical paper and gently tilted Mahmoud's head back as though he was a barber preparing for a straight-edge shave. The incision was four inches long but only deep enough to trickle blood. The bloody scalpel was left on Mahmoud's chest.

The ER doors closed and the engine of the Ford Ranger ambulance disappeared into background noise long before a distant siren was ever heard.

Mahmoud smiled as he considered the checkpoint guards. They wouldn't have the courage to check on "the Commando Colonel's wife" – supposedly the important "patient" in the ambulance – as she was driven through the main checkpoint gates of FOB Thunder, home to the 203rd Corps of the Afghan National Army and riding in a new Ford Ranger ambulance, bought and paid for by American taxpayers.

Mahmoud heard the approaching footsteps of Captain Henry and Miriam returning down the long fluorescent-lit corridor from the isolation ward. It was time to act terrified.

PART ONE

1

Section 60

The band leader stepped out in precision carrying a silver sword tucked in a ram-rod straight right arm that glistened against his dress blues. Behind him and off to the left the flag bearer carried the unit's colors followed by the conductor with baton grasped tightly.

The music from the United States Army Band echoed and consumed the fog that hovered over Arlington, partially masking the view of the Lincoln Memorial across the Potomac.

It wasn't just a band. It was Pershing's Own.

Five rows of four marched with the fidelity of one as though they played for angels. Three trombones next to a French horn in the first row, then two saxophones, another French horn and a clarinet. There was a trumpet, two more clarinets and another trumpet in the third. Trumpets only in the fourth row followed by a bass drum, trumpet, tuba and snare drum in the fifth.

US Navy Captain "Camp" Campbell searched the

souls lying in neatly measured rows of eternal rest, looking for heroes that might raise their heads and salute from their perches in heaven as yet another fallen soldier from a distant hell was brought home.

Six rows of two riflemen each followed like clockwork, white gloves pressed against freshly-oiled gunstock. The color guard trailed the rifle party and was anchored with riflemen on both sides, an Army flag bearer marched center left with stars and stripes center right.

The chaplain walked quietly behind the color guard, taking his place in a ceremony he had conducted twice that morning with five more yet to come.

Six fully tacked white Percherons led the 3rd US Infantry, 1st Battalion "Caisson Platoon" as the flag-draped casket, secured by two leather straps, rolled in step. The four old wooden wheels rotated bicep-high on the casket party, four on each side of the procession.

Eileen walked directly behind Jane. She was the older sister. She had always stayed a few steps behind Jane just to make sure she was okay even when they were children. Now Eileen could only wonder what her little sister was doing, who she was talking with, or if Jane was finally settled and just watching her own funeral in restful silence. Eileen's chin was up as she walked with purpose, never taking her eye off the flag that covered her little sister's war-torn body.

Camp angled his right arm in as Eileen's arm joined his tightly. Had Jane's Blackhawk not crashed in Iraq,

Camp and Jane would have been married by now. Instead, Camp prayed that God would forgive him for supporting Eileen's decision to pull Jane's life support five days earlier. For nearly 20 months after the helicopter crash in the deserts of Iraq, Jane slept in a persistent vegetative state until all hope was gone.

US Army Lieutenant Colonel Leslie Raines bowed her left arm in as Eileen's other arm hooked in tightly. Raines feared she might feel out of place, that she shouldn't feel so close to Jane, and that perhaps she should not have feelings for Camp. But her thoughts grew clear and singular as the procession rolled down a small road, past World War I vintage oak trees and came to a halt in the most recent of hallowed grounds.

This was Section 60, Arlington National Cemetery.

The rest of the mourners left their cars on the road and gathered around the simple canopy where Eileen, Camp and Leslie took seats in the first row. Camp's parents, Sea Bee and Ruth, sat stoically in the second row to bid farewell to the daughter-in-law they never had. Eileen and Jane had lost their parents years before. No other extended family members had the resources to travel to Washington, DC from Muleshoe, Texas. It would be a 20-minute funeral service for a war hero who died more than a year before she was ever pronounced dead.

The first of three volleys from the seven-soldier rifle party pierced the solemn Arlington air with a penetrating jolt. The other two volleys were anticipated.

A solitary bugler blew a solemn Taps from a crest on a nearby hillside, surrounded on three sides by simple white head stones.

The chaplain preached his sermon and held his Bible open though he never looked down for the words he already knew. The sermon was sincere, but the repetition of the words was ingrained and seared into his memory.

The flag from Jane's casket was folded with elegant tradition and accuracy. Three spent shell casings from the rifle party were discreetly placed into the folds of the flag.

Standing two rows deep, Brigadier General Jim Ferguson swallowed back a tear as the flag bearer moved closer to Eileen. Ferguson had been Jane's commanding officer in Iraq. He was Colonel Ferguson back then, when Captain Jane Manning flew MEDEVAC missions into the Balad Trauma Center as Navy Commander "Camp" Campbell, SEAL turned trauma surgeon, brought most of them back to life in a tent hospital during endless 20-hour shifts.

Eileen raised her eyes with the intensity of a battle-hardened ER nurse, a career she had embraced for many years, as the flag-bearer approached.

"Ma'am, on behalf of the President of the United States and the people of a grateful nation, may I present this flag as a token of appreciation for the honorable and faithful service your loved one rendered this nation."

Mourners filed past Jane's casket, some pausing to

remember, some reaching out to touch her for the last time.

When all had left the gravesite they paused at their cars to watch one solitary sailor who stood isolated, guarding Jane's casket while standing at attention.

Camp had given his heart to Jane in Iraq. He had slept on the floor by her bed in Gettysburg on and off for nearly 20 months, as she lay silently. Now he was forced to say good-bye.

Camp rendered a final salute. He removed his lid and knelt next to her one last time. He smiled as he remembered getting down on his knee in scrubs, proposing to Jane between surgeries and her flight missions. She had laughed at his chivalry while all of the nurses, medics and recovering soldiers applauded in the recovery bay.

There were no jewelry stores in Iraq and no time to shop in the Haji mart. So he used a black Sharpie and drew a ring around her finger and asked the love of *his* life to spend the rest of *her* life with him.

And she did.

"Fair winds and following seas, Captain Jane," he said as tears trickled down his cheeks. "And long may your big jibs draw." The seafarer's prayer and blessing gave Camp little comfort, but he hoped it would release Jane to take her rightful place in both Arlington and in heaven.

Camp kissed her casket and caressed her face through the wood one last time.

General Ferguson was offering his condolences to Eileen when Camp walked up. Raines walked over and grabbed Camp's hand.

"Are you okay, sailor?" Raines whispered.

Camp looked over into her eyes and lit up her heart with a reassuring smile. "Jane's finally home...she's at peace." He was torn by a million emotions but relieved that Leslie Raines was at his side.

"Sir, I suppose you have attended far too many funerals at Arlington," Eileen said as General Ferguson walked up to extend his condolences.

"Yes, young soldiers like Jane are the most difficult. When I was a boy, my father was the attending veterinarian for the Old Guard. I saw far too many funerals here, young boys who came home from Vietnam one last time. I practically grew up on Fort Myer. For 15 years, my dad took care of Black Jack."

"Black Jack was a presidential celebrity," said Camp as he joined the conversation.

"Indeed he was. A Morgan-American quarter horse, he was the rider-less horse that carried turned in boots for almost 30 years. I never cried so hard as when Black Jack died in 1976. He almost made it to his 30th birthday."

"General, we're having a reception for Jane out in Gettysburg tomorrow afternoon. I hope you'll join us," said Eileen.

"I wish I could. I really wanted to see your infamous 'research lab.' But I fear duty calls. The

Chairman of the Joint Chiefs needs to see me, something about a tularemia outbreak."

"Rabbit fever?" asked Eileen.

The general seemed surprised.

"Eileen's an old ICU nurse, general; she knows her diseases," said Raines.

"Well, I hope this is *just* a disease."

Camp moved closer to General Ferguson. If the chairman was involved, serious issues were at stake.

"In Afghanistan, sir?"

"As a matter of fact, yes, the battalion surgeon on a FOB in RC-East reported three Afghan patients with tularemia this week. One case of tularemia gets you a phone call, two requires a meeting. But three…that's a damn convention full of generals. So, my sincere regrets for tomorrow, Eileen, but duty calls."

Ferguson held Eileen's hand for a passing second, and then he and his coffee-pouring majors got into their car for the quick ride back to the Pentagon.

"Junior, your father and I are going to stay at Lightner Farms tonight so we'll see you tomorrow?"

"Okay, mom. Pops, you good to drive?" Camp asked with a wry smile.

"I haven't started drinking yet, boy, but I plan to."

Raines stepped forward and took Ruth's arm. "I'll walk you over to your car."

As Raines, Ruth and Sea Bee headed toward the Campbell's old Ford Galaxy, Eileen turned to Camp.

"You were Jane's knight in shining armor, sailor.

She loved you, and she loved that you loved her. This was the right thing to do, Camp. It was time to let her go."

Eileen and Camp embraced as the sounds of Pershing's Own kicked in on a distant hill for the next funeral.

Raines tucked Ruth into the passenger seat and made sure she was all buckled up. Sea Bee opened the driver's door then stopped. He held his car keys in his open hands but just stared at them. He was confused. He looked at the keys, then the car, and then back down at the keys. He was lost.

"Seabury Campbell…just what in God's name are doing?" Ruth nagged at her husband. She was half teasing but half perturbed.

He didn't respond. Sea Bee's old hands started to tremble.

"Seabury!" Ruth yelled.

Raines closed Ruth's door and walked around to Sea Bee.

"Sir…Mr. Campbell? Are you okay, sir?"

Sea Bee looked up and into Leslie's eyes.

"These? What are they? I don't know what I'm supposed to do with them," Sea Bee stammered.

'They're your keys, you crazy old fool," Ruth scolded.

Sea Bee ignored her.

"They're your car keys, sir…for your Ford."

Sea Bee looked perplexed. Raines and Ruth

exchanged concerned glances.

"I'll tell you what…this has been an emotional day, Mr. Campbell. Why don't you sit in the backseat, and I'll drive y'all out to Lightner. Let me just check with Eileen and make sure she's got a spare room."

Leslie walked back to Eileen's car where Camp was holding the door for Eileen.

"Hey Eileen, can I follow you out? I'm going to drive Mr. and Mrs. Campbell to Lightner."

"Is there a problem? Is my dad okay?" Camp asked.

"I think so. It's been an emotional day for them. I'd like to drive them over to Gettysburg, if that's okay with you?" Raines said.

"I've got four extra rooms, Leslie, so the more…the merrier."

Camp looked back at his parents' car. Leslie was right. He had just buried the woman that was to be his lifelong soul mate. Camp wasn't the only one whose heart was broken or whose thoughts were confused.

2

Lightner Farms
Gettysburg, PA

Sea Bee and Ruth Campbell occupied the oversized leather chairs in front of the Civil War era hearth as Eileen and Lieutenant Colonel Leslie Raines scurried back and forth from the kitchen to serve the 20 or so who had gathered to celebrate Jane's life.

Camp was trying to make small talk with a way-too-slick Army aviator who went to flight school with Camp's now deceased fiancée. He suspected the guy had probably cast his line several times to hit on Jane, and she was probably just as nauseated then as Camp was now.

Raines carried the tea pot over to Ruth.

"Can I warm you up, Mrs. Campbell?"

"Leslie, please call me Ruth, or I'm going to have to start calling you colonel. You wouldn't like that, now would you?" Ruth said smiling.

"No, ma'am, I wouldn't."

"Maybe she'll be calling you 'mom' if your son ever gets his act together," Sea Bee said quietly to Ruth, not aware, and not the least of which caring, if Raines was still standing within earshot.

"Seabury, your manners! This is Jane's wake for goodness sakes."

"Bury one, marry the other. Get busy, boy. Stop wasting time," Sea Bee said in his typical unrefined and urgent fashion as he stared mesmerized into the flickers of flame that danced randomly in the fireplace.

Raines was embarrassed. Ruth just ignored him as she had done so well during the natural ebb and flow of a 58-year marriage to a farmer.

Eileen scrubbed some food off the plates as she worked the sink with her sweet bed and breakfast hospitality and charm. The sounds of car doors shutting pulled her eyes to the pane glass window in front of her.

"Camp? You'd better come here," Eileen said as she waved a drying towel toward the window.

Camp got up from the table as "Slick" kept telling his war stories to anyone still interested in listening.

"What's up, gorgeous?"

Eileen pointed out the window and toward the driveway.

"Well I'll be...Raines! It's General Ferguson and his two coffee-pouring majors."

Camp opened the side kitchen door and walked out

followed by Raines and Eileen.

"General, I am so thrilled that you would make the drive all the way out here to honor Jane. Please come in and join us," Eileen said from several feet away.

"Thank you, Eileen. We certainly want to honor Jane. The captain was a hero. There are thousands of wounded soldiers who owe their lives to her steadfast work in Iraq. How many missions did she fly, Camp?"

"Sir, one day she flew combat wounded into Balad on eight flights within two hours…officially, 860 missions…unofficially, who knows."

"Gentlemen, please come in and join us for some home cooking," Eileen said as she opened the kitchen door.

"Eileen, we'd be delighted. Perhaps you could take care of my staff first. I'd like to borrow Captain Campbell and Colonel Raines for a minute, if you don't mind."

Eileen smiled and hooked an arm around each of the two majors and led them into Lightner Farms.

"Walk?" Ferguson asked.

"Sure," Camp said. "There's a nice trail out back."

The three walked behind the lodge and onto the bark chip trail that crawled in and out of poplars, evergreens and white birch trees. Ferguson unwrapped an Ashton Belicoso 52-gauge cigar, bit the top off and flared it five times with his lighter.

"Sir, is there any new information on the tularemia report out of Afghanistan?" Raines asked trying to ignite the conversation.

"Yes, I'm afraid so, but not with the tularemia. The battalion surgeon sent samples to the medical lab at Bagram, and it came back as garden variety. Probably undercooked meat or infected water."

"Sounds about right for three guys in a cave," Camp said. "Were they Taliban or local Pashtuns?"

"Taliban."

"So that's why you're concerned?" Camp asked.

"Maybe. The three Taliban boys were put on a standard antibiotic regimen there in the regional hospital. They'll be released within the week."

"Then what's the problem, general?" Raines asked.

"The battalion surgeon…he's been kidnapped."

"That's impossible," Camp said.

"Should be…supposed to be. He and his medic and interpreter had just met with the three Taliban patients. They were even joined by the Afghan physician. Our Army major went back to the ER to prepare the IVs and antibiotics. An ambulance arrived carrying the wife of an Afghan Commando colonel in it. She was apparently suffering acute pain, and the Afghan physician asked our guy if he could help."

"Why our battalion surgeon? We don't treat their people in their hospitals," Camp said emphatically.

"Because 'our guy' happens to be a gynecologist stateside. He agreed to consult – to mentor – so he went behind the curtain with the Afghan doc while his medic and translator went back to the isolation ward and administered the antibiotics for the tularemia. When they came back, the ambulance was gone, the patient was gone, the Army surgeon was missing, and the Afghan doc was strapped to the gurney, duct tape over his mouth and his throat cut."

"Geez. Always go in sets of two – never see the locals alone, if ever."

"I know, Camp, I know. This guy is Army Reserves, been in theatre less than a month. Developed an unhealthy trust with the locals. Rookie move."

"Sir, the Afghan doc…is he dead?" Raines asked.

"No, he'll be fine. Couple of stitches, I suspect, and he'll be back to work in a day or so."

"Quite the plan. Ambulance, Afghan Army base, a Commando's wife with female pain…this was staged," Raines surmised.

"Agreed, but why? Why such an elaborate plan to kidnap a God-blessed gynecologist?" General Ferguson asked.

Ferguson and Raines stopped walking as Camp stepped over to a bird house nailed chest-high on a white birch. He unlatched the clasp on the door, reached in, and pulled out a Browning 9mm.

"What the hell, Camp?" General Ferguson asked. "Now you're hiding 380 ACPs in the forest? Once a SEAL, always a SEAL."

"I got it for Eileen. She won't keep it in the lodge. Scared to death of guns. But she knows where to run if she needs one."

"Hope she runs fast," Raines said as Camp checked the magazine then put it back in the birdhouse.

"Les, you have a weapon at home, don't you?" Camp asked.

"Yes, dad," Raines said sarcastically, "but I haven't fired it in almost four years. So I plan to run instead."

The three shared a quick laugh as Camp closed the birdhouse door.

"Sir, do you think the kidnapping has anything to do with the tularemia?" Camp asked.

"Don't know. That's what I need you to find out."

"Sir?"

General Ferguson reached into his coat and pulled out an envelope.

"Your orders, Campbell…we're heading to theatre tomorrow."

"Sir…we?"

"Yes. I've been asked to serve as one of the Deputy Commanders for the International Security Assistance Force Joint Command. They're going to put me at ISAF in Kabul. My mission will focus on the organized crime circuits in Afghanistan."

"With all due respect sir, *you* have a background in security. I'm just a former SEAL with a medical degree."

"I know who you are Camp. That's why I've chosen you to replace Major Banks at FOB Lightning. They're short a battalion surgeon right now, and I need your boots on the ground, your nose in the air, and your head up. We need some clues. This feels like a criminal kidnapping."

"Sir?"

"Yes, Raines."

"What will I be doing? You want me to focus on the tularemia?"

"No, ma'am. You're staying stateside. Doctor's orders. No combat-related missions for one year after a chest flail."

"Sir, I feel −"

"Save it Raines. You're being assigned to the NIBC at Fort Detrick."

"National Interagency Biodefense Center?"

"It's a full level-four biocontainment facility. I need you there in case we're dealing with something more than just garden variety tularemia."

"Sir, it's a fabulous BSL-4 but −"

"Colonel, you're going to Detrick. The animal rights groups are still trying to shut down our chemical weapons research at Aberdeen Proving Grounds, even though the president lifted the Executive Order. They're after Detrick as well. If we get some Jihadists hell-bent on weaponizing Marburg, smallpox, Crimean-Congo or any other God-forsaken hemorrhagic diseases, then I'll need you in place. We need your expertise with non-human primates."

"Yes, sir, but I'm good to go. I'm ready to travel now."

"We'll keep you busy, colonel, not to worry. Camp, I assume you still have a 'go bag'? Well, we go at 0400 from Andrews. Better let your parents know."

"Actually general, my mom and dad are inside enjoying Eileen's freshly baked blueberry muffins. I'm sure they'd love to hear the good news first-hand from my boss."

Ferguson raised his eyebrow and snarled his lip. A sarcastic smile lit his face as he took another pull on his cigar.

"Have I ever told you that you're an ass, Campbell?"

"Every day, sir, every day."

Ferguson led the way back to the lodge steadily working down to the last draw on the Belicoso before going inside the lodge. Camp and Raines looked at each other as a million unspoken words were said in one long glance. He reached out softly and caressed the side of her face. She closed her eyes and printed his touch to her heart.

Old Town Alexandria
Virginia

Camp lathered his face with shaving cream the old fashioned way with a silver tipped pure badger brush, just like his father had taught him to do so many years before.

Shaving wasn't a chore or a task. It was an event. A perfect symphony of precision with each instrument conducted to perform in harmony with the others.

The glycerin got down to the roots of his morning beard. The coconut oil aroma filled his senses more than his first cup of coffee would before he headed out the townhouse for Andrews. The iPhone was docked, and Mumford and Sons split the morning haze.

With the gentle, calculated strokes of a trauma surgeon, Camp contorted his face to the proper angles as he pulled and pushed the French Thiers-Issard straight-edge razor along the contours of his reflection in the mirror.

The pounding at the front door interrupted his singular moment of self-indulgence. He wasn't happy as he stomped to the door in boxers and shaving cream.

"Leslie?"

Raines was out of uniform, dressed in a tight pair of Levis and an oversized Army sweatshirt. Her long brown hair was pulled back in a ponytail.

"Morning, sailor."

"What the hell? You drove all the way down here from Gettysburg for a booty call before wheels-up at 0400?"

"Booty call? You're nasty!" Raines said laughing. "I thought you could use a ride to Andrews so you don't have to park your girlfriend in the elements for six months."

"Hey, that's a great call. I'd rather leave my Defender 90 in the garage here. But you didn't need to do that."

"Nice boxers."

"Let me finish shaving. You wanna brew some coffee?" Camp walked into the kitchen and pulled some beans out and set them next to the grinder.

Raines walked past him and into his bathroom, grabbed the straight-edge and a towel.

"Sit down, sailor."

Camp sat down in a kitchen chair as Raines wrapped his shoulders with the white cotton towel. She tilted his head back slightly. As the blade touched his skin a subtle hint of Leslie's perfume blended with the coconut from the cream and filled his senses as he closed his eyes. With each stroke she wiped the razor clean on the towel until his face was fresh, smooth and ready to fly. She held his face in her hands and wiped away the last remnants of cream with her finger. He opened his eyes as she brought her face against his, first the left side, then the right.

Camp's mind was racing and his emotions were out of control. He felt guilty. Camp had never been in love until he met Jane. The war in Iraq prevented Camp and Jane from intimacy or even sharing a date together. Though they shared a few meals with each other in an over-crowded chow hall between shifts, Camp wanted Jane, like fire wants oxygen to burn. His love for Jane never stopped burning while she lay in her bed waiting to die. First-love never dies, Camp reasoned, but sometimes it fades. He wasn't looking for another woman when he was ordered to join the working group that Lieutenant Colonel Leslie Raines chaired in San Antonio. He wasn't looking for love when he and Raines shared a hotel room in Morocco during their covert mission under assumed identities. And Camp wasn't prepared for the guilt he was feeling when his feelings for Leslie Raines became raw and vulnerable.

"There, you're within the regs now. Better get dressed," Raines proclaimed as the shave was complete.

Camp was silent as he walked to the bedroom. The coffee grinder shattered the ambience that neither Mumford nor his Sons could repair. As Camp stared into his dressing mirror, he was acutely aware of something unusual, something that had not happened to him in years.

He had feeling again.

Captain Campbell emerged from the bedroom in his service dress khakis and a carry-on "go bag." Raines held out a mug of steaming fresh coffee as he walked into the kitchen. He dropped his bag. Reaching out with both hands he held Leslie's face for a brief moment then wrapped his arms around her. Neither of them wanted to let go. Neither of them knew what to do with all of the emotions that were finally unpacked.

But Captain "Camp" Campbell was packed for another mission. He knew that the heart must wait when duty calls.

3

Bagram Air Base
Afghanistan

General Ferguson and Camp were the first ones to deplane the USAF C-17A Globemaster inbound from Ali al Salem Air Base in Kuwait. Boarding first and getting off first were some of the few perks afforded senior military officers. The burdens of long hours, immense pressure and self-imposed guilt more than compensated for the occasional MILAIR benefit.

A small fixed-wing plane was staged and waiting to transport Ferguson on the 20-minute flight to KIA, the Kabul International Airport.

"Check in with the flight office across from the USO. You're already listed on the ring route for Lightning today. If the weather changes, there's a fixed-wing mail run into Gardez tomorrow morning. Here's the contact information at Lightning's TOC. They can send a ground movement to pick you up if necessary."

"Thank you, sir, I'll check in with you as soon as I'm billeted at Lightning."

After a quick, yet somewhat casual salute between friends, Ferguson got on board his fixed-wing and Camp followed all of the others who were making their way to the palletized luggage holding area. With only a go bag, Camp walked up to the counter and was first in line.

"Captain Seabury Campbell, Jr.," Camp said as he opened his envelope from General Ferguson. "Looks like I'm on mission Tango Charlie Fifty-Seven."

The staff sergeant behind the desk pointed to the mission board on the wall.

"Sorry, sir, TC57 has been cancelled due to heavy snow in the pass. I can get you as far as FOB Shank today, but you'll need to take a ground convoy from there or wait for the weather to clear."

"What about the fixed-wing mail runs into Gardez tomorrow morning?"

"Questionable at best. With temperatures this cold and mountain elevations as they are, weight becomes an issue."

"What would you do staff sergeant?"

"Sir, I'd take the ring to Shank. It's less than 20 clicks from Shank to Lightning. A ground convoy might be your best bet until the weather breaks."

"Then let's do that."

"Sir, I need your orders and your CAC card."

The staff sergeant entered all of Camp's information into the computer and asked him to step onto the scale holding his bag. He recorded the total weight and put Camp on the manifest.

"Seems a bit late for snow."

"Sir, it's been warm and comfortable here in Bagram. Chilly at night. But mid-March can bring some heavy snows in the Khyber Pass and Hindu Kush region."

"How long have you been in theatre, soldier?"

"Nine months, 17 days, and – judging by the clock – 11 hours and 13 minutes, sir."

Camp laughed.

"I assume that's your best guess?"

"No, sir. That's what my donut girl says." The sergeant turned his computer monitor around so that Camp could see the countdown clock that featured a scantily clad pin-up who took more clothing off as "in country" time counted down. The "donut girl" was an animated PowerPoint clock that helped thousands of soldiers endure multiple deployments.

"Khyber Pass…so you're pretty familiar with the terrain around here?"

"Yes, sir, but only as it pertains to flights. FOB Lightning is pretty damn close to Pakistan and the North Waziristan region. The Taliban should be heading back down from their caves after the winter."

"How far?"

"Sir?"

"How many miles from Lightning to Pakistan?"

"Fifty miles top, sir, right up the Tochi Pass, unless you prefer to take the Silk Road."

"Pesh Habor," Camp said to himself.

"Sir?"

"It was called Pesh Habor in the Bible. Khyber is both a Hebrew word and a Pashtu word. Means fort. Darius the First, Alexander the Great, Genghis Khan, the Israelites, Arabs and even the Russians; they all tried to conquer this place."

"And now the Americans?" asked the sergeant with eyebrows raised.

"We don't make the policy, staff sergeant, that's for the geniuses in Washington. We just enforce it."

"Roger that, sir, you're all set. We'll call the flight about 1330 hours, so you've got about 90 minutes to blow."

Camp took his bag and walked across the street to the USO hoping to find a computer so he could let Raines know he had arrived safely, albeit 14 long hours later.

Datta Khel, Miran Shah District
North Waziristan, Pakistan

Major Banks was rolled up like a mummy in the back of a small pick-up truck. His mouth was still covered with duct tape. His eyes felt swollen. His left cheek was throbbing, probably beaten during episodes of consciousness. His hands were still tied behind his back.

The three-vehicle convoy made its way out of Miran Shah and into the distant but neighboring village of Datta Khel. Finally stopping outside a sheet metal house, partially constructed of rocks and mud, they saw smoke pouring out of the fire stack.

Four men grabbed him and hoisted his rolled body over their heads. He heard the voices of several people inside, but nothing was said in English.

They placed him on a long table, maybe a bed. He was face down. The ropes that cinched the Afghan floor rug together were untied and he was rolled out of the rug in two or three swift pulls. The quick spin sent his body to the mud floor where his forehead and nose hit first. Blood poured from his nose.

Three men pulled him up to his feet then slammed him down in a chair. His eyes started to adjust to the light, as he squinted to shield himself from the bright open fire in the pit against the back wall.

The leader barked out some command and one of the men ripped the duct tape away from his mouth, which quickly filled with the unmistakable taste of blood from what was probably a broken nose.

"Hawale karna!"

One of his captors pulled out a knife, a Pesh-kabz, and held it in front of his eyes. With a wicked smile, he turned him around and cut the plastic ties that bound his hands together. He pulled his hands forward and rubbed them as he tried to loosen his shoulder joints.

His feet were still bound. Another man handed him a cloth and pointed to his nose. He applied pressure with the cloth and tilted his head back, never taking his eyes off the Pesh-kabz.

His eyes looked past the knife where he saw another bed. Someone was in it. The body was covered with a long, black burka, hijab and black face veil.

A man approached from the back of the room. He had a smile and a bounce to his step.

"Major Banks…you're a doctor, no?"

Banks said nothing.

"A female doctor, a gynecologist, no?"

Banks said nothing.

"My name is Kazi. I attended university in Alabama. Have you heard of Auburn?"

Banks stared at him, pinching his nose, blinking without showing fear though frightened to the core.

"I must apologize for my friends, no? They treated you harshly. But we need help. When we heard that someone like you was so close, well, we couldn't wait to meet you."

Banks struggled to swallow.

"Pani!" Kazi yelled as one of the other captors ran over with a cup of water.

Banks looked into the dirty cup. The water was discolored and foul. He pulled it to his lips and took a swallow.

"What?" Banks managed to cough out a word.

"I'm listening, Doctor Banks."

"What did you study?" Banks asked, hoping to establish a bond with his abductor that might lead to the preservation of his own life.

A large smile broke over Kazi's face.

"Microbiology."

"Are you a doctor?" Banks asked as he finished the water.

The smile left Kazi's face.

"The woman...over there...she is very important to us. She needs surgery."

"If she's so important to you, then why is her mouth covered with tape?"

"You can't see her mouth, Dr. Banks."

"And I can't hear her either. You folks seem to like your duct tape."

Kazi looked back at the woman then down at the mud floor.

"What kind of surgery, Kazi?" Banks finally asked.

Kazi got up and walked over to the table near the woman's bed. He picked up two small implant devices and caressed them as though he was holding bags of precious diamonds.

"Female surgery, Dr. Banks, female surgery."

FOB Shank
Regional Command – East, Afghanistan

Camp finally made it to the front of the line at Forward Operating Base Shank's MILAIR counter. Shank was a large and sprawling base in

Regional Command – East and one of the only bases other than Bagram that had a runway long enough for large military aircraft like the C-17.

"Ma'am, this is getting older than dirt."

"I'm sorry, Captain Campbell, but I have no control over Mother Nature."

"I understand that, Sergeant Delaney, but seven days in temporary billeting, sharing a bunk room with 14 Air Force individual augmentees gaming on their PlayStations until 0200 is about more than I can handle. Anything going out today?"

"Back to Bagram, yes…over the pass to Lightning… no."

"Ma'am, the Deputy Commander of ISAF is –"

"Captain Campbell, even if Pope Benedict wants you at Lightning, I can't do anything about it if the birds aren't flying. I'm sorry, sir; I know it's frustrating."

"No, what's frustrating is that you make me get out of my rack, pack my gear and my roll, put my full kit on, hump a click down the road and check in here every morning at 0500, so you can tell me the same damn thing. *That's* what's frustrating."

An older man, African-American with a receding hairline and dressed in civilian tactical 5.11 khakis, overheard the conversation from his vinyl seat in the waiting room. He was reading an old, well-worn and heavily circulated copy of Stars and Stripes.

"You headed to FOB Lightning too, captain?" he asked. Camp turned and saw the slight man still scanning through the old newspaper.

"Theoretically," Camp said turning his attention back to Sergeant Delaney.

"A ground convoy came in late last night from Bagram. They're leaving at 1500 today for Paktya Province, passing right through Lightning," the man said.

Camp stepped out of line.

"They got room?"

"They've always got room. I'm already on the convoy but thought I'd see if anything was going up and over instead of going ground through the pass."

"How do I get on the manifest? Where do we muster?"

"Muster is at the truck lot right behind your barracks, Captain Campbell."

Camp dropped his head and raised his eyebrows.

"Do we know each other?"

"Not yet. But Jim Ferguson described you as a confident, border-line arrogant at times, Navy Captain with good looks. I mean, how many of you can there be?"

Camp smiled. "You work for the general?"

"And with you, apparently," the man said as he stood up. "Billy Finn, Special Agent, FBI, retired agent that is, now Schedule A civilian for this tour."

"Pleasure to meet you, Billy. Did Ferguson send you to rescue me from FOB Shank?"

"Actually, I was on a bird that got diverted here last night. I was supposed to meet up with you at Lightning, but then again you were supposed to be there seven days ago."

"Tell me about it. I've been in transit from Bagram for more than a week. The weather just doesn't want to cooperate. What did you do for the bureau?

"Organized crime rings, worked in the Manhattan field office for 17 years, Montreal for a dozen before that."

"Organized crime? So, I guess that means our kidnapping at Lightning wasn't the work of the Taliban?"

Finn smiled and gathered up his pack and kit. A well-worn Glock 22 was holstered on his hip.

"Depends. No one knows where the Taliban ends and the Haqqani network or Pakistani intelligence begins out here. Afghanistan is the wild, wild west Captain Campbell, the wild, wild west."

"Well, if I'm going to be stuck with your sorry ass for a few days you might as well call me Camp."

4

National Interagency Biodefense Center
BSL-4 Facility
Fort Detrick, Maryland

Raines walked up the sidewalk to an unusual looking four or five-story brick and glass building. By design, the building was somewhat ambiguous in appearance and its size was unclear. The checkpoint guard reviewed her orders, verified her credentials and gave her the map. The $105 million facility certainly didn't look like anything else she had ever worked in before.

The atrium was enormous, and sunlight filled the room through expansive glass windows and skylights. Deep leather chairs and couches filled the space where scientists, military veterinarians and infectious disease experts lounged and discussed their work. Raines knew all about Fort Detrick but this was her first tour to actually work in the facility.

She stopped momentarily as her eyes gazed at the ceiling and absorbed the craftsmanship of the building.

"Lieutenant Colonel Raines?"

"Yes, sir," she managed to say somewhat startled.

"The guard desk called and said you had arrived. I'm Doctor Groenwald," he said with a faint Dutch accent.

"Yes, Dr. Groenwald, it is a real honor and pleasure to finally meet you, sir. You are a legend in the fields of infectious disease. I hardly think I'm qualified to assist your research work, but I am so honored to be here."

"Nonsense. I've read your folio, and it is I who should be honored to meet the one who uncovered the Malak al-Maut."

"Yes, well, that was quite an adventure. We were very fortunate only to be dealing with the Black Plague. An Ebola-Plague hybrid would have been catastrophic."

"Indeed. Well, let's get a coffee, and I'll give you the tour and show you where your office will be."

The atrium coffee bar was buzzing with activity and a line seven deep stood waiting for a caffeine concoction or a freshly baked pastry.

"Well, we have slightly more than 11,000 square feet here. This is an IRF. The atrium looks pretty, but I can assure you that she's built like a submarine."

"I've never worked in an Integrated Research Facility like this before. How many agencies are under the same roof?"

"The IRF basically holds three agencies. From NIH, we have the National Institute of Allergy and Infectious Disease. And, of course, we rolled the Army's Medical Research Institute of Infectious Diseases into this facility as well as the National Biodefense Analysis and Countermeasures Center; Homeland Security, Department of Defense and the National Institutes of Health, all under one roof. Ah, pick your poison, colonel."

"Sir?"

"Your coffee…pick your poison."

"Sorry, a tall skinny latte, ma'am."

"And I'll take a *grande* mocha, double shot, please," Groenwald ordered and narrated in the same breath, "so this is the crown jewel of the nation's biodefense research program, Colonel Raines. Every day we try to understand, treat and hopefully prevent any number of infectious, immunologic, and allergic diseases that threaten hundreds of millions of people worldwide."

"What did you do during the president's ban on animal research? Did you shut down?"

The barista handed them their drinks, and Groenwald left a $5 bill on the counter as they walked away.

"What ban?" Groenwald said with a sly smile on his face.

"Roger that!"

"So in a nutshell, we're trying to develop new and improved diagnostics, treatments, and vaccines for diseases caused by naturally occurring infectious agents as well as microbes that may be intentionally released into a civilian population."

"Very impressive, Dr. Groenwald; I can't wait to get started."

"Colonel, please forgive me, but I'm required to give you a very basic briefing. I'd have to do this even if you were the Secretary of Defense."

"I completely understand."

Groenwald led her over to some open seats.

"We have all biosafety level laboratory suites in this facility. In the BSL-1, we generally do *not* deal with agents typically associated with disease in healthy *people*. In the BSL-2 labs, we *are* dealing with agents associated with human disease. You'll see biohazard signs, and you need to take extra precaution with sharps as most of your work done in a BSL-2 will be done on a bench top. In the BSL-3 labs, we'll be working with agents associated with human disease caused by contamination through the air, or aerosol. These diseases have serious, sometimes lethal, consequences."

"I presume decontamination of all waste?"

"Waste and decontamination of all lab garments and PPE before laundering is mandatory. You'll see Class One and Class Two biological safety cabinets, and the labs are physically separated from access corridors. These labs have self-closing, double-door access. The exhaust air is not recirculated but negative air is pumped into each BSL-3 lab."

"And your BSL-4? Based on my orders, I presume

that's where I'll be assigned?"

"It's the smallest lab in here but the most potent. We'll be working with agents that spread disease through aerosol contamination, and in many of them we don't know the cause of transmission. They are usually life-threatening and possibly on a global scale. All clothing is changed upon entry including undergarments. Shower on exit, and all material goes through decontamination on exit. I presume you have worn the suits?"

"Yes, sir, but only in a facility that wasn't 'hot'. It was a training exercise."

"Your breathing suit weighs about 10 pounds, and that'll add an extra six inches to your natural height. Both BPS 400 suit options are full-bodied, air-supplied, positive-pressured personnel suits. You'll be tethered to an overhead air hose at all times. Our BSL-4 labs are in separate, isolated zones within the building. The labs have a dedicated supply of exhaust, vacuum and decontamination systems. Throw in two-foot walls of solid concrete, and I can assure you, Colonel Raines, that nothing is getting out of this building."

Raines smiled but was hardly relieved. Nothing from the federal government seemed reassuring.

"That's my briefing, any questions?"

"No, sir. I'd love to see the facility and my office. Sir, my orders don't delineate exactly what infectious disease I'll be working on."

"Well, according to the classified information I

received from General Ferguson's office, I think they want to exploit your expertise on hemorrhagic fevers – Marburg in particular."

All levity vanished as Raines began to process the work at hand.

"Marburg. A far cry from working with dolphins or second-guessing SARS."

"You are familiar with Marburg, are you not?" Groenwald asked with some hesitation.

"Seven days after infection, patients suffer flu-like symptoms before the virus multiplies. Blood starts to seep from the skin, the mouth, the eyes and the ears. Internal organs hemorrhage into bloody, unrecognizable masses. Up to 90 percent die within weeks, and it can be passed to another person by a kiss, a touch or even a sneeze. Yes Dr. Groenwald, I'm familiar with Marburg; it's a highly communicable pathogen."

"Your mission is to understand it, defend against it, and hopefully limit it to an outbreak, God willing, and not an epidemic…God forbid."

An elevator with card reader and a biometric took them automatically to the appropriate floor. No floor buttons were displayed within the elevator car. Raines and Groenwald emerged and stood in a dividing corridor between two labs. The outer lab was the BSL-3 where scientists, medical doctors, researchers and veterinarians were busy working on dangerous infectious diseases. The inner lab was the BSL-4 where Raines would work on the most dangerous pathogens in the world.

"Your old friend and his sister, the bubonic plague, are in there," Groenwald said as he pointed to BSL-3. "Ebola, Marburg and a few others that I'm not permitted to identify are here in the inner sanctum. These killers are transmissible, currently incurable and under quarantine."

"How long have you been at Fort Detrick, Dr. Groenwald?"

"Thirteen years now, mostly doing infectious disease work before this facility was built."

"Before that?"

"Baltimore at the ADRC, the Johns Hopkins Alzheimer's Disease Research Center. Mostly mouse models, Drosophila and some non-human primates."

"Fruit flies for Alzheimer's disease? Amazing."

"Unfortunately AD will kill 79,000 Americans this year, and next year, and more the year after that as our population ages. Let's just hope that Marburg fever doesn't ever exceed those numbers, or we'll all be in trouble."

FOB Lightning
Paktya Province, Afghanistan

The convoy of Mine Resistant Ambush Protected, MRAPs, long-bed flats and a wrecker team paused outside the checkpoint at FOB Lightning. Camp and Billy Finn exited the back access door of their MRAP. They showed their badges to two AK-47 toting Gurkha guards and walked up the gravel walk between T-walls to the checkpoint turnstile where US Army guards welcomed them in. Passing the path to Terp Village, they unbolted the wooden gate as the convoy drove out and exited the main checkpoint on FOB Thunder next door, before driving over to the city of Gardez.

US Navy Captain "Camp" Campbell fired off a stiff salute to an approaching soldier, a salute that was instantly, though hesitantly, returned.

"Specialist, where can I find the Mayor Cell?"

"Sir, veer to the right, about 700 yards up and on your right, next door to the Tactical Operations Center. And sir?"

"Yes, specialist."

"This is a non-salute base, so…you know."

Camp rolled his eyes and shrugged his shoulders as he and Finn made their way up the gravel road toward the Mayor Cell. The ominous hilltop fortresses of Alexander the Great began to emerge over FOB Lightning as they knocked on the Mayor's door.

First Sergeant Ramirez was the Mayor of FOB Lightning and was responsible for heating, air conditioning, plumbing, and food and billeting.

"Good morning, sergeant, Mr. Finn and I just arrived by convoy, and we'll be needing some rooms."

"Rooms? Would you like carpeting, granite counter-tops, a mini-bar and indoor plumbing, too?" Ramirez asked with less than subtle contempt for a high-ranking military officer. "This ain't no Hilton, captain. How long will you be here?"

"Several weeks, a couple of months, not really sure."

Ramirez looked at Camp's insignia badge.

"You're a doctor. Replacement for Major Banks?"

"Yes, something like that."

"Civilian or contractor?" Ramirez asked Finn.

"Civilian," snapped Finn. He hated the question.

"GS level?"

"Fifteen."

Camp got agitated. "What difference does that make?"

"Sir, I'm not going to bunk a GS nine with an O-six, but a 15 is equal to your level."

Ramirez handed them two keys to Building 89.

"Soon as you stow your gear, you need to check in with the XO and then in at the TOC. Bring your orders. The DFAC serves lunch from 1100 to 1300 hours."

Building 89 was a standard size B-hut. A long corridor down the middle was lit with two fluorescent light boards, and plywood walls were eight feet high on both sides. Camp and Finn had rooms across from each other. After getting past a simple key padlock on every plywood door, inside each soldier had an open closet with a bay for six hangers and two cubby holes for folded clothes. Four lines of three-inch plywood shelves would hold their toiletries, DVDs and batteries. Beneath the shelves a larger boxed-in bin stored weapons and ammo under separate lock and key. A three-foot by two-foot plywood desk was against the cement wall and beneath the window that was covered with black paper to prevent any light from being seen outside. Lightning was a dark base; no lights at night limited what a sniper might be able to get away with. The extended twin bed mattress sat on a plywood frame and was lifted four feet in the air so that sea bags and battle rattle could be stowed beneath. A 220-to-110 converter and a power strip were on the floor between the desk and the elevated bed.

"You unpacked yet, Finn?"

"Home sweet home. All done. Can we hit the head on the way to the XO's office?"

"Aye, aye…let's roll."

The XO was a National Guardsman from Minnesota. He had attained the rank of a full bird Army colonel on the weekends, but was a full-time literature professor at Gustavus Adolphus College by trade. The longest war in American history required several rotations of reserves and National Guard in addition to active duty enlisted. Even on the front lines.

A long line of local Afghan Pashtuns, each wearing a blue janitor's smock, stood watching two of their brothers emptying the trash out of the XO's metal can as two more replaced the liner bag. They were expressionless as Camp and Finn walked past them into the building.

"Ah, Captain Campbell and Special Agent Finn, we've been expecting you. The Mayor said you'd be over so, I took the liberty of inviting Captain Henry to join us."

Camp read the name tag.

"Colonel Kierkendahl, pleasure to meet you, sir. Sounds like a good Nordic name."

"Sixth generation Lutherans from Minnesota don't ya know. Campbell, that's Scottish right?"

Camp tired of the small talk he had initiated.

"Henry? You were with Banks the day he was abducted."

"Yes, sir, I run a MEDEVAC mentoring program for the Afghan Army with a team of six medics from the 82nd Airborne Division. I was assisting Major Banks that day."

"On the tularemia outbreak?" Camp asked.

"Yes, sir, it's been contained. The patients got their full treatment of antibiotics and have been released."

"Released? Or do you mean arrested?" Camp asked.

"Sir?"

"The report says all three were Taliban."

"Roger that, sir. The commanding Afghan general on Thunder is well-known in the province, and he thought it would be viewed as an act of compassion to let these patients go."

"How did the ambulance manage to leave Thunder with an American inside?" Billy Finn questioned.

"Sir, the checkpoint doesn't usually inspect outgoing vehicles, especially an ambulance with emergency lights on. They ambulance comes and goes throughout the day. The Paktya Regional Hospital is the most sophisticated hospital between here and Khost."

"How about coming on to the base? Do the Afghan Army guards inspect the ambulances then?" Finn continued.

"Affirmative, Mr. Finn. They do a quick inspect and release. Just to make sure there's no car bomb."

"So Captain Henry, the guards know who comes on to Thunder. The guards' commanding officer knows who comes on to Thunder. And by extension, the commanding Afghan general knows who comes on to his base too."

"Roger."

"Once you verified that an abduction took place, who pursued?"

"I can answer that one," Kierkendahl chimed in, hoping to satisfy Finn's interrogation. "We immediately called the Afghans and asked for ground pursuit and requested alerts for the various checkpoints in the province. We sent ground units out as well."

"Air?" Camp asked.

"Unfortunately, no. We don't have air assets here, and by the time the weather cleared, it was pretty pointless," Colonel Kierkendahl answered.

"Did the Afghan Army find anything? Any clues? Any leads?" Finn asked.

Captain Henry and Colonel Kierkendahl shifted in their chairs as the colonel abruptly stood and started to pace the room.

"Well, sir, the Afghans were not able to pursue that day," Henry said.

"To be fair, they complained that they were out of fuel. There was really nothing they could do," Kierkendahl added.

"Captain Henry, have you had other tours in Afghanistan?" Finn asked.

"Yes, sir, 13 months in Kandahar two years ago."

"Did you come across any corruption problems with the Afghans you worked with then?"

"Roger that, every week. In fact, most of the time, the issue was fuel. We'd bring in a fully loaded tanker. By the time the generals and the colonels and local government officials siphoned off what they wanted for personal use, there was hardly anything left for the Afghan Army vehicles."

"When was the last time Thunder was re-supplied with fuel, colonel?" Finn asked.

"The day before the abduction."

"And they were already on 'E'? How often do they send patrols out, colonel?"

"They typically send out a three vehicle patrol on a humanitarian mission once a week," Colonel Kierkendahl said as his agitation grew.

The colonel sat down behind his desk. "Listen, bottom-line, we did everything within our power. We immediately notified the ABP, Afghan Border Patrol. I'm certain that no American soldier has left this country out their back door."

"The ABP? You're not serious, colonel. Two TVs, a smart phone, a pack of smokes and some pirated porn, and they'd let you smuggle Jimmy Hoffa into Pakistan," Finn said as he stood up quickly and walked out of the HQ building, slamming the door behind him for dramatic effect.

"Captain Henry, can you take me over to the base clinic? I'd also like to meet the Terp."

"Roger that, Captain Campbell. I'll have my team escort her over to the TMC now."

Camp got up to leave then hesitated.

"Hey Captain, where do I go on Lightning to make a Skype call back home?"

Kierkendahl and Henry were amused.

"Captain, this Forward Operating Base isn't quite on the edge of the Earth but we can see it from here. One satellite dish provides barely enough bandwidth for all of our computers to run, let alone 'shits and grins' for the folks back home. Better send a letter and hope for good weather to get it out of here."

Camp had never been on any mission where basic communications were so difficult to come by. His heart wanted to reach out and touch Leslie Raines. But American bandwidth in Afghanistan wouldn't allow that connection to be made, at least not on FOB Lightning.

5

Datta Khel Village, Miran Shah District
North Waziristan, Pakistan

A Taliban guard bent down and cut the plastic straps that bound Major Banks' feet together. He stretched his legs and knees out for the first time in what seemed like months. He had lost track of time. When he finally regained consciousness from the hit on the head in the ER, he was already out of the ambulance, gagged and rolled into an Afghan rug and was bouncing in the back of an old pick-up truck. The temperatures were extremely cold, so he figured that he had been moved over the mountain pass and into the lawless villages of North Waziristan in Pakistan.

The windowless room in the building refused to betray either night or day.

Kazi was the only one who spoke English. He seemed friendly enough, American educated, but Banks didn't trust the others.

The captor walked him over to a wooden table that was covered with a few rudimentary operating room devices. Six bottles marked diethyl ether were sitting on the back of the table. Several dozen Ethicon Prolene visi-black M3 surgical suture cartridge spools were scattered around.

Kazi walked into the room.

"Dr. Banks, I'm sorry for your difficult treatment earlier. I apologize. I hope you have enjoyed your meal and some water."

Banks said nothing.

"This woman is very important. She is the wife of a Taliban commander. We do not have the expertise that she requires."

Banks looked at the table and the woman on the bed next to him. Her eyes screamed but her mouth was covered with tape.

"She needs surgery, Dr. Banks. Do what they need done, and these brothers will take you back to Paktya, completely unharmed. They can't take you back to Thunder the same way they took you out, for obvious reasons, but they will drop you off on a nearby road where the ANA will pick you up."

Hope started to build. Banks stretched his fingers to make sure his hands weren't injured.

"Yes, we made sure your hands were protected," Kazi said with some pride.

Banks walked closer to the woman.

"What's wrong with her?" he said in a raspy voice.

Kazi and the other captors in the room nodded and smiled with each other. This was progress. Perhaps they finally had a cooperative hostage.

"This is difficult to explain, Dr. Banks, but the woman does not bring her husband pleasure. She has been married one year but has not brought him children. He is not attracted to her."

Hope disappeared as fast as it had arrived. Banks looked at Kazi with contempt.

"The commander is not satisfied with her breasts?"

Kazi pointed to the two devices on the table.

"The commander wishes that you implant one of these in each breast. The commander has acquired these Poly Prothese PIPs from France. They are industrial grade silicone. The best."

Banks examined the packaging around the PIPs.

"Let me get this straight. You want me to put this woman to sleep with a couple of bottles of diethyl ether, then open her up in here, in this room, and insert industrial grade silicone PIPs? All to make her more satisfying and attractive?"

Kazi smiled. "Precisely, Dr. Banks."

"I assume you're aware that the United Arab Emirates and all other civilized countries have recalled these industrial PIPs because they rupture? Does he want his attractive, faithful, and satisfying wife to die in three to four years?"

"Dr. Banks, this is not your concern. Three to four

years is ample time to give him a son. She won't live even that long if she does not bring him a son."

The Army major started to grasp the purpose of his abduction. But he couldn't fully process the notion of performing cosmetic surgery on a Muslim woman under such harsh conditions. There had to be other options. Banks mustered enough saliva in his mouth as he could then spit on the floor near Kazi.

"Screw you," Banks snarled seconds before the butt of an AK-47 opened a gash on his head as he fell to the dirt unconscious.

The captors carried him over to his bed and threw him down as Kazi warned them not to hurt his hands.

Level One Clinic - TMC
FOB Lightning, Afghanistan

Camp was sitting on the edge of an exam table in the clinic. Seven soldiers were in line at the window waiting to get another week's supply of Ambien. Two young Army medics walked Miriam into the clinic and over to Camp.

"Salam," Camp said gently covering his heart with his hand.

Miriam smiled.

"Miriam, I am Captain Campbell, and this is my associate Billy Finn."

"It is my pleasure to meet you."

"Your English is excellent. You were Major Banks' interpreter?" Camp asked.

"And four more doctors before him. I have been working for coalition forces for five years now."

"Where do you live, Miriam?" Finn asked.

"Interpreter village."

"Well, your file says that you work seven weeks straight then take one week off every two months. Where do you go when you're not in Terp Village?"

"My home is in Khost, Mr. Finn."

"Do you have family, Miriam? A husband? Parents? Children?"

"Such questions are interpreted as rude in Afghan culture, Mr. Finn."

"Well, then pardon my damn potty mouth and answer the freaking questions. In American culture, kidnapping is hardly interpreted as high-brow social etiquette either."

Miriam nervously stroked the single glass bead on her necklace.

"I have one son, he is six years old. My husband is a farmer."

"What tribe are you, Miriam?" Finn pressed.

Miriam was now irritated with the excessive line of questioning.

"I am Pashtun, Mr. Finn, my father was Mezi clan of the Zadran tribe."

Finn smiled and shook his head slightly. He got the answer he wanted. The interrogation was over.

"Am I in trouble Dr. Campbell?" Miriam asked trying to stop the questions. "I desperately need my job to feed my family and take care of my parents and cousins. Many people depend upon my salary."

"No, Miriam, you're not in trouble," Camp said trying to be reassuring. "Mr. Finn and I are here to help figure out what happened to Major Banks. Do you know of any reason why the Taliban would want to kidnap an American doctor?"

"No. He was a good man."

"Was?" Finn asked.

"He *is* a good man. Dr. Mahmoud and the rest of the staff think highly of him."

"Dr. Mahmoud…I'd like to walk over and see him. I presume that's the hospital we saw across the street when we were pulling up to the checkpoint?" Camp asked.

"Yes, but I'm sure Dr. Mahmoud has gone home for the day. It's almost four o'clock," Miriam said.

"Geez, nice hours. Then tomorrow morning, 0900 hours?" Camp asked.

"Yes, I'll be waiting for you at the checkpoint."

Camp nodded, and the medics took Miriam out of the clinic and escorted her back to Terp Village. Finn got up and followed behind her for several steps, stopping only when she had left the clinic.

"Anything?" Camp asked Finn, as he searched for useful conclusions.

"Mezi clan. Zadran tribe. Jalalludin Haqqani became a powerful military leader back in the day, during the Soviet occupation. He also got tight with our CIA, Pakistan's ISI and the new Afghan government. His son Sirajudin Haqqani runs military operations for the old man now with capable help from his little brother Badaruddin. The Haqqanis are also Mezi clan, Zadran tribe. In fact, Sirajudin selected Sangeen Zadran to be the shadow governor for one of the provinces."

"Let me guess…for Paktya Province?" Camp asked as Finn touched the tip of his own nose.

"Bingo."

National Interagency Biodefense Center
BSL-4 Facility
Fort Detrick, Maryland

Raines was examining Phase One study results on Marburg's fever when the call came in.

"Lieutenant Colonel Raines."

"Ma'am, this is Sergeant Perkins at the Fort Detrick visitor's center. You've got a visitor here, says she doesn't have an appointment."

"For me?"

"Yes ma'am, says her name is Ruth Campbell."

"Ruth Campbell…oh my gosh, Mrs. Campbell?"

"Yes, ma'am."

"Okay, ah, tell her I'll be right over. It'll take me 10 minutes to get there."

"Roger that, ma'am."

A million things went through Leslie's mind. None of them seemed good. Certainly she would have heard directly from General Ferguson if something had happened to Camp. She rode the elevator without buttons down to the atrium, walked quickly past the coffee bar and the leather chairs, out the atrium and down the sidewalk past the parking lots to the visitor's center.

"Mrs. Campbell, what a lovely surprise."

Ruth looked around at all of the empty chairs in the visitor's center waiting room.

"I don't see a Mrs. Campbell in here, Leslie, do you?"

Raines laughed and gave Ruth a big hug.

"How are you, Ruth? Did you drive all the way over here from Lancaster County?"

"All 95 miles from Bird-in-Hand. The old man was driving me nuts, so I needed a drive. I've got exactly 20 minutes before I need to drive back home, so I can get supper on the table by five. Seabury gets persnippity if he's not served supper before the evening news. We always ate, washed the dishes by hand and fed the animals before Walter Cronkite came on."

"Well then, let's not keep Mr. Campbell waiting. Is something wrong, Ruth?"

"I took Seabury to see our doctor, Harry Tasner. He's been practicing medicine in Lancaster County since 1963. Fine man, really. His wife Doris passed a few years back. Harry has never been the same, but he still shows up for work every day."

"Is something wrong with Mr. Campbell?"

"Two days ago he was out in the barn. The girls

and their husbands had already come over for the evening milking. They had just fed the cows. Seabury hasn't worked — actually worked — in the barn for 10 years. After supper he went out to the barn. He didn't even turn on the news. I went out into the barn, and there he was, holding a bucket of feed. He didn't know what to do with it. He didn't know why he was even out there."

"Well, Ruth, I wouldn't get too worried. Mr. Campbell is getting up there in years. Maybe he was just a little tired, a bit confused after a long week."

"Maybe so. But yesterday was different. He said he grabbed his coat and went outside about eight-thirty last night. Never even took a flashlight with him. I think I dozed off in my chair while I was crocheting. I never heard him leave. Well, something on the blasted TV woke me up, must've been nine-thirty. Seabury was nowhere to be found. I checked the porch. I looked in the barn. I even rang the dinner bell. Nothing. I called the girls, and they came over. We looked for a few minutes, and finally we called the sheriff. The sheriff came over in his pick-up. It's a beautiful new four-wheel drive truck. Not sure how he can really afford that kind of a truck on his salary, especially with all of those fancy off-road lights and everything."

"Ruth…did he find Mr. Campbell?"

"Well he drove around the 40 acres for 10 minutes with the girls. Down by the creek, on the far end of our land, there was Seabury. He was sitting on a tree stump, shivering and all upset."

"Was he hurt?

"No, not that we could tell. The sheriff brought him back to the farm house. After I hugged him, I just about knocked his head off I was so mad. I said, 'Why didn't you come home?' He said he tried to but just got lost."

"Lost?"

"We've lived on those same 40 acres since the 1950s. You can't get lost out there. It's all row crops and grazing pastures."

"What did Dr. Tasner say, Ruth?"

"Said he thinks Seabury's got hardening of the arteries."

"Atherosclerosis?"

"No, he didn't mention that one. Maybe. I don't know, all those fancy words confuse me."

"It's a reasonable diagnosis from a small-town family physician. What does Dr. Tasner want to do?"

"Says I ought to cut back on the pure butter I use in Seabury's food and that he should have his pressure checked every week over at the drug store."

"That's it? Cut out butter and get his blood pressure checked?"

"Well, that didn't seem like enough to me either, Leslie. That's why I wanted to talk to you. Junior is out gallivanting around the globe playing Army men, and Eileen is still mourning over Jane. I didn't know who to call."

"You did exactly the right thing, Ruth. Are you okay to drive home?"

"Oh, for heaven's sakes yes. I may be seasoned, but I'm not an invalid."

"Okay…let me make a few calls. I'll call you tomorrow, no later than supper, I promise."

Ruth stood up, grabbed her purse and reached over to kiss Leslie's cheek.

"You are a wonderful person, Leslie. I knew that the first time I met you. You would make a wonderful daughter-in-law."

Raines blushed as Ruth summoned one of the guards behind the desk.

"You there, sergeant, walk this old woman out to her car," Ruth called out to one of the uniformed guards behind the desk. Regardless of their rank, all soldiers were "sergeants" in Ruth Campbell's mind.

Lieutenant Perkins looked over at Raines who lifted her hands in defense since she was innocent of issuing the order.

"Yes, ma'am," Perkins said begrudgingly as he locked arms with Ruth and walked her out to her Ford Galaxy sedan for the 95-mile drive back to Bird-in-Hand, Pennsylvania.

Raines watched Lieutenant Perkins help Ruth into her old Ford Galaxy. She knew Camp would want to know that his father's health was failing. But just like every military family that deploys, sometimes decisions are made to protect warriors from having to deal with more than one war at a time. Raines decided to step in and handle the family problem herself, a situation Camp knew nothing about.

6

When Banks regained consciousness, he realized that he had been placed in a chair at a table. Two AK-47 toting captors stood above him on both sides. A long knife was the only object on the table. He looked up to his left and realized that the guard's face was completely covered by a Shemagh that was tied around his head, face, nose and mouth. Only his eyes were exposed. He kept looking straight ahead. Banks looked to his left, and the other terrorist was equally as stoic. The wall behind him was covered with a black and white flag. Based on what Banks remembered from the pre-deployment briefings he tried to sleep through, he thought he was probably sitting in front of the Islamic Khilafah – Shahada – the flag of jihad.

"Dr. Banks, I hope you're feeling better since your

nap."

Banks glared at Kazi. His jaws clenched, and he was determined to take his execution like an American, like a soldier. He said nothing.

Kazi bent down in front of him and placed his forearms comfortably across the table.

"Dr. Banks…there's a couple of ways we can do this. It's entirely your choice. But before you choose, I want you to know what a marvelous invention Facebook is. Oh yes, it clearly helped fuel the Arab Spring in Tunisia, Egypt, Libya and perhaps even in Syria. What would the Occupy Wall Street movement have been without Facebook? Do you have a Facebook page, Dr. Banks?"

Banks remained silent.

"Let me think…hmmm…yes, yes now that I think of it you do, don't you…Dean Banks, MD…Board Certified Gynecologist practicing with the Bucks County Women's Health Clinic, US Army Reservist on a four-month deployment to Afghanistan. Nice of you to wish all your friends goodbye and a Merry Christmas."

"Banks is a common name. Nice try," Major Banks said.

"That was my concern too…but when my friends in Philadelphia finally got your 14-year-old son Chad to 'friend' them well, then we knew. The family photos are precious, Chad and Brittany look like lovely children. And your wife, Meg – or do you still call her Peggy – she is very attractive Dr. Banks…very attractive."

The major's heart sank to the floor.

"Did you know that your Chad is in the *same* Phillies Baseball Fan Club as *my* friends? He likes baseball! I prefer cricket myself, but baseball is close. Now, Dr. Banks…you have a beautiful home in Doylestown, on Bergstrom Road, no? I saw the photos. It must be very close to the Country Club and Golf Course. Does Brittany still take tennis lessons there? I read one of her posts on your wall. It sounded like tennis lessons to me."

Banks began to panic. He felt nauseated as his mind wandered through a million possibilities over what could happen to his family.

"Okay, stop…stop! I'll do what you want."

"We're going to film a little video for your family, Dr. Banks. My friends will gladly post it on Chad's wall, if you like, or Brittany's. You do this surgery, and if the commander's wife lives…then we will drop you off on a road by Thunder, just as I promised. Refuse to perform this surgery, or if the commander's wife doesn't make it through the surgery…then neither will you. So think of this as possibly a 'goodbye' video, or possibly not. But the only way that Chad, Brittany and your wife Peggy will ever see your thespian skills depends on how you act now. Don't be stupid, Dr. Banks, and don't be sloppy."

Banks swallowed hard and said a quick prayer.

"One final thing, Dr. Banks…if this doesn't go well,

and go well quickly…my friends will be visiting your house tomorrow morning, while everyone is asleep in that four-bedroom, three-bath house of yours on Bergstrom Road. But I promise you that Brittany will live…she will certainly be able to please a man, don't you think?"

Kazi put two sheets of scribbled English on the table in front of the knife.

"Read them, Dr. Banks…and sound convincing. This is the performance of your life."

Paktya Regional Hospital
FOB Thunder, 203rd Corps, Afghanistan

US Navy Captain "Camp" Campbell, Billy Finn and Captain Henry walked through the main entry doors and into the Paktya Regional Hospital. The Afghan day workers stood and greeted the trio with the same morning ritual. Miriam was 10 feet behind just as she had been for almost five years. Five other American medics were in the main lobby as well as three more interpreters from Terp Village.

"Geez, looks like a Shriner's convention in here. Where's Mahmoud?" Camp asked in no mood for small talk, hot tea or cultural pleasantries.

Miriam yelled out the Captain's question in Pashtu, as she removed the solitary bead from her necklace and put it in the glass vase on her desk.

"Dr. Mahmoud is down in the emergency room, Captain Campbell. I can take you down there now," said

Miriam as she entered the long fluorescent-lit corridor that led down to the ER.

"He's back to work already?" Camp muttered to no one in particular.

Mahmoud was restocking bandages and wraps in the first-aid cabinet as the three Americans and Miriam walked into the ER. Captain Henry walked over to Mahmoud as Camp and Finn examined the layout of the ER, especially the ambulance access doors.

"*Salam,* Dr. Mahmoud."

"*Salam,* Captain Henry. Who are your friends?"

"Dr. Mahmoud, this is US Navy Captain Campbell and Bill Finn from ISAF in Kabul."

Mahmoud covered his heart with his right hand and lowered his eyes in respect.

"Is there any news on Major Banks?" Mahmoud asked.

"Nothing yet," Camp said.

"I'm sure this was a very traumatic event for you, Dr. Mahmoud," Finn questioned.

"I came close to death, Mr. Finn. Allah was faithful, and I was spared another day."

Camp walked over to Mahmoud and stood right in front of him. "Captain Henry says that when he and Miriam returned from starting the IV antibiotics for your tularemia patients, they found you bound and gagged on the gurney."

"That is correct, Captain Campbell. After they hit Major Banks over the head, he fell onto the woman. She got up immediately and covered his mouth with duct tape. They rolled one table out and another one in. I thought they would kill me right there."

"But they didn't."

"No. They made me get on the gurney, and they strapped me in with leather restraints. They covered my mouth with tape as well."

"And then they cut your throat?" Finn asked.

"Yes."

"Did you see it?" Finn asked.

"See what Mr. Finn?"

"The blade. Was it a knife…a sword…a letter opener? What did they cut you with, Dr. Mahmoud?"

"I'm afraid I don't know. I was trembling with fear."

Camp raised his hands slowly toward Mahmoud's face.

"May I?" Camp asked as he tilted Mahmoud's chin up.

Mahmoud nodded. Camp examined the thin red cut line and scab.

"You're lucky to be alive, Dr. Mahmoud, they missed your carotid artery by less than a centimeter."

"Really?"

"Good thing Captain Henry and Miriam returned when they did. You could have bled out," said Campbell. "Is that the door they brought the woman in?"

"Yes, and the same one they took Major Banks out of."

"The woman…did you recognize her?" asked Finn.

"No. I was told she was the Commando colonel's wife. But we have since learned that was a lie," Mahmoud said as he gently rubbed his neck.

"Any idea who would have wanted to do this?" Camp asked.

"No. Major Banks was a very nice person. But I don't think this was about Major Banks," Mahmoud reasoned. Camp paused and waited for the explanation.

"Okay. What's it about Dr. Mahmoud?" Camp asked.

"War. Afghanistan has been at war since 1980. These things happen in war all the time," Mahmoud said.

"Not with American Army doctors who are here to help," Camp lectured.

Mahmoud dropped his head. "War doesn't care who you are, Captain Campbell," Mahmoud said sadly.

Camp, Finn and Captain Henry walked to the doorway and Miriam followed.

"I'm sure we'll have more questions, Dr. Mahmoud. Can we talk to you again tomorrow?" Camp asked.

"Yes, certainly, Captain Campbell. I'm here to help."

Finn exited then took a few steps back into the ER. "Dr. Mahmoud, looks like you scored a new pair of Air Jordans. Nice shoes."

Mahmoud beamed with pride.

"Yes, I love American shoes. It's very difficult to get Nike brand in Afghanistan. Usually it's only Puma, sometimes Reeboks."

"Nice."

Finn caught up to Camp and Henry as they walked down the other fluorescent-lit corridor past recovery and the sick bay. Miriam walked closely behind.

"What do you figure they pay a government physician from Kabul to work at the Afghan Army hospital in Paktya?" asked Finn.

"Two hundred, maybe two hundred and fifty US dollars a month," Captain Henry responded as Camp rounded the corner into the surgical recovery room.

"Looks like Doc Mahmoud just came into a bit of a windfall then. Even on the black market those Jordans had to set him back a hundred," Finn added. "What do you think Camp, just a lucky guy?"

"What do I think? I think it was a number seven beaver...a surgical scalpel for internal organs. Precise and accurate. They could have cut him deep and separated his neck from his jawbone. But Dr. Mahmoud wasn't even stitched up after they slit his throat. He was lucky alright, or maybe he knew exactly what he was doing."

Miriam kept her head down and remained focused as the four walked through the recovery room.

"We need more answers. Who else can we talk to?" Camp asked.

"Checkpoint guards?" Captain Henry offered.

"What about the colonel who runs the commandos? They said it was his wife?" Camp asked.

"How about the commanding general? It's his base.

Nothing gets on, nothing gets off, unless he knows about it," Finn added.

"What about some grunts and medics, regular Afghan Joes that work around the hospital?"

"Captain Campbell, our Army medic team is doing trauma and triage training drills with their Afghan counterparts next Tuesday morning. Might be a good time to ask some questions," Captain Henry said.

Miriam stepped up and changed the direction of the conversation.

"Excuse me, Captain Henry, I just want to remind you that I delayed my leave. I go home this weekend. I have not seen my son in almost two months."

"I'm tracking, Miriam. Three days, right?"

"Yes, sir, I will be at the Thunder checkpoint Tuesday morning and ready to work during the drills."

7

University Hospital, Clinic and Research Center
Philadelphia, Pennsylvania

Sea Bee Campbell, his wife Ruth, and Lieutenant Colonel Leslie Raines occupied three seats in the expansive yet elegant waiting room. Leslie held Ruth's hand as Sea Bee stared at the BMW advertisement in his US News & World Report magazine.

"Planning to buy a new car Seabury?" Ruth asked.

He didn't answer, nor did he turn the page.

"Have you heard from my son?"

"He Skyped me from the USO in Bagram, but that was a couple of weeks ago," Raines said.

"Do you miss him?"

"Oh, maybe a bit," Raines said with a smile.

Sea Bee just glared at the BMW.

"You like him," Ruth said contently as she looked around the room at the other patients.

The office door opened and a nurse called for Seabury Campbell. Ruth took the magazine out of Seabury's hand and the three of them stood up. The nurse led them to Exam Room #3. The room was large and included the exam table, the doctor's desk, two leather patient chairs, a magazine rack and a coat rack. The walls were littered with diplomas, advanced degrees, board certifications and awards.

"Dr. Blauw will be with you shortly."

Raines stood while Ruth and Seabury took the two seats.

"Look at all of these degrees, Seabury."

Sea Bee looked at the walls and suddenly seemed engaged. He got up and started to read the inscriptions.

"Pieter J. Blauw, Bachelors of Science, Biology, University of Leipzig; Pieter J. Blauw, MD, Boston University; board certified in neurology and psychiatry? This guy's a shrink?" Seabury said.

"He's a geriatric psychiatrist and neurologist Mr. Campbell. My colleague said he is the best of the best," Raines said trying to defend the credentials of a man whom she had never met.

"Best at what?"

"Honey, Leslie says he's a professor, the director of the hospital's memory center and the associate director of the Alzheimer's Disease Center," Ruth summarized.

The exam room door opened, and Dr. Blauw extended his hand to greet all parties. Though he had earned his advanced degrees in the states, he still couldn't hide his German accent.

"You're German!" Sea Bee said dismissively.

Blauw gazed quickly at his wall of fame.

"Born and raised in Hamburg, medical degree in Boston, residency at Columbia Presbyterian in New York, a fellowship in Behavioral Neurology and Cognitive Neuroscience in the Netherlands, now I cheer for the Eagles and Flyers in Philadelphia," Blauw said.

"Did you hear that, Seabury, said he's a Presbyterian," Ruth emphasized with assurance.

"Well, actually," Blauw started, but decided it was better to just let it go. "Mr. Campbell, why are you here today?"

"My wife thinks I'm nuts!"

"Do you think you're nuts?"

There was a long pause. "I'm not as sharp as I used to be."

"In what ways?"

"I can't find the words I used to know…I can't find the doors I once walked through…and I'm not real sure what to do when I finally find those doors."

"Does that bother you?"

"That's a pretty stupid question for such a smart Presbyterian with a bunch of fancy degrees on his wall…Of course it bothers me."

"Seabury!" Ruth interrupted. "Mind your manners."

Dr. Blauw raised his hands in a calming manner. "No, that was a fair response. In fact, the fire in your belly is helpful. We can use that. There's nothing I've seen in your medical records over the last 40 years or in just a few minutes of talking with you that would suggest we're dealing with a severe mental illness. "

"Well then we're in good shape, Dr. Blauw, because my husband has an endless supply of piss, fire and vinegar!"

"Mr. Campbell, let me explain what I do from the 30,000-foot level, then I'll bring it back to what I want to do with you."

"Now he wants to drop me out of an airplane."

"Not exactly. I both see patients – as a doctor – and I also conduct research on the diseases I treat in a laboratory, as a scientist. I'm a clinician, and I'm a researcher. When I'm not seeing patients like you, then I work in my lab with mice and other animals that have been genetically bred to have the same diseases people develop. In the clinic, I treat patients who mostly have neurodegenerative diseases; those are fancy words for diseases that usually attack us when we get older. In the laboratory, I focus on cellular and molecular neuropathology and the clinical biomarkers in aging."

"So what have I got, Doc? Harry Tasner said it was hardening of the arteries. Do you think I have Alzheimer's?"

"AD, Alzheimer's disease, is hard to diagnose; it's more of a judgment first, then followed by some specific tests that would confirm if you have AD. Your family doctor has taken great care of you for many years. But now you're suffering a little bit of dementia. I need to figure out if that's due to Alzheimer's or something else."

"What kind of tests can you do, Dr. Blauw?" Ruth asked.

"Today we'll do a complete physical exam to check Mr. Campbell's overall neurological health. Reflexes, muscle tone and strength, ability to get out of a chair and walk across the room, sense of touch and sight, coordination and balance."

"But you ain't gonna check my nuts to see if I'm nuts, are you?"

"Seabury!" Ruth scolded.

Blauw laughed. "It's okay, Mrs. Campbell. I can assure you that it's nothing compared to surgeon talk in an operating room. No, you should still see your family doctor for all your annual physicals. My nurse will draw some blood so we can rule out thyroid disorders or vitamin deficiencies. If you're okay with all that, then I'd like to get started with a 10-minute 'mental status test.' Colonel Raines, you're welcome to stay for the mental test but only family members during the physical portion."

"She's our daughter-in-law," Ruth blurted out before Raines could speak. "She *is* family."

"Look who's nuts now, woman!" Seabury quipped.

"I understand, Dr. Blauw," Raines answered amid subtle embarrassment.

"Okay, this should take 10 minutes. You can use the clipboard for the written answers. Are you ready?"

Sea Bee nodded.

"Number one; draw the face of a clock with the hands showing four-thirty."

Sea Bee looked over at Ruth and rolled his eyes.

"Two, what's today's date, and where are you right now?"

Sea Bee answered but couldn't hide his contempt. Blauw held up a laminated sheet of paper with a picture on it.

"Three, here is a picture of two pentagon shapes intersecting. On your paper draw the same thing, or as close as you can come."

Sea Bee looked at the picture and reproduced it on his clipboard.

"Number four, Mr. Campbell; I'm going to hand you a note card with instructions on it. Please read the card silently and then follow the instructions written on the note card."

Blauw handed him the card. Sea Bee stood up and walked over to the door. He knocked on the door two times quickly.

"I have 40 cows in the field," Sea Bee announced to the room then knocked on the door two more times, turned around in a circle and sat down.

"Number five, Mr. Campbell, here is a blank note card. Write down one complete sentence that tells me about your family."

"Can't do it in one."

"Please, try to limit your thoughts to one complete

sentence."

Sea Bee looked at Ruth for inspiration, but she refused to make eye contact with him. He started to write fast and furiously then handed the note card back to Dr. Blauw who read it to himself.

"Okay, two more and we're done. Mr. Campbell, count backwards from 100 by sevens, out loud."

A strange gaze grew over Sea Bee's face.

"I'm not following you."

"Start with 100 and count backwards by sevens. For example, take 100 and subtract seven, which would give you 93, then keep subtracting sevens."

Sea Bee didn't speak. His breathing became more pronounced. He started to panic.

"Seabury, you've always been a math whiz. Just count backwards," Ruth said trying to encourage him.

"Mrs. Campbell, please," Blauw stopped her as the intensity with Sea Bee started to ramp up.

"Well he is," Ruth whispered to Raines. "He was the one who always helped the children with their math problems."

Leslie held up her hand to help quiet Ruth who was starting to panic more than Seabury.

"Mr. Campbell? Can you count backwards from 100 for me...by sevens? I've already given you the first answer."

Sea Bee looked down at the floor in defeat. He said nothing.

"Okay, number seven, the seventh and final

question, Mr. Campbell. Are you up for one more?"

Sea Bee nodded his head.

"I'm going to say three words out loud with a pause between each word. Once I've said all three words, simply say them back to me. Okay?"

He nodded again.

"Sliding…slippery…sidewalk…"

Sea Bee moved his lips. He was trying to say the words. Both Ruth and Raines could see the anguish on his face as he struggled to recall the pattern that flashed through his brain but quickly disappeared.

Sea Bee was lost.

"That's okay…I understand that you are a farmer so let's try these three words instead. Cow…barn… pasture."

Sea Bee smiled as he searched for the words. Finally it came.

"Junior…my boy. He used to help me on the farm. He was a good boy, Dr. Blauw, a good boy."

The room was silent. Dr. Blauw recorded some notes and then stood. "Mr. Campbell, I'll give you a couple of minutes to change into this hospital gown for your physical exam."

"And I really need to get back to Fort Detrick," Raines said as she gathered up her things.

Blauw walked over to Raines as Ruth tended to Sea Bee.

"Colonel Raines, I'll walk you out. You must have gotten a very high level referral. It's not often that we can take new patients on such short notice."

Raines and Blauw emerged in the corridor away from the exam room.

"Actually my boss, Dr. Ernst Groenwald, said you were the best on the East Coast."

"Ernie? He's a great guy. I haven't seen him in years."

"He said you two once worked together."

"A hundred years ago in The Netherlands. Ernie was one of many brilliant minds who rotated in and out of Rotterdam. I worked for a few years in the Daniel den Hoed Clinic, part of the Dijkzigt Hospital, while Ernie researched infectious diseases and pandemics. Once you get accustomed to the American way of life, even an impressive place like the Brezden University Medical Center can't keep you."

"Well, I hope you can do something for Mr. Campbell."

"Hard to say, colonel, we'll see how the tests come back."

"I presume you'll do the standard battery: CT, MRI, and PET?"

"Colonel, the best hope we have for AD is early diagnosis and prevention. By the time we cinch the diagnosis of AD we're already in trouble. Too late. Think of the fireman holding the hose, spraying water into your living room, and yelling 'fire' while you're sitting on the couch reading a book. It's kinda too late to be at the bedside when the fire department shows up. That's why

I work on the bench as well. We've got to find better diagnostic tests, biomarkers, vaccines, early detection and prevention."

"I work with infectious diseases and bioterrorism. Prevention is the name of the game."

Blauw pulled the note card out of his lab coat and handed it to Raines.

"Colonel, hang on to this. Guess his son must be a Navy SEAL. The family will appreciate it one day, but probably sooner than they would like to admit."

8

Datta Khel, Miran Shah District
North Waziristan, Pakistan

The table next to the woman's bed was set. Ether, surgical sutures, a scalpel and two industrial grade silicone breast implants were staged for the operation.

"Why were these taken out of their packages? It's hardly a sterile environment in the first place," Banks said with full irritation as he pointed to the silicone implants just lying on the wood surface of the dirty table.

"They are fine, Dr. Banks. The commander wanted them modified," Kazi defended as he turned on two more lights, all powered by an outdoor generator. "I want to introduce you to Dr. Ja'far. He will be assisting you."

Ja'far had arrived the night before. He was an older man, bespeckled, and of slight build. He wore the traditional salwar kameez.

"What kind of a doctor are you, Ja'far?" Banks asked as the old man looked back puzzled.

"He does not speak English. Dr. Ja'far is a professor, a scientist by trade," Kazi said. "Tell me what you're doing, how you're doing it, and I will translate everything for Dr. Ja'far. Perhaps he can learn to do the procedure himself in the future."

Banks took a long glance at Kazi and shook his head with not-so-subtle contempt. He figured his only ticket out was to perform the surgery and hope that Kazi was telling him the truth.

"Well, Ja'far, then it looks like we'll learn this thing together. I operate on women, but usually I'm working on the other end. I don't know of anywhere in the world where they still use ether for anesthesia, but that's what we're going to do today, Ja'far. Pour some on these rags and hold it over her nose. I'd recommend you boys take the tape off now so she doesn't gag, choke and drown in her own vomit. Better hold her down too. I have this feeling she's not anymore thrilled to be here than I am, so she's going to fight you."

Kazi told Ja'far what to do and nodded to two of the abductors. They held her head down as Kazi pulled the face veil and hijab off before pulling the duct tape from her mouth. Her blood-curdling scream filled the entire village until Ja'far covered her nose with the ether rag. Slowly, she stopped fighting and settled down into a slightly disturbed sleeping pattern.

"Normally we do this sort of thing in a hospital," Banks said as he reached for some alcohol and swabs.

"Most women have the procedure done as outpatients, Dr. Banks, in less than two hours." Kazi's reassurances were hardly reassuring. "This will be fine."

"Thanks for the news flash, Kazi."

Banks stopped working and stood still as he stared at Kazi.

"Well?"

"Well what?"

"Would you like me to perform the surgery by cutting directly through her burka or are you going to take it off?"

Kazi looked over at the woman, now unconscious, and at the two captors who stood guard.

"It's called a chadri, Dr. Banks. We are not permitted to take it off her. You'll have to do that."

"You have got to be –."

Banks closed his eyes in boiling anger and walked over to the woman. As he started to pull the chadri up and over the woman's head the guards looked at him in disgust. He was fulfilling their vision of the Great Satan, the infidel. Under the burka the woman was wearing the traditional trousers and black shoes. Banks removed her shirt and her bright blue bra.

Kazi, Ja'far and the two armed men were obviously disturbed by the sight of the bare-breasted woman.

"Sorry guys, but this is the only thing I can think of doing for this particular surgery. Better keep the ether handy, Ja'far."

Banks poured rubbing alcohol on some Q-Tip swabs and scrubbed the area around each nipple.

"What are you doing, Dr. Banks?" Kazi asked.

"I'm trying to sterilize the area before I cut."

"I realize that, but why are you going to cut there? Shouldn't you be under her arm?"

"Transaxillary? In this dirty hellhole shed of a surgical suite? Give me a break. A transaxillary incision under the armpit tissue requires a channel up to the breast. We'd need an endoscope, and I certainly don't see one here on my table of barbaric Barney Rubble tools."

"Endoscope?"

"It's a small tube and inside is a light and a camera that's embedded in the end of the tube. If I had one, I could watch the movement of the endoscope on a TV monitor so I could position the implants at the exact spot, planted and centered behind each nipple."

Kazi shook his head as he and Dr. Ja'far traded epiphanies in Pashtu.

"Perhaps that's what we did wrong?" Kazi said to Ja'far.

Banks kept cleaning the breasts.

"Thought he didn't speak any English?"

Ja'far moved in closer.

"You make incision *on* nipple?" Ja'far asked in broken English.

"It's called a periareolar incision. I've never done this myself, Ja'far, but I've watched several when I was in school. Can't be that hard, I guess. Plastic surgeons do this procedure. You cut right at the edge of the areola. We want the incision between the dark areola and surrounding breast skin so it can be hidden. Most women – maybe even this one – would rather not have visible scarring on their breasts."

"This is better method?" Ja'far asked.

"Yes, for two reasons. First, we can place the implants in a precise pocket formation. They'll be exactly where we want them to be and, ah, where your commander wants them to be. Second, absolute controlled bleeding. Bleeding is our enemy, especially in here."

Ja'far smiled. It was all making sense now.

"Unfortunately, we have to get these huge-ass PIP implants in and through a very small incision."

"How big the cut?"

Banks picked up the number seven beaver scalpel. He pressed the edge of the blade down on her right breast and started to cut.

"Five centimeters, seven at most. Kazi, I don't have the skills or the tools necessary to do this thing submuscular. I've gotta go subglandular."

"Whatever," Kazi mumbled as he observed the first incision.

"I can't put these things behind the pectoralis major muscle. I'm placing them in the retromammary space – subglandular – it's like a pocket between the gland of the breast tissue and pectoralis muscle."

"Is that bad?"

"Can be. Can cause capsular contracture of the immune system. Her body might reject the implant."

"How long, Dr. Banks? How long before she could reject the implants?"

"I don't know, six months, a year, two years. You need to get her to a hospital if she starts to run a fever, feels pain, or develops hematomas or the settling of blood in her breasts."

"We'll let the commander worry about all of that," Kazi opined.

After an hour with each breast and a couple of doses of ether from Ja'far, Banks sutured the woman up with the Ethicon Prolene cartridge spools. He walked over to his bed and sat down followed closely by his two armed captors.

"There you go, Kazi. Tell the commander that his woman will be good as new in a week or so. He should go easy on her for the first month. She's gonna be sore to the touch."

"I will let him know, Dr. Banks."

"So how 'bout that ride back to Thunder? When do we leave?"

"Dr. Ja'far...do you have any more questions?" Kazi asked as Ja'far walked away.

Kazi nodded to one of the captors.

"Right now, Dr. Banks."

Banks sensed the motion and felt the cold steel as a single AK-47 gunshot broke the village calm and jarred the burka–clad woman momentarily from her ether sleep and recovery.

Paktya Regional Hospital
FOB Thunder
Afghanistan

The PA speakers above Thunder and Lightning crackled to life simultaneously, Pashtu on the Afghan base and English on the American base.

"لوکرو نیږمت, لوکرو نیږمت, لوکرو نیږمت."

"Drill, drill, drill."

Camp was sitting with Billy Finn, Captain Henry and Captain Sylvia Dawkins in the middle dining room of the DFAC when the PA announcement came in.

"Are you kidding me? My omelet is still hot. I thought this thing was gonna happen at 0930," Camp jawed as he pushed back from the table and stood.

"It's the first time in history the Afghans have done anything early," Henry quipped.

Dawkins grabbed her US Air Force-issued Nikon D3S and stood as Finn kept eating.

"I'll take care of your trays while you three go play disaster triage with your Afghan buddies," Finn said as he reached over and forked a bite of Camp's fresh cheese and mushroom omelet.

Miriam was waiting at the gate outside of Terp Village as Camp, Henry and Sylvia Dawkins ran up. Ten medics from Captain Henry's team rushed through the turnstile one at a time, running down the gravel path between T-walls, past two Nepali Gurkha guards and across the street to the Paktya Regional Hospital.

Barracks building 59 on Thunder opened up as a steady stream of bearded Afghan men in military uniforms ran down the hill between enlisted barracks, through the open field and over to the hospital. Unlike their American counterparts, the Afghans did not carry weapons.

Miriam was bundled up in a winter parka and stayed her typical 10-foot distance behind Camp and Henry as they jogged over to the front entry doors of the hospital.

Two Ford Ranger ambulances were staged in the parking lot and another five Ford Ranger army trucks were loaded with Afghan men pretending to have various forms of injuries and wounds.

The main lobby of the hospital was quickly converted to a disaster triage center. More seriously wounded "patients" were wheeled down the long fluorescent-lit corridor to the ER or alternatively, over to the sparsely-equipped and seldom sterile operating room. Minor injury patients were treated in the lobby.

American military medics mentored their Afghan counterparts as each team's Terp translated between Pashtu and English. The scene was chaotic. Aside from occasional laughter from some of the Afghan soldiers who were medics by assignment, rather than by interest or training, the drill unfolded flawlessly.

Miriam retreated to her cubicle behind the lobby wall and desk but close enough and within earshot of

Camp if he needed translation services. Unlike Captain Henry, Camp was largely unengaged and somewhat disinterested in the whole training exercise. It came with the new turf, but his main job was to find Major Banks.

Miriam removed her winter parka and placed it on the back of her desk chair. She had modified her sweater vest earlier in the morning. She had configured a solitary green fabric strap that lifted up from the left side of her vest, wrapped around and behind her neck, then connected back down to the front right side of her sweater vest like a halter. The straps were sown into the vest where three empty water bottles sat snugly in three neatly sewn pockets.

Miriam reached over and pulled the vase on her desk closer and removed the artificial flowers. Camp looked over briefly and smiled as Miriam admired her flowers.

The lobby was overflowing with emergency orders and instructions yelled out in two different languages. No one heard Miriam pour the glass beads into the three empty water bottles – a bead that had been deposited into the vase each day for almost four years – and born from a single bead necklace worn one day and replenished the next.

Out of the top center drawer, Miriam removed two packages of cotton shoe laces she had purchased from one of the Haji stores in Terp Village. She had spent several long nights in her Terp Village hooch corning the black powder she had scoured for on Thunder. Using water as a binder, she had dried the black powder into cakes, crushed them again and again, and screened them into smaller sizes. The fine-grained, dried slurry of black powder covered the cotton shoelaces along with a light coating of glue from the hospital's supply cabinet, and together created an archaic black match fuse with an ignition burn rate of nearly 20-feet per second.

The cotton shoelace had 10 inches of common single stem on top. Three extending stems were sewn together into the common stem, and all were covered and prepped with the dried slurry. Miriam staged each of the coupled stems down through the narrow slits she had cut into the blue plastic water bottle caps and then into the glass bead-filled water bottles already sitting in their customized pockets in her colorful wool vest.

She removed the iced tea bottle from her lower desk drawer, unscrewed the cap and emptied a new flask of oriental spice perfume into the bottle. She poured the mixture into the water bottles where it blended with the beads and the dried slurry laces. Miriam gently screwed the blue plastic caps back onto the water bottles.

She waited for several minutes until she saw him coming.

Dr. Mahmoud walked quietly down the long corridor and into the front lobby so he could inspect the triage drill. She bowed her head, said a quick prayer, then reached back to grab her parka. She put both arms in and zipped the parka up a few inches.

Camp looked over at Miriam and smiled again.

"What's the Pashtu word for cold?" he shouted to Miriam over the mayhem and din in the lobby.

"Same as in English…brrrrr," Miriam laughed without the slightest hint of betrayal in her voice.

Miriam got up and walked around the six-foot wall separating her cubicle from the front desk. She moved past triage cots where more than 40 Americans, Afghan soldiers and local Paktya role-players were conducting the emergency drill. She stepped to the center of the room.

She stopped.

Without speaking a word she reached into the pocket of her parka and pulled out a cigarette lighter she had found discarded on the picnic table between Terp Village and the checkpoint.

"What's up with Miriam?" Camp whispered to Sylvia Dawkins who was sitting next to him as she snapped photos for her Armed Forces Network story.

Camp's legs froze in situational awareness cement as Miriam lit the dried slurry cotton shoe lace that peeked out from the parka zipper. The flame raced up her coat and disappeared.

The initial "explosion" sounded more like a muffled backfire from an old pick-up truck.

The parka expanded with a violent heave of gas vapor then flames shot up through the collar, out the sleeves and through the zipper as Miriam screamed in pain.

Camp found his legs and after two steps was

airborne through the front lobby until his body came crashing down on Miriam. The lobby erupted in panic as 40 people jumped for cover and 10 medics reached for M9s and M4s.

Sylvia Dawkins kept shooting photos.

Camp smothered Miriam with as much force as possible. In a split second, he wondered if he would actually hear the final detonation or feel his body disintegrating into a thousand tiny little pieces.

Flames poured through the open spaces between Camp's arms and chest as an Army medic standing nearby grabbed a blanket and jumped onto the burning contortion of US Navy Captain "Camp" Campbell and Miriam the interpreter who was buried and hidden on the cement floor in a melting parka.

The flames were extinguished. The room was eerily silent. Everyone waited for the final blast that never came.

Camp rolled off of Miriam. His hands were burned and his uniform was smoldering and frayed.

Miriam moaned in pain. She was alive but semi-conscious.

The medics rushed over. Two medics tried to attend to Camp before he brushed them aside. Four others went to Miriam. They gently cut off the remains of her parka and rolled her over. The three water bottles had melted to her chest. The glass beads were still perfectly lodged against her chest as they carefully removed the improvised explosive device from around her neck.

"SECURE THIS BUILDING. No one leaves. No cell phones. No comms. No one moves," Camp yelled as he got to his feet. "Everybody go to red." The words echoed in the cinder-block hospital as medics took their weapons off of safety.

"She's alive, Captain," one of the medics yelled.

"Get her down to the ER," Camp said as he ran next to the cot she was being carried on.

Miriam was delusional, moaning, and trying to speak. She was saying something in Pashtu.

"English, Miriam," Camp prodded as they hurried down the single fluorescent lined corridor.

"My husband," she uttered through her brown crusted face which had already started to swell.

"Your husband? Did he make you do this?" Camp yelled through her moans as she started to go into shock.

Inside the ER, Camp grabbed an intubation tube as Miriam was moved to a gurney. She writhed violently as Camp jammed the tube up her nose to make sure her airway stayed open before massive swelling set in.

The medics moved in to cut away the clothing that hadn't already melted to her skin.

Camp checked her vitals on both wrists and ankles.

"Check out her right arm, sergeant, she's going to need an escharotomy, or we'll lose that pulse," Camp barked to the lead medic.

"I don't think I can do that, captain."

"Better learn quickly."

Captain Henry ran in from the drill location in the

operating room down the other corridor just in time to see the carnage in the ER.

"Get me a scalpel and some large dressings, sergeant," Henry barked. "Someone take a look at the captain's hands."

Camp was already on the cell phone he was issued at Bagram.

"Finn! Get over to the hospital now! We've had an attempted homicide bombing."

"What the hell?" Finn said as he got up from his table in the DFAC and sprinted out the back door with his phone glued to his ear.

"Finn, find some C4 and bring it."

"Where the hell am I supposed to - ."

Camp hung up as Finn changed directions and ran toward the EOD B-hut.

"Captain Dawkins!" he screamed down the corridor. Sylvia Dawkins came running carrying her Nikon with M9 pistol still in her thigh holster, while six other American medics stood guard in the lobby with weapons pointed at Afghan army soldiers, hospital workers and the local citizens who were participating in the drill.

"Yes, sir."

"I'm going to need a story and some photos ASAP. This is going to be released to the Afghans only. Do NOT send it up the chain for approval. This is not for Coalition Forces. Afghan eyes only!" Camp yelled.

"Sir?"

"That's a direct order, captain."

"Roger, sir, I have some great photos. Do you want me to run back to the PAO shop now?"

"Negative. Write your story here from the ER computer. But there'll be a few more photos to take."

Billy Finn came running down the corridor with two Explosive Ordnance Disposal soldiers from the 753rd National Guard unit out of West Virginia.

"Holy shit!" Finn said as he rounded the corner into the ER where Miriam was being treated and Camp managed the disaster wearing a burned uniform.

"Dawkins come here," Camp said as he pulled Finn, the two EOD soldiers and the Public Affairs Officer against the wall opposite of where Miriam was being treated. "I need an explosion outside the front door of the hospital. Big, but not ridiculous."

"Sir, is this authorized?" asked one of the EOD technicians.

"I'm your authorization, sergeant. Dawkins, I need you to get a photograph of the blast."

"Photograph, my ass, all of Thunder and Lightning will go ape-shit, Camp. What the hell are you thinking?" Finn asked.

"Miriam was sent to blow this place up. For all they know she will, and she'll be dead. Give them what they want. If we can keep Miriam alive, we might be able to find Banks."

"Sir, what about damage to the building?" the EOD sergeant asked.

"Put the brick far enough out that it soils the wall and blows out a few windows. Finn, move everyone into the operating room and away from the front and the glass."

"Camp, what about the Afghan soldiers and locals out there?"

"Don't worry about them, Finn, they still think this is all a drill."

"What about the story, captain?" Dawkins asked as she prepared her story.

"Suicide bomber detonates at the Paktya Regional Hospital today, killing an undisclosed number of Afghan soldiers, locals from Gardez and some American military personnel. Tell them no one has claimed responsibility for the bombing. Tell me about the local media here, Dawkins."

"Well, sir, Radio Television Afghanistan has terrestrial TV and a long-reach radio signal. Al Aribya is here as is Al Jezeera. Not much in the way of print."

"Good. Get the story over to the Afghan PAO and have him distribute with photos immediately. I want this on their TV news and radio within an hour. Don't let anyone else beat you with the story, Dawkins. Finn, I need 10 minutes before detonation."

Finn and Dawkins ran down the corridor as the EODs followed behind. Finn cleared out the front lobby and moved everyone over to the operating room.

"Captain Henry, we need to get Miriam loaded into an MRAP and over to the clinic on Lightning," Camp yelled as chaos in the ER became more intense.

"Roger that, we should be ready in 30 minutes," Henry said as he applied loose bandages to the new incision on Miriam's right arm.

"We don't have 30, gotta be now. No ambulance, sirens, or lights, and no urgency as we move through the checkpoint."

"Roger."

"They're going to have plenty of fireworks to respond to in a few minutes." Camp walked out the back door of the ER to look for a Mine Resistant Ambush Protected vehicle he could borrow for a quick ride.

FOB Lightning – XO's B-Hut
Paktya Province, Afghanistan

Colonel Kierkendahl paced back and forth in front of his desk as Camp, Finn and PAO Dawkins sat around his conference table.

"You walk onto my base and start blowing up Afghan hospitals like you're Dustin Hoffman or something. Who the hell do you think you are, Campbell?"

"I wasn't the would-be suicide bomber, colonel. That was the interpreter your boys cleared, vetted, housed and fed for the last four years," Camp said with obvious contempt.

"We've got all of the Afghans on Thunder in full code red, Lightning is on lockdown, and I'm stuck here with the mission creep producers of Wag the Afghan Dog. What am I supposed to do now?"

"I'd wait it out, professor. Never know what snake might crawl out of the hole on his belly to claim responsibility," Finn replied with a not-so-subtle jab at the Minnesota National Guardsman and his day job at Gustavus Adolphus College.

Dawkins' cell phone rang.

"Got it. Thank you," she said as she ended the call. "RTA just ran the story. Photos are up on TV, and Al Arabiya and Al Jazeera are running it shortly."

"Running what?" Kierkendahl demanded as he pounded his desk.

"Suicide bomber detonates at the Paktya Regional Hospital, undisclosed number of Afghan soldiers, locals and American military killed," Dawkins said as she recited some of her copy.

"That's it! I've had enough of this wild, wild west crap from you two. I want you off my FOB first light tomorrow."

Finn and Camp looked at each other and smiled.

"Oh how we'd love that, colonel," Finn said sarcastically, "but no can do."

The colonel's desk phone started to ring.

"Colonel Kierkendahl...yes, yes good afternoon General Ferguson...yes, sir...they're in my office right now...so you've been briefed?...yes sir, but do you realize what these two have...come again, sir?...Roger that, sir."

Kierkendahl hung up the phone and sat down in the chair behind his desk and swiveled around so that his back faced the others. He sat silently for several seconds then exhaled loudly.

"Let me know what you need. My assets are at your disposal."

Dawkins looked over at Camp and Finn with astonishment as Camp stood.

"What about Miriam the Terp?" Camp asked Colonel Kierkendahl.

"You mean the one RTA is reporting as dead? You saved her life then killed her off for the entire world to see. Looks like she's your problem now, Captain Campbell. Dismissed."

9

A crowd of 14 protesters with signs and posters were gathered outside the main gate to Fort Detrick as Lieutenant Colonel Leslie Raines pulled her Jeep Wrangler into the checkpoint queue. The Jeep window was already down so Raines could hand her credentials to security when a protester started shouting at her.

"Rot in hell, lady, you animal killer!"

Raines never looked at the young man who was hurling the venomous insults.

"Here we go again," she complained quietly as her nails tapped the steering wheel.

Dr. Groenwald was doctoring up his grande mocha with a double shot of espresso at the atrium coffee bar in the Integrated Research Facility when Raines walked up.

"Good morning, Colonel Raines. I would have gotten you a tall skinny if I knew you were here already."

"Who sent the greeting committee?" Raines asked as she got in line.

"Pardon me?

"The animal rights protesters at the gate…is today PETA day?"

Groenwald put the plastic lid back on his cup after three more packets of raw brown sugar and stood in line next to Raines.

"No, they're not just the domestic protesters *du jour* this time. Seems like we have an international operation today," Groenwald said with a lowered voice.

"International?"

"This crew is from SHAC, kissing cousins to the hooligans in London."

"The SHAC Seven are out of jail now, right? Is this part of the same old crusade?" asked Raines.

"Not really. Shall we sit?" Groenwald motioned to an empty couch. "Looks like some of the peaceful groups are trying to recruit a bit of the fringe in order to add some bite to their bark. Another 15 are over at Aberdeen Proving Grounds this morning as well. The British Union for the Abolition of Vivisection has gone to great lengths to ramp up their intelligence gathering, especially on the issue of transporting research animals. They've even blogged about a top secret shipment we received last month. Animal Aid is now making in-roads in the states, even mounting a campaign against the

American Cancer Society and the Susan G. Komen Breast Cancer folks. Worse than that, the public believes what they tell them."

"Why Aberdeen?" Raines asked.

"Vervet monkeys, mostly. SHAC got a hold of some training video a couple of years ago, and every few months they pull it back out to gin up discontent."

"Nerve agent training, wasn't it? I thought the Army stopped doing the training program with vervets several months ago."

"They did. But protesters aren't inclined to let facts get in the way of a TV news camera and some potential donations now are they? Then they got wind of a USDA report that mentioned 94 guinea pigs and 54 rats. Nothing unusual, all by the book really, but written by a clueless science geek who forgot the reports are public domain. His written report came across like he was a heartless bastard."

"BIO or CHEM?" Raines asked.

"Chem for these. They were checking lethal doses for inhalation. You don't know what's really lethal until, well, you know. Anyway, the guy cites a 1984 Clement and Coperman study in his report and asserts that even though the chemical agent induced convulsions and death, that did not necessarily mean the animals went through any pain or suffering. Well, they certainly weren't enjoying a Saturday afternoon playing in the park! The American Humane Fund gets the report, goes international with all of the animal rights underground, some groups align, and today they trot out the vervets. When the Army denies, it comes across as the liar."

Raines took another pull on her latte.

"I don't like the use of guinea pigs and rats, but how would they like us to protect our troops, or the innocent Kurds in Anfal, or the Serbs or any other group? So why Detrick, why today?"

"Aerosolized inhalation. A young community newspaper reporter has apparently been getting some pillow time with one of our scientists who apparently forgot he had an oath along with a single-scoped, polygraph security clearance when he just happened to mention that we would be conducting aerosolized Ebola tests on primates this week. Front page story in the *Bethesda Weekly* this morning; local citizens are going nuts."

"I don't subscribe."

"Well, there are plenty of copies around today so help yourself. It'll be unusually quiet as everyone speculates as to the identity of our sex offender with the big mouth."

"Pretty remote, isn't it?"

"What?" Groenwald asked, as they got up and headed for the elevator.

"That a band of terrorists could aerosolize Ebola effectively as a WMD? They'd have to get the appropriate strain of the disease pathogen and know how to handle the organism correctly. They'd have to grow it in a way that would produce the appropriate characteristics, and then they'd have to store the culture and scale it up to production capacity. Aerosolized or not, dispersing a perfectly lethal recipe for inhalation and widespread destruction is next to impossible."

"That's what we thought, too, until three weeks ago. An Illinois company gets an order for two commercial misting machines for pesticides, something called SkitoMister. The municipality in Hamburg, Germany buys them for mosquito control. Hamburg takes delivery last April just in time for mosquito season. But there's a problem. The two 101-pound machines are nowhere to be found in the maintenance garage when the mosquitoes start to hatch. The city officials get busy with other work, get sloppy and finally file a police report in September. The Bundespolizei contact the American company to verify shipping and get the serial numbers. Next thing you know BPOL says the serial numbers showed up at a port in Jakarta, Indonesia. The local Polri checks out the importer who quickly compensates the Indonesian National Police with an appropriate bribe and confesses to shipping both machines black market to Islamabad."

Stunned, Raines asked, "Oh my God, could this really work? I mean, do they have the competence to formulate the organisms to really be able to facilitate aerosolized particles?"

The elevator door opened and Groenwald swiped his card as did Raines. They both did their biometric scans and the elevator without floor buttons closed and climbed to their floor.

"That's the million dollar question, Colonel Raines. We're not running a Dark Winter or a Top Off, but that's why we're testing aerosolizers this week."

"Do we have any clues on the biologicals? Ebola? Smallpox? Marburg's?"

"No clue.   But two American-made, high performance, aerosol misters, sold to Hamburg, stolen and shipped to Jakarta before black market transit to Islamabad, can't be a good thing."

"And the protesters?"

"Right now, the least of our worries…they're just the detritus of our storm."

FOB Lightning – Level 1 Clinic
Paktya Province, Afghanistan

A short-straw Army specialist was about to end his evening shift guarding the prisoner-patient when Camp walked through the doors of the clinic.

"Good morning, specialist. How's our patient?"

"She seems fine, sir; she woke up about an hour ago."

"She's awake?" Camp asked as he moved quickly toward her private room.

"She said something all whacked out in that Afghani shit and then, all of a sudden like, she says 'my son' in like perfect English, you know?"

"I've got it from here, specialist. Go hit your rack."

"Doc, I was wondering if you could get me some

Ambien. I'm having a real hard –."

"Big bottle behind the counter, little round blue pills, help yourself. One per night. Got it?"

"Yes, sir."

Miriam's face was crusted and more swollen. Blotches of red covered her neck and forehead. Her arm was heavily bandaged from the escharotomy, but Camp could feel a pulse. The IV bag kept a constant flow of antibiotics, pain meds, sedation and fluids flowing. The intubation tube was uncomfortable, but it was better to have it in, especially if the airway should close from swelling. The Level 1 clinic on a Forward Operating Base was intended for PT sprains, colds, diarrhea, flu and Ambien. It was hardly a burn center, but Miriam was luckier than most burn patients. Camp and the medics got the fire extinguished quickly. The patient would be in recovery for several weeks; there would be scarring, but she would live.

"Miriam, can you hear me?"

Her eyes were swollen shut with bandages and ointment covering them.

A weak raspy whisper pierced the silence.

"Yes."

"How are you feeling?"

"My son…my husband will kill him if he finds out that I lived."

Camp walked around to the other side of her bed.

"You're dead, Miriam…we sent reports to the Afghan media about the suicide bomber who killed

herself and several others at the hospital. So relax…
you're dead."

"I wish I was."

"But your son may not be as lucky as you, Miriam."

Her body writhed, and she grew agitated.

"What have you done to him?"

"Nothing yet. But I intend to hunt him down and
kill him myself unless you tell me what I want to know."

Camp heard the clinic door open. He saw Billy
Finn walk into Miriam's room just as Camp bent over
toward Miriam's ear.

Miriam became still.

"Mr. Finn is here," she said to their mutual surprise.

"How are you, Miriam?" Finn responded though
not really caring if she was feeling well or ever would.

"Your husband, Miriam, who is he? Why did he
make you do this?" Camp continued the interrogation.

Miriam did not speak.

"Did he have something to do with Major Banks'
kidnapping?" Finn asked.

Miriam stayed silent.

"Does he live in Khost? Does he live there with
your son and his family?" Camp asked.

She did not respond.

Camp walked away from Miriam's bed and over to
the desk phone in the room. He looked up at the phone
numbers on a sheet of paper taped to the plywood wall.
Pressing the speaker button, dial tone filled the room
before Camp punched in the numbers.

"Task Force Duke, this is Sergeant Melendez," said the voice on the other end.

"Melendez, you've got Khost in your area of operations, do you not?"

"Affirmative, sir."

"Great. Operation Baby Bird is now green. Send your team over right now. Dead or alive, doesn't matter to me," Camp said as he pulled the handset up and disengaged the speaker phone.

"No!" Miriam pleaded as urgently as possible through the pain.

"Sir, what the hell are you talking about? You've reached the medical clinic at TF Duke in Khost," Sergeant Melendez shot back into Camp's handset and ear.

"Excellent. Let me know as soon as the mission is completed."

Camp hung up the phone and walked closer to Miriam who was starting to twitch uncomfortably as Finn pinched the bridge of his nose, closed his eyes and held back the laughter.

"I'll tell you."

"Too late, Miriam, you're nothing but a suicide bomber with a dead kid. You certainly didn't care whose sons you were going to kill yesterday. Why should you care if your son is killed today?"

"Datta Khel, Miran Shah District, in the northern tribal regions."

"Pakistan?" Finn asked now fully engaged.

"He is called Khyber Abbasin."

"Is he Talibani?" Camp asked.

Miriam did not answer.

"Haqqani?   He deals in the Haqqani network, doesn't he Miriam?" Finn prodded.

"ISI…Inter-Services Intelligence," Miriam said as Finn bolted out of the room.

"Okay, Miriam, I'll trust you on this one…we'll call off the mission for your son."

"No…please rescue him…bring me my son."

Camp reached down and touched her left hand by the IV drip, the only part of her upper torso that wasn't burned.

"Inshallah."

10

Kabul, Afghanistan

Camp and Finn exited the Blackhawks on the LZ at Camp Phoenix and made their way to the Rhinos for the six-mile ride through the streets of Kabul and over to ISAF where General Ferguson was waiting for them. The Rhino was an up-armored "Winnebago on steroids", virtually indestructible in both Iraq and Afghanistan, and served as a civilian and military personnel carrier. It was presumed to be indestructible until the Taliban sent a vehicle-borne improvised explosive device into one a few months earlier. The VBIED car bomber knocked the Rhino over and left a morass of twisted steel scattered among 14 dead and 11 wounded civilians and military personnel from three different NATO nations.

Ferguson and two coffee-pouring majors were seated and waiting for Camp and Finn when they arrived.

"Camp! Billy Finn! Great to see you, boys," Ferguson said as he got up to shake their hands then stopped abruptly as he saw the bandages wrapped around Camp's hands.

"Good God, Camp…your AAR said nothing about being wounded."

"I must've forgotten to write it down, sir."

Ferguson leaned over to one of his majors. "Make a note and file the paperwork."

"Sir, really it's nothing."

"That's another Purple Heart, captain…your nation is paying you jack shit for dollars. The least we can do is to give you a damn medal when it's earned."

"Why don't you just send me a bottle of cabernet, and we can break General Order Number One together and call it good."

Ferguson smiled and lit a cigar. No one was about to tell him he couldn't smoke in his own office in the middle of a war.

"What do we have, Billy?"

"Well, Miriam the Terp straps on three plastic water bottles, loads them with what I'm guessing was acetone peroxide – kitchen table TATP, the woman always smelled like bleach to me – and then coupled a homemade fuse out of some cotton shoelaces and lit the candle."

"What about the Afghan doctor?" Ferguson asked.

"That one puzzles me a bit. The guy sports a brand

new pair of Air Jordans, not a speck of dirt on them, had to cost him a month of salary, even in the black market. But he was standing in the middle of the kill zone when Miriam lights up the room."

"Finn's right. Clearly Miriam didn't mind killing Mahmoud, so it's hard to know if they were in bed together, figuratively speaking of course," Camp added.

"Base commander at Thunder?"

"Well, that's an interesting study in itself. He refuses to send any Afghan army troops after the ambulance claiming he's out of fuel but calls for a full investigation of his checkpoint and medical crew."

"That's good," Ferguson reasoned.

"It would be, except he's still thinking about who he wants to appoint to that committee. As far as he knows, Miriam blew herself up and killed an undisclosed number of Afghan soldiers, Afghan civilians and American military."

"That was the point of the ruse, right?"

"That's correct, general, but wouldn't you think he'd like to reclaim and identify some bodies or notify next of kin? Nothing. Not a peep about the casualties. But he's on all of the Afghan radio and TV stations promising retribution to those who committed the cowardly act on his base," Finn said.

"Me thinks he doth protest too much," Camp quipped.

"Responsibility?"

"Less than 30 minutes after the news broke the

Taliban spokesman claimed responsibility and threatened more actions."

"Pretty standard, Billy. The Taliban will claim responsibility for a car accident, goat flatulence or runny scrambled eggs in the DFAC."

"But this was different, general. The Taliban referred to the bomber as being a woman, an interpreter who had been hidden within Coalition Forces for four years. Sir, we never described the bomber," Camp added.

"So, they had no doubt that it was Miriam. Have you gotten anything out of her? Can she talk?" Ferguson asked.

"I spent some time with her yesterday morning, sir, and was able to, ah, persuade her to cooperate with us," Camp said.

"Does she know anything about Banks?"

"Sir, it looks to us like her husband may be the common denominator in all of this. Miriam says that if she didn't fulfill her role, her husband would kill their son. She apparently lives for the kid," Camp said.

"She's from Khost. Khost and Paktya are all Haqqani turf. They've got shadow governors in place wherever you look. As far as I'm concerned, I'd bet you the commander at Thunder is Haqqani, too."

"You don't know that Billy."

"No, but this much we do know," Camp added, "Miriam said her husband is ISI."

"Pakistani intelligence? Now what the heck am I supposed to do with that?" Ferguson grunted as he got up and paced the room. "Major Spann...play the video."

Camp and Finn looked at each other.

"Video, sir?"

"Major Banks is a reservist out of Bucks County, Pennsylvania. Board certified gynecologist for a women's health practice. He's got a son, Chad, and a daughter, Brittany. Two days ago Chad gets a video posted to his Facebook wall from one of his new 'friends', a friend he thought was part of a Philadelphia Phillies Baseball Fan Club."

Major Mitchell dimmed the lights then started the two-minute video clip as Camp and Finn watched intently. Spann brought the lights back up. The room was silent.

"Well?" Ferguson asked trying to stimulate discussion.

"Well, at least they didn't chop his head off in the video," Finn said with some degree of honest relief.

"Camp?"

"He's alive...at least he was...that's a start. Maybe we should show it to Miriam and see if she can tell us anything about it."

Finn stood up and walked toward the TV monitor.

"Major Spann, would you play that one more time? Let me have the remote control this time."

Spann dimmed the lights and started the DVD over again from the beginning. He handed the remote to Finn.

"Watch his hands…his hands are on the table but he's doing something with his fingers."

They watched the video again and saw Major Banks contorting his fingers while he was speaking. The DVD ended and Spann turned the lights back on.

"Looks kind of random to me," Ferguson said less than excited.

"Does anybody know sign language? You know, for deaf people?" Finn asked.

The coffee-pouring majors looked at each other, but there were no takers.

"You think he's saying something, Billy?"

"I don't know, but the movement of the fingers isn't natural. Something's going on there. General, can you see if we have someone at Eggers or ISAF or even the Embassy who's familiar with sign language?"

With a quick nod from General Ferguson, one of the majors scrambled out the door and down the hallway.

"Okay, why don't you boys find some billeting and get some food. Let's reconvene back here at 1400 hours. Camp, if you'd stay an extra second or two, I'd appreciate it."

Finn stood up and left with Major Spann as Ferguson moved closer to Camp and sat on the front edge of his desk.

"You okay?"

"Hmm? Oh, this? Fine. Not much worse than a sunburn," Camp said dismissing his burns.

"No, I mean about Jane. Unfortunately we had to deploy you only a few days after her funeral. Not much time to grieve," Ferguson said, sounding more like Camp's friend than a commanding officer.

"Yes, sir, I'm fine. The grieving started and ended a long time ago. This was just the letting go part. I'm at peace with the whole thing. Really, I'm okay."

"So have you talked to *her* since you deployed?" Ferguson asked with special emphasis.

"No. As a matter of fact I haven't. I need to call and see how she and dad are doing."

Ferguson laughed.

"I wasn't talking about your mother, idiot. I was asking about Raines."

"Raines? No, I haven't contacted her recently. I 'Skyped' her from FOB Shank when I was stuck there in the snow last month. Not much bandwidth out of Lightning. Is something wrong?"

Ferguson shook his head in disbelief.

"Yes, something's wrong…she likes you, Camp, and you're too damn dumb to see it…too blind to appreciate it. The woman has been sending me nonstop emails. Why don't you head over to the MWR and call her? I think she'd appreciate it."

"Is the old grizzly playing matchmaker now?"

Ferguson took a long pull on his cigar and filled the room with a billow of smoke.

"You can't wear the uniform forever, Camp. There's life after combat boots. Maybe it's time to start thinking about that."

Camp got up and walked toward the door.

"With all due respect, sir; I don't think *Mrs. Banks* is interested in my lack of a love life right now. But I'll call Raines if that will make you happy. See you at 1400."

Camp walked out and down the middle sidewalks of the ISAF compound. The Kabul air was heavy, dirty and disgusting. The local villagers burned wood fires in their cooking pits just about year round. The heavy winter air kept the smoke from escaping over the mountain passes. It took less than two weeks for every American to fall prey to the "Kabul Krud", an upper respiratory cough that would seldom subside and hardly ever go away until the deployment was over.

Walking into the Morale, Welfare and Recreation building, affectionately known as the MWR, Camp checked in with the Filipino contractor who handled computer check-outs. A piece of wood with the number "7" written in Sharpie ink was Camp's 30-minute ticket to computer number 7. Twenty-three other soldiers, civilians, contractors and NATO partners were already in the computer room, most of them on Skype talking to friends and family around the world as the war in Afghanistan raged all around them.

"Hello, sailor," came the voice on the other end as Raines' image finally caught up with the bandwidth burst. "I was wondering when I might hear from you again."

"Hello, Leslie. I hope I didn't call too late."

"Just getting ready for bed. It's only 2130 here, but I start at 0600 in the morning. A girl's got to get her beauty sleep."

"Well, then you should only need about a half hour. Looks like you're gorgeous already."

"That's coming from the man who currently sees nothing but burka babes."

Camp laughed and readjusted his headset.

"Geez, Camp…what happened to your hands?" Raines said as she moved closer to her computer monitor.

Camp had forgotten about the bandages.

"No big deal. Just a little grease fire in the DFAC when I was making French fries."

Raines gave him a dirty look.

"This from the 'king' of microwaveable dinners? I don't think so. But I suppose you'd have to kill me if you told me what happened."

"How's the new job going, Les? Do you like it?"

"It's interesting, not terribly exciting, but fine. Couple of crazies at the gates with posters, but nothing we can't handle."

"Typical PETA stuff?"

"More of an international flavor these days. Some kind of loose alliance between BUAV, Animal Aid, SHAC and the Animal Liberation Front. Where did they finally send you?"

"Paktya Province."

"Is that where the tularemia outbreak was? Where is it?"

"Eastern border with Pakistan, maybe an hour southeast of Kabul as the crow flies. The tularemia thing turned out to be nothing. Hey, could I ask a favor of you?"

"Anything for a sailor. Did you want me to steal a couple hundred lab mice or something?"

Camp laughed as he watched Raines cradle a cup of hot tea with her soft hands.

"Would you mind checking up on my parents some time, you know, just give them a call or something and see how they're doing?"

"I'd be happy to, Camp. I'll give them a call. Should I tell them about the bandages on your hands or just lie?"

"Save the bandages for another day. Well, General Ferguson wants to see us in a few minutes, so I'd better get going."

"Us? Have you replaced me already?" Raines protested with an exaggerated upper lip pout.

"No one could replace you, Leslie. Ferguson sent a retired FBI agent out to work with me. Billy Finn – he's actually a decent guy."

"Hmmm…that makes a lot of sense…send an FBI agent out with the trauma doctor SEAL who burned his hands while making French fries in the DFAC. Some things never change, do they Camp?"

"You look beautiful, Leslie…talk soon?"

"I miss you Camp…not so long between calls next time, okay?"

General Ferguson and his coffee-pouring majors were already sitting in his office. The video posted on Chad Banks' Facebook account was up and playing as a young woman from the US Embassy watched it. Finn and Camp took their places.

"Tina, this is US Navy Captain Campbell and retired FBI special agent Billy Finn," Ferguson said. "Tina works in the public affairs office at the Embassy. She is fluent in dactylology."

"Dacty what?" Camp feigned.

"Sign language for the deaf, captain," Tina said. "There's really not much to see in the video, and I wasn't sure if his hand gestures were intentional or coincidental, until this part. I'd say it was coincidental if it weren't for the letter z."

"Z?" asked Finn.

"Major Banks' fingers spell four letters, k-a-z-i. The k, a and i are very discreet and could be random. The thumb between the index and middle finger for the 'k', the fist with the outward thumb for the 'a', and the fist with the pinky finger up for an 'i' could all be random. But the sign for z basically requires that you trace the outline of the letter in the air. You have to make three distinct movements with your finger to communicate the letter z."

General Ferguson stood as did all of the other men in the room.

"Thank you for coming over here on such notice, Tina. We really appreciate it," Ferguson said as Tina left. One of the majors walked her out and closed the door.

"So what the heck is kazi?" Ferguson asked.

"Could be the name of the village they took him to," Camp guessed.

"Could be an acronym, could be a weapon, could be random just like the lady said," Finn added.

"Maybe it's a name. Maybe he got the name of the kidnapper," Camp speculated.

"Why don't you run that name past Miriam…see how she responds when you say it," Ferguson suggested.

"Maybe that's a nickname," Finn added. "Or then maybe this is all random, a red herring and a waste of our time."

The remaining major in the room raised his hand as though he was in school and needed permission to contribute to the discussion.

"What is it, major?"

"His file…I've been reading Major Banks' file, and I just found something interesting. His wife…Peggy… she's deaf."

"Well, that eliminates random. So was he trying to communicate some type of love code to her?" Finn said as he stood up and paced the room. "Maybe they do the 'kazi', or something."

"General Ferguson, Miriam said we could find her husband in Datta Khel, Miran Shah District. If her husband is there, maybe there's a good chance that Major

Banks is there as well," Camp said.

"Where's the village?"

"North Waziristan region, sir, in Pakistan," Camp explained.

"Okay, so we send some drones over and look for them."

"Jim, with all due respect, no one in Datta Khel, Miran Shah District thinks Miriam is still alive. They have no idea that we know anything. If drones all of a sudden start snooping over their heads we might lose the element of surprise," Finn reasoned with his old friend General Ferguson.

Ferguson got up and walked over to the classified maps on his wall. The major had already planted a red push-pin flag on top of Datta Khel, Miran Shah District.

"Element of surprise, Billy? What element of surprise? Do you think you two are just going to head over to Hertz, rent a sedan, drive over a few miles of IEDs, pass by the Afghan Border Patrol, present your passports to the Pakistani ISI border agents, then conduct an unauthorized incursion into a sovereign nation, while you go knocking cave to cave looking for a dude named Kazi and our Major Banks?"

Camp and Finn looked at each other and considered the scenario without speaking a word.

"Something like that, sir," Camp finally said.

Ferguson removed his glasses and rubbed his forehead and eyes.

"Make it small. Minimal team. No fireworks. In

and out. If it goes bad, you two need to know this mission was never officially sanctioned. If it goes well, it never happened either."

"Roger that, sir. What about the Terp?"

"What about her, Camp?"

"She can't stay at Lightning. If she goes back to her village, she'll be dead within an hour. If she helps us, we need to do something for her."

"Helps us? Hell, she's probably neck deep in the whole damn plot. Camp, she was trying to be a suicide bomber. She tried to kill everyone in the hospital. As far as I'm concerned, send her back to her village and let them administer some Sharia Law on her ass," Ferguson gruffed as he paced the room.

"Sir, I can use the leverage of her son to make her talk, to make her cooperate. But if she talks, and if she leads us to Major Banks, I want refugee status for her," Camp said.

"SIV? Right, the Ambassador's staff is going to love that. She failed in her suicide attack, so we'd like to bring her to the states so she can be a greeter at Wal-Mart. You're asking too much this time, Camp, too much."

Camp stood and headed to the door as Finn followed behind.

"Finn, how fast can you grow a beard?" Camp asked as Finn turned around and smiled at Ferguson. "Looks like we're going hiking in the Hindu Kush."

"Campbell, I never said I would officially sanction

this," Ferguson yelled as Camp walked out.

"Sanction what, sir?   This whole thing never happened!" Camp's voice trailed off down the hallway as Ferguson lit up another cigar.

11

The nurse walked Seabury and Ruth Campbell into Exam Room #3 and opened the window on Dr. Blauw's computer screen so the doctor could look at the results from the CT, MRI, and PET scans when he arrived.

"Dr. Blauw will be with you in just a few minutes," she said as she closed the door behind her.

Old Sea Bee tapped his fingers relentlessly on his thighs. Ruth reached out and grabbed his hand to stop the fidgeting.

"Stop it. You're driving me crazy, Seabury," she said as the held hand stopped and the free fingers doubled their speed. The door finally opened.

"Good afternoon, Mr. Campbell, Mrs. Campbell. I trust the process this morning was quick."

"Everything was fine, doctor. We're just a bit anxious to get the results," Ruth said.

"Were you able to stop in our cafeteria for lunch? There are lots of great restaurants in the area, but I think our cafeteria serves the best food at a good price," Blauw said as he looked at Seabury's scans from the CT, MRI and PET.

"I had the soup...Navy bean...my son's in the Navy, you know," Seabury said with a great pride.

"Yes, that's what Colonel Raines was telling me a couple of weeks ago. I'm sure he's seen a lot of things during his career."

Blauw looked at the images for several more minutes then closed the screens.

"Okay...let's talk. The positron emission tomography, or PET scan as we like to call it, measures how much sugar is taken up and into the brain. Before the test, we injected Mr. Campbell with glucose, a diagnostic flourodeoxyglucose called FDG. It's a short-lived radioactive form of sugar and it illuminates activity within the brain. What we see in the scans is very low activity in the front of your brain. In my opinion, we're looking at FTD, frontotemporal dementia."

"What the hell? First you talk about pets, and now you want to send flowers. Can you just speak American?" Seabury said with fierce irritation as the finger tapping tripled in speed.

"I'm sorry, but based on these scans and the psychometric tests we did a few weeks ago, I think you have AD, Alzheimer's disease. The FDG-PET images are, unfortunately, rather conclusive. But I think you may have had these symptoms longer than you both realized. We may be moving from mild- to moderate-AD rather quickly."

Ruth reached over and took both of Seabury's hands and held them tightly.

"What can we do, Dr. Blauw? Are there pills he can take, or can we try herbs? One of my lady friends in Sunday school class started doing crossword puzzles and that seemed to help her some," Ruth asked desperately grasping at straws.

"Yes, Mrs. Campbell, we should try everything. Let's start taking over-the-counter Vitamin E supplements each day. Vitamin E is an antioxidant and it might protect some of the nerve cells in the brain from damage. We might be able to delay severe AD with a Mediterranean diet of fish, fruits, beans, high-fiber grains and olive oils. You need to avoid meats, cheese and sweets. I'd also recommend an increase to your exercise, two brisk walks every day."

"Hell, I'd rather die!" Sea Bee yelled to the shock of both Ruth and Dr. Blauw. "Almost 50 years on a dairy farm, and you want me to give up bacon and cheese and hop on a treadmill? Why? Just so I can live another four years?"

Blauw lowered his eyes and stayed silent as Seabury calmed down.

"We'll also start you on some medications, Mr.

Campbell. I'm going to start you with Donepezil, or maybe Aricept, and see if your system can handle it. We may go to Memantine in order to regulate the glutamate if we need to."

"Dr. Blauw, will any of these pills cure Alzheimer's?" Ruth asked.

"No, no I'm sorry, but currently there's no cure for AD. We're working on it, all over the world in fact, and we've had breakthroughs but no cure yet. I spend almost half of my time here doing research with animals, trying to find the next puzzle piece in the equation."

"Are there any other options? Fish, beans, walks and pills, anything else?" Ruth asked.

"Well, there are some clinical studies."

"What do you mean?" Ruth asked.

"It's one of the last phases of the biomedical research process. A scientist has an idea and writes a grant to NIH. NIH awards money, and researchers, oftentimes at universities, conduct basic animal research. The discoveries are then acquired by pharmaceutical and biotech companies as intellectual property. Then they try to develop a medicine or a therapy that targets your disease and is also safe to take. If those applied animal studies are successful, then the Food and Drug Administration authorizes a limited clinical trial where patients with that disease take an experimental medicine, therapy or procedure. That's a human clinical trial."

"Well, I don't think Seabury will be a human guinea pig," Ruth said.

"Now wait a minute, Ruth, I like it. My son's out there on the front lines of God-only-knows-where. The least I can do is get on the front lines of this damn thing," Seabury said with a new sense of purpose. "When do I start?"

"Well, there are several trials we can choose from. I can make some calls and see which ones will take you. You're not what we call 'early-onset,' so options are limited. I can call you in the next week, to discuss what's out there."

"Dr. Blauw, please just set it up with Colonel Raines. She understands all of this gobbledygook better than we do," Ruth rendered as she stood up and reached for Seabury's hand.

"I appreciate that, but due to doctor-patient confidentiality, I can only discuss this with immediate family members unless you provide a waiver."

"Well, I'll sign whatever you want."

"Very well," Blauw said as he wrote out a prescription for Aricept.

Ruth signed the waiver at the nurse station then pulled Sea Bee out of Exam Room #3 on her hand-leash.

FOB Lightning
Paktya Province, Afghanistan

US Army Captain "Sonny" Sanchez closed the door to the private dining room in the DFAC and then put a chain and padlock through the two metal door handles. Fourteen men sat around the four dining room tables, including Camp and Finn.

"Gentlemen, next time y'all call in Special Forces, please make sure you get here on time. We don't like to wait," Sanchez said to start the meeting.

"Sorry, captain, but we're at the mercy of your Army's ring routes. The birds get here when the birds get here," Finn said with a little irritation.

"Once we got the order from General Ferguson, we drove 180 miles through the mountains and IEDs at night in the middle of March and made it here on time. I expect the same moving forward from both of you."

"Captain, I presume you're aware that Captain Campbell here is a Navy O-6 and a former SEAL?"

"I don't care if he's Santa Claus, and you're his elf. This is my mission, and we go by my book and my clock. Clear?"

"Crystal!" Camp said with a reassuring smile. He liked Sanchez already.

"And no more ranks and honorifics. 'Sanchez' is good enough. We're Special Forces Operation Detachment Alpha, based out of Kandahar for now, soon to be your best friends. Before we get started, I need to ask who else knows about this mission."

"What mission?" Camp recited with a straight face.

"Let's keep it that way. Campbell and Finn, any nicknames we should use?"

"Call me Camp."

"Well, Finn is kinda short as is. Call me Billy if you

need to."

"Camp and Finn it is. Before we do the brief and work on the plan, just want you both to know that we muster in the truck pool at 0200. We'll leave sometime after that. One assault pack each, bring your own food, medical and kit for at least seven days. We'll restock later. We have extra gear that you'll receive at the appropriate time. Questions?"

Neither Camp nor Finn flinched. It wasn't their first rodeo.

"All of us read the SITREP ya'll wrote for Command in Kabul with regard to your female IED and the intel gathered. Likewise, we have a copy of the video you saw at Command, and we've already begun to assess clothing, flags, weapons – including hi-res serial numbers – backgrounds and acoustics. We've also asked for an assist from Langley for video upload plot points. What about the Terp? Does she expect anything or assume anything is going to happen?"

"We literally walked over here from the LZ. I haven't even stopped in the Troop Medical Clinic to see her. She might be dead for all I know," Camp said.

"Roger, then stay away from the TMC and do NOT, repeat, do NOT have contact with her again until mission completion."

"Aye, aye Sanchez…but she traded information for the safe return of her son. What are we going to do with that?"

"Not a damn thing, Camp, but when you return

from this mission you can tell her whatever you think she wants to hear. No other rescue than Major Banks has been authorized for the mission. Anything else? Good. First we cover mission planning, then we roll for rehearsals, mission and re-entry. Brick?"

"Gentlemen, I'm the CW2 on this detachment. Sanchez will take Team One, and I've got Team Two. I've created the mission plan for both and will run the rehearsals. Once I say we're prepared to execute the mission, Sanchez will then brief the plan to Command. Once they approve, we stage and go," Brick said as he searched the room for questions.

Brick was a tactical expert, a Chief Warrant Officer, grade two as commissioned by the President of the United States.

"Fine, let me introduce the team," Brick continued. "Manson is our Master, he and Colt have weapons; Geek and Chip have intel; Ham and Dex take the comms; Dino and Jazz run demolitions; while Country and Bulldog handle engineering. Lynch and Veggie have medical. Camp, you're going to shadow Veggie since you're a Doc, and Finn you work with Geek on intel. We normally roll in two seven-man elements, but with you two added we're going eight each with this mission," Brick finished and took his seat.

"Just in case anyone decides to get loose lips on Skype or with Terps in the TMC…the mission plan will be spelled out once we hit stage at the rehearsal point. Questions? Good. See you at 0200," Sanchez said as he walked over to the front of the private dining room, entered his combination and pulled the chain and padlock off the DFAC door.

University Hospital, Clinic and Research Center
Philadelphia, Pennsylvania

Lieutenant Colonel Raines walked quickly through the front doors of the University Hospital, Clinic and Research center and took the elevator to the fourth floor where a glass-enclosed sky-bridge walkway would take her over to the research center and labs.

The sign on the door read: Pieter J. Blauw, MD, PhD Lab.

Blauw was holding court with three of his post-doctoral research staffers and the veterinary technician who cared for his research animals.

Raines walked in and stood to the side as Blauw finished up.

"Colonel Raines, I trust you found the lab without great difficulty."

"Yes, sir, exactly as your map and instructions indicated. Looks like you have quite the operation going on in here."

"We do. I'll give you the 50-cent tour as we walk over to my office."

"Is this all Alzheimer's research?"

"We have an Alzheimer's focus but neurodegenerative diseases in general. I have three post-docs, a microbiologist and a few vet techs on my team.

Nothing like I had back in the days at Brezden but really quite ample."

Raines explored the stacks and stacks of Allentown XJ cage and rack systems.

"Transgenic mice?"

"Well, genetically modified at least. They have additional, artificially-introduced genetic material in every cell. We call that foreign DNA. It gives us a gain of function, for example the mouse may produce a new protein. But we're also looking for a loss of function if that foreign DNA interrupts another gene."

"Are you buying transgenics with Alzheimer's knocked-in from the breeders, or do you create your own?"

"Actually both, Colonel Raines. In our research, we're using genetically modified mice with inbred strains so that we have a stable genetic background, and then we add novel strains carrying alleles of genes that have been identified as potential targets for Alzheimer's therapies. At the risk of being too technical, in our mice the transgene contains a tetracycline operator that drives four repeats of the protein 'tau' gene."

"Yep, you just lost me."

"Well, the microtubule-associated protein 'tau' is the most commonly misfolded protein in human neurodegenerative diseases like Alzheimer's, Parkinson's, dementia, Pict's and palsy. Our focus is on the mechanisms behind the pathogenesis, or neurodegenerative diseases similar to, when prions spread through the nervous system."

"Okay, sorry I asked," Raines said as she laughed and took a seat in Blauw's research office at the far end of his lab.

"I understand. Try this on for size…almost 80,000 Americans die from Alzheimer's each year, the fourth leading cause of death in the US after heart disease, cancer and stroke. That's why I do this. Just like Mr. Campbell, four million are diagnosed each year at a cost to the nation of $100 billion. One of my heroes from Germany, Alois Alzheimer, was the neurologist who first described the pathology of the disease nearly 100 years ago, and we're still working on it."

"Are we any closer to solving this disease now, than we were back then?"

"Each day we add a new piece to the puzzle. We just don't know how many puzzle pieces are in the full disease picture. The brain is one of the last frontiers in medicine. But thanks to these mice, we have increased the speed of discovery. In a six-month old mouse we can see AD disorders in the hippocampus and spatial learning deficit. In a 13-month old mouse we can see memory deficits. Breakthroughs are a function of time, money, good people and a lot of luck. Every day we hope we're going to find something that makes it to a clinical trial."

"And that's why I'm here. Mrs. Campbell wanted me to help them select a human clinical trial for Mr. Campbell. What do you recommend?" Raines asked.

"I prepared a file for you," Blauw said as he handed

Raines a manila folder. "Three studies are currently recruiting patients. Given the fact that Mr. Campbell is 77 years old, he might be suitable for a trial out in Baltimore. Essentially, they are looking at the influence of age on amyloidal load in Alzheimer's and in atypical focal cortical AD."

"Are they using experimental meds?"

"No, not with this one, they're injecting a radio-tracer to measure age-specific deterioration factors for both early-onset and late-onset as well as atypical cortical AD. They look for brain lesions through PET scans and try to measure cortical brain atrophy and the glucose metabolism that correlates to neuronal activity."

"Doesn't sound like this will help him get better."

"Colonel Raines…he may see some marginal improvements with the medicines, diet and exercise… but he's not going to get better. He's an old-school fighter. So if he wants to contribute to the body of information on Alzheimer's, this is a great start. This is a two month study. I'll keep looking for others if he's interested. You can also check out clincialtrials.gov and see if others come up."

"I assume he would be qualified for this trial in Baltimore?"

"Yes, his clinical dementia rating is 1.5, his cued Grober and Buschke recall test was 10 of 48 and his total recall was 30 out of 48."

"I take it that means yes." Blauw smiled and checked his watch. "I know you're a busy man. Thanks for taking so much time with me."

Raines stood and shook Dr. Blauw's hand and started to leave.

"Colonel Raines…he's 77 years old…there's not much time."

Raines walked out through the aisle in the long lab, over the jet-walkway, down the elevator and out to the parking lot where she sat in her Wrangler wondering what she should tell Camp, or even if she should tell him anything at all.

12

Combat Outpost Chergotah
Khost Province, Afghanistan

Afghanistan's border with Pakistan careens 450 miles down the eastern portion of Regional Command-East. It was inundated with extreme mountainous terrain and perilous conditions along the Hindu Kush mountain range which topped 16,000 feet in some places.

More than 2,000 footpaths ran across the border in RC-East and another 200 paths could handle a mule depending on weather conditions. The people of the area weren't as much Afghans or Pakistanis as they were tribal members with interconnected family ties sitting on both sides of an invisible border.

Combat Outpost Chergotah sat at 8,000 feet where oxygen was hard to come by and western comforts were non-existent.

Chergotah was just two miles from the border with Pakistan.

Less than 100 war-weary soldiers from the 4th Brigade Combat Team, 25th Infantry Division out of Fort Richardson, Alaska worked, mentored and trained a rag-tag group of Afghan Border Policemen to sustain border security and maintain peace among the local tribes and villagers.

MRAPs with Common Remotely Operated Weapons Stations secured the area with .50-caliber machine guns and Mark 19 grenade launchers that used precision computer video targeting systems controlled with a 10-inch TV screen by each gunner sitting in a warm cabin cockpit below.

Special Forces Operation Detachment Alpha had taken over a vacant Afghan house on the outpost. An open wood fire warmed the air to a balmy 45 degrees. Classified maps hung impaled into walls of mud, wood and straw with oversized nails.

An old wooden table sat in the center of the room as ODA Troopers staged for the rehearsal. Manson and Colt laid out the M4A1s for Camp and Finn. Master Sergeant "Manson" sported a wandering and half-crazed eye that never seemed to align with the other, and his laugh was as demonic as his namesake's which seemed to fit as he mounted the M203 grenade launcher to his 9-inch barrel M4. The only thing fancy for Camp and Finn's weapons were aftermarket buttstocks and vertical forward grips. If everything went according to plan, neither would need to fire so much as a round.

Geek, Chip, Ham and Dex worked on the intel and communications components for high elevation technical mountain movements, while Dino and Jazz prepped C4 explosive bricks and an assortment of small-charge door busters. Country and Bulldog had enough rappelling equipment and mountaineering gear to run a 6-month survival course for Outward Bound. Lynch and Veggie packed up their medical supplies including a MEDEVAC 4 combat tactical stretcher, just in case Major Banks was found wounded or unable to walk. They packed an entire extra set of outdoor gear for Banks. What the Taliban didn't finish, the extreme weather would if they didn't pack accordingly.

"Alright, listen up," Brick said as he called the meeting to order. "Manson has pegged our movement at point-six kilometers per hour based on the terrain maps and satellite imagery of the trails. We're 100-percent snow-covered up there, but we have to move in and move out. We've got 22 miles from ingress to target at Datta Khel Village in Miran Shah District. People, that's 59 hours of high-terrain hiking and one four-hour sleep break on the way in and the same thing on the way out."

"No trips to the bazaar, Brick?"

Brick didn't even acknowledge Staff Sergeant "Dex" or his wise-ass attempt at humor.

"Geek, you've got the floor," Brick said as he took a seat next to Camp.

"Human intelligence is a major component of this mission. We can't simply rely on the Terp's recollection of a particular house in some alley. Nothing from the birds can really help us out at this point. Omid?"

Geek's eyes lifted and a man of solid build entered from the back of the room.

"Good afternoon, Alpha, Camp...Finn," Omid said as he took center stage in the chilled room.

Finn quickly put his glasses on and gave Omid the once over inspection. Omid looked to be about Camp's age. His chest was well-developed and he carried himself with poise and bearing. He was shorter than Camp. His boots were new and his clothing was both rugged and stylish. Omid's eyes didn't dart around the room, but rather focused in on each subject with laser-guided precision.

"Persian?" Finn asked Omid who was not given the chance to reply.

"Details are not important, Finn. Omid will be helping us with this mission. He knows the route, the people, the risks and the village in Miran Shah District. We've been working with Omid for several years and his HUMINT work is second to none, reliable above reproach," Geek said as both he and Omid sat down.

"At 0400 our rehearsal goes green. We're going four miles up and only half a click in to the Paki's side of the border. We'll simulate the extraction, load the Tac4 with 200-pounds of rocks to simulate Banks, and egress. Total mission time is 24 hours. We may encounter hostiles so we're lock and load, yellow and red, as needed. If the rehearsal goes according to plan, I'll brief Command, and if we get the approval, we go. Questions? Get some chow, hit your rolls, and we go at 0400," Brick said as Omid stared at Camp.

"Navy SEAL now a doctor?" Omid asked.

Camp picked up his things and stood. "I believe the man said details are not important."

Ham and Dex walked back into the open room carrying a huge pot of steaming soup and placed it on the open fire. The ODA team lined up followed by Omid, Finn and Camp. They all filled their tin cups with hot soup and found places around the abandoned house to sit on their folding metal tripod ruck stools. Omid ate quickly as Finn looked over somewhat disgusted by his hunger and his etiquette.

"You know there's pork in the soup, right?" Finn teased as Omid stopped eating for a second and then increased his eating speed.

"Really?" Omid said as he continued eating. "I cooked this soup, but I don't remember putting pork in the pot. We were short of broth, so, yes, I did have to piss in the kettle first, but I don't remember adding any pork."

Finn looked over at Omid then down at his soup as Finn's appetite escaped the room. Camp was finally smiling.

"Let me guess, Iranian Revolutionary Guard," Finn said triumphantly as though he had made a significant investigatory discovery.

"You're good," Omid said not taking his eyes off the next spoonful of soup. "And you?"

"Retired," Finn said.

"Finn…when you were in the FBI's New York field office, was Dalton Fischer still the director?" Omid asked.

Finn looked shocked but said nothing.

"I worked for Dalton on many occasions. Tell him Pablo says hello," Omid finished his soup and ladled out some more. Camp looked over at Finn as the dynamic had just taken an unexpected turn toward exciting.

"You know Pablo?" Finn finally stuttered.

Omid looked up and into Finn's eyes.

"I *am* Pablo."

"Okay will someone clue me in here," Camp injected. "The Iranian intelligence officer from the Revolutionary Guard who pissed in our kettle of soup knows your former boss?"

"For the last 15 years or so, the FBI has had some noteworthy double-agents from Iran, none more accurate or trustworthy than a man they simply called Pablo. Dalton Fischer and one of our intel guys met with this Pablo a few times in Europe and even twice in New York."

"It wasn't a guy, Mr. Finn. You must be talking about Susan Francis. She was the intel specialist Dalton brought along. Last I heard from Susan, her father had cancer," Omid said as he devoured another cup of soup.

Finn leaned back on his ruck stool.

"He died…Susan's father died of colon cancer."

"Okay Finn…so I'm guessing you're okay with all this now," Camp asked. "So are you Omid or Pablo?"

"Neither actually, but you probably could figure that out by now."

"So how do you manage to just waltz out of Iran and into other countries for these covert assignments?" Finn asked.

"I tell the authorities that my father needs constant help, Finn. He was wounded in an attack in 1981 and left a paraplegic. He's in a convalescent home in Islamabad."

"Oh, sorry to hear that," Camp said.

"Don't be, not anymore at least. The truth is that he died in 1981 after the attack. I was only six, just after the Revolution began. He was ambushed, shot, and then died several months later. I kept him alive in my reports and it became a convenient story. I even have nurses, doctors and caregivers who call and send letters from my father to the authorities. Works out nice."

"How did you get in this time?" Finn asked.

"Commercial flight to Islamabad, rode out with Pakistan troops to the Federally Administered Tribal Areas, and they dropped me off in Miran Shah District. Did a little business then changed and geared up in my safe house and rode over to Datta Khel Village in the back of a truck. Spent a few hours, located where I think your major is, hiked through the Hindu Kush and then pissed in your soup."

Finn and Camp looked at each other in utter

amazement. Finn got up. "I'm gonna hit my roll. Early morning coming." Finn placed his dirty cup in the ammo box and found his place against the back wall of the room as the rest of Operation Detachment Alpha were winding down with iPods and PS3 portable play stations so they could play combat war games until they fell asleep.

Camp moved closer to the fire as Omid stoked the flames.

"So tell me Omid, why do you do this? For the money?"

His brown eyes fixated by the fire, Omid smiled and shook his head.

"I love my country. I love the Iranians and the Persian people. I would gladly die for my land. The revolution in 1979 hijacked the soul of the Iranian people and plunged all of us into a black hole of religious fundamentalism under the Ayatollah Khomeini. But we have never lost hope; there will be a Persian Renaissance…someday…inshallah."

"Before or after you drop nukes on Israel?" Camp asked with no hint of pleasure in his voice.

"You Americans," Omid scoffed as he kicked a small branch into the fire pit. "You still have a Cold War mentality. You still act like Kremlinologists, you read the tea leaves, listen to the rhetoric as sabers rattle and then try to interpret events with no evidence at all, no understanding at all."

"You've got to be kidding me. We've got inspectors

from the IAEA and satellite imagery of your nuclear facilities and our intel is somehow tea leaves, interpretation without evidence? Give me a break."

"You miss the point. You churn out college graduates who can make video games, manage museums and run hamburger stores. Do you study philosophy? Do you study religion? Do you understand history? No, you study for jobs so you can buy big cars, get fat and use credit cards."

"You're right, Omid. I'm just a dumb, fat American with a Visa card and a Cadillac. Enlighten me!"

"Of course they are building nuclear weapons...of course they plan to bomb Israel...and if possible, they will bomb you with long-range intercontinental ballistic missiles and with bombs inside cargo containers at your ports. You know all of this, yet still, you know nothing."

"They? You may be playing double-agent for some quick cash, but 'they' is 'you', Omid, whether you like it or not."

"That's where you are wrong, Camp. That's where your leaders have made major miscalculations. Iran has two governments, two populations of people. There is no unitary structure or sovereign power that makes our decisions. There are many competing factions within Iran. Yet you continue to say 'Iran will do this' and 'Iran will do that'. The formal government was stolen from the people during the last election and is still run at Ahmadinejad's pleasure. But the religious and ideological command is the domain of the Supreme Leader,

Ayatollah Ali Khamenei."

"Is this supposed to be new information?"

"Power is decentralized. Everyone is vying for power in Iran, even the Russian mafia, even Muqtada al Sadr in Iraq. You think one voice in Tehran speaks for all Iranians? You think one threat from Tehran is a threat from every farmer, teacher, mother and child? You know nothing."

"Sorry, Omid, but nut jobs run your country hell-bent on destroying Israel at any cost. Any way you slice it, Islamic extremism runs rampant and unchecked both in Iran and throughout your proxies like Hezbollah. You may have some romantic notion of a Persian Renaissance after a nuclear winter, but as far as I'm concerned, you still view us as the Great Satan, and you still want death for the infidels. It's in the Holy Koran, Omid; it's in your book. Look it up and read it."

Omid grew silent and shrugged his shoulders. He closed his eyes as though he was praying.

"Yes, Camp, it's in there. I can't deny that. Some fanatics and terrorists believe they must help Allah, that it is their duty to purge the world of infidels. But the vast majority of Muslims are content to let Allah solve all of that in the next life. Are you a good Christian?"

Camp reflected on his answer for several seconds. "I believe in God. I used to go to church; at least I did when I was a boy. I try to do the right things, but – I don't know – I'm not sure I'm a very good Christian."

"Some might read your Holy Bible or listen to a

preacher and conclude that you help Jesus by killing your sinners in prison with the death penalty. Some might read your Holy Bible and decide that they can help Jesus by killing doctors who perform abortions. You can argue that those words are in your Holy text, too. But do all Christians believe that? Do they all act on that? Your Holy Bible says that it is easier for a rich man to pass through the eye of a needle than it is for him to get into heaven. But you still have nice cars, nice homes, and what you call 401Ks? By any standard, American Christians are rich. Do you read that Holy text and decide to remain poor? Of course not. But it's in your book, Camp. You can't deny it. Perhaps most Christians are willing to let Jesus solve everything in the afterlife. Most Muslims feel the same way."

"Omid, there's a difference between moderate Muslims who are willing to live in peace and radical Islamic fundamentalism through state-sponsored terror."

"You see satellite images and think you understand everything. You do not. If you did, you would act differently….if you did, you would have come to our aid during the people's protest and the democratic uprising…if you did, then you would understand why I betray the regime so I can embrace the people. How can you be so smart, so educated, yet still know nothing?"

Omid walked away from the fire, unrolled his bed and curled up against the wall near Billy Finn.

13

National Interagency Biodefense Center
BSL-4 Facility
Fort Detrick, Maryland

Lieutenant Colonel Raines got her coffee from the atrium's barista, scanned her security card and processed her biometric as she rode the elevator without floor buttons to her cleared location.

Groenwald's door was open, and he was talking with a man and a woman she didn't at first recognize, but she offered a smile and a wave as she passed by nonetheless.

"Colonel Raines? Can you join us?" Groenwald called as she did a one-eighty. The two guests stood as Raines entered.

"Special Agent Daniels," Raines said with a bit of surprise in her voice as Daniels turned to greet her. "Nice to see you again."

"Colonel, looks like you've made a full recovery,"

Daniels said. "This is Agent Fallon Jessup with the bioterror directorate."

"Pleasure to meet you, ma'am." Raines looked over at Dr. Groenwald and explained. "Special Agent Daniels was key to the mission last year that took us through Algiers, Morocco and Yemen. He was there the night I was wounded."

"Well, I'd like to hear the whole story some day. Colonel, can you take a seat and join us?" Groenwald asked as he pointed to the last remaining straight back desk chair in the room.

"How is Captain Campbell doing?" Daniels asked.

"The last I heard he was working on a special project in Afghanistan."

"Well, please tell him Daniels says hello next time you speak with him."

"Colonel Raines, Daniels and Jessup have come to us for some help," Groenwald said.

"Colonel, we have reason to believe that scientists in Pakistan have made some major strides in weaponizing tularemia. We've already been in touch with General Ferguson, and he suggested we visit both you and Dr. Groenwald," Daniels said.

"The attending physician at FOB Lightning concluded that their tularemia cases were garden variety…uncooked meat, contaminated water…the usual," Raines said somewhat defensively.

"You're referring to Major Banks, the physician who was abducted shortly after his conclusions."

"Yes."

"Agent Jessup is a Naval Academy graduate and now handles our bio desk in the region. If you don't mind, we'd like to brief you."

Fallon Jessup was a tall and slender blonde, a head-spinner who wore a cute figure and carried a "back off" gaze that turned meat market heroes into playground boys. Raines had no reason to be threatened by her beauty, but she wasn't inclined to take an intellectual backseat either. But Raines was a career officer. She didn't like Academy "brats" that served one tour and then switched jobs for more money. Raines didn't have much interest in former military officers who took the "one and done" career path.

"Please Agent Jessup...school me."

Groenwald's eyes flared ever so slightly. He had taken Raines to be a recovering pacifist. Nothing in her file suggested she could morph into a street-fight brawler that quickly.

"Well, we first recognized tularemia in the early 1900s. It was a plague-like disease in rodents and a severe, sometimes fatal, illness for humans. But it's potential for epidemic emerged in the 1930s and 1940s in Europe and the Soviet Union. Water systems were contaminated, and tularemia was characterized by waterborne outbreaks."

Raines cleared her throat.

"Agent Daniels, I've been studying the ecology, microbiology, pathogenicity and prevention of tularemia

– and others – for my entire career. Did you happen to bring any useful or current information with you today?"

The cat fight was on as Dr. Groenwald and Special Agent Daniels were reduced to mere spectators.

"Colonel, I understand that you are an expert in the confined safety of a biocontainment laboratory, but I'm talking real world here. In World War II both the Soviet Red Army and the German Wehrmacht forces suffered hundreds of thousands of casualties from infectious diseases."

"Oh my gosh," Raines said expressionless.

"A former Soviet scientist and defector – Kanatjan Alibekov – asserted that the Soviets used tularemia as a causative agent during the Battle of Stalingrad in 1942 and 1943."

"A biological weapon," Daniels said hoping to add a layer of depth and texture to the history lesson. "But once unleashed, it killed as many Russians as it did Germans."

"Folks, based on the clinical cases and the nature of the pathogen we all studied from Stalingrad during vet school, I must tell you that I disagree. It was a natural outbreak."

Raines stood abruptly and reached for her brief case.

"Millions died in the siege of Stalingrad, Colonel Raines," Fallon Jessup said with a burst of fury. "For some of us in this room, we'd like to prevent a reoccurrence of that disaster."

"Listen Jessup, I didn't raise my hand and put this uniform on to see anyone die, so don't lecture me."

"Kanatjan Alibekov was the former deputy director of the Soviet Russian Biopreparat. He claims that tularemia was deployed against Nazi troops during the battle of Stalingrad. Hundreds of thousands of tularemia infections quickly arose at the beginning of the siege and there was a high – more than 70 percent – pulmonary involvement among those infected with tularemia from both sides, suggesting man-made air-borne dissemination."

"That's the biological weapons part," Daniels added.

"Geez, you two must be a real hoot on a Friday night glued to the history channel. Listen, I'd really love to stay and listen to more. I'm sure you have some fascinating stories about food and dysentery from Valley Forge as well, but I've got to get back to some current work on hemorrhagic fevers."

"Colonel Raines…please sit down," Groenwald said softly. Raines was shocked more by the verbal evidence of his spinal column than by the command itself. She sat.

"Listen…I apologize for being abrupt," Raines said, "but history reveals that the Rostov region already had 14,000 confirmed tularemia cases long before the siege of Stalingrad. With all due respect, mosquitoes carried the pathogens, and what the mosquitoes didn't cause initially, inhalation of dust from the unharvested straw in the fields completed the delivery of the toxins. I'm sure your Soviet defector has enjoyed his 15 minutes of fame, but it was a natural outbreak of tularemia. Regardless, we already have vaccines and antibiotics."

"Colonel, we have vaccines for laboratory workers like you. That's all. Do you really think we have enough vaccine doses or even antibiotics for a city of five million people if there's an outbreak?" Daniels asked. "The numbers of casualties could easily overwhelm existing capacity to treat both the sick and the worried well. Hell, colonel, in the 1950s we put tularemia in aerosol cans. But nobody messed with this stuff like the Soviets."

"Your scenario is highly unlikely, Agent Daniels. Sanitation and pest control is far more advanced than in the fields of Stalingrad in 1942."

"In 1982, the Soviets developed a vaccine-resistant recipe for tularemia," Daniels countered.

"And in the 1990s the Russians asserted they destroyed their tularemia stockpiles," Raines added.

"And of course we all believe the Russians."

The room was silent. Daniels had a valid point.

"Colonel, in the now defunct US bio-weapon program, tularemia was weaponized by freeze drying bacteria-laden slurry and muting it into a flue powder for aerosol delivery," Jessup said.

"Whoa, another info gem. Who knew!"

"The Soviets had an aggressive BW program during the Cold War. So did the United States. We had massive stockpiles of tularemia. The Soviets had 52 clandestine sites employing 50,000 people. They were producing as much as 100 tons of weaponized smallpox every damn year. Colonel Kanatjan Alibekov ran their program in the Kirov Oblast, a town of 470,000 people west of the Ural Mountains along the Vyatka River. Colonel Raines, Kirov is a 36-hour ride on the Trans-Siberian railway connecting to the Trans-Caspian and on into Ashgabat, Turkmenistan."

"Oshkosh? Either way I'm sure it's a lovely trip."

"Ashgabat is on the Iranian border. Colonel Raines, why would the Russians send boxcars of tularemia to Ashgabat? Why would they send a lethal bacteria, weaponized or not, to the border with Iran? Let's just blue sky this for a minute, shall we? Let's say the Russians are looking to make some cash. And let's say a bad state actor is interested in buying tularemia – rabbit fever – just because they know the world will blame it on a natural outbreak caused by mosquitoes and rodent dust inhaled from dirty grass and straw, just as you assert even now that it was a natural outbreak in Stalingrad way back then. Hell, you may be the first one to stand up and exonerate the Iranians, assuring the world that the outbreak was natural. That, Colonel Raines, is what we're looking at. If you'd shut up for six seconds you might, in fact, get schooled."

Agent Fallon Jessup finished with a flurry and added the exclamation point. Raines was silent for a few seconds.

"How do we know it's tularemia and that it's headed for Turkmenistan?" Groenwald asked.

"We're on that train right now," Daniels said, "and the shipment is verified."

"The Iranian connection?" Raines asked.

"Pure speculation at this point as we try to connect the dots. But Ashgabat is a relatively large transportation hub; trains and trucks, all just 21 unfettered miles to the northern Iranian border," Daniels said.

"General Ferguson is in the loop?" Raines asked.

"He's been briefed and in turn he's passed the intel on to the Alpha Team heading up Camp's mission."

Raines glared at Special Agent Daniels.

"What mission?"

Daniels looked over at Jessup, and they both fell silent.

Raines got up and paced over to Groenwald's white board. She pulled out a black marker and began to draw.

"Two SkitoMisters are sold by an Illinois company to the City of Hamburg, Germany. The machines go missing and are reported stolen. A port in Jakarta, Indonesia records the serial numbers and a black market importer hocks them to a buyer in Pakistan. Now a Russian train carrying Cold War stockpiles of tularemia along with a CIA informant on-board is heading for the Iranian border. Whether or not the tularemia can be aerosolized is irrelevant because we have no capacity during three to five days of an outbreak to meet the medical demands of people infected with rabbit fever.

The world can logically blame nature and poor sanitation for tularemia. One nation collects cash for an old bio-weapon while another state kills, or at least terrorizes, millions."

The room was silent as Raines continued.

"So let me guess…you want to see if we can create an aerosol version of tularemia? Better than our Rabbit-Fever-In-A-Can from the 1950s. You want something toxic, effective and lethal – not garden variety – but pandemic and widespread."

"Something like that…we need to know what they might try," Jessup said.

"You want me to play Terrorist Raines and cook up something they might reasonably cook up. Existing vaccine doses and antibiotic supply? I'm sure you've done the numbers…what do we have?"

"We're working on that part," Daniels said begrudgingly.

"And ground zero for all of this? The target? Let me go way out on a limb…Israel?"

FOB Lightning
Paktya Province, Afghanistan

Captain Henry walked into the Level One clinic carrying a handful of letters from the post office. He made his way through the Ambien slug-line at the counter, and set the mail down on the exam bed before walking down the 40-foot corridor toward Miriam's room. A young specialist was finishing his shift guarding her door.

"Anything new?" Henry asked.

"Sir, she's taking her walks up and down the hallway as you requested. She seems to have a good appetite and slept most of the night."

"Thank you, specialist. Hit your rack and get some sleep. We've got her until the night duty guard comes in."

Henry opened the door and entered the room. Miriam was sitting in a chair and reading the same four-month-old newspaper from Kabul that she had read a hundred times before.

"Good morning, Miriam. I understand you slept well and are getting some exercise."

Miriam said nothing. She was both a patient and a prisoner, something the US Army was having difficulty defining with an official designation.

"Well, I have some news for you."

Miriam looked up from her newspaper.

"We're moving you to Kabul."

"I don't want to go to Kabul," Miriam snapped. "I'm from Khost."

"You're dead, Miriam, and don't forget that…it was in all the papers and on Radio Television Afghanistan. If you go back to Khost, you won't live five minutes, especially after you provided some intel to the infidels. I'm guessing the Haqqani network would not be pleased with that."

"What about my son?"

"Captain Campbell is working on that as we speak. As soon as we know something – you'll know something."

"I'm not going to Kabul without my son."

Henry reached down and pulled the sleeve on her hospital gown up so that he could examine the dressings from the escharotomy.

"You're healing up nicely, Miriam…no infection. That's nothing short of a miracle. Infection kills most burn victims. Fortunately, Captain Campbell put you out before you could melt like the wicked witch of the west, or wherever the hell we are."

Miriam spat on the floor and returned to her old newspaper.

"Miriam, the gratitude and humility leaves me speechless. We are so going to miss your cheery smile and happy heart around this clinic," Henry said with a full dose of sarcasm not lost on Miriam. "You'll be on a bird in the morning at 0730 hours whether you like it or not. Kabul can figure out what to do with you next."

Miriam threw her paper down, stood up and walked to the door and opened it.

"Going somewhere?"

"My doctor told me to exercise, so I walk up and down this hallway a hundred times a day. Every step I take I curse the day when I first met an American."

Miriam disappeared down the hallway.

"Seriously, lady, you are welcome. It was our sincere pleasure saving a suicide bomber from herself. Hope you have a great life!"

Miriam paced up and down the hallway as Captain Henry retreated to his back office. The Ambien candies were all dispensed, and the line was gone. The on-duty medic was behind the counter resupplying the cabinets with bandages, dressings and pills. Miriam ventured a bit further out into the open bay before doing her 180 and heading back to the other end of the hallway near Henry's office. She turned again and walked completely into the exam bay the next time where she noticed the day's mail scattered on an exam bench. One envelope caught her attention. It was addressed to Captain Seabury Campbell, Jr. with a return address of only a first name, Eileen, then Lightner Farms, Baltimore Pike, Gettysburg, Pennsylvania. She did her turn and headed down the hallway again. She looked into Henry's office and saw him on his computer as she turned again. The medic still had her head buried in the medicine cabinet as Miriam brushed past the exam bed, picked up Camp's letter and tucked it into her hospital gown as she headed back down the hallway. She walked into her room and placed the envelope inside her Koran.

14

Hindu Kush
North Waziristan, Pakistan

The 14 soldiers from the Special Forces Operation Detachment Alpha Team, along with Finn, Camp and Omid, made their way across an unmarked border from Afghanistan into Pakistan. The footpath had been narrow and snow-covered all the way from their ingress 42 hours and 17 miles earlier.

The expanded Alpha Team was dressed in snow camo they had borrowed from a German NATO unit stationed with them in Kandahar. The white masks at least kept parts of their cheeks from freezing as goggles prevented wind-whipped tears from icing over.

Captain "Sonny" Sanchez led Team One and kept a quarter-mile pace ahead of the CW2 and Team Two. Two scouts with M4A1s took point in the front of the formation, spread eight feet apart and separated from the middle core by thirty feet. Manson and his best sniper pulled up the rear with Manson's M203 grenade launcher on his 9-inch barrel ever at the ready. Camp walked ahead of Veggie, the medic carrying the MEDEVAC 4 combat tactical stretcher, and behind Omid who was closest behind the scouts since he knew the mountains and the footpaths.

Brick's Team Two stayed a quarter-mile back down the trail as they moved up, over, and through the Hindu Kush and into Pakistan. The spread formation in snow camo was the best way to mitigate any possible ambush, though Billy Finn was eager to peel off a few rounds if the situation warranted.

Operation Detachment Alpha was hoping the Taliban fighters would be sleeping in their warm little caves at 0300 hours and, for at least another three hours, until Alpha took their only sleep break before the final push into Datta Khel Village.

Omid's ears were only a few feet from Camp's mouth.

"Iran is too unpredictable right now."

"Not Iran, the Hojjatieh and the Twelvers," Omid said.

"You keep yakking about both. Who are they?"

"You're American so I suppose you want the 30-second drive-thru window version?" Omid said sarcastically.

"We've got three hours until rest and first light so how about just the Cliff Notes?"

Omid smiled and fell back next to Camp, so they could talk and walk softly as their boots crunched on the snow covered trail. Clouds were gathering in the sky as stars reflected off the snow and the rock outcroppings of the Hindu Kush. The wind was still and death seemed to lurk around every cutback on the footpath.

"The Hojjatieh Society was a clandestine group of traditional Shia followers that began in 1953. They felt the Bahá'í Faith that was growing in Persia was a heresy and the only immediate threat to Islam. With the permission of the Ayatollah, a mullah from Tehran named Halabi created the Hojjatieh. In the beginning, Halabi and his 12,000 followers in the Hojjatieh Society were loyal to the Shah of Iran since they both hated the Communists. But Halabi thought the Shah was too friendly and open with the Bahá'í so they supported Khomeini during the overthrow and the subsequent Iranian Revolution in 1979. Khomeini forced the Hojjatieh to dissolve in 1983. He wanted to consolidate all Islamic power. Halabi took his movement underground where it grew until his death in 1998."

"Was Halabi martyred?"

"Quite the opposite. He lived to be 98 years old. In our culture the older you are the wiser you are. Every word that mullah Halabi spoke was like a word directly from the prophets. He opposed Sunnism. He opposed Khomeini's form of *velayat-e faqih*, or Islamic government by Sharia Law. In fact, he wanted no form of official government at all. Some say the Hojjatieh was nothing more than an underground messianic sect; that they wanted to quicken the apocalypse so they could hurry the return of the Mahdi, the prophesized future redeemer of Islam. But others claim that Halabi was content to wait for the Mahdi's return in peace."

"What happened when he died?"

"As with any movement there are always other leaders who try to rise up when a power vacuum emerges. Ayatollah Yazdi was the most notable. Camp, this Yazdi is the center of the crazy power in Iran. He is a hardliner who heads the ultraconservative faction. Yazdi is a member of the Assembly of Experts, the body who chooses the Supreme Leader."

"Crazy?"

"Yazdi is the spiritual leader in the city of Qom. He is opposed to democratic reforms. He opposed the people's uprising and the reform movement after the presidential elections in 2009. And he believes that Iran has become too liberal, and too open, since the Revolution in 1979."

"Too liberal? Doesn't sound any crazier than the rest of the bastards in power over there."

"And he's a Twelver."

"You keep saying that."

"Twelvers are the largest branch of Shia, the second denomination of Islam and the followers of Ali. Iran, Iraq, Yemen, Azerbaijan, Bahrain, and Lebanon have very large Shia populations. The rest of the Muslim countries are mostly Sunni. Sunnis make up nearly eighty percent of the world of Islam. But there are more than 200 million of us."

"Two hundred million Muslims?"

"No, two hundred million Shia, maybe more. There are 1.6 billion Muslims. Twelver Shiites believe that the descendants of the Prophet Muhammad, but only from his daughter Fatima and his son-in-law Ali, offer the best ways of knowledge about the Holy Koran, the most accurate protectors of Muhammad's traditions, and are the most worthy of emulation."

"At the risk of being called a 'drive thru' American intellectual, I'm still not tracking the whole twelve thing, Omid. The 9/11 hijackers were Sunni. Bin Laden was Sunni. Al Qaeda and the Wahhabis are Sunni. Now I'm supposed to be afraid of Shiites and the Twelvers?"

"Do you want fries with this education?"

Camp and Omid laughed a bit too loud as one of the scouts turned back and glared. Camp could hardly speak as the two squads of Alpha Team passed through the 12,000 foot peaks between Dabgay, Kazen Kalay and Zakarkhel passing over an invisible Afghanistan border and into the lawless region of Pakistan, the Federally Administered Tribal Areas of North Waziristan. Omid spoke without constraint, as though walking casually in Tehran.

"An Imam is a worship leader, a spiritual leader at a mosque. In Islam, there are twelve Imams who are considered the political and religious successors to

Muhammad."

"Like Jesus and the twelve apostles."

"Similar. Allah guides the Imams, and the Imams guide the people. According to Twelvers, there is always an Imam of the Age. Ali was the first Imam in the line from Muhammad, and in the Twelvers' view, the rightful successor to the Prophet of Islam. Each Imam thereafter was a male descendant of Fatima and Ali. The twelfth and final Imam was Muhammad al-Mahdi. He was born in 869, and anointed as the Twelfth Imam when he was only five years old. Then came the occultation."

"The what?"

"Occultation…it means a hiding. For more than 1,200 years Allah has hidden the Mahdi from our sight. He never died. The Mahdi – the Twelfth Imam – is the ultimate savior of humanity, and he will return with Isa, the Islamic name for Jesus Christ, and together they will rule the world."

"Christians and Muslims side by side? Including Jesus?" Camp asked.

"Not exactly. Jesus will convert to Islam when he returns."

"That's convenient if not improbable. So the Mahdi has been hiding in a cave?"

"Or perhaps living in the open as one of us, waiting for the right moment when Allah reveals him."

"Okay…that's a bit out there…a bit hard for my Western mind to grasp…how does all of this add up to nuclear weapons in Iran…and a double-agent wanting to save his people?" Camp said as he struggled for oxygen.

"It is now the Age of the Coming, my friend. It is now our calling to prepare the way for the Twelfth Imam. Certain things must now happen before he can reappear."

Omid dropped his head and stared at the starlit snow covered path in front of him as they started a steep climb. The footpath grew very narrow.

"What things, Omid?"

"Things your diplomats, White House and the United Nations Security Council don't seem to understand. You study our policy. You assume we won't attack other countries, Europe or even the United States. You assume we would never launch bio-weapons or nuclear weapons because the world's retaliation would destroy Iran. Perhaps you should study the regime's theology instead of their politics."

"Theology?"

"Our theology *is* our policy. Our theology requires destruction. It's the only way for the Mahdi to return. So Mister Smart American Navy man…would you like to sit down and negotiate with us on theological terms? Or perhaps you think you can change our theology with sanctions?"

Camp was quiet.

The cave complex was right where Omid said it would be. Alpha Team had made good time and arrived four minutes ahead of schedule. Three members of each team cleared the caves as the rest of the team hugged the rock walls of the frozen Hindu Kush. The team quickly unrolled and climbed into their sacks for four hours of rest.

Camp couldn't shake the despair. He reflected on his schooldays when his father assured him he could talk his way out of every fight. Camp had never even considered the notion that one could be lured into fighting an inferior opponent because that opponent had a death wish.

Camp reached over to Omid's bed roll and touched his arm.

"Omid," he whispered. "What makes you so sure that this – right now – is the Age of the Coming? Why not in five years, in 50 years or even 500 years?"

Omid pushed himself up on his elbows.

"Signs and technology, analysis from the Hadith and the promises of the Ulema, our religious leaders, all point to The Coming."

"Technology? You mean nukes?"

"Partly. One intercontinental ballistic missile can only kill thousands. We don't have unlimited missiles. But biological weapons can kill millions, and we have the technology to put them into the air you breathe and the water you drink."

"You're crazy, Omid. Your people are crazy. There's no way on God's green earth that your little Safir ICBMs are going to hit the US. Your calculations are way off."

"We don't need to attack *you*, Captain Campbell.

You will attack *us*, and it will take only 10 minutes."

"What the hell?"

"Imam Ali said it best…Waging war against enemies with whom war is inevitable, and if they might attack Muslims, then war is a duty of Muslims. The Holy Koran says in Albaghara 2:191-193: *And slay them wherever ye find them, and drive them out of the places whence they drove you out, for persecution of Muslims is worse than slaughter of non-believers … and fight them until persecution is no more, and religion is for Allah.*"

"Since 1979 we've been dealing with you when the Shah was exiled and our Embassy was attacked. Now you think we'll just lose our patience with you in 10 minutes?"

An eerie glow from the snow and the morning light breaking into the cave covered Omid's face. His steel brown eyes pierced Camp's face.

"The calculations are in place. The plan has been created. It will take us eight-minutes and 53-seconds to destroy Israel."

Camp was sick to his stomach just hearing the words spoken with calm and ease. "Why are you telling me this?"

"We've been telling you for years. You just don't listen."

Camp knew that the radicals controlling Iran had more than 1,000 missiles. They were close to achieving success in their designs for intercontinental delivery technology. If there was a secret military program, on a parallel path with the domestic energy program, then Iran could have enough enriched uranium for at least three to six nuclear bombs.

"Armageddon? Really! Just to pave the road for the Twelfth Imam?"

"You did us a great favor in Iraq. You eliminated Saddam."

"You're welcome."

"For when the Islamic Messiah returns, he will set up his reign in Iraq. That's why we were so involved in the Iraq War. Now Iraq is free and waits for the Twelfth Imam."

Camp closed his eyes and tried to soak it all in. Nothing was logical. A suicide bomber that welcomed martyrdom was not a logical enemy. There was no diplomatic track with a suicide bomber hell-bent on mutual destruction, all in the name of God.

"Iran is a suicide bomber, Omid. How does anyone stop it?"

"There are only two answers, Camp. Reformation. Islam needs a reformation, a Martin Luther who will lead Muslims to a new way of viewing God."

"Great, that only took about 200 years."

"Or shoot the suicide bomber before he detonates."

"After Iraq and Afghanistan, the Americans are sort of tired of wars, Omid. I don't think we have any plans to shoot you first."

"That's because you don't know what you're looking at. You don't understand that you are looking at a suicide bomber. The vest is on. The button is ready to be pushed."

"America won't do it," Camp said shaking his head at the insanity.

"Then perhaps Jericho 3," Omid said in a hushed whisper.

"Israel? If your president keeps threatening Israel, you may give them no other choice. The Jericho 3 is their newest missile and I'm sure they're pointed at every hot spot in Iran this very minute."

"Is that *your* logic or *our* theology? Israel would not attack our people. They would drop their Jericho missiles on our nuclear sites and weapons factories. It would delay the Age of the Coming. It would delay the Shoeib."

"Who?"

"The prophets said the role of the Shoeib is to be the deputy, the one who prepares the way for the Mahdi. He is the mythical figure in centuries-old Hadiths, Shoeib-ebne Saleh, and he is the Islamic commander who attacks Israel in the Age of the Coming to set the stage for the reappearance of the Twelfth Imam. The Hadith says that the preparers will come from Yemen, Lebanon and Iran. The annihilation of the Zionist regime and the conquering of Beitol Moghadas are of the most important events that must happen in the Age of the Coming."

"Beitol what?"

"Beitol Moghadas. It's our word for Jerusalem."

"Is President Ahmadinejad a Twelver?"

Omid nodded. "You heard him speak of the aura he witnessed when he spoke at the United Nations General Assembly. He is not quick to admit it, but we know, we all know, that he is part of the Hojjatieh Society, and he is a close follower, maybe even protected by, the most dangerous hardliner in Iran, Ayatollah Yazdi of Qom."

"So Ahmadinejad is a Twelver, but that's hardly shocking," Camp said as he pulled his blanket up. "He's a certifiable nut job, denies the Holocaust and advocates the annihilation of Israel. One missile on Tel Aviv, and his precious Tehran will be a smoldering pile of rubble."

"There's your logic again, Captain Campbell. It won't be one missile; it will be one thousand within 8-minutes and 53-seconds. Your first missiles – Israel's first missiles - will fall on Iran…10 minutes after we have fired everything we've got."

Camp's fingers started to tremble in spite of the cold.

"The suicide bomber accepts death, if he can kill the enemy as well," Omid said.

"Do all Muslims believe this? Do they all want this?"

"Many Muslims are Twelvers, but only some believe the apocalypse will trigger the Mahdi's return. Many Islamic countries are content to wait in peace for the Mahdi's return. And many Muslim governments are afraid of Ahmadinejad too. They know what he believes.

They know what he wants. They know what this self-proclaimed deputy of the Twelfth Imam is willing to do."

"Do you want to stop him, Omid?"

"Did some Germans want to stop Hitler? Let's just say we do enough to slow him down every now and then. Sometimes a mysterious man on a motorcycle pulls up next to the car carrying a nuclear scientist. Within seconds a magnetic bomb is placed on the car and detonates 30-seconds later as the motorcycle disappears down an alley."

"You do that?"

"No…but sometimes we don't see it when others do it."

"Mossad?" Omid wouldn't answer. "Why don't you just assassinate him?" Camp asked.

"He is not the only one within the many factions fighting for power in Iran. If not Ahmadinejad, then there will be others. He may not ultimately be the one who gets to press the button on the suicide vest that sends nuclear fire raining down on the heads of the Zionists…but someone will."

Omid closed his eyes and laid back down as Camp rolled over to catch a few hours of sleep.

15

Bird-in-Hand, Pennsylvania

Lieutenant Colonel Leslie Raines had been driving for nearly an hour on old Highway 30, passing through Stonybrook and finally past the Smoketown Airport into Bird-in-Hand. The headlights on her Wrangler illuminated the reflective letters on the mailbox which read SEABURY CAMPBELL, SR. Even though it was a few minutes shy of 4:00am, the farmhouse kitchen lights were on as were the lights in the barn for the morning milking. Camp's two sisters and their husbands kept the dairy farm going while Seabury supervised from his porch swing.

Ruth waved at the approaching headlights coming down the gravel driveway as she flipped four strips of bacon and fried two eggs over easy for Seabury. Leslie tapped on the door glass and walked in on her own.

"Good morning Ruth. Good morning Seabury."

"Hello Leslie, how's my favorite colonel doing?" Seabury asked as he got up and kissed Raines on the cheek.

"I'm doing great, and you sound great!"

Ruth placed a plate of bacon and eggs with white toast and a heaping slab of butter in front of Seabury.

"As you can see, Leslie, Seabury is quite faithful to the Mediterranean diet that Dr. Blauw prescribed." Ruth's sarcasm was not lost on Sea Bee.

"I'm not changing my life for this damn disease. I'm exercising more, but I'm going to eat what I always eat. For the love of God, I'm a farmer."

Ruth put another slab of butter in the frying pan as it quickly sizzled to life. "Farmers grow and harvest Mediterranean fruits and vegetables too, Sea Bee. How do you like your eggs cooked, Leslie?"

"Oh, well I wasn't planning on –"

Ruth broke two eggs into the pan. Raines knew that resistance was futile.

"How about sunny side up," Raines said as she took a seat at the table across from Sea Bee.

"How old are you, Leslie?"

"Seabury Campbell! That's rude. You know better than to ask a woman her age," Ruth scolded as she dropped some bacon into the cast-iron skillet.

"That's fine. I'm 39, but I'm feeling more like 59 since the injury. Takes a long time to recover and get back into shape."

"You know, Junior is 41. You two are close in age."

Leslie blushed and lowered her eyes as Ruth put a cup of coffee in front of her.

"You like cream, right?"

"Yes, ma'am."

"Where do your parents live?" Ruth asked as she pulled a fancy plate out of the cupboard and rolled the eggs and bacon onto the plate.

"Well…that's a complicated story, Ruth. My father was killed in Vietnam when I was only two months old. He never saw me. He and my mother were not married when I was born. She was very young. They were both young. When my mother got the news, she cried for a few days then drove over to Lester's house."

"Lester?" Ruth asked as she put another slab of butter in the frying pan and cracked two more eggs for herself.

"Lester was my dad's name, hence I got Leslie. Lester's parents didn't even know their son's girlfriend was pregnant. My mother handed me over to my grandmother, said 'good luck' and walked out the door. She never returned."

"That's horrible, Leslie. Did you ever try to find her?"

"No…I've never even been curious. If she didn't want me then, well, I guess I don't want her now. But I was blessed with an incredible childhood. My grandparents are my heroes. They gave me more love than a human being deserves."

"Are they still living?" Sea Bee asked as he added

more butter to his toast.

"As a matter of fact they are. They still live in the same house they were married in, up in New Hampshire. My grandfather Karl just turned 90 years old. The man is amazing, and he still goes to work five days a week, eight hours a day. My grandmother is 89 years old. Lydia is slowing down a bit now, but she still keeps Karl fed and in line."

Ruth smiled and nodded her approval and understanding.

"Karl sounds like he might be World War II era. Did he serve?" Sea Bee asked.

"That's a story! He had been working in a hospital as an orderly after he and Lydia married. When he was drafted, they put him through training as a medic. I guess they figured medic-by-orderly osmosis or something. December of 1944, Karl was sent to the Ardennes Forest on the German-Belgium border."

"Oh my, was he in the Battle of the Bulge?"

"He was, Seabury. He and the rest of the American divisions were so green, so new. They hadn't seen any combat yet."

Seabury grabbed Ruth's hand and explained.

"Hitler chose the Ardennes Forest and purposefully left it soft, hoping to draw the Americans and British in," Seabury recounted from his World War II history. "Then he sent in more than 250,000 men and hundreds of Panzers. It was a blood-bath."

"Was Karl wounded, Leslie?" Ruth asked.

"Worse than that, Ruth, he was captured by the Germans and spent five months in prisoner of war camps. At first, he was taken to Stalag 9B at Bad Orb, Germany. But 350 of them were pulled out from the thousands of other POWs. If you were Jewish or even looked ethnic, you were given special treatment."

"Is Karl Jewish?" Ruth asked.

"No, but he had a longer nose, a darker complexion, and the Germans decided he was ethnic enough."

"Hell, I've got a schnoz bigger than an Amish buggy. Guess I'm Jewish, too."

"Karl and his 350 buddies were put on railroad boxcars in the middle of winter and sent on a week-long journey with no sanitation, food or water to Berga-an-der-Elster, a little village maybe 50 miles south of Leipzig. Berga was a slave-labor camp that was full to capacity at 400 men, but with more than 1,000 it was unthinkable. They worked 12-hour shifts, slept two to a bed in lice-infested bunks, and were fed starvation rations as they dug tunnels into a mountainside for German munitions."

"Oh, Leslie," Ruth gasped.

"Seventy men of the original 350 died within the first two months. After the beatings and the work and limited rations, Karl weighed 84 pounds when the Americans finally liberated them in April of 1945, but not before the Nazis forced them on a 150-mile death march."

The old farm kitchen was quiet. No one had any

words to utter as all contemplated what a poor American soldier must have gone through almost 70 years before.

"Well, on that happy note, we have some work to do, don't we Seabury?" Leslie concluded.

"I've never done anything like this, Leslie. I'm not a TV anchorman."

Leslie laughed as she removed a small digital video camera from her backpack and a small tripod.

"No experience necessary, Seabury. I'll set the camera on the tripod, press the RECORD button, and I'll walk away. It won't hurt at all."

"You still think this is a good idea?" Seabury asked as he pushed his chair back from the farmhouse kitchen table.

"Well, sir, you said that you don't want Camp to know while he's serving in Afghanistan. You may be right; it may distract him from his mission. But he'll be upset that he wasn't told," Raines said as she took her fancy plate to the sink.

"Don't you worry about those, Leslie, you two get to work," Ruth added as she gathered up the coffee mugs.

"Leslie, do you think Junior tells us everything he's doing over there in the war? Or do you think he holds things back so his mom and dad won't be upset?"

Raines couldn't look Seabury in the eyes. She knew he was correct, but she knew Camp would want to know, and she knew he would be upset. It seemed like the best thing to do.

"Dr. Blauw said that since you were older when the Alzheimer's was detected, it may progress fairly rapidly… you may get worse, faster. Now's the best chance, Seabury, to tell your son what you're feeling…what you're going through."

"Let's get going while I'm still sharp. Things get a bit fuzzier as the day gets older."

Seabury grabbed his red jacket off the hook behind the kitchen door and his John Deere cap.

"Honey, where are you going? Leslie has the camera in the house," Ruth said not sure if Seabury's mind was fading already.

"I want to film this in the barn. It's where my boy and I spent most of our time together."

Seabury walked out the door and headed to the barn. Leslie grabbed the camera and tripod and followed out the door.

Seabury pulled a milking stool over in front of the stalls. The barn was empty now that all of the cows were out in the pasture grazing. Leslie put the camera on the tripod.

"Ready?"

Seabury nodded.

Raines pushed the record button and verified the framing. She backed up, waved, and walked out of the barn. As she was closing the barn door she heard Seabury start to speak.

"Hello, son…this is your daddy…Seabury Campbell, Senior…that makes you Junior…well, I'm not sure how to start this so, here goes…I've got some bad news."

ISAF Headquarters
Kabul, Afghanistan

General Ferguson returned to his office at 2330 hours with his two coffee-pouring majors waiting for the telephone call. It was 1400 hours back at Langley, an odd nine-and-a-half hours behind. Ferguson knew that Langley had no intention of being inconvenienced with an off-hours call, so it was his job to suit up and go back to the office before retiring for the evening. Whatever the issue was, it was worthy of a late night call.

The call finally rang in on Ferguson's desk. The telephone was right next to him, but he motioned for one of the majors to answer it.

"General Ferguson's desk. Major Spann speaking… yes, sir…please hold, sir."

Spann put the call on hold and handed the phone to Ferguson. He shuffled through some papers he hadn't been looking at before the phone rang, then finally took the call off hold and answered with his 'busy' voice.

"Ferguson."

"General Ferguson, this is Special Agent Daniels, and I have Agent Fallon Jessup with me. My apologies, sir, for the lateness of the call."

"What can I do for you this evening?"

"Sir, you've already received our classified briefing

regarding the shipment on Russian rails heading toward Ashgabat, Turkmenistan. There's another component that may or may not be related, but I wanted to bring it to your attention. Actually, we met with Lieutenant Colonel Leslie Raines at Fort Detrick, and she asked if you had been informed."

"I'm listening."

"Sir, Agent Fallon Jessup here. Two commercial mosquito misters were sold by an Illinois company to the city of Hamburg, Germany. The sprayers were stolen out of the warehouse in Hamburg, and the serial numbers showed up at a port in Jakarta, Indonesia. The police in Jakarta tracked the sprayers down to a black market importer who sold them to an unknown party in Islamabad, Pakistan."

"That's a very nice story, Agent Jessup; thank you for sharing it," Ferguson said with no attempt to hide the contempt in his voice.

"Sir, if someone was trying to cook a special recipe of a biological agent, then a commercial sprayer, a misting device like this, might be the ticket to creating an aerosolized bio-weapon," Daniels added.

Ferguson grew silent.

"Sir, I know you have your finger on the pulse with Special Ops missions going in and out of Pakistan. Perhaps you could include this information in your ops planning and briefings. We sure would like to see these two SkitoMisters immobilized. Has Captain Campbell's mission launched?"

Ferguson and his two majors looked uncomfortable.

"Special Agent Daniels…when did you acquire this intelligence?" Ferguson asked.

"Sir, we've been following this paper trail for several weeks now. With the stockpiles on a Russian train headed for the Iranian border, we've been connecting some dots."

"Well, perhaps you should have connected a bit sooner. You're well aware of the fact that Campbell's operational detachment is moving into North Waziristan as we speak. Unfortunately, they only have unit comms with contingency plans to use their SAT phones if the situation on the ground warrants. We've got a drone watching from above and tracking all 17 beacons. We intend to see 18 beacons on egress. But there's no way to initiate communications while they're navigating the mountain passes. It would have been nice to get this information a bit earlier. Anything else?"

"No, sir, just the SkitoMisters."

"Well, glad to know the Agency is spending our time and money trying to protect the Taliban from a mosquito infestation. Sounds like an important mission. Goodnight."

Ferguson rubbed his eyes and pulled a cigar out of his top drawer. He was irritated and tired but mostly tired of separate US government agencies and their reluctance to share intelligence with each other in a timely manner.

"Major Spann, get Creech Air Force Base on the

line. I want a status report on Alpha Team."

"Roger."

Ferguson lit up and paced back and forth in front of the classified maps that filled two walls in his rectangular office. He paused to review Alpha Team's mission plan and time markers which were laid over the Khost – Miran Shah map with great detail. Checking his watch, Ferguson ran his finger from the northwest starting point and stopped where the time marker said the team ought to be as Spann talked with the Tactical Operations Center at the stateside Nevada base.

"Sir, all 17 beacons gathered in Toledo according to plan. Final leg of the ingress, six dials from Sherwood Forest."

Ferguson traced the mission plan from the cave complex called Toledo, through the riverbed complex of caves, over Bannu Road and into Datta Khel Village. They were only six hours away.

16

Miran Shah District
North Waziristan, Pakistan

At 0930 the two squads of Alpha Team mustered in the largest cave. The weather was cooperating perfectly for the final six hour push into Datta Khel Village. Weather conditions were miserable. Heavy snow was falling, the wind had picked up and was whipping around the rock walls of the Hindu Kush. The daylight traverse to the village would require as much cloaked transparency as both snow camo and blowing snow could afford. Once out of the Hindu Kush, the Alpha Team would have limited cover. Omid would lead them directly to the house he had surveyed a few days before, so the team wouldn't have to remain exposed for very long.

"Listen up," Manson said as he placed the map in front of Alpha Team. "We're two clicks out, but at point-six kilometers per hour we could be there in two-and-half hours. We've allowed six hours in case of hostiles. We stay spread out along the river bed so snipers have a more difficult kill zone. Once on Bannu Road, we stay smart. Any vehicles, military or other, we go down and hold until they pass. Do not engage. Clear? If we have to engage before Datta Khel, then kiss Major Banks goodbye as we scurry back over the Hindu Kush."

"Gentlemen, take a look outside," Sanchez said pointing to the cave opening. "The weather has gone red. Ain't nobody flying a bird up here in this white-out to save our sorry asses. The blowing snow will cover us, but if momma nature warms up, we could be looking at rain. The mission is right on track, 20 clicks in 53 hours. Two more clicks and, as Manson said, we only need two-and-half dials, but we will use six full dials if we need them. Once we find Banks, get a beacon on him immediately. The drone boys are watching our 17 beacons, and they're expecting an eighteenth. It's the only way 'eyes in the skies' can distinguish us from Haji. Questions?"

Camp pulled some ice out of his three-week beard as everyone pulled their snow camo masks over their faces for the rapid descent into Datta Khel Village.

In less than 10 minutes Alpha Team had descended the steep footpaths that merged with the riverbed. The trail was completely covered with blowing and blinding snow. The two squads were spread out, but the two scouts with the M4A1s were moving too slow for the clock ticking in Manson's head. Manson gave a hand signal to Brick, and the CW2 stopped his unit. Manson walked over to Omid who was 30 meters ahead of Camp.

"I need you on point with the scouts, Omid. You know the route. We can't see shit."

Omid nodded and ran to the front. "I thought you'd never ask."

Omid took point, and the pace doubled. No one in Alpha Team could be sure that Omid was actually keeping them on mission, but the blinding snow gave them few options.

The medic in Brick's squad yelled up to Dex who was carrying the SAT phone package.

"You trust that Iranian?" Lynch asked.

"I don't even trust *your* fat duff."

Emerging from what seemed to be a thousand switchbacks along the riverbed, Alpha Team reached Bannu Road. One set of fresh tire tracks in the snow was heading in the direction of Datta Khel Village. A truck going into the village could mean a truck leaving sooner or later.

The smell of burning wood fire pits wafted in and out of the wind. The smoke hovered low from the heavy snow and couldn't blow out and over the Hindu Kush.

The first house was visible on Bannu Road. A brown wall made of rocks and mud surrounded the house where a tribesman could make sure his livestock remained close.

Omid stopped. The two squads of Alpha Team stopped behind him. There was nothing to see. No one could hear anything other than the howling wind. Suddenly Omid gave the down sign, and he dove to the side of the road. Sixteen other Alpha Teamers were down and still before Omid's body even settled.

Camp peered up through his snow camo mask. Nothing.

Out of the blowing snow, Camp started to see an image emerge. A donkey started to break through the wall of snow seemingly coming from infinity. As the donkey walked closer, Camp's eye caught a glimpse of a tribal elder, bundled up with blankets and scarves across his face and eyes. A Pashtun Pakul was tucked on top of his head. He was sitting on a perch behind the donkey which pulled him and the rusted steel bed of an old Toyota pick-up truck slowly down Bannu Road. The donkey, driver and Toyota bed passed within feet of Omid, Camp, Billy Finn and 14 other members of Operation Detachment Alpha Team.

When the donkey caravan had disappeared from sight, Ham got on the unit communications.

"Clear," came the whisper from Ham which was heard over every headset in the unit. The team rose as one.

Omid led them past the first house then gave a quick hand signal that was repeated down line. Omid didn't like the conditions for the main mission plan, the one he had crafted, and decided to utilize the fall-back option, an option he had created as well. With so much snow, local tribesmen would be more inclined to use Bannu Road if they were even outside in these conditions. The six-hour contingency plan allowed them some flexibility.

One hundred fifty meters past the first house and beyond the first street in Datta Khel Village, Omid took a hard right to the southwest and away from their southeast plan. The team cut through a field as a large grove of trees started to emerge in the distance where the walls of more houses came into view.

Once inside the grove, code-named Sherwood Forest, Geek pulled out his binoculars to assess the four houses that lined the near side of the second street. The team needed to cross the second street. The second house on the second street was their target-rich environment.

Smoke was pouring from three of the four houses on the first street. Omid watched for Geek's sign. The second house seemed to be vacant or at worst, no one was up cooking or warming themselves by a fire yet.

Omid climbed the backyard wall of the second house followed by 16 more men. No animals greeted him in the backyard, so that was a good sign. Sheep at the first and third houses started bleating. A goat rose up over the wall as Alpha Team hustled past.

As the two squads of Alpha Team passed over the outer wall of the second house, Chip pulled out his thermal imagery scope and pointed it at the house.

There was nothing "living" in the house. No heat.

Omid approached the front wall of the second house. He scanned up and down the street. There was no activity.

The target house was now clearly visible across the street. There was a large house on the corner of Bannu Road and the smaller street. On the other side of the target house, another property seemed to sit with a vacant area between them.

The target house looked different than the seven houses on the street. Datta Khel Village had less than 200 tribesmen and families. The target house looked half sheet metal and half rock. It had more of a commercial feel to it, if anything in North Waziristan could be called commercial.

Geek's binoculars were fixed on the smoke that rose out of the stack on the target house. He gave the signal. Chip moved up to Omid's spot, checked both ways, then crossed over the short front wall, over the street, over the target house wall, and up next to the house. He pulled out his thermal imagery scope.

Four people. Chip gave three long clicks and a short click over his comms. Each member of Alpha Team knew the code that they would soon face three adults and a child. Camp had already lobbied for the preservation and rescue of Miriam's son. He was denied. But Ferguson did provide an acceptable condition. If the boy could be saved, Alpha Team could bind and gag him, put him in a different location, and hope that the child's discovery was made long after the team's egress back through the Hindu Kush.

Three adults and a child meant the team had to go in with silence and surprise. Manson and Colt were the weapons specialists. Master Sergeant "Manson" would not be using his M203 grenade launcher mounted on the 9-inch barrel of his M4 for this part of the mission.

Manson and Colt moved over the wall past Omid, crossed the street, and over the wall and next to the building where Chip was crouched. Chip showed them the imagery. Manson used hand signals to send Colt to the rear southwest corner of the house.

Manson put three short clicks in burst over the comms as the explosives guys crossed and joined Manson and Chip. They looked at the imagery, and Manson sent another soldier to the back of the house with Colt.

On signal, Manson and his soldier would enter from the front as Colt and his soldier entered from the rear. Chip would hold back and watch the imagery unfold. The comms guys stayed back across the street in case things got out of hand and a drone was needed. CW2 "Brick" along with three of the Alpha soldiers stayed at ready distance across the street. If things went bad, Brick and his team would have to deliver some quick justice.

Sanchez, Billy Finn, Camp and three more soldiers crossed the wall, then the street, then the last wall. They would either be the second wave of support or the janitors to clean up the mess.

There were seven sheep, a goat, and an old burro within the walls of the compound. The sheep were bleating but not anymore than usual. The animals huddled close to Alpha Team members on both sides of the house.

According to Omid's intelligence report, the building was a rambler with two long hallways of interconnected rooms and shorter hallways. The imagery suggested that an adult and a child were in the second room up from the rear door. The second adult was in a center room, and appeared to be working at a table. The third adult was sitting in a chair in the front of the house next to the heat glow that was the open fire pit.

If Alpha Team simply kicked in the doors and started shooting, the Taliban, tribesmen and Pakistani forces, if there were any in the area, would be at the house within seconds.

A soldier held a lamb in his arms as Manson slid the front door open. Colt opened the back door as his soldier held another sheep. On cue, Manson and Colt battered the tin on the door. A loud metal clang echoed from both sides of the house as two sheep entered bleating from both ends of the complex followed by Manson in the front and Colt in the rear.

The man warming himself by the fire cursed at the animal barging in through the front door in search of warmth. Before he could make it to his feet, Manson pushed the Carson flipper on his razor-sharp, triple-point, serrated Tanto M16T tactical knife and with a swift thrust cut through the man's throat with decapitating force. Manson quietly laid his lifeless body back into the chair as his head snapped back and blood gushed through the gurgling crevice that was recently his neck.

Both sheep bleated louder and ran panic-stricken down the hallways.

The man in the back bedroom emerged through the doorframe looking down the hall as one of the sheep ran past him. He kicked wildly at the passing animal as Colt's white titanium spearpoint penetrated the back of the man's neck and out the front side of his throat somewhere around the fourth cervical vertebrae, just as Colt had hoped. He fell to the floor where Jazz finished the work.

Seeing his father fall to the ground surrounded by two men who looked like snow, the boy screamed from his bed.

The man in the center room heard the scream and picked his AK-47 up from the table in front of him and managed one step before another Alpha soldier grabbed his head from behind, and with one violent heave, broke the man's neck as the lamb jumped over his crumpled body on the dirt floor.

Colt got his hand quickly over the boy's face before another scream could sound. Within seconds a rag was in the boy's mouth, and two rounds of tape covered the boy's mouth, head and hair. Colt flipped the boy on his stomach and plastic restraints joined his hands behind his back and around his two ankles.

Colt carried the frightened boy out of the room and over his father's body as he took him to the main room. Within seconds, eight soldiers along with Billy Finn and Camp stood by the fire as three terrorists lay dead in the house. Manson sent four short clicks – all clear – across the headset comms and Omid moved over the wall, across the street, over another wall and in through the front door.

The boy's face was filled with terror.

"Tell him we're not going to hurt him," Camp said as Omid entered the room. "We're here to find an American soldier. Tell us where the soldier is, and you'll live."

Omid spoke to the boy in Pashtu. The boy seemed confused by Omid's Persian accent with extra Dari words.

"Does he know where the American is?" Camp demanded.

Omid translated. The boy nodded and head-pointed down the hallway toward the room he had been in with his father. Colt carried the boy down the long hallway with Manson in front, Omid and two others trailing behind. When they got to the door near his father's body, the boy shook his head and nodded toward the rear door instead.

"Outside?" Omid asked in Pashtu. The boy nodded.

Manson opened the door. In the backyard, next to the far wall, they could see a small shack.

"In that building?" Omid asked. The boy nodded again.

Colt took the boy back to the main room by the fire. Manson and two others – followed by two sheep that appeared much happier outside of the building than they were inside – approached the shed. Chip followed the three Alpha Teamers from the front after he saw them heading outside in the snow toward the shed.

With four weapons drawn, Chip pulled out the thermal imaging scope.

No heat. Nothing in the shed. The boy was lying.

Manson unhitched the door and walked into the six-by-eight wood cobbled feed shack. Light pouring through the wood boards illuminated the frozen stiff body of Dean Banks, MD., Board Certified Gynecologist with the Bucks County Women's Health Clinic, and US Army Reservist on a four-month deployment to Afghanistan, and a single, solitary AK-47 gunshot wound to the head.

Camp and Billy Finn walked into the main room where the man with the broken neck was still sprawled out motionless on the ground.

"What the hell?" Camp said in muted tones as Finn inspected the table next to the bed.

"Some kind of a laboratory?" Finn asked.

"Or a Flintstones-era surgical suite."

Camp picked through a box of assorted trash. With

his knife he pawed at discarded items, bloody gauze, injectibles, syringes and packaging.

"Poly Prothese PIPs?" Finn asked as he read the label on the packaging Camp pulled out of the trash. "What's that?"

"Silicone breast implants," Camp said in bewilderment.

Finn walked over to the cabinet next to the prep table.

"Check it out...ether, rubbing alcohol, and several bottles of *this* stuff."

"Ether? Looks like they were putting someone to sleep for surgery," said Camp. "A bit archaic, but I guess it would do the trick. Looks like Russian scribbling on the bottles."

Finn pulled out his small digital camera and started taking photos of the room, the trash and the mysterious bottles with Russian labels.

The body of Major Banks was carried inside and placed gently on the floor near the open fire pit. Colt moved the boy and placed him on a chair next to the man with the slit throat and nearly decapitated head. Veggie removed a body bag as Lynch unfolded the Tac4 foldable stretcher.

Camp walked into the room as the team prepared the body of Major Banks for his final return home. Camp moved closer to the major and slowly dropped down to one knee. The Alpha Team stopped their work and paused. Camp reached out and touched the frozen hand of Major Banks. He closed his eyes.

"God…we give thanks for this fallen warrior. He was a soldier, a father, a husband, a son, and our brother. Guide us as we bring him home." Camp touched the face of his comrade then rose to his feet.

"This won't stand, gentlemen," Camp said to every eye in the room that was fixated on his leadership. "This man was a healer, a physician; a man who dedicated himself to providing medical care. Every man, woman and child on this earth is entitled to freedom. Major Dean Banks gave his life in the great cause of liberty. This will not stand. Let's get him home."

Camp walked over to the boy, smiled, and bent over by the child's face.

"Which way are you going to go, son? Which path are you going to choose?" Camp rubbed the boy's head and walked away as the child's eyes followed him in horror. The boy didn't understand a word Camp said or why Alpha Team had just killed his father. Alpha Team resumed their preparations for egress.

Omid glanced at his watch and became instantly agitated. "He's dead. There's no reason to move him out and through the Hindu Kush," Omid said as he stood over Banks. Veggie jumped up and got in Omid's face.

"We aren't a bunch of Iranian dogs. We're American soldiers, and we DO – NOT – LEAVE our soldiers behind!"

Manson motioned Veggie off and, with one eye

seemingly fixed on his kill and another staring down Omid, he spoke. "Quick check of the house as Veggie and Lynch bag the major. We're out in three."

Omid left the room and wandered into the center room where Camp and Finn were back examining the lab.

"Breast implants? They kidnap a gynecologist and bring him to hell's living room to do a boob job on a burka queen?" Finn asked.

Camp looked at the wall behind the bed.

"Looks like this is where they made the Facebook video," Camp said.

"The Islamic Khilafah, the Shahada, the flag of jihad," Omid said from the back of the room.

"Clearly the boy was with Miriam's husband back there. I guess one of these other guys is Kazi," Camp said to Finn.

"Kazi?" Omid asked. "How do *you* know the name Kazi?"

Camp and Finn moved quickly to Omid.

"How do you know the name Kazi?" Finn asked with full FBI investigatory tone.

"Kazi is a business consultant to Iran. He is used on several projects. He was educated in the states, a microbiologist who fashions himself as a doctor, a scientist type. He's Pakistani but worked in The Netherlands before he was recruited."

"Recruited? By whom?" Camp asked.

"ISI…Inter-Services Intelligence, Pakistan," Omid

answered.

"And the Iranian Revolutionary Guard?" Finn pressed.

"A freelancer, yes…but not to the Revolutionary Guard…he works with MISIRI."

"MISIRI?" Camp asked.

"The Ministry of Intelligence and National Security of the Islamic Republic of Iran," Finn answered.

"Kazi is not one of the dead guys, Captain Campbell. But you don't want to be here if he comes back. He'll be in the company of ISI."

"Master Sergeant Manson! You'd better take a look at this," a call came from the back of the house. Camp put one of the PIP packages in his pocket and followed Finn and Omid.

In the back room, behind a wall of curtains, Chip wheeled out a machine.

"What is it?" Sanchez asked. Manson put his flashlight beam on the side of the machine.

"The label says SkitoMister…made in Illinois," Chip said.

"What the hell is that for? Do the Paki's have a mosquito problem up here, Omid?" Manson asked.

"At this elevation? I doubt it," Camp said as he moved in to take a closer look. "A mister…takes a liquid and turns it into a mist. Basically a sprayer."

"How much does it weigh?" Manson asked.

Chip picked it up awkwardly.

"Eighty, maybe a hundred pounds."

"Okay, we've got to get moving," Sanchez said as he left the room.

"What do you want to do, Camp? If we blow it, the gig's up. Everyone in Datta Khel will come outside to see the fireworks," Manson said.

"Get Dex."

"Dex!" Manson yelled as running boot steps approached down the hallway.

"Dex, did you put a beacon on Major Banks when you bagged him?" Camp asked.

"Affirmative, sir."

"Unzip him. Hide the tracking device on the SkitoMister. Once we get back into the Hindu Kush, we'll have the drone blow it up."

"Roger that, sir."

"What about the boy?" Manson asked. "He's not coming with us."

"I understand, Manson. Let's put him in the vacant house across the street. It'll take them a day or two to find him."

The mission timer on Geek's wrist watch indicated 19-minutes and 23-seconds. Three men, presumably Taliban or Haqqani Network were dead, the body of Army Major Dean Banks was bagged and mounted to the Tac4, and Miriam's son – now orphaned from his insurgent father and his suicide bombing mother – was placed in a chair in a vacant house with no heat.

The Alpha Team climbed the back wall of the vacant house on the north side of the target street. Back in the grove of trees, tension grew as the snow subsided. The winds were howling and blowing, but the snow was diminishing. Camp couldn't tell if his body was warm from adrenaline or if the temperatures were rising from the midday warm-up. The clouds had breaks in them but looked much darker.

The temperature gauge on Camp's watch registered 33-degrees Fahrenheit. The moisture was borderline snow and rain.

Crossing out of Sherwood Forest and through the field, Alpha Team returned to Bannu Road. There were two more sets of tire tracks.

The pace increased as the two squads spread out. Lynch and Veggie were on either ends of the Tac4 as they double-timed carrying Banks.

Suddenly, the two scouts on point raised their hands and dove into the ditch on the east side of Bannu. Fifteen other Alpha members did likewise and settled. Veggie and Lynch covered the white body bag and the Tac4 with their own bodies.

Three pick-up trucks full of Pakistani ISI drove past them. Alpha Team, sprawled out in the water ditch next to Bannu Road, remained motionless and undetected.

"They'll follow our tracks in the snow. Call in the drone." Omid whispered to Captain Sanchez lying next to him.

"And cause an international incident by attacking members of a sovereign nation's military? Not on your life. We roll!" Sanchez said as Alpha erupted out of the ditch and sprinted down Bannu Road.

"Brick, when we get to the riverbed take squad one up and along the road, and we'll head down through the riverbed. Give us cover if you can. Muster at Toledo," Sanchez said into the helmet comms while running at full speed.

Three, four-wheel drive Toyota pick-up trucks pulled outside in front of the second house on the south side of the second street in Datta Khel Village. Six men emerged from the cabs, and another 12 jumped out of the truck beds anxious to warm themselves by the fire that certainly would welcome them beneath the smoke stack pouring out from above.

Seventeen men carrying weapons and another unarmed man sauntered through the gate and up to the house. They were in no particular hurry. The Pakistani ISI soldiers were oblivious to the conditions on the ground as Kazi's eyes examined the snow-covered ground. He held up his hand, and everyone stopped as he pointed to numerous sets of waffle-like boot prints in the snow.

AK-47's rose immediately, and the men spread out front and back around the house. Within seconds they realized the full carnage of an event that had taken place 30 minutes before they arrived. The bodies of three of their comrades were still warm to the touch. But the boy was missing.

The Commander sent a detachment of six to follow the tracks in the snow which led over the wall, across the street, and over the next wall to the vacant house. Within a few short minutes, the Pakistani soldiers found the boy and brought him back and quickly removed the tape and rag from his mouth and cut the plastic restraints.

"White suits, white suits," the boy screamed in Pashtu.

Kazi walked up to the boy as the ISI Commander was trying to calm him down.

"How many?" Kazi asked.

"I don't know…maybe eight," the boy said. "I told them. Then they took him."

"Told them what?" Kazi demanded. "They took what?"

"They were looking for the American. They came for him."

Kazi ran out of the room and down the long hallway to the room with the curtain walls. The SkitoMister was exactly where he had left it. Kazi stroked the machine like a woman's face.

"They can't be far. Four on the ground, the rest in the trucks," the Commander said as he walked toward the front of the house.

"Put the machine in my truck. We'll head to Miran Shah right now," Kazi said as two soldiers picked up the SkitoMister and carried it out to Kazi's truck.

The boy knelt down alone next to his father's body and started crying as ISI soldiers and Kazi left the house as fast as they had arrived.

The four ISI runners were standing on Bannu Road after emerging from the grove of trees in Sherwood Forest and running through the field. The footprints they followed led north toward the Hindu Kush, the border with Afghanistan, and the same direction they had just driven in from.

The Commander slowed down, and the four got into the back of the two vehicles. Kazi and his two soldiers turned the opposite direction and headed south toward Miran Shah.

Sanchez took his squad down along the riverbed. Omid stayed up with the scouts at point since he needed to chart a different egress on the fly. There was no visible trail, and the conditions had gotten worse. Camp and Finn ran on opposite ends of Veggie and Lynch who carried Banks on the Tac4.

Brick's squad was running at full speed when they heard the sounds of approaching vehicles. The 40-mile-per-hour speed of the ISI Toyotas was no match for Brick's team, Special Forces or otherwise.

They had just crossed a one lane bridge over the shallow mixture of water and ice from the Hindu Kush run-off when AK-47 fire sprayed the fields wildly all around them.

"Dino, Jazz...C4 discharge on the bridge, now!" Brick screamed as he and three other Alpha soldiers kept running.

Dino and Jazz descended the banks on both sides of the one-lane bridge and mounted their C4 bricks, then took off running. AK-47 fire danced on Bannu Road as Dino and Jazz ran z-patterns up the winding road.

"Above their heads, no shoot to kill," Brick yelled as his team turned on a dime and opened fire at the Pakistani soldiers.

The nearly simultaneous C4 explosions sent the wooden bridge and a cloud of fire, ice, water and snow 70 feet into the air as the Toyotas veered to each side of the tributary trying to avoid open water below. The Commander's vehicle flipped over sending four ISI soldiers airborne and down the embankment into the frigid water.

Brick and the squad kept running as bullets fell harmlessly to the ground behind them.

The explosions and fireball illuminated the riverbed as Sanchez kept his squad moving on the parallel path below.

"All clear," Brick yelled into his helmet comms as the split Alpha Team kept humping toward muster at Toledo, a cave complex less than two clicks away and at the base of the Hindu Kush.

The snow turned to freezing rain as midday approached. It hid the mountains behind a gray, wind-whipped scrim of water and threw hailstones chattering to the earth. It flooded the gravel yards of the hillside and transformed the footpaths into freeways of chocolate-colored water.

Inside Toledo, the tempest knocked out comms and turned their muster into a dark, flooded cave, soaking body armor and wrecking bags full of electronics. Soaked soldiers stood miserably as Camp, Billy Finn and Omid gathered with Sanchez and CW2 "Brick." The half-crazed, wandering eye Manson stood guard over the Tac4 holding Banks' body bag.

"How's the SAT phone?" Sanchez barked to Geek.

"Checking it now, sir."

"We can't stay here...these conditions are nothing for the Taliban and the tribesmen. You can count on 20 of them less than two kilometers behind us already," Omid said as he pled his case for urgency.

"We need to get a strike on that beacon in the house," Finn said to no one in particular.

"Screw the damn mosquito machine. We've got to go now!" Omid yelled.

"Geek? Give me something, brother," Sanchez begged.

"Nothing, sir...maybe we'll have better luck higher up."

"Brick...we're too damn wet. We've got to do better than point-six kilometers per hour, or we're going to freeze up here," Sanchez said as Brick nodded. "Let's move."

The Alpha Team started up the Hindu Kush and spread out for Taliban snipers. They were soaked to the bone. Veggie and Lynch carried Major Banks on the second leg of his long journey home. Camp grabbed Omid's arm as they headed up the trail.

"I want to trust you, Omid."

"Why?"

"I'm not really sure. Tell me the plan. I want to understand."

Omid looked deep into Camp's eyes. "Do you really think that we can ever become friends?"

Camp smiled and extended his hand. "Why not?"

PART TWO

17

The desk phone in General Ferguson's office rang. He waved off Major Spann and took the call himself.

"Ferguson."

"Sir, First Sergeant Morris in the Creech TOC."

"Go, Sergeant."

"Sir, we have 18 beacons on the move."

Ferguson let out one of his very few smiles and fist pumped the air.

"That's great news, sergeant."

"Maybe not, sir. The 18th beacon is heading in the opposite direction of Alpha Team. Looks like it's on the road to Miran Shah."

"Any comms from Alpha?"

"Negative, sir. What would you like us to do with

air support?"

Ferguson put the call on speaker and walked over to his classified wall map.

"Sir?"

"I'm here, sergeant…stay with Alpha Team until safe egress and comms. Maybe hostiles moved Major Banks before Alpha arrived."

There was silence on the other end of the call. Sergeant Morris at the Creech TAC finally spoke.

"Sir…with all due respect…if hostiles moved Major Banks, then someone had to put a beacon on him. Is there any chance that we have a broken arrow, sir?"

Ferguson sat slowly in his chair and rubbed the fog of war out of his eyes. He thought about Camp's penchant for going outside mission plan which is why he put Billy Finn on his hip. If Camp went all John Wayne on him then Billy Finn would have been riding shotgun.

"I don't know, sergeant; I just don't know."

National Interagency Biodefense Center
BSL-4 Facility
Fort Detrick, Maryland

The technicians were fully dressed in their BSL-4 body suits, yellow oxygen tubes connected to the ceiling grid, as Lieutenant Colonel Leslie Raines watched from the command center's video monitors.

A SkitoMister from the manufacturer in Illinois was in the room. Four rhesus monkeys were in their cages nearby as the technicians hooked up the tularemia recipe into the tank on the SkitoMister. Cooking up a toxic rabbit fever blend that was lethal by inhalation was anything but easy. But if it could be simulated in Raines' BSL-4 lab, then an antibiotic or vaccine could be cooked up too.

Tularemia was a less than glamorous bio-weapon. The world was focused on other leading actors like anthrax, the Black Plague, Marburg's and smallpox. Even though rabbit fever was a Category A pathogen, the words "rabbit" and "terror" never seemed to go together.

Tularemia was first mentioned as a plague-like disease of rodents in 1911 when it killed a large number of ground squirrels in the area of Tulare Lake in California. The lake gave the name to the disease – tularemia. Scientists determined that tularemia could be dangerous and humans could catch the infection just by touching an infected animal, dead or otherwise. The illness became more frequent among hunters, cooks and agricultural workers. If any of the pathogenic organisms penetrated a body through damaged skin or mucous membranes, then a potentially severe and fatal illness developed for infected people.

It was one of the key reasons why BSL-4 facilities were designed and created, biocontainment labs where epidemics *inside* could be prevented from escaping *outside*.

Raines knew that tularemia was one of the fastest sprinters among all infections. It took only 10 microbes of the bacterium to cause an extremely dangerous disease. The disease had a very fast and acute beginning. It was the three-to-five day infection window that caused her the most angst.

A weapon using airborne tularemia might not even be detected within five days. Without treatment, the clinical course could progress to respiratory failure, shock, and death. By the time a true diagnosis was rendered, millions could be ill if not dead.

But the most alarming conclusion for Raines was the status of the vaccination: incomplete. In volunteer studies, the live attenuated vaccine did not protect all recipients against aerosol virulent tularemia.

This was the aspect of animal research that bothered Raines the most. If she and her technicians had cooked up a lethal recipe of inhalation tularemia, all four rhesus monkeys would be sick within three to five days and dead soon thereafter. If not, then they had to go back to the biological pantry of ingredients and try a new recipe.

If the monkeys died, then the research team knew they had achieved sufficiently lethal inhalation tularemia. They could then get busy developing vaccines and antibiotics to protect the next batch of monkeys *from* dying.

Dr. Groenwald walked into the command center as Raines watched her technicians load the SkitoMister with the fourth recipe they had concocted of inhalation tularemia.

"What's the plan, colonel?" Groenwald asked.

"We've cracked the so-called vaccine-resistant tularemia the Soviets developed in 1982. Now we're trying to cook a recipe that even we can't solve. We're simultaneously working on microbes of bacteria and vaccines."

"Progress?"

"Not yet, all four NHPs have handled each recipe thanks to their vaccines."

Groenwald looked out over the TV monitors feeding images of the technicians working with the SkitoMister and the non-human primates.

"Keep me posted, colonel."

Four rhesus monkeys or four million people? In order to save four million people, Raines needed to make sure four monkeys died.

It was an easy choice, even if she didn't like to make it.

Combat Outpost Chergotah
Khost Province, Afghanistan

Emerging out of the Hindu Kush, Alpha Team stumbled into the Combat Outpost, deprived of a badly needed, four-hour sleep break and pushed to cover almost a kilometer an hour through the high country, all the while fearing that they were being chased by a hot pursuit.

Dex unpacked the SAT phone as the others stripped out of their frozen snow camo and into warm battle dress uniforms. The soldiers from the 4th Brigade Combat Team, 25th Infantry Division stoked the fires and put some water on the cook stoves for the weary Alpha Team members.

Dex connected with Creech Air Force Base and confirmed that all 17 had indeed made successful egress over the Hindu Kush. The duty sergeant asked him to hold so he could patch in General Ferguson at ISAF headquarters in Kabul.

"Captain, need you here, sir," Dex yelled. "They're patching in Command at ISAF."

Captain "Sonny" Sanchez grabbed the SAT phone as Camp walked over to listen.

"Captain Sanchez."

"Major Spann here at ISAF, please hold for General Ferguson."

"Captain, this is not a secure transmission," Ferguson barked.

"Roger that, sir, all 17 safe and warming up at base camp."

"Seventeen?"

"Affirmative, sir. We recovered the mission target, sir, that was a KIA, and we have returned with that mission objective."

"Captain, Creech has been tracking 18 beacons. One went the opposite direction of your team."

"Affirmative, sir. I'm going to put Camp on the phone."

"General."

"Welcome back, Camp. What's the story on the 18th beacon? We picked it up about two and a half days ago," Ferguson asked.

"Sir, can't really get into that on this transmission for security reasons. Suffice it to say, I authorized placing a beacon on an item. Sir, I'd highly recommend that you turn that beacon off…permanently, sir."

Ferguson and his coffee-pouring majors appeared puzzled.

"I can't really authorize that until I have some more information. How long before you get to a FOB and get on SIPR?"

"Twenty-four to 36 hours, sir. Air is red, roads are red. Nasty weather."

"Understood. We'll continue to keep an eye on number 18."

Camp paused and thought for a few seconds. "Sir, I wanted to let you know that I need to cancel my leave."

"Your leave? You just got here."

"Roger that, sir, but you know I was planning to take Marcy and the kids to International Falls, Minnesota for some canoeing. But Marcy said the mosquitoes are out, and they'd kill us. So we're going to have to postpone that trip."

Ferguson got up and paced the room.

"Roger that, Camp, roger that. Listen, I know how much this trip means to you and Mary – ah, correction – Marcy, so I'm going to send my birds to pick you up.

Sometimes the air for my birds isn't quite as red as it can be for those boys who fly the ring routes."

Camp hung up the SAT phone wondering if his old friend and former XO from Iraq understood what he was saying or concluded that he had finally lost his mind.

Major Spann was at the phone and dialing Special Agent Daniels' home number even before Ferguson could issue the order.

"What time is it in Virginia, major?"

"Sir, 0240 hours."

Ferguson smiled.

"Perfect."

18

ISAF Headquarters
Kabul, Afghanistan

General Ferguson's two Blackhawk helicopters made the round trip flight to and from Combat Outpost Chergotah, with one stop on the return to Bagram Air Base, in less than two hours. Camp and Billy Finn remained on their bird at Bagram in respect until six soldiers from mortuary affairs removed the body of Major Dean Banks. A throng of 40 soldiers, sailors, airmen and Marines stood ramrod straight and held their salutes until Major Banks was placed in an ambulance on the tarmac.

At just past 0930 hours Major Spann greeted Camp and Finn at the ISAF helo pad and walked them over to Ferguson's office. The hot shower and warm meal could wait until they briefed the General. Ferguson rose from his desk as Camp and Finn entered.

"You need a shave, sailor."

"Aye, aye, sir, it's on the schedule," Camp said as he shook Ferguson's hand.

"How are you, Billy?"

"Cold, wet and hungry, but I'll survive," Finn chided.

"Well, let me guess," Ferguson said as he took a seat behind his desk. "You found a SkitoMister."

Camp and Finn were surprised.

"You knew about it?" Camp asked.

"Not in time, unfortunately. Special Agent Daniels from CIA called me while you two were hiking up the Hindu Kush. The Agency traced two of these units from Illinois, to Hamburg, to Jakarta and finally Islamabad. Had no idea you'd stumble across one in North Waziristan, not that that would be much of a surprise given the FATA. What did you see in there, Camp?"

"Basically a laboratory and a barbaric third world surgical suite."

"I took 20-some pictures if you want to take a look?" Finn said as he handed the SD card from his camera to one of the coffee-pouring majors who put it in the general's laptop and warmed up the projector.

"I found this in the trash," Camp said as he handed Ferguson the Poly Prothese PIP packaging.

"What is it?"

"Industrial grade silicone breast implants, made by a French company. We suspect they abducted Major Banks probably because he was a female surgeon," Camp said.

"You can't be serious," Ferguson responded.

"Boob jobs for burka babes, general. You can't make this shit up," Finn cracked with a sly grin on his face.

"Ready, sir," the major said as the first of Finn's photos appeared on the screen. The major handed Finn the remote clicker.

"There were two or three bottles of ether. Ether was used for anesthesiology way back in the day, maybe 40 years ago, but it still gets the job done. Here you see surgical sutures, scalpel, bandages, gauze and rubbing alcohol," Camp said as he narrated the photos.

"What are those? Looks Russian?"

"No clue, sir. Finn found three of these bottles, but the labels were in Russian," Camp said to Ferguson.

Ferguson waved his hand at Major Spann. "Get me an American or British Russian speaker right now."

"Sir, many of the Afghans speak –"

Ferguson cut him short. "I don't want a damn Afghan who kinda speaks Russian, then tries to translate what he's thinking in Dari Persian or Pashtu and then over to the English he kinda speaks."

Spann left the room before Ferguson could finish ranting.

"How'd they kill Banks?"

"Single shot to the temple. At least they didn't make him suffer. Then again, not sure what he may have gone through before they shot him," Finn said.

"Looks like he was performing some surgeries based

on the PIPs and the ether," Ferguson answered. "What about the Terp's son? Did you find him?"

"Yes, sir, at least we were pretty sure that was her kid. We put him in a vacant house across the street, bound and gagged. I'm sure they found him within minutes. Any word on Miriam?"

"She's here in Kabul. Recovered nicely, no infections, but I'm told some ugly scars on her face and arm. You certainly saved her life," Ferguson said.

"Right, not every day that you can save a suicide bomber. What's going to happen to her?"

"Well, the geniuses from the State Department are trying to find another country for her. She's a dead woman walking in Afghanistan or Pakistan...literally. I'm guessing she'll go into the SIV program and be resettled as a refugee in Virginia. She's highly educated and speaks fluent English."

"Not to mention she only tried to kill 40 Americans," Camp said with sarcasm duly noted by Ferguson and Finn. "Sir, why don't you just email the photo to the Russian desk at the Pentagon, State or CIA. I'm sure they could give you an answer in 60 seconds. I'd really like to get a hot shower."

Ferguson nodded to the sole remaining major who took the SD card out of Ferguson's laptop and sat down at the PC on his desk.

"Were you able to immobilize the SkitoMister? I had our intel guys hide a GPS beacon on it so the drone could lock in," Camp said.

"It was the 18th beacon, Camp. We thought it was Banks until it headed in the other direction. Until I spoke with you, there was no way that I was going to authorize an airstrike."

"Other direction?"

"It moved. First to Miran Shah, then Islamabad… then we lost it."

"Do you think the Paki's found the beacon?"

"No, they put the whole machine on an airplane and then we lost it…until it landed in Tehran. Now it's in Damghan, 300 kilometers east of Tehran…close to the Caspian Sea and not far from the border with Turkmenistan."

Ferguson stood up and paced rapidly in his office.

"General?" Camp asked.

"Crap," Ferguson grumbled as he rubbed his balding head. "Raines."

"Leslie Raines?"

"Daniels and some other agent from Langley briefed her on some biologicals a few weeks ago at Detrick. Raines called me afterwards and told me the Agency was tracking a rail shipment of stockpiled biologicals from the Kirov Oblast west of the Ural Mountains along the Vyatka River on a 36-hour ride on the Trans-Siberian railway to Ashgabat, Turkmenistan."

Ferguson walked over to a different classified map on his wall as the full picture started to emerge and dots were connecting themselves.

"Ashgabat is less than 700 kilometers from

Damghan," Ferguson said.

"What's on the train?" Finn asked.

The major got a quick response from the Pentagon.

"Sir, we have a translation on the Russian labels. But it's more like Latin than Russian. *Francisella tularensis*, or something like that."

Ferguson looked Camp straight-on square in the eye.

"Tularemia. That's what Major Banks reported from FOB Lightning. That's what Colonel Raines is working on right now in the BSL-4 at Detrick. That's what you found in Datta Khel Village. And that's what's on this damn Russian train."

National Interagency Biodefense Center
BSL-4 Facility
Fort Detrick, Maryland

The slightly chubby technician got in the elevator without buttons, swiped her card, scanned her biometrics and rode the car down to the first floor. Running through the atrium, past the coffee bar, leather chairs and couches, she ran out into the parking lot as Lieutenant Colonel Raines was getting out of her Wrangler.

"Colonel...Colonel Raines," she yelled as she got closer.

"Tina, are you okay?" Raines said as she picked up her pace.

Tina was out of breath and bent over in exhaustion.

"Ma'am...four...dead...monkeys!"

Raines looked up toward the secret floor in the NIBC.

"Oh my…Tina are you sure?"

"Positive…we suited up and verified."

"We did it. A vaccine-resistant strain of tularemia. If we can do it, they can do it. Let's go girl. Now we need a new vaccine and new antibiotics. Now we're even. Gotta get one step up and ahead."

"More dead monkeys?" Tina asked as the redness started to leave her swollen cheeks.

"I hope not, not anymore…Now I want them to live!"

Dr. Groenwald was standing in the Command Center looking at the BSL-4 TV monitors when Raines burst in.

"No skinny latte today, colonel?"

"Champagne if they'd serve it," Raines responded as she looked at the four non-human primates dead in the bottom of their cages.

"What's next?" Groenwald asked.

"Now we cook vaccines. The variations shouldn't be that far off from our existing protocols. Get the recipe out to a pharmaceutical company and manufacture supply."

"Who do you plan to work with?"

"Haven't even thought that far, Dr. Groenwald."

"Well, I know of both a French and German company who have done bio vaccines and antibiotics in the past. I can make some calls."

"That would be great," Raines said as Tina ran into the Command Center.

"Colonel Raines, you have a telephone call on the SIPR line…Afghanistan…a U.S. Navy Captain Campbell."

"On the SIPR? Okay…," Raines said as a warm flush filled her face. She thought the news couldn't be *that* bad if he was well enough to call her, though he always called on her personal cell phone.

"Camp? Are you okay?"

"Hello, Les…I'm doing great. Took a little backpacking expedition with Outward Bound through the Hindu Kush and finally got a hot shower and three bowls of chili in the DFAC. Feeling great."

"Are you still at Lightning?"

"No, ISAF headquarters in Kabul. Here with Ferguson and my new best friend Billy Finn. Les, I just wanted to call and talk to you. I wanted to hear your voice. How are you doing?"

Raines lost her breath. *I wanted to hear your voice?*

"Crazy busy. I assume Ferguson has filled you in?"

"Roger that. Sounds like you're cooking up some recipes for death. Ferguson told me about the Russian train and tularemia. Hey Les, I found one of your SkitoMisters in North Waziristan."

"Camp, are you serious? Did you blow that sucker up?"

"Too close for comfort, couldn't afford the fireworks. We put a GPS beacon on it, and the drones watched it move to Miran Shah, then Islamabad."

"Guess they can't bomb it in the capital, can they?"

"Nope, because it's not there anymore. It was flown to Tehran and then driven to Damghan."

"Damghan? Isn't that where the Iranians do all of their biological and chemical weapons work?"

"One in the same."

"These guys really freak me out, Camp. I just have a hard time believing that they'd be so stupid as to attack other countries with biologicals or even nukes."

Camp paused and thought about the many conversations he had with Omid.

"You have no idea, Les…this regime doesn't have a western logical bone in their collective body."

"So, when are you coming home, sailor?"

"I'm not sure; just met with Ferguson after lunch. He's heading back to the states to meet with the SECDEF, the SECSTATE and hopefully the US Ambassador to the United Nations. Billy Finn and I are heading to Turkmenistan to see what we can find out about the Russian freight train. After that…if I were a betting man…I'd say Tel Aviv."

"Israel? Oh my gosh."

"When will you be done with your work, Les?

"As soon as we can cook up a vaccine recipe. Just this morning we got four dead NHPs, so we know we have a strain that is now vaccine-resistant. Now we need the other side of the equation. Once we've got that, we hand it off for manufacturing and let the Pentagon, State and maybe the FDA take it from there."

"Well, work fast...I may want you to join me in Tel Aviv."

Raines smiled and lowered her voice.

"Another undercover assignment in a crowded double-sized bed like our escapade in Morocco last year?"

"I don't know about all that...the last one didn't end so well for you as I recall. You're the expert on the biologicals. I'm just a trauma doc."

"And a former SEAL...that's the part that seems to bring trouble your way."

Camp laughed out loud. He knew she was right.

"I'll be in touch, Les...but get your suitcase out...just in case."

"Hey, Camp? Call your parents, okay?"

There was a brief pause.

"Why? Is everything okay?"

"Yeah, sure...I mean I think so. You know, they just want to hear from you. Let 'em know that you're okay, that's all."

19

Tehran Imam Khomeini International Airport (IKA)
Tehran, Iran

Emirates flight 977 from Dubai pulled into the gate as the ground crew marshaled in the Boeing 777-300ER. Omid was exhausted from the two legs of the journey back home. After the 9:00am flight from Islamabad's ISB airport into Dubai, Omid had a nearly seven-hour layover before the Tehran flight.

The seatbelt sign went off, but his traveling companion was still asleep.

"Hey, wake up…we're at the gate," Omid said as he gently tapped the man's shoulder.

Omid grabbed his backpack out of the overhead bin, and the two of them shuffled down the aisle with the rest of the passengers, out the plane, over the jet bridge and into the terminal toward customs.

The customs agent looked at Omid's passport and

the military ID he presented with it.

"Colonel Farid Amir, welcome home. You weren't gone as long this time," the customs agent said to Omid as he quickly assumed his true identity. "How is your father doing?"

"All praise to Allah, he continues to live, but his days are numbered. I am thankful that he's getting good care."

The agent stamped his passport, and Omid proceeded to baggage claim.

Omid and his traveling companion waited as the carousel began to spin. Omid's large bag came first.

"It was nice to see you again. Will you be in Tehran long this time?" Omid asked the man.

The man was lost in his thoughts as he waited for his luggage.

"No. Actually I'm heading to my lab in Damghan. Not sure when I'll return to Islamabad."

"Damghan? I haven't been there in a long time. I was stationed there early in my career for a few years. I hope you enjoy your time."

Omid and the man exchanged good-bye kisses on each cheek.

"May God be with you, Farid," the man said. "I will pray for your father."

"And with you as well, Kazi," Omid said as he touched his heart, picked up his suitcase and hoisted his backpack over his shoulder before exiting the terminal.

ISAF Headquarters
Kabul, Afghanistan

Camp had an hour to spend before the 30-minute Suburban ride with Billy Finn over to Kabul International Airport. The nameplate on the door said Major John O'Brien, so he knew he had found the right place. He was only slightly embarrassed that he didn't know how to find the chaplain's office given that he had no clue where the chapel was even located.

Camp was not a publicly religious man. But faith was an important part of his life as a child, growing up on a farm in rural Lancaster County, Pennsylvania. He hadn't forgotten his roots.

According to the bio on the DOD website, O'Brien was born and raised in Texas, did his undergraduate studies in religion at Texas Christian University and earned his Masters of Divinity at the Southern Baptist Theological Seminary in Louisville, Kentucky.

Camp tapped lightly on the door, perhaps secretly hoping that the chaplain might have stepped out or was running late from a previous appointment.

"Come in," came the warm but soft voice from the other side of the door.

Camp opened and walked in.

"Camp? I'm so glad you stopped by. I'm John. Have a seat."

O'Brien was in his early 30s and seemed quite affable and approachable. He had a welcoming smile with none of the formalities or honorifics that other military officers were accustomed to using.

Camp sat down on the edge of his chair. He didn't want to appear too comfortable.

"Chaplain, I have to head to the airport for a flight at 1800 hours, so I can't take much of your time."

"Please call me John. I prefer to keep my counseling sessions informal."

Counseling session? Camp wasn't really looking for a counseling session or even pastoral advice as much as he wanted some theological insight.

"John, I really just have a question or two that I thought maybe someone like you could answer."

"Try me."

"Well, my mother used to haul my ass, um, me out to church every Sunday – usually against my will I might add – and I remember my Sunday school teacher talking about the end times and Armageddon, and all that stuff. Do you believe in that, John?"

Chaplain O'Brien sat back in his chair across from the coffee table that separated him from Camp. With interlocked fingers in a praying position, he looked quite pastoral.

"It's a perfectly natural fear. We face war and death every day. Certainly within the Southern Baptist tradition we believe in the end times, a final battle of Armageddon and ultimately the second coming of Christ. But we could spend hours debating all of the timing, whether or not we believe in the rapture, or if the second coming would be pre- or post-tribulation."

Camp was sure his mouth fell open with all of the unfamiliar words the chaplain spoke with matter-of-fack ease.

"I don't have a clue what you just said, John."

Chaplain O'Brien laughed and leaned forward.

"What part are you specifically interested in Camp?"

"Armageddon. Do you believe there will be a final battle?"

The interlocked fingers danced with renewed fervor. Chaplain O'Brien lowered his brow and spoke with implied theological authority.

"Personally? Yes, I do. The scriptures say that there will be a final battle between the nations of the world. Some Christians take that battle figuratively, others take it literally."

"And you?"

"Well, I'm sure the folks living during World War II thought it was Armageddon back then. Based on what I read in the newspapers today, I'd say mutual annihilation and destruction is possible, perhaps even literal."

"The entire world would be destroyed?"

"Not as far as Baptist theology is concerned. The battle of Armageddon would include armies of the world trying to conquer Jerusalem."

"What armies?"

"Well now, we're getting down into detailed speculation. No one but the Lord really knows that."

"What do the Baptists say?"

"Depends which Baptist you talk to, I guess, but the leading candidates have always been Russia, Syria, parts of Lebanon and, of course, Iran."

"Iran?"

"What other government in the world today is calling for the absolute annihilation of Israel?"

"So Armageddon is the name given to this final battle?"

"More than that really. In the Book of Revelation, chapter sixteen, verse sixteen, the Apostle John writes that the battle will take place in an area called *har megiddo,* or mountain of Megiddo. It's in the Valley of Jezreel where many historic battles have already taken place, even one with British Field Marshal Edmund Allenby in World War I when he took control of the Holy Land from the Turks in 1918. Jezreel is where Gideon fought his famous battle with armies from the east."

Camp was deep in reflection, thinking about Omid's words to him as they hiked through the Hindu Kush.

"Tell me, John…would Christians do things intentionally to try to tempt the apocalypse?"

"Overtly? I hope not. There are plenty of preachers who have sold books on the subject, but I don't think anyone's planning to literally blow up Jerusalem or the Dome of the Rock Mosque in an attempt to start Armageddon."

"No one?"

Chaplain O'Brien withdrew and a serious scowl covered his otherwise jovial demeanor.

"No one other than, perhaps…Iran."

The Pentagon

General Ferguson landed at Andrews Air Force Base and was immediately shuttled to the Pentagon where he was awaiting a meeting with the SECDEF and the Undersecretary of State's Near East Bureau. Special Agent Daniels from CIA was already in the SECDEF's waiting room when Ferguson arrived. Daniels and Ferguson exchanged brief pleasantries before the executive secretary ushered them both into the conference room where Secretary of Defense Pennington was finishing a private discussion with Undersecretary Miller from the State Department.

"Ah, Jim Ferguson, great to see you my friend. Do you know Katherine Miller from State?"

"Pleased to meet you, ma'am. May I introduce Special Agent Daniels from Central Intelligence."

"Ma'am…sir," Daniels said as all took their seats.

"Alright Jim, what's going on and what do you need from us?" the SECDEF asked in his trademarked bottom-line style.

"Sir, three Afghans diagnosed with tularemia – rabbit fever – at a remote FOB in eastern Afghanistan, less than 50 clicks from Pakistan. The US battalion surgeon sends samples to Bagram, and they declare it garden variety tularemia, probably under-cooked meat or contaminated drinking water. A few days later that same battalion surgeon is kidnapped in a fairly complicated abduction plot. I sent a US Navy Captain and former SEAL to the FOB to investigate. While he's there, one of our Afghan terps – a female – rigs up a homemade suicide vest and detonates. The Navy Captain saves her life and, in turn, gets some valuable intelligence. Turns out her husband put her up to it, and he's part of the Haqqani Network working hand-in-hand with the Taliban in North Waziristan. The Terp gives us enough details to send Operation Detachment Alpha Team up through the Hindu Kush to rescue the abducted doctor. Meanwhile, Special Agent Daniels reports that commercial aerosol misting devices have found their way from Illinois to the black market in Indonesia and ended up in Islamabad. Simultaneously, CIA reports that the Russians are sending stockpiles of tularemia, a biological weapon that they were quite fond of, by rail down to Ashgabat, Turkmenistan. The Alpha Team finds the location in North Waziristan. The battalion surgeon has a bullet in his head. But in a back room, Alpha Team finds one of the missing commercial aerosol mosquito misting machines. The center of the house has a laboratory in it, almost a surgical suite. Three bottles of Russian-labeled tularemia are discovered. Alpha Team can't blow the machine without risking egress, so they put a GPS tracking beacon on the unit. By the time our drones and satellites knew that they were tracking a machine and not a man, the device goes silent for a few hours and suddenly re-emerges in Damghan, Iran, home of the Iranians' biological and chemical weapons facilities. Fort Detrick is working on the tularemia bacteria and a vaccine in their BSL-4 even as we speak."

"Geez Jim, our hands are full enough with the Iranians over the nukes. Now tula-whatever?"

"Sorry, sir."

"What do you need?"

"I've got the Navy captain and a former FBI agent in the air right now, Kabul to Dubai, Dubai to Istanbul, Turkey, then Istanbul to Ashgabat, the capital of Turkmenistan. They need a meeting with the US Ambassador there, then support to investigate the rail yard and verify the shipment."

"I'll arrange the meeting with the Ambassador," Undersecretary Miller said. "What are their names, and when do they arrive?"

"Captain Seabury Campbell, Junior and William Finn. They land at 1348 hours tomorrow afternoon."

"I think it would be prudent to put a drone over Iranian airspace. We have a new stealth drone that's deployable and ready for this type of mission. I want to make sure we keep an eye in the sky on this latest development," SECDEF Pennington offered. "Any other resources, Jim?"

"Yes, as soon as we have a verifiable vaccine, we need to move to manufacturing. We'll need your help, sir."

"How soon will you know?"

"I'm heading to Fort Detrick right after this meeting. I'll know more within a few hours."

"Keep me posted. No surprises going forward."

Ashgabat, Turkmenistan

Turkish Airlines flight number 324 landed precisely at 1:48pm on runway 12L and taxied immediately to the gate as a green-tailed Turkmenistan Airlines jet took off for Minsk. The orange and tan airport was much more modern than either US Navy Captain "Camp" Campbell or Billy Finn had imagined.

The US Embassy sedan was waiting curbside to take them to the Turkmenistan Hotel to rest and refresh before their morning appointment with American Ambassador Annette Pfister and her counterparts from the government of Turkmenistan.

Literally translated as the "city of love" in Persian, Ashgabat's nearly one million people and relatively modern city served as a refreshing detour for Camp and Finn on the back-end of a brutal march up, over and back from the Hindu Kush in freezing weather. Situated between the Karam Kum desert and the Kopet Dag mountain range, Ashgabat was the capital of Turkmenistan, the last of the Soviet bloc's to declare independence before the former Soviet Union collapsed.

Ashgabat was a major stop on the Trans-Caspian railway, a point that was of utmost importance to Camp and Finn as they rode in the back of the black sedan on the 23-minute ride to the hotel.

"Finn, can I ask you a question? What compels a group, or a country, to consider launching a bio-weapon that kills thousands, maybe millions, so indiscriminately?"

"That's a bit heavier than the 'wanna get a beer at the bar' I was expecting."

"Seriously, you FBI guys profile this sort of thing. How does anyone even think this way?" Camp asked.

"You can't get your arms around it because you're a rational warfare guy, Camp. Rationalist theory says the actors are rational and able to project their likelihood of success or failure. The Cold War was a stand-off between two rational players, armed to the teeth with nuclear weapons, but each actor embraced the inevitable notion of mutual destruction. Hence, no war...both actors were rational."

"I spent a lot of time talking to the Iranian... Omid."

"I know...so let me jump to the chase; Iran is not a rational actor," Finn said.

"But they are, Finn! They are completely rational within the constructs of their own brand of Islam. They rationally believe that they have a moral and spiritual obligation to usher in the Age of the Coming. It is their rational desire to trigger the annihilation of Israel in order to rationally pave the way for the Twelfth Imam. It's all quite rational...for *them*."

"Every Muslim?"

"Oh, no. Not even close. But the current Iranian regime...the Muslims in control of Iran today...they want rational annihilation."

"They're a bunch of radicals!"

"Billy, one man's 'radical' is another man's 'rational.' But here's the problem: what about the 200 million more Shiite Muslims who follow this same brand of Twelver Islam? Do they secretly disagree with the interpretations of this Iranian regime? I haven't heard any other Twelvers *condemning* them. Now add in the other 1.4 billion Sunni and Shiite Muslims. Would any of them be terribly upset if Iran wiped Israel off the map? Or would they reject Israel's destruction on the grounds of being Islamic pacifists who preferred instead to live side-by-side in peace, content to wait for the Islamic messiah to reveal himself later on?"

"So...*you* think a type of quasi-rational theory is in play," Finn concluded. "The west is using *their* rational *diplomacy,* and the east is using their rational *theology*?"

"Exactly! We try to discourage Iran with western rational theory actions: sanctions, rebukes, then more sanctions...Iran responds with rational eastern theory and theocratic policies: shut down the Internet, suppress the popular revolt, then prepare the nukes and bio-weapons for the rationally-required annihilation of Israel that ushers in the Mahdi," Camp said with almost complete exasperation.

"So, what if we think outside our rational western

box and deny them first-strike capability?" Finn asked.

"Shoot the suicide bomber before he detonates?"

"It won't change their theology...but it will slow them down," Finn reasoned.

Camp stared out at the passing streets, cars and buildings without really seeing anything as he grew introspective.

"I've spent my entire career wearing this uniform, Finn, and here I sit not really sure why nations go to war in the first place."

"Well, Rome marched into Carthage to crush a resurgent rival. Prussian General Von Clausewitz waged war as an act of force designed to compel his enemies to do his will. But the Jewish Talmud says it best," Finn theorized. "There are only three universal reasons for war."

Billy Finn fell quickly silent as he leaned forward and looked into the driver's rearview mirror at the same unmarked car that had been following their sedan through the streets of Ashgabat since they left the airport.

"What is it?" Camp asked referring to his silence.

"Money, ideology-religion, and power."

The sedan stopped curbside in front of the Turkmenistan Hotel, a comfortable Soviet-era three-story cinder block hotel with 90 rooms and five suites, all packaged from the outside with sea foam green paint and dark green awnings covering petite wrought iron patios.

Finn noted the trailing sedan as it pulled a u-turn after passing the hotel then parked on the opposite side of 19 Bitarap Turkmenistan Street.

"So be western irrational for a second, Finn," Camp said as they exited the sedan, tipped the driver and made their way into the hotel and the reservations desk. "You heard what Omid was saying about the Twelvers. What would you do?"

"There's only one way, Camp…cut the head off of every snake that comes out of that pit. Shoot the suicide bomber before he pushes the button."

"But don't blow the entire snake pit up?"

"Nope. That'll piss off every other snake and make 'em even more aggressive."

"And how do you suppose we just chop off heads, Mister Irrational?" Camp asked.

Billy Finn smiled as he laid his passport down on the counter.

"Look the other way when the chopping starts. Get someone inside the pit to chop the heads, or just get it done yourself."

The front desk clerk smiled and greeted the two American guests.

"You gotta be kidding," Camp whispered as she processed Finn's room. "CIA?" The clerk handed Finn his room key as Camp put his passport down on the counter.

"You have a beard now, Mister Campbell. It's hard to recognize you from your photo," the clerk said as

Camp smiled and stroked his fledgling beard from the Hindu Kush mission that he'd all but forgotten. Finn leaned over and whispered.

"Mossad."

20

General Ferguson and a new detail of coffee-pouring majors from the Pentagon pulled through the security gates at Detrick. The checkpoint guards called Lieutenant Colonel Raines immediately as instructed. Raines grabbed Dr. Groenwald, and they headed down the elevator without buttons to the atrium where they waited for Ferguson.

"General Ferguson, welcome to Detrick, sir, it's great to see you again," Raines said as she shook the general's hand and introduced herself to his majors. "This is Dr. Groenwald who runs the facility."

"Pleasure to meet you, doctor," Ferguson said. "Colonel, how's your health?"

"Medical cleared me to start running again and,

other than being a bit winded I feel just about 100 percent."

"Glad to hear it, colonel." Ferguson's eyes fixated on the coffee bar in the atrium. "Think we can grab a cup of high octane before you give me the briefing?"

Five cups of coffee in hands, Dr. Groenwald conducted the standard briefing then the entourage entered the elevator without buttons and rode it to the floor where a card reader and Raines' biometric scan allowed her to go. Everyone took their seats in the conference room. Ferguson hesitated and almost seemed lost when Dr. Groenwald took the chair at the head of the table, so Ferguson quickly sat side saddle across from Raines.

"Last we spoke…you had successfully cooked up a vaccine-resistant recipe for tularemia. 'Four Dead Monkeys' I believe was the headline on your brief. Where do we stand today, colonel?"

"Sixteen. Sixteen more dead monkeys, sir."

Ferguson rubbed his balding head.

"Well, that's not good. Obviously, you have created quite a recipe. I suppose you don't want to work on the manufacturing side of the equation until you master the vaccine."

"That is correct, sir."

"Do you think we should manufacture domestically, colonel?" Ferguson asked.

"The issue is FDA oversight and additives. Could be dicey, sir. Dr. Groenwald has put me in touch with two pharmaceutical companies in Europe, one in Germany and one in France. I've spoken with both, and I believe the one in Lyon, France – called LyonBio – has the manufacturing capacity we would need and lacks the public visibility, scrutiny and potential hysteria that we'd prefer to avoid."

"Animal testing?"

"Yes, sir, they are equipped to handle the necessary applied research with animal testing to make sure the vaccine is effective, efficacious and safe."

"Animal rights groups?"

"Not so much in southern France, sir."

"Transportation?"

"For the vaccines, we ship at intervals when supply is ready. Antibiotics? If an outbreak occurs in the Middle East, northern Africa, or Europe, LyonBio could drop and ship five million doses within 48 hours. That's not for manufacturing – that's the time needed to ship. They'd need 72 hours for shipping to Southeast Asia, the Pacific Rim, North and South America. But our outbreak models suggest that the Middle East is more likely."

"Israel in particular?"

"Yes, sir."

"Dr. Groenwald, is 48 hours good enough?" Ferguson asked.

"As you know, the incubation period is three to five days from exposure. That's the time window before health officials connect the dots and identify it as tularemia, unless someone announces they released this bio-weapon, which in that case, we can move very quickly. But the colonel is correct. Prevention is a better option than treatment."

"What symptoms are we looking at?"

"The patient experience starts with chills, pus in the eyes, fever, headache, muscle pain and joint stiffness. Most will assume they have the flu. Unless a physician orders a blood culture for tularemia, it could go undiagnosed."

"Then what?"

"If they contract the bacteria through the skin, then we'd expect ulcers and open sores to start appearing. That would be the best kind of tularemia to contract."

"Inhalation?"

"If they breathe it in, then fever, sore throat, abdominal pain, diarrhea and vomiting for sure," Groenwald described. "Untreated or undiagnosed, five-to-15 percent will die. If the lymph nodes swell and pneumonia sets in, mortality could reach 60 percent without antibiotics."

"General Ferguson, the problem is that you only need 10 to 50 microscopic bacterial organisms in order to be infected," Raines added. "With vaccines and antibiotics, the survivability tables look good. But the panic and fear will be more contagious. Most people will live – but everyone will be scared to death."

"Colonel, I asked you to run some outbreak models for an aerosolized attack on Israel."

"Yes, sir. Israel has a population of roughly seven million people with another four plus million living in the Gaza Strip and the West Bank."

"You think they'd attack Muslims?"

"Perhaps not overtly, general, but tularemia bacterium is no respecter of persons. It doesn't care if it infects Jews, Muslims, Christians, men, women, the elderly or children on a playground."

"How many doses, colonel?"

"It's not practical to vaccinate nearly 12 million people against something that might not happen or to prepare 12 million antibiotic treatments without an outbreak. But given the geographical constraints, Israel is a target-rich environment."

General Ferguson stood up and walked to the door.

"Colonel, Rhode Island is the smallest state in the union, both in terms of land mass and total area. You could fit Israel inside of Rhode Island...two and a half times."

Groenwald and Raines followed Ferguson and his entourage out into the hall. They rode the elevator with no buttons down to the atrium and then outside into the light rain.

"You're on the clock, colonel. I need a vaccine," Ferguson said as he started to walk away.

"Sir, I'm working as fast I can. I want to get the research done so that I can join Captain Campbell in Tel Aviv as soon as possible."

Ferguson stopped on a dime, turned and walked

back as the majors covered his head with an umbrella.

"Colonel, unless you two are planning to honeymoon in Israel, no one is going to Tel Aviv. Am I clear?"

The general didn't tarry for an answer. A clear and direct order had been given.

21

Caesar's Palace Casino
Las Vegas, Nevada

Brady Kenton kissed his wife Karen goodbye in the rear parking lot employee entrance where she worked as the assistant front desk manager at Caesar's Palace.

"Love you, babe. See you in a few hours."

She smiled and caressed his cheek.

"Be careful up there today, okay?" she said as she left for her eight-hour shift.

"Chinese carryout tonight; its Tuesday you know," Brady said as she winked and walked into the Palace.

Brady plugged in his iPod and headed off to work, 40 miles down Highway 95 toward Indian Springs, Nevada. The driver's window on his Chevrolet Silverado stayed down the entire drive as the warm desert air blew through Brady's short, cropped hair. He stopped at the main gate and showed his badge.

"Good morning, Captain Kenton," the checkpoint guard said as he greeted U.S. Air Force Captain Brady Kenton back to Creech Air Force base for another day of work.

General Wilbur "Bill" Creech was a trailblazer. During the Cold War era it was Creech who encouraged the military to pursue a new era of modern weapons and tactics coupled with decentralized authority and responsibility.

Captain Kenton was about as decentralized as any Air Force combat pilot could possibly be. Kenton moved quickly into the main gaming room where third shift aviators were more than thrilled to see their replacement crews.

"Good morning, Jack. Kill any bad guys last night?" Kenton asked as he moved into the 17th Reconnaissance Squadron's large brown leather swivel chair in front of the video screens, computer monitors, keyboard and flight throttle.

"Not much going on, Brady. Late afternoon Kandahar time we had an MRAP pinned down on patrol with small arms fire. They got ground back-up within minutes, so no hellfire's from 'Kate.' She's back sun-tanning on the ground and waiting for you."

Captain Brady Kenton was a drone pilot. Since these modern day, remote Air Force pilots couldn't paint traditional naming signs on their UAVs, Captain Kenton had affectionately named his drone after the latest swimsuit model sensation, Kate Upton.

More than 7,000 drones were in use during the height of the wars in Iraq and Afghanistan. Every one of them were given unofficial nicknames, depending on the shift and the pilot. As Iraq wound down, many of those drones and the MQ-1 Predators were transferred to joint Air Force / CIA control over the lawless regions of North Waziristan, Pakistan.

But Kate was different. She was wearing hardly anything at all and was practically naked, at least on a radar screen. Built by Lockheed Martin, Kate was a bat-winged RQ-170 Sentinel, a sophisticated stealth spy drone.

Shift Commander Lieutenant Colonel Abrams walked in and took the seat next to Captain Kenton briefly.

"Brady, we just received a special joint mission request from the SECDEF and Langley."

"Pakistan?" Kenton asked eagerly hoping to get some heat drops on a special Al Qaeda target or two.

"Negative. Kate's going over Iran."

"Whoa," Kenton said as he quickly punched up Iranian maps and topography on his computer screens. "Nukes?"

"Bio. Special Ops got a tracking beacon on a machine they think the Iranians might want for aerosolizing a biological weapon. The satellites picked up the device in Damghan."

Kenton quickly honed in on Damghan.

"North 36, east 54, got it. Chemical and biological weapons production facilities. Bet you didn't know this, colonel," Brady Kenton said with schoolyard delight.

"School me."

"Damghan is the pistachio nut capital of Iran, in the Khorasan Province," Captain Kenton said as he read from his computer screen.

"One of many nuts in the area I'm sure. I need a flight plan by 0830 and Kate in the skies by 0900."

"Roger that, sir."

Kenton developed his flight plan based on the most recent tracking from the birds in orbit. It would take less than 90 minutes for Kate to get to high altitude and beyond Iran's rather advanced radar systems and reach Damghan where the machine appeared to be stationary and parked in a warehouse. Kenton was excited. He had never flown over Iran before.

Careful not to fly over Turkmenistan, Kenton flew the RQ-170 Sentinel over Herat and Gurian before flying over the Iran-Afghanistan border, up toward Mashhad and then almost directly down over Highway 44 and into Damghan.

Kenton checked his satellite imagery one more time before allowing Kate to track on to the signal. He blinked twice and refreshed his screen. The target was moving.

"Colonel, are you seeing this?" Captain Kenton said into his headset as Colonel Abrams was watching the same thing in the Tactical Operations Center two buildings down on Creech.

"Roger, the target's moving too fast for ground, looks like she's getting a lift."

"Sir, I've got it heading south, by southwest at 140 miles per hour."

"Helicopter," Abrams confirmed.

"Slowing down now, sir and…stopping. Looks to be a rural area between Khomein and Aligoodarz."

"Brady, we've got an intel officer looking at the area now, stand by…" Abrams said as his computer screen came to life with information from the intelligence officer on duty. "Five small villages…Dehno, Khorzend, Farajabad, Bahmanabad and Sangesfid. The area is called the Bourvari."

"Anything significant?" Brady asked.

"Maybe, hard to tell, but these are all Persian-Armenian settlements."

"And that's somehow important, colonel?"

"They're Christians, Brady…not a great country to be living as a non-Muslim, if you know what I mean."

Captain Kenton and Kate circled above the Bourvari for 20 minutes. The video images from Kate were fed to the TOC at Creech for Abrams and his team to watch as Special Agent Daniels and Agent Fallon Jessup watched the same video feed from a CIA command center at Langley.

"Sir, you seeing this?" Brady asked as Abrams, Daniels and Jessup all listened to the anxiety in Brady's voice. "The machine is on a truck and appears to be driving up and down the village streets."

"Roger that, looks like the village of Dehno. Can we get the camera in closer?"

"We're getting a view that feels like 2,000 feet up, sir. Can't get any better optics unless I take Kate down closer."

Lieutenant Colonel Abrams stood and took aggressive command in the TOC.

"I need some close range satellite optics. Give me the radar ceiling in the area."

Abrams reviewed the information on his computer screen seconds after he asked for it.

"Negative Brady, Kate needs to fly high on this first one. We're just observing today."

Abrams received a still satellite photo that sucked the wind out of his lungs. The image looked straight down on top of what appeared to be a maintenance truck. The vantage point could have been from the top of an oak tree, if it weren't for the fact that it was a military camera on a spy satellite.

Three intelligence officers had also gathered in a joint command center at the headquarters of the Directorate of Military Intelligence in Tel Aviv as they watched the same Iranian event unfold through images from their Ofek 9 military spy satellite. The officers were from Agaf Ha Modi'in, otherwise called Aman, as well as Mossad and Shin Bet. Aman was tasked with Israeli military intelligence; Shin Bet handled internal security; and Mossad handled intelligence collection and covert operations. Launched from Palmachim Air Force base on Israel's coast south of Tel Aviv in 2007, the Ofek 9 had a high resolution camera second to none in the world.

Ofek 9 could clearly see the man in the back of the maintenance vehicle spraying a light mist from a tank of fluid as local children played in the mist and chased the truck passing up and down the dusty roads of the Bourvari villages. The camera resolution on the Ofek 9 was so clear that each of the Israeli intelligence officers wrote down the same word on their paper tablets at the exact same time: SkitoMister.

Lieutenant Colonel Abrams and Captain Brady Kenton sat captivated by the video feed from Kate as Kenton flew the drone.

"Okay captain, let's take Kate home."

Kenton pulled back on the stick and took off for Kandahar with intermittent thoughts of Chinese carryout when his combat mission was over. It was, in fact, Tuesday he reminded himself.

U.S. Embassy
Ashgabat, Turkmenistan

The sedan carrying US Navy Captain "Camp" Campbell and Billy Finn pulled up in front of the Embassy at Number 9 1984 Street. Formerly named Pushkin Street when Soviet influence permeated the capital, the American Embassy was understated but efficient.

"Some things never change in the former Soviet bloc," Finn said as they passed through the gate complex watching the same unmarked car park on the other side of 1984 Street. "You look good today, Camp. Get some sleep, a beer and a hot shower?"

"I look good because you can see my gorgeous face again. Felt great to finally shave the jihad beard."

As promised, Undersecretary Miller had cleared Ambassador Annette Pfister's calendar for Camp and Finn. She had been briefed on the rail shipment from the Kirov Oblast down the Trans-Siberian, over to the Trans-Caspian railway and into Ashgabat. Their 9:30am meeting would be a brief get-acquainted session before they would be joined by the Deputy Ministers of Railways and Trade for Turkmenistan and their entourage.

The Ambassador's scheduler entered the office where the three were having coffee and swapping stories about where they all grew up in America.

"Madam Ambassador, the Deputy Ministers and their staff are seated in the conference room."

After a few social courtesies, Ambassador Pfister got down to business.

"Allow me to start first with the railways. I sent a letter of request to Minister Seyitgulyyew earlier this week. I hope you have some information for us."

The Deputy Minister of Railways had never been to the US Embassy before and couldn't speak a lick of English other than "movie English." He spoke through a translator.

"Madam Ambassador, we routinely receive freight and rail shipments from all parts of Russia, including the Kirov Oblast. The shipment in question was transported on the Trans-Siberian from Kirov to Koshagyl, Russia. It passed through Kazakhstan where it was transferred to the Trans-Caspian railway, and was rerouted in Beyneu, and then down to Bekdash where it was placed on a cargo vessel, crossed the Caspian inlet and then here to Ashgabat. It was more than 3,700 kilometers for the trip and perhaps a three day transport with switching."

"Sir, is the shipment still here in Ashgabat?" the Ambassador asked.

"No. A few weeks ago we transferred six boxcars filled with 55-gallon drums onto the IRIR where it was moved through Mashhad. The shipment was transferred to Damghan."

"IRIR?"

"The Islamic Republic of Iran Railways."

"How many of these 55-gallon drums were in the boxcars?"

"The bill of lading was for 500 drums."

"And the contents within those drums?"

"Pesticides. Iran is rich with agriculture, Madam Ambassador."

Ambassador Dunn turned her attention over to the Deputy Chairman of the Cabinet of Ministers for Trade, Commerce, Textiles and Customs.

"Sir, does Deputy Chairman Gurbannazarow

conduct a lot of business with Iran?"

"We are very close trading partners. But Turkmenistan is more of a trading gateway, an intersection of world trade for the region. We collect a tax for all goods traveling between Russia and the region. We take great pride in our rail system."

Billy Finn nodded to the Ambassador and took the floor.

"Sir, do you ever inspect the contents of shipments that pass through your yards, to verify that the contents match the freight bills?"

"Do we taste the tea to make sure it's tea? Do we turn on the radios to make sure they're radios? Do we test the pesticides to make sure they kill the red palm weevil bug that eats away at Iranian date palm trees and pistachios? No."

"You mentioned Damghan as being the final destination. Isn't that where the Iranians produce their biological and chemical weapons?" Camp quizzed the Deputy Minister of Trade.

"I know nothing about weapons, Mr. Campbell, but as for trade, Damghan is a manufacturing city. There are many chemical factories and distributors for plastics, petroleum products and additives."

"Do the IRIR trains come to Ashgabat for switching, or do you transfer loads off the Trans-Caspian onto IRIR once they reach Mashhad?" Camp asked.

"We transfer here…onto IRIR trains in the main rail yard."

"Do Iranians come here to conduct business often?" Finn asked.

"Of course, we are friends. They especially enjoy holidays close to the Caspian Sea."

The meeting was adjourned, and the Ambassador thanked the Turkmenistan staff and Deputy Ministers for their time and candor. The Ambassador's scheduler stepped into the conference room and handed Camp a note as final farewells were being exchanged.

CALL GENERAL FERGUSON AT ISAF ON SECURE LINE ASAP.

Camp and Billy Finn were escorted to a small video conference room. The vapor locked door made a swishing sound as they locked themselves in.

Major Spann answered the SIPRNET line that was ringing less than a foot away from Ferguson.

"General Ferguson's Office, Major Spann speaking."

"Major, Captain Campbell and Billy Finn."

"Please hold, captain."

Ferguson took another 45-seconds shuffling through the papers that he wasn't even looking at prior to the call.

"Camp, what did you find out over there?" Ferguson finally asked.

"Sir, the Kirov Oblast shipment passed through here about two weeks ago. Five hundred 55-gallon drums of red palm weevil pesticides transferred over to the Islamic Republic of Iran Railway and moved to Damghan."

"So CIA was correct; it did originate in Kirov?"

"Affirmative."

"Okay, well that's not good then. I just received a classified briefing from the SECDEF's office. They've put a new stealth drone over Iran and were tracking your SkitoMister. The drone was en route from Kandahar when the SkitoMister went airborne. A chopper set it down in the Bourvari District, a compilation of five villages full of Persian-Armenians. The SkitoMister was placed on a maintenance truck that drove all of the roads in the five villages. According to the video feed it appeared as though they were spraying."

"Spraying what?" Camp asked.

"The SECDEF is adamant that we not jump to conclusions on the whole tularemia thing. For all we know these are pesticides and a legitimate use of the SkitoMister. We don't have an exactly stellar record of intelligence in the region."

"Why these particular villages, general? Is this an agricultural area?" Finn asked.

"There's some agriculture in the Bourvari, Billy, but the only notable thing is the people."

"Persian-Armenians?"

"Christians, Billy…they're all Christians."

Camp and Finn took a few seconds to digest the news.

"What's next, general?"

"Get yourselves back to Kabul, and we'll take it from there."

22

National Interagency Biodefense Center
BSL-4 Facility
Fort Detrick, Maryland

Lieutenant Colonel Leslie Raines and two microbiologists were suited up and inside the BSL-4 lab. Tissue samples from all 16 dead rhesus monkeys were under the scope. The team needed to reverse-engineer what was clearly a vaccine-resistant strain of tularemia. The dead monkeys were living proof.

The challenge of vaccine development was more than developing suitable antigens, adjuvants and delivery methods. Numerous regulatory, technical and manufacturing obstacles needed to be considered in order to translate a vaccine candidate developed in a controlled lab over to a human setting in a clinic. It was the difference between the classroom and the streets.

Raines was focused on the adjuvants, substances that

could be added to existing tularemia vaccines to boost the vaccine's ability to produce an immune response. If Raines could cook an adjuvanted vaccine, then LyonBio should be able to produce more doses of vaccine with smaller amounts of the antigen, the active ingredient that delivered the immune response.

Even though the public demand for safe and effective vaccines remained strong, very few of the major pharmaceutical companies had the knowledge or facilities required to develop and manufacture new vaccine products. Most of the traditional work focused on small-molecule drugs and therapeutic proteins.

Raines had no choice but to choose an offshore firm. There were too many restrictions on which additives could be introduced into American-made vaccines. The complexity of the technology, the need for specialized facilities and the endless regulatory hurdles were major obstacles in the US. And with the emergence of an expanding animal rights movement that was waging effective battles on all five fronts – political, legal, social, violence, and psychological – basic science was anything but basic in America.

At her core, Raines was a biomedical researcher, a basic scientist. Raines started with *in silica* modeling. She used the finest Silicon Valley computers and software programs and looked for ways to exploit naturally occurring tularemia into a lethal bio-weapon. Based on some vulnerable areas she discovered within the gene make-up of tularemia, she cooked up an *in vitro* recipe that she hoped would be vaccine-resistant. *In vitro* was the research conducted in a Petri dish or within glass. Raines developed both her toxin and her vaccine inside test tubes. She had to find a delivery mechanism that would spread an aerosolized version of the bacteria that could be inhaled. Aerosolized tularemia was tricky. If the bacteria broke down too much during physical alteration, it would lose its potency. Raines then needed to test both the toxin and the vaccine in a living organism. She gave the existing baseline vaccine to four rhesus monkeys and delivered the inhalation tularemia. It was a pre-clinical animal trial, or what was called *in vivo* research conducted within a living organism.

When the first recipe failed, as evidenced by the fact the monkeys were still alive, Raines had to go back to the computer modeling and revise her assumptions.

She manipulated the genes in the tularemia and created a bio-hazard that had to be restrained within the cement walls of the BSL-4 facility. With formula in hand she produced the new strain in glass. The aerosolized delivery produced inhalation tularemia without breaking the strength of the bacteria. The pre-clinical animal trial was successful. All four rhesus monkeys were infected and symptomatic within three to five days, and dead with complications from pneumonia within a week. The vaccine did not preserve their immunity. The monkeys were not immune from the tularemia.

Raines then had to produce a new vaccine, one that would keep the next group of monkeys alive.

It took great skill for Raines to successfully produce a lethal strain of tularemia, but creating the new super vaccine would require innovation normally reserved for Nobel winners. Evolving and translating the procedures Raines was developing in her basic BSL-4 research laboratory into a process that could be scaled up in a manufacturing environment to make millions of doses would require as much luck as it would skill.

Success would require a scientist with dedication and a willingness to be patient. There would be failure and disappointment. No one was more patient or dedicated than Lieutenant Colonel Leslie Raines.

When the first four monkeys were rolled into her BSL-4, she knew they were in a death chamber. Raines went above and beyond the enrichment requirements that her staff gave the four rhesus monkeys and made sure they had extra treats to eat and toys to play with while they waited for a lethal dose of tularemia. If millions of people and animals were going to live, she knew that four monkeys had to die first.

When Raines got the great news that the rhesus monkeys had died, she suited up and went into the BSL-4 and quietly thanked the non-human primates and stroked their fur from the openings in the cages. Raines was an animal lover at heart, but her mind was full of science.

Sixteen more dead monkeys cut her to her soul. She hadn't found the right vaccine formula yet. She hadn't found the correct immune response mechanism. She killed those monkeys, and she felt horrible, personally responsible.

Losing the animals she was desperately trying to save gnawed at her relentlessly. She worked many nights until 0400 hours, slept on the couch and got back into the lab by 0600. She was moody, short and irritable. Nothing else mattered. She couldn't even comprehend a tularemia bio-weapon killing millions of people.

She had to save the next four rhesus monkeys.

Maybe it's the adjuvants, she reasoned.

A small-molecule drug had a molecular weight of less than 1,000, whereas the virus-like particle Raines was using as the basis of her new vaccine was more than 10,000-fold greater in size. The dosage amount would be based on both weight and biological potency.

In the four failed vaccine tests that caused 16 dead rhesus monkeys, Raines took scrupulous notes. Every procedure, piece of equipment and data discovered was documented. Raines knew each process had to be described and characterized in great detail, including the nature and performance of the specific equipment used for every step of the process. The requirements created an essential rigidity to her approach which was necessarily unforgiving of an error in judgment. Any misstep along the way could result in a very time-consuming and expensive correction in the manufacturing process as soon as the vaccine product candidate left the Fort Detrick BSL-4 and landed in France at LyonBio.

In normal vaccine development, Raines and her team might have required five-to-nine years in repetitive pre-clinical trials. The FDA would demand the studies prior to moving the vaccine for rapid evaluation in human clinical trials.

But developing a vaccine for a bio-weapon was different than a vaccine intended for universal pediatric use. A bioterrorism threat was an emergency situation and testing for efficacy was not always as practical, and not always possible.

LyonBio was equipped to be the pilot plant for the Phase 1 human clinical trials that might not ever happen. Bulk preparation of the Phase 3 final vaccine for full-scale manufacturing was the most likely scenario.

But if Raines couldn't save four rhesus monkeys, none of it would matter anyway.

Qazvin University of Medical Sciences
Ghods Hospital
Markazi Province, Iran

Ghods Hospital, built in 1991, was a fairly small, but modern regional hospital. Iranian doctors were well-trained, and the equipment in the hospitals was quite modern. Even though the Islamic Republic of Iran was estranged and isolated from the west, the universities, hospitals and businesses were anything but third world.

Markazi Province was Kazi's favorite province in Iran. It was also his family name. Literally translated,

Markazi meant central, as in the central province of Iran. With Azak as the capital city of the province, more than 1.3 million people called Markazi home.

Kazi fashioned himself as being middle of the road, in the center. He was born in Pakistan to Iranian immigrant parents, then raised in Iran by his ultra religious grandparents, and educated in the United States before his career took him to The Netherlands, Pakistan and back to Markazi Province in Iran.

Kazi's parents were murdered in cold blood by Pakistani terrorists in 1981. They broke into the house in the middle of the night looking for food and money. He always assumed the thieves allowed him to live because he was only a 12-month old infant at the time. He couldn't remember anything about his first year in Pakistan. He never heard his mother's screams as the men slit her throat or the single gunshot that was fired into his father's head.

His grandfather flew to Islamabad to collect him from the orphanage. Forty-eight hours after his parents were murdered he was living in Markazi Province with a grandfather he had never met.

Kazi's grandfather was a highly educated man and worked as the Dean at the Arak University of Medical Sciences. AUMS did train some doctors, but their specialty was research, especially training doctors who were both clinicians and basic science researchers.

Kazi spent his formative years playing in his grandfather's lab, mixing chemicals together and dissecting every dead animal he could get his hands on. Kazi was fascinated with the similarity and interconnectivity of organs, between both humans and animals.

Kazi's grandfather, Qazvin, was also a religious zealot. He was a member of a secret and clandestine religious group which he co-founded with several others in 1953 called the Hojjatieh Society. They were an underground messianic sect which hoped to quicken the coming of the apocalypse in order to hasten the return of the Mahdi, the future redeemer of Islam who had been hidden through occultation since the 7th century.

Qazvin and the others wanted to bring back the Imam through violence rather than waiting piously for the Imam's eventual return on his own schedule. But after the Iranian Revolution began, the Hojjatieh Society was banned and persecuted by Ayatollah Khomeini's government. The Hojjatieh rejected both democratic and Islamic forms of government. They preferred to wait and be governed by the Islamic Messiah. Any form of government to the Hojjatieh was illegitimate or unnecessary at best. They were not interested in democratic reforms or totalitarian regimes. They wanted no government at all.

The Hojjatieh Society was important but unfulfilling to Kazi's grandfather until he attended a mosque in Qom and heard an Imam who was a Twelver. By the end of that Friday's holy day, Qazvin and his 14-year-old grandson Kazi were radical Twelvers. Kazi had centered every dream on the return of the Twelfth Imam, the Mahdi.

Kazi's grandfather encouraged him to pursue college studies in the medical sciences. He applied to many universities in Europe and in the United States with his Pakistani passport and credentials. He was accepted to every university he applied to but one stood out: war eagle.

Kazi knew nothing about Auburn University, let alone the state of Alabama, but the name "war eagle" matched his own self image. He, too, was raised to be a war eagle and entered Auburn in the fall of 1998 as an 18 year old.

Kazi thrived for three full years and made hundreds of friends across the Auburn campus and throughout Alabama and neighboring Georgia. Everything changed for Kazi on September 11, 2001. In one swift instant he became a suspicious Middle Eastern man. The terrorist hijackers were Sunni. He was Shiite. Most of the 9/11 terrorists came from Saudi Arabia, but Kazi was from Pakistan and Iran. Eight months shy of graduating Auburn with a bachelors of science in microbiology with honors, Kazi was ostracized and discarded. He was as angry as a war eagle.

The job market in the United States for Middle Eastern men after 9/11 was very challenging. Kazi applied all over the world before finally getting a job at Brezden University Medical Center in The Netherlands where he worked as the microbiologist on a team that studied avian influenza. Though he was brilliant and perhaps one of the most gifted microbiologists in the world – thanks to his early years in Qazvin's laboratory – Kazi couldn't shake the anger.

His frequent trips back to Islamabad and Tehran allowed Kazi to meet people who were willing to pay for his significant expertise while he put his Brezden job in jeopardy by missing so many days of work. By the time he was terminated, Kazi was an international freelancer, a Shia Muslim Twelver with an angry past and a "war eagle" attitude.

In 2006, the executive branch of the Iranian government, as well as elements of the vaunted Revolutionary Guard, fell under heavy influence by a resurgent Hojjatieh Society. Kazi's grandfather, Qazvin, became more valuable to the radical government the older and wiser he became. When the elderly Qazvin assumed an advisor's role to the Iranian president, the university was named after him. By extension, Kazi became the nation's "war eagle" who had the power to travel freely as an eagle among all nations.

Kazi and Qazvin looked through the charts of the 47 people from the Bourvari District of villages that had already been admitted to the 130 rooms of Ghods Hospital in Markazi. More than 400 other Persian-Armenians had filled the waiting rooms and were spread out in lines under tents and trees onto the hospital grounds and parking lot.

"Many of the children have ulcers, open sores on their hands, arms and faces," Qazvin said as he reviewed the charts.

"They were infected by contact to the skin. Many of them played in the mist and followed the truck. The adults?" Kazi asked.

"Swollen glands in the throat, shortness of breath, cough, fever, and some with chest pain. We have one fatality, but probably from a heart attack," Qazvin said.

Kazi stood up and paced back and forth in the administrator's office while looking out through the glass walls at the Persian-Armenian patients who lined the corridors.

"Okay, grandfather…this is a very effective Phase One clinical trial. Let's call in the BBC now and other Arabic media outlets. Start all of these patients on intravenous ciprofloxacin and then send them all home with a seven day supply of streptomycin. Make sure that you announce all of the precautions."

"And you?" Qazvin asked his grandson.

"This exceeded my expectations. It proves we can produce an aerosol version without degrading the bacteria. I must head back to Damghan and make the corrections. Soon we will test the new strand in a Phase Two trial. God be with you, grandfather."

Kazi kissed his grandfather and walked down the corridor, out the door past hundreds of panic-stricken and infected Persian-Armenians and their children – the same ones who had played innocently in the cool mist just three days before in the villages of Dehno, Khorzend, Farajabad, Bahmanabad and Sangesfid.

23

General Ferguson, US Navy Captain "Camp" Campbell and retired Special Agent Billy Finn were on a conference call with Lieutenant Colonel Leslie Raines back at Fort Detrick.

"Colonel, again my apologies for keeping you up so late," General Ferguson said as he transitioned to her part of the call.

"No problem, sir, I'm getting ready to turn-off the lights and hit the couch right here in my office. All tucked in with the blanket my grandmother Lydia knitted for me," Raines said as the energy in her voice started to fade. With fingers crossed and a voice less than hopeful, Raines announced that she had just launched her fifth preclinical test with the vaccine-resistant tularemia she had created. Each of the four new rhesus monkeys were injected with the fifth generation of the vaccine designed to trigger an immune response to the lethal inhalation tularemia Raines had developed. Within five days, they would all know if they had four more dead monkeys or if Raines had finally cracked the code.

Major Spann opened the door to Ferguson's office unannounced and burst into the room. The general was immediately angry.

"Major!"

Spann was out of breath.

"Sir, BBC right now, tularemia outbreak in Iran."

Spann fidgeted with the remote controls and finally got the TV on and tuned to the BBC as Raines kept the line open and listened from Maryland.

"Again, Iranian health authorities have announced a natural outbreak of tularemia. Tularemia is known by several societal names including rabbit fever, deer fly fever, Pahvant Valley plague, and Ohara's fever. But today, more than 400 people living in the villages of Dehno, Khorzend, Farajabad, Bahmanabad and Sangesfid – mostly in the Markazi Province – call it torment. Authorities at Ghods Hospital are appealing for calm. This is not – I repeat – not a fatal condition if infected patients receive antibiotics immediately. Health officials are stressing that this is also a very preventable disease, and some vaccines may already exist. Tularemia bacterium is found in wild animals and can occur from undercooked meat and in infected drinking water supplies. The people in these villages should make sure their meats are thoroughly and sufficiently

cooked and should boil their drinking water before consumption, at least until this outbreak is under control. Authorities stress that this is a sanitation issue, and no one should panic."

Ferguson nodded and Major Spann turned the TV off.

"Brilliant…just brilliant," Billy Finn said as he got up rubbing his head.

"But you said the drone and the satellite took photos of the Iranians using the SkitoMister to spray these people. How is that a natural outbreak?" Raines said as her voice erupted over the open telephone line.

"It's nothing short of a perfect explanation. Iranian authorities are now *concerned* with the poor *sanitation* in these rural villages. *Cook* your damn meat and *boil* your water and you too can prevent a natural outbreak," Ferguson said with high notes of sarcasm punctuating each word.

"Now they can justify the Russian 'pesticides' because they're really just trying to take care of their own people," Camp said.

"Certainly we can take this intel to the UN Security Council. We've got to sound the warning bell," Raines lobbied.

"So the Russians can veto any resolution while boasting they supplied the pesticides and insecticides on humanitarian grounds to their friends and allies in Iran? That dog don't hunt, Colonel Raines," Ferguson said.

The room fell silent.

"Well, in case anyone cares…we just witnessed a

Phase One human clinical trial. Better get your drone back up in the sky, general. Phase Two is coming. Goodnight, gentlemen," Raines said as she terminated the call.

Three mid-level intelligence officers from Aman, Shin Bet and Mossad in Tel Aviv, who had been watching the same news coverage of the tularemia outbreak in Iran, turned their televisions off as well and started writing their reports.

Islamic Azad University of Damghan
Damghan, Iran

The Ja'farī council of religious leaders and scholars convened the meeting in the Shura room at the university. Kazi was well known among them and though only 32 years old, he was respected for having knowledge, intellect and wisdom beyond his years.

Kazi's extreme and committed faith was endearing to the elderly scholars. Kazi was a Twelver, and he knew his role in the Age of the Coming as the world prepared for the coming of the Twelfth Imam, the Mahdi.

Kazi carefully explained the events from the Bourvari District, the 436 patients that were seen at Ghods Hospital, and the one unfortunate fatality, an elderly man who was predisposed to congenital heart disease.

"When will your portion of the Coming be full-scale and ready to proceed?" an elder from the Ja'farī council asked.

"The first test is complete. The world now knows that natural outbreaks are common, and if people will remain clean they will not be infected. The world knows that modern medicine has the vaccines and antibiotics to prevent this disease. Now we must conduct the second test, the lethal test," Kazi said.

"The infidels are by their very nature unclean. The Zionists are unclean. Can you protect Muslims against infection?" another elder asked.

"With the grace and power of Allah, I say yes. It took many months, but Allah provided the path. We can vaccinate the entire Palestinian territory. I pray that they will be spared Allah's judgment when the wind of torment comes."

The members of the Ja'farī council nodded in approval and spoke quietly among themselves.

"Where will you conduct the second test?"

Kazi made eye contact with each member of the council.

"I submit to your wise counsel," he said as he lowered his eyes.

"Perhaps Rasht would be a good choice," one elder said as the others considered his selection. "It is there that the young Muslim man lost his way and was tempted by the devil. He converted to Christianity and became a pastor. He started many Christian home churches in Rasht, he conducts Christian services and has baptized others including himself. He has broken Islamic law. This pastor has been arrested and faces hanging for apostasy and blasphemy. He was given the chance to recant his faith and return to Islam but he has refused. Perhaps this would be the place to purge the devils that follow him."

The Ja'farī council nodded it's approval. Kazi stood and walked over to each and kissed their hands with sincere respect.

Creech Air Force Base
Indian Springs, Nevada

U.S. Air Force Captain Brady Kenton and "Kate" were on their fourth day of surveillance missions over Iran. The tracking beacon on the SkitoMister had remained stationary in the Damghan warehouse since it returned from the Bourvari District.

The CIA and the SECDEF took advantage of "Kate" being in the neighborhood and authorized that she and her combat pilot friend take photos and sign autographs over Iranian nuclear sites in Arak, Natanz and Bushehr.

Colonel Abrams' voice over the comms from the Tactical Operations Center jolted Kenton back to reality.

"Okay Brady, let's get Kate back to bed in Kandahar."

"Roger."

Kenton pulled back on the stick and turned Kate east back toward Afghanistan.

24

National Interagency Biodefense Center
BSL-4 Facility
Fort Detrick, Maryland

Lieutenant Colonel Leslie Raines drove her Wrangler through the Fort Detrick checkpoint and into the parking lot. It had been five days since the new vaccine was injected into the latest round of four rhesus monkeys. The monkeys had already lived a full 24 hours longer than the previous 16 monkeys. Raines was prepared for more disappointment but remained cautiously optimistic. She questioned her own skill, her own ability to produce an effective vaccine. Self-doubt was a greater enemy than vaccine-resistant tularemia.

Her eyes were shallow, and her shoulders sagged from the fatigue and weight of the world as Raines ordered her skinny latte in the atrium coffee bar surrounded by leather chairs and couches. She hated the informal living room furniture. She hated the entire atrium and the stupid little coffee bar. She hated her miserable life as a solitary tear streaked down her face as she entered the elevator without buttons.

Raines emerged on the only floor her card and biometric scan would allow her to enter.

Dropping her bag off in her office, she quickly checked her voice mail and emails. There was nothing, nothing of significance anyways. There was nothing new to hate.

Raines walked slowly down to the command center. It was empty. On the TV monitors she noticed four technicians gathered around the rhesus cages in her lab.

They're dead, she thought to herself.

Two of the technicians pulled away from the cages carrying four vials of blood as the other two moved in closer. They had treats in their gloves...and toys.

Then she saw it. The monkeys were still alive.

The two technicians moved over to the bench and placed several blood samples on slides. One of them waved through the thick glass as they noticed Lieutenant Colonel Leslie Raines who was now standing in anticipation.

Moments later both technicians turned and gave thumbs-up through thick gloves.

Tears gushed out of the colonel's eyes as her hands covered her face.

Dr. Groenwald walked into the command center

and saw the raised thumbs and the emotion pouring out of Raines. He leaned forward and put a consoling hand upon her shoulder.

"You did it, colonel; you absolutely did it."

Raines reached up and grabbed his hand without saying a word.

"Come on, we have some calls to make," Groenwald said as he left the command center.

Raines and the team poured over the toxicology reports. Other than the strain of tularemia proteins cooked into the vaccine recipe itself, the toxicology was clear. No tularemia. Raines made the first call up the chain of command to General Ferguson, who in turn notified the SECDEF's office and the CIA.

Within six hours Raines was sitting in economy class on board an Air France flight to Paris connecting on another Air France flight to Lyon.

Rasht
Gilan Province, Iran

Rasht, affectionately called the Seattle of Iran due to all the rain, was the largest Iranian city on the Caspian Sea coast. With almost 600,000 citizens, Rasht was once known as the Gate of Europe and the preferred trade route with Russia. In earlier centuries Rasht was the center of the silk industry and was buzzing with commerce from the textile workshops.

An industrialized town, Rasht had begun to fall out of favor with the religious authorities as their culture of consumerism seemed far too western for clerical comfort. With modern hotels and hundreds of tourist attractions, Rasht was becoming a favorite international tourist destination that attracted thousands of Austrians, Germans, Dutch, French, Australians and Japanese each year.

It was also a comparatively open city that seemed to look the other way as Christian house churches sprang up with a touch of evangelical fervor, especially in the suburbs of Golsar.

The Iranian Supreme Court had been considering the fate of Pastor Khani after the provincial court convicted him of apostasy and sentenced him to death. Even the Supreme Leader had grown agitated to learn that perhaps more than 100,000 Christians were living – and growing – in Iran.

Rasht was getting out of control. With seven universities, a thriving media, multiple cinemas and musical concert halls, Rasht was too cosmopolitan. Modesty was at risk in Rasht.

The helicopter carrying the SkitoMister touched down on the outskirts of Golsar and was quickly loaded onto a maintenance truck. The helicopter crew carried a fiberglass tank full of liquid and hooked it up to the SkitoMister.

With a technician in the back, the truck drove down several specific streets in Golsar, streets that had been identified by the MISIRI, the Ministry of Intelligence and National Security of the Islamic Republic of Iran, as being suitable for pesticide application.

Captain Brady Kenton and "Kate" watched from above as the truck spent less than 20 minutes in Golsar. Three intelligence officers from Mossad, Shin Bet and Aman watched similar images they were receiving from the Ofek 9 in their Tel Aviv monitoring stations. A surveillance satellite could observe a site for only a few minutes at a time given the complexities of orbit distance and speed. But "Kate" and all of her collegial drones could loiter for hours at high altitude and send a continuous video feed of the people working on the ground. "Kate" delivered the complete pattern of life, giving critical clues of the work being done, the equipment being used and the people on the ground.

Almost as fast as it began, the maintenance operation was over. An entire tank had been dispersed and Captain Brady Kenton watched the SkitoMister get loaded back on the helicopter for the return flight to Damghan.

Kenton followed the chopper all the way back to the warehouse. Hovering 30,000 feet over the Damghan warehouse, Kenton became amused. A man appeared to be out in the field next to the warehouse, and he was flying a gas-powered remote-controlled airplane. "Kate" watched the man take the four-foot winged craft on high banks, barrel rolls, steep dives, and vertical climbs. The man was incredibly skilled, and it brought back memories of when US Air Force Captain Kenton was just "little Brady," flying his airplanes and gliders in the grass fields near Lake Winnebago in Oshkosh, Wisconsin.

Brady grew up an experimental aviation nut. Captain Brady Kenton watched the incredible toy fly for a few more minutes before he and "Kate" needed to head back to Kandahar, Afghanistan.

The man in the field brought his airplane in for a landing as the helicopter touched down, and the SkitoMister was rolled into the warehouse.

Captain Kenton pulled "Kate" up and turned her east toward Afghanistan. They had only been flying a few minutes when something happened. Somewhere in the mountains between Neyshabir and Mashhad, Brady lost control of his drone. "Kate" disappeared.

"Brady…Kate just dropped off our screen…you still got her?" Colonel Abrams asked from the TOC at Creech Air Force Base in Indian Springs, Nevada.

Brady was frantically working his stick and resetting computer images.

"Roger that, sir, still working it. Kate seems to have lost her connection with the GPS satellite. Stand by."

The video feed from Kate was intermittent, but clearly she was descending and getting closer to the two mountain ranges of Binalood and Haser-Masjed. She was too close.

"Talk to me, Captain Kenton," Abrams yelled as he stood with greater urgency.

"I have no controls, repeat, I have no control over Kate."

"What the hell? Has she been hit?"

"Negative, sir, she is disconnected. Sir, she's on autopilot. She's landing herself."

Seconds later the video feed was gone. Kate laid in three pieces on the ground in the most level place she could find in the Binalood mountains of northeastern Iran.

The Ofek 9 sent Kate's photograph to Tel Aviv where the three intelligence officers stared at this technological wonder in amazement. Special Agent Daniels and Agent Fallon Jessup ran down the corridors of Langley to brief the Director as phones around the world were dialed and picked up simultaneously.

"Get me the SECDEF's office now!" Colonel Abrams screamed as combat pilot and US Air Force Captain Brady Kenton unbuckled himself from his tan leather swivel office chair, stepped back and ejected from the virtual debris.

25

ISAF Headquarters
Kabul, Afghanistan

General Ferguson, US Navy Captain "Camp" Campbell and Billy Finn were positioned and waiting for the video conference call connection to the Pentagon. Whatever Secretary of Defense Pennington wanted to talk about, it must have been important because the Chairman of the Joint Chiefs was joining the call as well.

"Mister Secretary, I'm joined by Captain Campbell and retired FBI special agent Finn," Ferguson said as the video feed came to life.

"Jim, we've got a big problem, an international situation," SECDEF Pennington began. "Our classified drone, the RQ-170 Sentinel crash landed an hour ago in northeastern Iran."

"Hostile fire?" Ferguson pressed.

"We don't think so, but we're looking at a technological glitch with the guidance satellite as probable cause. Jim, the Israelis are going bat-shit. Their Ofek 9 has been tracking the events in Bourvari District and now this. They also got hi-res images of the crashed drone. They want some explanations."

"How can I help, sir?" Ferguson asked.

"Get your team to Tel Aviv as soon as possible. Tell the Israelis everything you know. Be candid with them but keep them calm. We don't want to trigger a damn war over this. Undersecretary Miller is working with the Knesset and the Prime Minister's office. CIA is sending Daniels and a gal named Jessup to meet with Mossad. I need you to brief Aman and Shin Bet."

"Affirmative, sir, we'll keep your office posted."

Camp raised his hand to make sure the call wasn't prematurely ended.

"Secretary Pennington?" Camp asked.

"Yes, captain."

"What about the drone, sir? If the Ofek 9 could track her and photograph her that means we've still got a good signal on her. Are you planning to destroy the drone before the Iranians find her?"

"That's above your pay-grade captain. We've presented three options to the president, and that'll be his call and his alone to make."

"Sir? What are those options?"

Pennington seemed perturbed. Even the Chairman of the Joint Chiefs thought the Navy O-6 was out of his lane.

"Send in a covert mission to destroy it, send over another drone to blow it up with a hellfire missile, or let it be."

"Sir, what's the realistic window for any of those options?" Camp pushed.

"This is the latest stealth technology, Captain Campbell. This is a top secret military weapon. We'll do everything in our power to make sure that this technology is not compromised," Pennington said.

"But what's the window, Mr. Secretary?"

Pennington paused and blew a sigh of disgust and subtle irritation out of his mouth.

"Seventy-two hours...tops."

Lyon International Airport
Lyon, France

Lieutenant Colonel Leslie Raines was thrilled to be out of uniform and dressed in casual attire as she exited the jet bridge and walked into the beautiful and modern terminal at Lyon. She had already cleared customs at Charles de Gaulle Airport in Paris and was tempted to take advantage of the duty free shops, boutiques and spas that adorned the terminal.

Raines sported a tight pair of designer blue jeans tucked into a new pair of suede UGGs with her straight brunette hair pulled back in a pony tail. She wore an expensive white, fine gauge cotton cable sweater with a plunging neckline and just a hint of a tan t-shirt below.

Raines was turning heads, and she knew it. She couldn't afford a massive wardrobe on military O-5 pay, but she made sure every piece that made it to her closet counted. She was the queen of thrift stores, outlet malls and second chance stores. Leslie Raines was not a woman who would pay full retail for brand names and designer labels. But she sure looked like it.

A crowd of people that had gathered beneath one of the overhead flat-panel TV screens pulled her away from any self-indulgent "duty free" ideas she may have been contemplating.

The breaking news was broadcast in French, a language she knew precious little about. But the subtitle of the news story screamed at her in Latin: *Francisella tularensis.*

The television images were from a city on the Caspian Sea coast of Iran, a thriving somewhat modern-looking town called Rasht. Raines saw images of Iranian medics carrying sheet-covered bodies out of their homes. The number featured in the on-screen graphic was 42. She didn't need to be fluent in French in order to understand that 42 people were dead.

Raines pulled out her cell phone and took a wild chance of connecting with Camp on his Afghan cell.

He answered.

"Hey, I know this number," Camp answered.

"Camp, I just got off my flight here in Lyon."

"France?"

"Yes, I'm standing here looking at some breaking

news coming out of Iran, looks like it's a story about tularemia. Do you know anything?"

"On this telephone line I can't really say anything, Les. But let's just say whatever you're thinking is probably correct, and it's probably worse than you think."

"Are you driving? I hear cars."

"Yes ma'am, on the way to the airport."

"Where are you off to?"

"Can't say that either, darling. How long will you be in Lyon?"

"Two weeks, maybe four months. Who knows. Wanna come visit?"

Camp smiled and thought about the last time they had been to France together, a fancy restaurant in Marseille.

"Les, remember that restaurant in France?"

"The Sofitel Marseille Vieux Port hotel, at Les Trois Forts restaurant with Chef Dominique Frerard."

Camp was stunned.

"Good God, woman, how do you remember that kind of stuff?"

"Because I *am* a woman, and I pay attention to details, Mister SEAL. What did I drink that night, Camp? Or do you not pay attention to details?"

Camp did not hesitate.

"There we were, in the south of France along the Mediterranean, a romantic dinner with twelve of our closest SEAL friends and CIA spooks, and Raines orders an *Italian* Pinot Gris."

Now Raines was shocked.

"You remembered," she said softly, almost romantically as bodies from the tularemia poisoning were being carried out of more houses in Rasht on the TV screen in front of her.

"I remember every detail, Les…especially when it's important…see you soon?"

Raines heard the line click off. She folded her phone and held it close to her heart as her thoughts filled with tularemia. The Iranians weren't bluffing, and Raines knew it.

26

Palmachim Airbase
Rishon LeZion, Israel

The C-17 carrying Ferguson, Camp and Billy Finn from Kabul to Kuwait and into Israel landed and taxied to a stop on the tarmac closest to the military terminal.

The faces of Camp and Finn were glued to the small portal windows in the back of the military transport as they tried to get glimpses of the famous Palmachim Base.

Palmachim Air Force Base was an Israeli military facility and spaceport located near the cities of Rishon LeZion and Yavne on the Mediterranean Sea, named after Kibbutz Palmachim on the Mediterranean shore.

The base was home to several Israeli Air Force helicopter and UAV unmanned drone squadrons, and served as the rocket launch site for the Arrow missile.

The Israelis used Palmachim to launch the Shavit space launch vehicle into retrograde orbit by launching over the Mediterranean. It was their primary spaceport. The strategic location allowed rocket debris to fall harmlessly into the sea, and away from Israel's regional enemies that might have wanted access to their technology. Palmachim was also used to test ballistic missiles, including the Jericho 3.

Ferguson, Camp and Finn were escorted to a black Mercedes for the ride to Tel Aviv. The Israeli Defense Agency asked that the initial meeting be held at Shabak's Non-Arab Affairs Department offices in Tel Aviv. Shabak, or Shin Bet as the Americans referred to it, was responsible for internal security, but their missions often took them around the globe. Shin Bet served Israel as almost a mirror image of the FBI and Homeland Security in America. Special Agent Chaim Yariv was the lead investigator with Shin Bet, which made Billy Finn feel like he was back in the game.

General Ferguson had been briefed on the plane that his counter-part, Major General Moshe Shalom would represent Aman, the overarching military intelligence body of the Israel Defense Forces. Though Major General Shalom was an intelligence expert, he couldn't match the combat command experience of Brigadier General Jim Ferguson.

Mossad had at first declined to attend the meeting. But while the C-17 was refueling in Kuwait, word came that Mossad was sending two people. No ranks or titles were provided, just simply Yitzhak and Reuven, first names of two people from Mossad, one of the worlds' most ruthless, efficient and surgically precise intelligence agencies, easily on par with the CIA and MI6. Camp did not have the intelligence credentials and suspected that he would be an observant, perhaps subservient, bystander.

Originally, the Americans thought they would be meeting their Israeli counterparts in the Ben-Gurion Complex Givat Ram neighborhood of Jerusalem. But the Israelis were known for conducting a cat and mouse game of moving meetings from location to location. They had been fighting for their own self-preservation since 1948 and for centuries before that.

All the Americans knew was that they would be driven to an undisclosed location in Tel Aviv.

Leaving the Mercedes, Ferguson, Camp and Finn were led up 75 marble steps to an impressive building that was both ancient and modern. Once inside the expansive lobby, the three were consumed with an endless abyss of nothing. A few statues carved from marble seemed to hint at biblical characters. Sporadic and sparse oil paintings filled a few walls between enormous amounts of glass, modern steel and marble. It wasn't the least bit clear if the building was old or new, completed or still under construction. There were no names, no logos, and no signs.

Two sets of floor-to-ceiling, 16-foot wooden doors adorned both the north and south sides of the lobby.

Two Israeli security officers greeted them in the middle of the room and politely asked them for identification and then asked each to power down their cell phones and place them in a velvet bag. The officers turned and led them to the north wing where they opened the large doors and ushered the three into a chamber off the main lobby. Two rows of tables faced each other in the middle of the room. Five Italian leather office chairs were on one side behind two mahogany tables. Four Italian leather office chairs were neatly arranged behind two mahogany tables on the other side.

As Ferguson, Camp and Finn walked into the chamber, Special Agent Daniels and Agent Fallon Jessup rose from their chairs.

"Gentlemen, great to see you. Allow me to introduce Agent Fallon Jessup," Daniels said as Ferguson, Finn and Camp shook hands and made small talk.

Camp was mesmerized by Fallon Jessup at first sight. She was tall and thin, blonde with high cheekbone features and sported an incredible handshake and grip that Camp held one second too long. She wore a khaki skirt, white blouse and navy blue blazer. Her calves were toned, muscular, and strong but not obnoxious. Her voice was soft, but firm and her eyes pierced through Camp's with relentless intensity. For a split second he felt inferior, under-dressed, improperly groomed. He felt disheveled.

The room was bare. Not a white board, TV screen or telephone in sight.

A rear set of 16-foot doors opened promptly, and the Israeli delegation of 10 people walked in. Numerous pleasantries and handshakes were exchanged. No one offered business cards. As though they had gone through an elaborate rehearsal, Major General Shalom sat directly across from Brigadier General Ferguson and three aides stood several feet behind Shalom. Special Agent Chaim Yariv sat directly across from retired FBI agent Billy Finn as three of Yariv's aides stood behind him and next to Major General Shalom's aides. The Mossad agents, Reuven and Yitzhak, took their seats across from Agent Fallon Jessup and Special Agent Daniels. Camp sat at the far end of the American table. No one sat across from him. He was the odd man out.

Major General Shalom spoke first.

"We have some questions…some concerns…and some issues that we're hoping you can shed some light on."

"Major General Shalom, our Secretary of Defense personally asked me to meet with you and provide you with anything you need. We continue to stand with Israel as friends, allies and partners," Ferguson said with kiss-ass thickness that even made Camp sick to his stomach.

"Tell us about Kate."

Ferguson seemed perplexed. He looked at Billy Finn and past the eyes of Jessup and Daniels down to Camp. No one had a clue what Shalom was talking about.

"The RQ-170 Sentinel drone that crashed near Benalood. Her name is Kate," said Reuven as he stared straight ahead at Daniels who knew but said nothing.

"The drone was next-generation technology which we deployed over Iran for surveillance of their nuclear program. It was not shot down. There was technical malfunction."

"Nuclear surveillance, General Ferguson, or was it bio-weapon surveillance?" Chaim Yariv from Shin Bet asked.

Again, Ferguson looked down the row for help, but no one made eye contact with him.

"The short answer is both. We have reason to believe the Iranians are trying to weaponize tularemia."

"Run-of-the-mill rabbit fever?" Yariv pressed.

Billy Finn jumped in since his counter-part had taken over the questioning.

"No. We believe the Iranians acquired some tularemia stockpiles from the Russians, and they have cooked up a vaccine-resistant bacteria strand suitable for aerosolized dispersal equipment," Finn said perhaps releasing more information than what needed to be disclosed.

"The outbreak in the Bourvari District earlier this month was not lethal," Yariv stated.

"Phase One human clinical trial," Camp nearly yelled from the corner of the last table just to be heard and included.

"And Rasht yesterday? More than 46 dead…and

counting,"Yariv said.

"Phase Two human clinical trial," Camp sighed as he slouched back in his Italian leather chair.

"And what would be Phase Three, Captain Campbell?" Shin Bet's Special Agent Chaim Yariv asked.

"Phase Three would be Israel."

Ferguson interrupted and offered a soft rebuke for his American partner.

"We don't know that, Camp, that's only armchair speculation," Ferguson said as he turned his attention back to Major General Shalom. "General, we will share all information with you on this topic in a very timely manner. I urge all of us to remain calm, but vigilant."

"What about Kate? Are you going to blow her up before the Iranians discover her?" Shalom asked.

"We are evaluating our options right now."

"Options? What options do you have?" Mossad agent Yitzhak demanded.

"The American government is reluctant to drop a missile on the drone in Iranian territory. We don't want this incident to be perceived as an act of war."

Yitzhak laughed and leaned forward.

"And how will the presence of a spy drone be perceived if the MISIRI finds it first? We do not welcome the thought of stealth drone technology in Iranian hands."

"I'm sure your Ofek 9 has some good images. Why don't *you* blow it up if it bothers you that much?" Camp asked as he cleaned a speck of grunge from beneath his fingernail.

Reuven grew intense and directed his comments to the end of the table.

"Perhaps we wouldn't have an issue at all right now, Captain Campbell, if you and your Alpha Team had taken care of business the way you should have inside Datta Khel Village. I find it surprising that a SEAL would leave a machine like the SkitoMister intact, just to prevent some toothless tribesmen from firing off a few AK-47 rounds."

"I'm sorry, Reuven, but I looked all over the damned Hindu Kush, and I didn't see any Mossad boys out there doing the heavy-lifting. Please feel free to join us next time if you're ever in the area."

"Gentlemen, please," Major General Shalom called out, "you indicated a vaccine-resistant tularemia. If Captain Campbell is correct, the Phase Two trial must be such a bacterium."

"Not necessarily, General Shalom, there's no indication that any of the citizens in Rasht were previously vaccinated against tularemia. This would appear to be a lethality test," Ferguson said.

"So you're saying that we don't know this particular tularemia recipe, and nor do we know if an existing vaccine will cause an immune response?" Shin Bet's Special Agent Chaim Yariv asked.

"Not exactly," Ferguson said with much deliberation. "We have tried to create such a recipe in our labs and a corresponding new vaccine. It's still too early to know if we'll be successful…in time."

"In time for what? Phase Three?" Mossad agent Yitzhak questioned.

General Ferguson pushed his chair back slightly from the table. No one else moved.

"I can assure you that you have the full support of the American government, military and intelligence community. We will navigate these turbulent waters together. But in the mean time, we must remain calm, measured and vigilant."

Reuven looked over at Camp who was already staring back at him.

"Tell me, Camp…may I call you Camp? How long will it take Raines and her French biotech company to manufacture the vaccine she created? Two weeks? Two months? Two years? We have more than 7 million people in Israel. How many vaccines can they manufacture in a week? And tell me this, Dr. "Camp" Campbell, famous trauma surgeon from Balad and Navy SEAL from Tora Bora…how will we know that this vaccine is safe in humans? It's never been tested on humans, has it Camp? Or do you suppose that the entire country of Israel stands ready to be your guinea pigs?"

The entire room was silent. Two Mossad agents with first names and no titles knew as much about the situation as Camp did. Camp pushed his chair back and stood.

"Hey Reuven…how far along are you Israelis with this vaccine? Or are you just holding back and waiting for Uncle Sam?"

Reuven was silent.

"What's that? You're doing nothing? Just sitting back and waiting for the Americans to cover your ass again? Listen pal, next time, *you* boys get on a plane and come brief *us*. I'm not interested in your juvenile schoolyard games designed to prove that you know everything about jack shit. Millions of people are about to die while you play 'I've got a secret' with human scorecards. You may have some great intelligence, I grant you that. But if you even remotely understood the Age of the Coming, the Twelvers, or the Mahdi, you wouldn't be sitting here with half-shit-faced grins on your faces. Go play with somebody else."

Ferguson and Billy Finn fidgeted as Daniels dropped his head. Agent Fallon Jessup allowed a soft smile to percolate across her high cheek-boned face as Camp jumped out of his chair and walked out of the chamber toward the two 16-foot wooden doors. He ripped the velvet bag out of the hand of the guard at the door.

"Give me my damn cell phone," he said as he reached in and grabbed his phone shoving the bag back into the man's chest as he walked through the expansive lobby and down 75 marble steps to an approaching taxi.

"Hilton Tel Aviv," Camp said to the taxi driver as he pushed the car into gear. Within a few minutes they had turned down Arolzorov Street and into Independence Square where the Hilton Tel Aviv overlooked the Mediterranean Sea, less than a minute's walk to the beach.

Camp walked in through the double-wide revolving glass door and into the well-appointed lobby with exquisite leather seating and recessed golden glow light boxes. He looked through the glass walls against the back of the lobby. Tables and small living room suites filled the veranda lit by tiki torches painted up against the blue backdrop of the Mediterranean Sea. The view was simply spectacular. It was an oasis of relief given ISAF headquarters, Ashgabat, FOB Lightning, Chergotah and the laboratory and barbaric surgical suite in Datta Khel Village.

"Good afternoon and welcome to the Hilton Tel Aviv," the front desk clerk said with a warm and inviting smile.

"Hello, Seabury Campbell," Camp said as he handed her his tourist passport and an American Express card.

"Dr. Campbell, I have five in your party all together. Are you the first arrival?"

"Yes, they're probably behind me in another taxi. My meeting got out a little earlier than their meeting did."

"Your rooms are direct-billed. Would you like me to keep your card on file for incidentals?"

"Please."

Camp checked into room 711, threw his bag on the bed and opened the sliding glass door to the balcony. He closed his eyes and inhaled the sea salt air and temperate breeze. He had never been to Tel Aviv before.

The modern city set against the sea grew on him by the moment until he was overwhelmed by the notion that another country was planning its total and complete annihilation.

Camp walked back into the room, fell face-down and sprawled spread-eagle out on the bed as he dozed off into a deep sleep.

When his phone started ringing at 8:45pm Camp reached up and tapped the top of his nightstand clock, hoping from the depths of his slumber that he was hitting some type of snooze button.

The phone kept ringing.

"Hello," he finally said sounding fully asleep.

"Captain Campbell?"

"Who's asking?"

"Fallon Jessup."

"Oh, who?…ah, Fallon…what's up?"

"Listen, the four of us were going to have dinner in the King Solomon Restaurant, but it looks a bit stuffy, so we're going to meet down at the Sea View Terrace in about 15 minutes. Thought you might like to join us, if you're hungry, or anything."

Camp rubbed his eyes and sat up in bed.

"Yeah, um, maybe, we'll see…I'm working on some reports right now."

"Okay, well, the invitation stands."

"Fallon, was Ferguson pissed?"

She laughed.

"Not really. He said you've been going off like that

since the day he met you. Says you're a 'loose-cannon', but your shots always hit the mark, whatever that means."

Camp bolted for the shower and unrolled his tactical 5.11 khakis and a purple Ralph Lauren polo and hung them on the hook behind his bathroom door. The hot water soothed the tension in his troubled skin as the steam smoothed the wrinkles in his clothes.

Outside the elevator and into the lobby, Camp saw the sign pointing toward the Sea View Terrace. Fifteen feet from the door to the restaurant a man stepped out from behind the massive marble wall and approached within inches of Camp's face.

"Reuven…well, if it's not my favorite intelligence spook. Are you here to tell me where I'm going or just where I've been?" Camp said with as much sarcasm as he could muster.

"Your Fallon Jessup is quite attractive, young and naïve, but definitely attractive."

"Is that your *official* intelligence report?"

"If you go in there you'll have to do battle with three other men and an array of waiters for her attention. Besides, she and Daniels have a thing going on."

"Do you have an alternate suggestion that you already know I'll choose?"

"Perhaps a brief walk and chat along the sea. My favorite bar is just a few hundred yards down the beach. They serve seafood scampi that will amaze you. Then perhaps a Macallan single malt whisky, served neat, and a fine 54-gauge Cuban cigar?"

Camp shook his head and laughed as Reuven smiled for the first time.

"You certainly do your homework, Reuven. I'm all yours."

Reuven and Camp walked south along the beach on a warm August night and made small talk until they came across a taxi stand at the next hotel down the coast.

"Let's get in," Reuven said.

"I thought you said your favorite place was within walking distance?" Camp asked.

"I lied. Besides, an Israeli never goes to the place he mentions first. Life is an endless series of back-up plans."

Reuven handed the driver a slip of paper, and four minutes later they pulled up in front of Molly Bloom's, directly across from the US Embassy.

Molly Bloom's was an Irish pub, an Anglo-establishment with real beef and stout whisky in their Shepherd's Pie. Reuven and Camp took a wooden booth against the back wall of the very loud and raucous pub.

"Kind of hard to talk in here," Camp said above the din.

"Harder for others to listen to us, as well. No agencies or countries while we're in here, okay?"

"Got it."

The waitress rolled up and threw two drink coasters

down on the table. She didn't bother to greet her two new customers and nothing about her convinced Camp that she really wanted to be waiting tables, especially theirs.

"I'll take a pint of Guinness," Reuven said, "and two menus."

"Newcastle Brown if you have it," Camp said as the waitress left without speaking.

"You might be the first American I have ever met who gets it."

"I thought we weren't mentioning agencies or countries."

"Touché."

"Get what?" Camp asked.

"Twelvers. All the men and women who sit in elevated and elected chairs across the world can't fathom such an irrational act with mutually destructive consequences. 'Who would even consider such a thing' they say as they rattle their sabers and authorize more sanctions. No one in their right mind purposefully triggers mutual annihilation. It defies logic. It defies game theory. No one would do it...no one other than the Twelvers."

"Can you stop it?" Camp asked as the waitress dropped off two beers and two menus then left.

"Stop what? Stop which wave? Stop which plan? We face hundreds from every border, thousands more within the reach of missiles. Which plan should we stop tonight? Which one tomorrow morning or the day after? All day – every day – I exist to stop hundreds of evil plans for our annihilation. One of these days, I will screw up. One of these days, I will be a step too slow. One of these days, I will make a wrong move on the board. One of these days, I will guess wrong."

The men were silent as Reuven's words echoed in their heads and cold beer quenched their thirst.

"Leslie Raines is an incredible scientist, Camp."

"She's an incredible woman."

Reuven lifted his glass to toast her.

"We were nearby when your mission went off the grid in Yemen last year. Obviously, Raines recovered quite well."

"Apparently you're not as good as you think you are. 'Nearby' isn't close enough when bullets start flying."

"When Raines landed in Lyon, we assumed she had mastered the vaccine. She works with a doctor at Fort Detrick who still works with us."

"Are you spying, Mister Molly Bloom?" Camp said with a laugh.

"That's what we do, my friend, that's what we do. Tell me about your hike up the Hindu Kush into Datta Khel."

"Not much to tell really. Dead soldier, a SkitoMister, a lab with foreign labels on bottles, ether and some surgical tools."

"And that's how you learned about the Twelvers?"

"No, that was on the hike up. An Iranian double-agent, Revolutionary Guard, was our escort. Omid was his name."

Reuven's face became focused and intense.

"Ah, the all-allusive Omid reappears every three years from self-imposed occultation."

"Who is he?"

"If I knew that then he wouldn't be quite as all-allusive. But I have my hunches. He has some authority. He seems to be able to come and go without drawing undue attention. And for some reason, he occasionally helps others slow him down. Not sure if he's sympathetic and helpful or if he's cunning and deceptive, toying with his prey and tempting them into a well-laid trap."

"Have you heard of Kazi?"

Reuven stopped his swallow and put his beer down on the table. He could hardly hide the contempt in his face or the clenched fist that was about to be covered by his other hand.

"That hit a nerve," Camp said as he took a long swig and stared at Reuven through the glass of his mug.

"Born in Pakistan, raised in Iran by his grandfather who had his son and daughter-in-law murdered as some type of honor killing. Educated in the states, Auburn University, as a microbiologist; worked for years at Brezden University Medical Sciences in The Netherlands where he earned a PhD and now floats around the world as a freelance terrorist. I'm not sure how, but this Kazi has access to the top. I'm talking the religious clerics, all the way to the president, maybe even the Supreme Leader for all I know. You met him?"

"No. He and his friends killed my Army doctor up in Datta Khel Village."

"We have our theories, with regards to Iran, but what do you think Camp? What's the grand plan?"

The waitress finally returned to the wooden booth against the back wall of Molly Bloom's. She held an ordering pad and a pencil as she stared at Reuven and Camp.

"Two Shepherd's Pies, extra 'whisky' for my brother," Reuven said as she gathered up the menus and left.

"I have a guess."

"Then you could work for the CIA. We don't guess."

"A vaccine-resistant tularemia is spread over Israel to rain down some death, widespread illness and uncontrollable panic. The world has seen two outbreaks of tularemia in the region already; there might be more. The UN will appeal for calm and claim it's a natural outbreak, the result of poor sanitation. That's T-minus ten, 10 days out. T-minus three, they send in a covert operation to assassinate the King of Saudi Arabia. T-minus two, they move 500,000 to 1 million Iranian soldiers west toward the border with Iraq. T-minus one, they launch as many as six nukes and 1,000 'regular' missiles. Proxy forces – Hezbollah - move in from Lebanon in the south. Hamas moves in from Gaza and the West Bank as loyalists in Yemen head for Mecca. Israel and the US launch retaliatory strikes as 500,000 to 1 million Iranian soldiers march into Iraq and set up the perimeter for the Mahdi and Jesus to reappear and bring peace to the world. That's D-Day."

Camp was intrigued by Reuven's personality. The secretive Mossad agent became silent, stoic and more unemotional than normal as the waitress dropped two bowls of steaming Shepherd's Pie down on the table. Reuven pointed to their empty beer mugs, and she disappeared.

"Eight minutes and 53-seconds," Camp said stirring his bowl. "The first outgoing retaliatory strikes won't rain down on top of Iran until 10 minutes have passed. They don't care about mutual annihilation. The Age of the Coming, the new Islamic caliphate, will be next door in Iraq."

"So we strike first. Jericho 3s take them out before their plan launches."

"You could do that. But world condemnation might deliver the annihilation they seek. Jihadists from all over the world and sympathetic nation states might accomplish what their 9-minute plan couldn't do."

"That's why we built the Jericho 3, to protect our survival at all costs…even the wrath of the world."

"But the world doesn't believe *them* right now. The world believes they are rattling sabers, mouthing off and spewing hate. Sure, the world believes that they'll send in their proxies; they'll supply the Katyusha rockets that'll rain down on your settlements; they'll supply the IEDs that blow up Americans in Iraq and Afghanistan; but would they *really* strike Israel first with six nukes and a thousand regular missiles and willingly accept mutual annihilation? The world doesn't believe that. That's not rational."

"But the Twelvers?" Reuven asked.

"For some of the Twelvers…some…not all…that's very rational."

"That 'some' could be as high as 200 million Muslims." The waitress slid two more beer mugs across the wooden table. "You got a better plan?" Reuven asked.

Camp leaned in close.

"What if T-minus ten *doesn't* go according to plan? What if the tularemia attack doesn't cause deaths, doesn't cause widespread illness and doesn't cause unprecedented panic and fear? What if a massive bio-weapon attack delivers nothing? There's nothing to trigger Hezbollah, nothing to trigger Hamas and an assassination in Saudi Arabia fails. There's nothing to trigger a rush to Mecca from Yemen, and nothing to trigger a million man march into Iraq."

"I'm listening."

"Raines has cracked the code. She has created a tularemia strain as bad, maybe worse than what Kazi can do. But she took it further than the apocalyptical microbiologist who only bought a one-way ticket. She made it round-trip. She created the super vaccine for the vaccine-resistant bacterium.   No one needs to die, get sick or be afraid. She can kill you, and she can save you."

"This is the magical vaccine that has yet to be tested on humans? Risk the future of Israel on a prayer?"

"Haven't you been doing that for 6,000 years? Oh, I'm sorry, I must've misunderstood the Talmud. God let the children of Israel annihilate Egypt with a first strike, *and then* the Pharaoh freed the children of Israel from bondage. Geez, I was under the false impression that God used supernatural forces like plagues and locusts to defeat your enemies. You know, you're as hypocritical as every other religion on the face of the earth. You only use 'god' when it's convenient for you…you don't really *believe* anything, do you."

Reuven was silent. He wasn't accustomed to being lectured on Hebrew theology by an American who was hardly religious, let alone Christian, to begin with.

"What do you need?"

"Time. Buy me time. Buy us time to manufacture millions of doses of vaccine and antibiotics. Give us time to place a biomedical shield over Israel. If you can slow them down, delay the start of their countdown clock, we've got a fighting chance."

"How much time?"

"Twelve weeks."

"Eight."

"I'll take eight."

"If they attack us with tularemia and we're not

ready, not vaccinated…if there's no biomedical shield over Israel…the Jericho missiles go in. I can't stop that."

"Understood."

Reuven stood up and left cash on the table as Camp followed him out of Molly Bloom's to the street curb. Reuven handed him a note.

"If you need me call this number. They will give you information. Follow it closely, and I will contact you. Separate taxis, okay, I'm sure you can find your way home."

Reuven got into the first taxi as Camp leaned in to say goodnight.

"Do you want my number?"

"I have it."

Camp shut the car door as Reuven lowered the window.

"Hey Molly Bloom, just so you know, I would have taken six weeks."

Reuven laughed.

"That's good because I would have granted 10."

27

Biotech Park
Lyon, France

Leslie Raines waved and smiled at Thierry Gaudin as she passed by the glass walls of the executive offices on the way to her lab and office.

In the heart of the Rockefeller University Hospital Center, LyonBio was one of 19 other health science companies in the biotech corridor of southern France, including a business incubator designed to move basic scientific discoveries to full-scale production and consumer products.

LyonBio had built its reputation on developing vaccines and 'one medicine' biologicals, drugs that uniquely measured and targeted an individual's specific genetic make-up and DNA. With an African lion as its logo, LyonBio had attacked market share and opportunities with unrivaled aggression and passion since it broke onto the world's biotech landscape in 2003.

Thierry Gaudin was identified in Le Monde daily newspaper's business section as one of the nation's top 10 up-and-coming chief executive officers in 2007 before he took his company public in 2009. LyonBio climbed to the top of the Euronext 100 and quickly became the darling of the French stock exchange, formerly known as *Bourse de Paris*.

Gaudin never forgot his humble beginnings and continued to reinvest in the revitalization of Lyon's industrial district which Gaudin helped transform into a technology corridor.

What Silicon Valley meant to hi-tech computer-based discovery, research and development in California, BioTech Park in Lyon meant to life sciences-based discovery, research and development in southern France.

Though wealthy by all standards, the 45-year-old Gaudin was a family man and a devout Catholic. His oldest son Bernard was 15 and an avid downhill skier and swimmer. Thirteen-year-old Marie was a vocalist in the school choir and had taken ballet training since she was four years old. Philippe was only six, but his passion was football, soccer as the Americans called it, and he wanted to be on the team that brought the World Cup back to France.

But the glue that kept his family together and fueled his business was his wife of 22 years, Rochelle. For the first seven years of their marriage, Rochelle worked day and night next to Thierry to help transform his dream into a reality. She worked two jobs to put him through graduate school. When LyonBio rocketed to success, Rochelle kept him grounded. No fancy cars, no exotic villas and no public displays of wealth were allowed as jewelry around her neck or on her fingers.

Rochelle's influence on Thierry was personified in the culture of LyonBio. Universities, corporations and even world governments wanted to do business with LyonBio, including the United States Department of Defense.

No one at LyonBio knew that Leslie Raines was, in fact, Lieutenant Colonel Leslie Raines. She dressed casual, but smart. She didn't have a pretentious attitude, but she was deliberate and expected order. Her demeanor was steady keel, never too high up, and never the least bit down. She had only been occupying the "developer's" office for three days, but the 540 employees were already talking about the "American woman" that Thierry Gaudin was trying so desperately hard to please. They didn't realize the financial potential of "the project" let alone the catastrophic risk of its failure.

Raines got the call shortly after 9:00am. She hustled down to shipping and receiving where two large GEFCO freight trucks were backing into the docks. It had taken an additional 48 hours since the project received a "green light" at Fort Detrick before a ground shipping company could be found that was willing to deliver almost 200 NHPs, non-human primates. The transportation of research animals, especially monkeys, was becoming a global nightmare and a hot-button issue, especially in Europe.

France, like much of Europe, wasn't real keen on the notion of using animals in research. Rats, mice, rodents, fruit flies and zebra fish were not as big of a deal as beagles, cats – and worst of all – monkeys. Less than half of LyonBio's 540 employees had any clue that the company they worked for needed to use rats and rodents in order to test the targeting and safety of the vaccines and drugs they were developing.

Word of almost 200 rhesus monkeys housed on the premises spread through LyonBio – and the rest of the second largest city in France – like wildfire.

But if everything went according to plan, Raines knew that she and her monkeys would be long gone in less than three months. She only hoped that she had that much time.

LyonBio didn't have a BSL-4 facility like Raines used at Fort Detrick, but their BSL-3 equivalent was deemed adequate, given Raines' amazing work in developing a vaccine product candidate. Biocontainment was classified by the relative danger to the surrounding environment in terms of "biological safety levels." Since tularemia occurred naturally, the Government of France gave "the project" a waiver on the grounds of it being an agricultural hazard. LyonBio's BSL-3 was appropriate for their clinical, diagnostic, teaching, research, and production facilities for all work done with indigenous and exotic agents which could cause serious or potentially lethal disease after inhalation.

Laboratory personnel at LyonBio had specific training in handling pathogenic and potentially lethal agents, and it took less than three days for Raines to assess that they were supervised by competent scientists who were experienced in working with these agents. If the work Raines did at the BSL-4 on Fort Detrick was valid, then she knew they only needed to build a neutral or warm zone for tularemia in Lyon, France.

Thierry Gaudin walked up to Raines as the handlers unloaded the NHPs and moved them to the vivarium.

"This is a great day, Mademoiselle Raines…I assure you that you will be greatly happy you selected us as your partners," Gaudin said in stilted English. "We will duplicate and verify the vaccine components today and make sure the adjuvants are as you have directed. We will replicate the lethality of the bacterium first to make sure that…you know, to make sure."

Raines *did* know. At least four more monkeys needed to die, just to make sure the vaccine recipe was creating an immune response against a truly lethal bacterium.

Damghan, Iran

Kazi was bent over a work table in the warehouse where his research and laboratory complex was housed. The others were outside waiting for him, but he wanted to finish painting the last three letters on the bottom side of the wing: G-L-E.

If he hadn't pursued microbiology as his grandfather Qazvin had insisted, his dream was to become an astrophysicist, or a combat fighter pilot at the very least. Kazi satisfied his passion as a nitro-gas, radio-controlled airplane pilot.   Fueled with nitro-methane and an internal combustion engine that screamed to life with glow plug ignition, Kazi was more than a hobbyist. He was a professional.

With painstaking precision he had assembled the brand new ARF P-51D Mustang WARBIRD as soon as the box arrived. The P-51 was his dream machine, a scalable model built on the famous American fighter jet platform from World War II. With a 65-inch wingspan and only 7.8-pounds of weight, the WARBIRD would be an impressive, perhaps daunting, sight in the sky. The model kit came with balsa wood wings and a fiberglass blend fuselage as well as all of the decals and paint necessary to decorate it like the classic American fighter. But Kazi intended to decorate the WARBIRD with his own creative meanderings, and the English lettering beneath the wings was just the start.

The SkitoMister had been removed from his warehouse three days before and just after the maintenance test in Rasht. The machine was flown to Turkey and then driven by truck down south into Iraq through Zakho District and into the village of Levo. Assyrians in the village had long-complained that insufficient attention was being paid to their agricultural needs, including their unanswered requests for pesticides and insecticides.

As Kazi finished painting the last letter on the undercarriage of the wing, his cell phone rang. The test in Levo was complete. The SkitoMister would make one more trip, to Ajloun village, 47 miles northwest of Amman, Jordan, before heading back to Damghan.

Kazi spoke his approval into the phone as a young man opened the warehouse door and yelled his complaint. The others were getting impatient.

Kazi put the phone down and ran outside where two teen-aged boys and another man in his mid-20s were standing with their RC airplanes waiting for Kazi. The large field behind the warehouse was set up like a circular track with four large pylons in each corner of the long rectangular field that would soon become an oblong race course. Each nitro-gas plane had been calibrated to have similar speed and matched performance. Each of the four planes on the track were constructed primarily of fiberglass with composites used at high load points. The wings were hollowed out to save weight. The .40 cubic engines had no problem reaching 150 miles per hour in the long straight-aways. The individual planes were identical and comparable.

It was the skill of the pilot that won each race, and Kazi had never been defeated.

28

Hilton Tel Aviv
Tel Aviv, Israel

Camp was the last one to shuffle into the King Solomon Restaurant for breakfast. General Ferguson, Billy Finn, Special Agent Daniels and Agent Fallon Jessup were deep in discussion with coffee and orange juice poured and breakfast orders already taken.

Ferguson glared at his Navy Captain in a manner that brought back many memories of then Colonel Ferguson giving Camp "that look" when he refused to leave his 18-hour shifts in the Balad trauma tents.

"You stormed out of a high level military intelligence meeting and failed to join us for dinner last night. Are you on official leave, Captain Campbell, or is there some other explanation for your juvenile behavior?"

The waitress walked up before he had a chance to

formally ignore Ferguson.

"Coffee, OJ, two eggs over easy, and a bagel with cream cheese…cinnamon raisin if you have it," Camp said as he rubbed his temples. "Finn, Daniels, Jessup… everyone sleep well?"

Camp couldn't help but notice Fallon's unbuttoned white blouse with a low-cut halter revealing most of God's natural creation. Camp was not a skirt-chaser and his military bearing provided all the discipline necessary to reject the double-look temptation of an attractive woman. Fallon Jessup reminded him of "home" where beauty was celebrated and honored, not hidden beneath a burka and limited to eye-slit connections between men and women. Camp looked at Fallon once and allowed himself a brief glance before turning his attention away like the officer and gentleman he was.

"You won't make admiral at this rate, Campbell." Ferguson said as his blood apparently continued to boil after Camp's premature exit from the meeting the day before.

Camp spewed a few ounces of freshly-squeezed orange juice all over his white china plate.

"Finn, please drop a slug of lead in my left temple if I'm ever so stupid as to solicit an admiralship. Sir, I've been telling you for two years that I have my years in, and I'm more than ready to retire and head back to Bird-in-Hand to milk some cows. If you're ready for me to go then – please – just say the word, and I'll have the paperwork on your desk yesterday."

Ferguson had learned to ignore Camp as well.

"Where were you last night?"

"Covert mission."

"Camp!"

"Seriously. Took a walk then took a taxi, some Irish pub named Molly Bloom's."

"By yourself?" Ferguson asked.

"No. I was on my way to meet up with you at the Sea View Terrace and I was, how shall I say, intercepted."

"By whom?"

"The tall Israeli spook with the glasses."

"Reuven? Why did he want to see *you*?" Daniels asked.

"Probably because none of you were making any sense. Hell, Daniels, you didn't even utter one damn word."

"You learn by *observing* Captain Campbell," Daniels added rather dismissively.

"Guess you didn't *observe* enough then, at least when it came to WMD in Iraq."

Ferguson raised his hands to stop the schoolyard argument while Fallon Jessup kept her attention on Camp.

"What did he want?" she asked.

"Nothing really, just wanted to know how I viewed the whole situation from 30,000-feet I guess."

"Need I remind you that your opinions do not constitute official US policy positions on this matter?" Ferguson lectured.

"I wasn't wearing my uniform, general, so you can relax."

The waitress and two assistants wheeled a cart next to the table and started unloading breakfast orders.

"Well, no more contacts with Reuven or any other Israeli officials. That's a direct order."

"Aye, aye, sir."

"Billy, I want you and this malcontent to head out to Lyon today. Make sure that Raines and this LyonBio outfit get the full support and cooperation of the United States government. You will both stay there until we have vaccines loaded on boats, trains, planes and automobiles bound for Tel Aviv. Clear?"

Finn nodded as Camp shoveled two eggs over easy into his mouth.

"Daniels, what's next for you two?"

"Back to Langley tonight, sir. We'll be in touch with the SECDEF's office with any new developments," Daniels said.

Ferguson took one bite of his toast, pushed back and placed his napkin on the back of the chair.

"I've got a MILAIR flight out of Palmachim within the hour and back to Kabul."

"You got this?" Camp said with a mouth full of food referring to the restaurant tab. Ferguson ignored him and walked out of the King Solomon.

Lyon Airport
Lyon, France

Billy Finn and Camp left baggage claim and scanned the waiting cars until they saw headlights flash on a white Peugeot. Camp's heart missed a beat with the smile that flashed his way from a familiar face partially hidden behind her Oakley's.

Raines got out and walked back to open the trunk as Finn and Camp threw their bags in.

"Bill Finn?" she asked.

"Yes ma'am, Billy Finn or Finn if you prefer. Pleasure to meet the world's greatest secret scientist," Finn said as he shook hands with Raines and started to get into the back seat of the Peugeot.

"And you must be US Navy Captain Campbell," Raines said with a wry grin on her face extending her hand to shake his.

Camp moved in and wrapped her in a full embrace and kissed her on the lips. Camp could hear every ounce of oxygen leave her lungs in pleasure as her arms fell limp. Camp let go, smiled and got into the front passenger seat. It was the first time Camp had kissed Raines. The kiss wasn't planned, nor was the longing and desire Camp was beginning to feel.

"Um, well, I guess you two need no introductions," Finn said as Raines pulled away from the curb after checking Finn out in the rear-view mirror. "And all this time I thought you were chasing Fallon Jessup's tail last night."

The Peugeot came to a screeching halt as Raines slammed on the brakes.

"What?" Raines demanded as she glared at the defenseless Naval Captain.

"No, no, no, and nope…never been alone with that woman a second in my life, not a drop of interest. Eye candy? Yes. Interest? No, no and no."

"How do you know Fallon Jessup?" Raines demanded.

"Oh boy!" Finn sighed from the backseat. "Stepped in it now."

"Me? How do *you* know her?" Camp responded.

"She and what's his name came over to Fort Detrick to school me about tularemia and some shipment of Russian stockpiles."

"Well, I have it from reliable sources that she and old 'what's his name' Daniels are mixing spying with pleasure, so please call the dogs off. I'm innocent…and I'm where I want to be, right now."

Camp watched Leslie's face soften as she checked Finn out in the rear-view with a raised eyebrow and a question that wasn't asked.

"I got it, lady," Finn said as he looked out the window as the Peugeot climbed through second and third gears and out of the "arrivals" section of Lyon Airport.

"Thanks, Billy," Camp said sarcastically from the front.

"Did you hear the latest?" Raines said as she drove out of the airport and onto the highway toward LyonBio.

"Another tularemia outbreak?" Camp asked.

"Explosion. Huge blast at the Alghadir missile base in Bid Ganeh, Iran. Seventeen members of the Revolutionary Guard were killed including the architect of their missile program. Witnesses said it sounded like a bomb was dropped on the site. Windows were rattling 30 miles away in Tehran."

"Any speculation on the cause?" Finn asked.

"Widespread speculation. The Iranians say Mossad did it. The Israelis say that it was an inside job by the Iranian militant group Mujahedeen e-Khalq, or MEK. Western diplomats say they probably mishandled their own munitions and set the explosion off accidently."

"Well that can't be good. Probably sets their missile program back a bit," Finn surmised from the backseat as Camp allowed a content smile to fill his face.

"What are you grinning about?" Raines said as she looked over at Camp.

"Because it sounds like Reuven to me. How's your work going?" Camp said deliberately changing the subject.

"They've replicated the tularemia strain I cooked up. Now they're replicating the vaccine in their pilot house," Raines said as she shook her head slightly with disgust.

"What?" Camp asked.

"They've already terminated twenty-four rhesus monkeys. I hate that part; I just hate it."

"Come on, Les, you know they gotta do it. If the bacterium doesn't kill or make them seriously ill, what good is the vaccine? Same with polio, same with cancer drugs, same with Alzheimer's."

"I know" Raines answered as she made intense and concerned eye-contact with Camp, a look that made him feel uncomfortable a few seconds.

"Where are we bunking, colonel?" Finn asked.

"Well, I have a furnished one-bedroom apartment at the Biotech Park complex. It's actually a pretty cool place, something like 19 other life science companies in the same area. You boys, however, have government billeting at the Hilton Lyon."

Raines pulled onto Highway A43 then exited onto Perpherique Laurent Bonnevay Boulevard for the 16 minute ride to the Hilton Lyon Hotel on Quai Charles de Gaulle.

"I'm going to drop you two off at your hotel, let you freshen up, and then you can take this American girl out for a fancy French dinner, as long as it fits within our per diem."

"Based on my professional observations during the airport greeting a few minutes ago, I think an old FBI guy makes three an odd number," Finn said.

"Nonsense. I'll be in the lobby at 1930 hours, and you'd both better be ready. The French are kicking and screaming, but I make them start at 0700 every morning."

"LyonBio will never be the same," Camp said as the Hilton came into view.

PART THREE

29

Rue Café
Lyon, France

Odette opened the door to the Rue with raw
nerves and emotions exposed. She knew her face
was flush and she couldn't stop her eyes from darting
from table to table as she walked through the restaurant.
Odette wasn't a child, but at 23 years old she hadn't done
anything like this before. It felt important. She fancied
herself as being a patriot on the front-lines of a
revolution.

Remodeled out of 100-year-old masonry and a
long-since defunct print shop, Rue Café was the new
trendy nightclub for "live" jazz and "*bar a tapas*" culinary
treasures in the old financial district in downtown Lyon.
The 16-foot ceilings, European-accented sconces,
narrowly-dipped ceiling fixtures, exhaustive wine list and
well-appointed bar made Rue Café the hottest

destination for the social elite.

Jason Timmons had taken the train down from London the same night he'd received the message from "Claude." Jason was one of the protest organizers for Animal Aid, a well-respected, highly organized and widely supported animal rights group in the UK. Claude, who didn't have a last name or at least wouldn't provide one, was a full-time musician and the part-time head of the *SPEAK, A Voice for the Animals* franchise in Lyon. Organized to end animal research at Oxford University, SPEAK and SHAC were often aligned in the common mission to end animal research throughout Europe, especially when it involved the use of primates.

While Animal Aid was content to lobby out in the open for an end to animal research, groups like SPEAK and SHAC were just as content to go underground with far more nefarious and direct actions.

The larger and more egregious the direct action, event or protest, the more effectively they could trigger media coverage and ultimately fulfill their mission.

Claude moved in and established "SPEAK-Lyon" as soon as the Lyon Biotech Park was up and running. But the use of rats, mice, rodents, fruit flies and zebra fish didn't really spark any controversy and the people of Lyon were largely apathetic and indifferent.

But that was before Odette, who worked at LyonBio, called Claude who, in turn, contacted Jason. The two men were seated at a high bar table in the back of Rue Café when Odette joined them. Claude was a friend from the music scene in southern France. Now they were warriors in a cause. Claude wasted no time getting started.

"Tell Jason what you told me," Claude said in English for the benefit of Jason.

"Last week we received a shipment – two trucks actually – full of non-human primates. Rhesus monkeys. There were 196 in all."

"Who supplied them?" Jason asked.

"I don't know, but I can find out. They came on two GEFCO trucks," Odette said as Jason took notes.

"If they shipped them, then *they're* going down. We'll put so much public pressure on them they won't know what hit them. Go on." Jason seemed excited to Odette. Claude had told her that his British friend loved to wreak financial havoc on companies who supplied animals to biomedical researchers.

"The first 24 were separated and taken to what we call 'the pilot house.' Only a few employees have badge access to that area."

"Do you?" Claude asked as he peered though his red-framed eyeglasses. He was still wearing his black leather jacket.

"No, but my best friend does. The first four monkeys were exposed to some sort of mist." Odette started to cry.

"It's okay, what happened?" Jason asked with a soft tenor of empathy.

"They got sick, real fast. The monkeys were

coughing, choking…my friend said they were suffering…and then they died. He pulled out his iPhone – he wasn't supposed to take it into the pilot house – but he did it anyways…here's the video of them dying."

Jason and Claude watched the 23-second video in horror.

"Bastards! Did they even try to save the damn monkeys?" Claude demanded.

"No. Nothing. They did nothing. But that's not all…they repeated the same test five more times. My friend said each time they gave them a different vaccine, a few times they gave the monkeys antibiotics as soon as they got infected. But nothing worked. Twenty-four… all 24 died. After the scientists did the necropsy on each of them, they were incinerated …as medical waste."

Odette wept uncontrollably as Claude tried to comfort her. Nothing seemed to help or calm her down.

"Odette, one more question…are they planning to murder the rest of the monkeys, too?" Jason asked as Odette's tears and anguish subsided.

"I don't know. That's why I called Claude."

Claude's face was filled with rage.

"Public pressure has worked well in the UK. Claude, it can work here, too," Jason said.

"Screw public pressure," Claude said with barely restrained anger. "Odette, who runs LyonBio?"

"Gaudin…Thierry Gaudin."

"Odette…thank you for letting me know. You did the right thing. This insanity will stop, I assure you. Jason and I need to talk."

Odette got the hint. Her mission was accomplished. She wiped her face and kissed Claude on the cheek and touched Jason's hand as she stood.

"What are you thinking?" Jason asked.

"You don't want to know," Claude answered as he wiped a tear from Odette's cheek.

"Listen, we'll blog about these atrocities the rest of the week, no doubt about that. The people of France will not stand for this. This will be a fundraising *coup d'état*," Jason said with great pleasure.

"We don't have the rest of the week. These monkeys will be dead by then." Claude got up and put 15 Euros down on the table. "That should cover my portion with a little bit left over for your fundraising *coup*," Claude said as he stormed past Odette and out of the restaurant.

Odette offered a sad smile to Jason and walked out of the Rue Café and down the narrow cobblestone walkway that separated the facing buildings, shops and restaurants.

Sainte-Consorce Suburb
Lyon, France

Rochelle Gaudin kissed each of her children good-bye as they marched out of the house to wait for the school bus. They were dressed in standard parochial uniforms for a traditional Catholic education. The Gaudins could have easily afforded prestigious private schools for Bernard, Marie and Philippe, but Rochelle wanted to keep the family well-grounded in the community. Thierry did whatever Rochelle wanted.

The bus pulled up on schedule, and the children got on for the 15-minute ride to Sainte-Luc's Catholic Church and school, a sprawling campus on 12-acres that served K-12 families in Sainte-Consorce.

Rochelle waived from the front steps of the home as six-year-old Philippe waved back from a window seat toward the back of the bus. Rochelle turned back into the house and never noticed the Volkswagen van that pulled out and followed the bus from a distance.

The school day ended promptly at 3:30pm, and the children were marched out to the circle drive where the buses were lined up for the afternoon drive home.

The Volkswagen van waited as well, from across the street.

Philippe and Marie got on the bus and waved to Bernard who had just started walking with two friends, each carrying a backpack full of school books, folders and papers. The boys walked off Sainte-Luc's campus, crossed the street and over to the center of town that was filled with small shops, cafes and restaurants.

Bernard never noticed the Volkswagen van that followed them for a short distance, stopped and let one passenger out, then drove past Bernard and his friends and parked in the back alley behind a bookstore.

Bernard stopped on the sidewalk in front of his favorite after-school café and called his mother. The man walking behind Bernard and his friends moved in closer and pretended to be looking at a sign in the café window as Bernard placed the call.

"Maman, je suis au café avec mes amis. Puvrez-vouse me chercher dans une heure?"

Smiling after gaining his mother's permission and promised pick-up, Bernard closed his phone and walked into the café with his friends.

Bernard and his friends were ordering their cappuccinos as a man approached from behind and joined their conversation.

He told Bernard that he was an engineering student at the University of Lyon in Saint Etienne working on his PhD. He asked the boys if they attended Sainte-Luc's and told them it was the same school he attended as a boy.

One of Bernard's friends asked the man what type of engineering he was studying, and the man said he was designing fighter jets. The young boys were enthralled with his story as he pulled out 10 Euros and told the waitress that coffees and sweets were his treat.

The boys were delighted.

The man sat down at the table with Bernard and his two friends as they all shared some dreams and tall tails about teachers at Sainte-Luc's until the back door of the café opened and a stranger ran in shouting.

"Does anyone in here know a six-year-old boy

named Philippe? He's outside crying. Says he got off the bus to follow his brother and got lost."

Bernard and his friends swapped looks of disbelief.

"*Il ma suivi? Il va avoir des ennuis avec ma mere,*" Bernard complained to his friends about the trouble Philippe would be in when they got home. Bernard followed the man out the back door as he prepared the words of scolding he was about to deliver to his little brother.

Bernard's friends kept talking with the engineering student.

As Bernard walked through the back door, the stranger pointed inside the Volkswagen van. Bernard looked inside then felt a huge shove on his back that pushed him into the rolling van as the driver took off and the sliding door slid shut behind him. Bernard's mouth was quickly taped, and his hands were bound.

The engineering student checked his watch, apologized to the boys for his quick departure and wished them well in their studies.

"*Dites a votre ami bonne chance a l'ecole,*" he said as he walked out of the café and down the street to the waiting van.

30

LyonBio
Lyon, France

US Navy Captain "Camp" Campbell, comfortably dressed in civilian attire and retired FBI agent Billy Finn were both bored stiff by the end of their first day "monitoring" the progress of tularemia vaccine development at LyonBio. They popped into Leslie Raines' office to voice their boredom.

"Watching paint dry," Camp started.

"Grass growing," Finn added. "Either has a million times more energy and action than biomedical research, Raines. How do you do it?"

"And this is *accelerated* work, gentlemen. How would you like to babysit this process for 15 years as a conventional drug or vaccine moves down the pipeline?" Raines answered not looking up from her computer screen.

Camp walked over to the TV in Raines' small office, turned it on and flipped through channels until he found some English. It was CNN world news.

"A nuclear scientist was killed in a blast in Tehran this morning, the Iranian news agency reported, the latest in a string of attacks that Iran has blamed on Israel. A motorcyclist placed a magnetic bomb under the scientist's Peugeot 405, the state-run IRNA news agency said. The blast also wounded two others. State television channel Press TV reported later that the scientist's driver had died in a hospital from his injuries. The Iranian ambassador to the United Nations condemned what he called 'cruel, inhumane and criminal acts of terrorism against the Iranian scientists.'"

Camp and Finn were jolted out of their fixated television news focus by a loud commotion outside and a stream of people running down the hallway past Raines' door.

"What the heck?" Raines said as she stood and leaned into the hallway.

"What's going on?" Camp asked nonchalantly.

"Beats me, but everyone looks pretty riled up," Raines said. "Wanna go take a look?"

Camp and Finn followed Raines out and down the hallway to the main lobby of LyonBio. A sizeable crowd of more than 200 people had gathered outside the CEO's executive offices as more streamed in.

Two police officers from the Bureau de Police, dressed in white shirts with light blue berets, stood outside the executive office. Two more agents with

Interpol and the Deputy Chief of Police for Lyon spoke with a distraught Thierry Gaudin on the other side of the glass walls.

Raines scanned the growing crowd and spotted Pipi Chandre, the client manager who served as her "go to" problem-solver and who spoke fluent English. Camp and Finn followed Raines as she made her way through the throng.

"Pipi, what's going on?"

Pipi was almost hysterical.

"Mr. Gaudin's executive secretary came out a moment ago and told some of the workers that Mr. Gaudin's oldest son, Bernard, was kidnapped after school today."

"Kidnapped?" Finn asked.

"Yes. Terrorists have taken him."

"For ransom? Money?" Finn asked.

"We don't know."

The investigators from Interpol led Thierry out of his office and out the front door into a waiting vehicle and away from the legion of his beloved employees as rumors and speculation flew wildly.

Tel Aviv, Israel

Mossad agents Reuven and Yitzhak poured through their daily intelligence reports. Nuclear inspectors were, once again, denied access to several of the Iranian nuclear sites.

Inspectors from the International Atomic Energy

Agency, or IAEA, were back in Iran doing the one-step, two-step dance. The steps seemed to be the same each time the dance music was played. Iranian officials always looked forward to IAEA inspections, and they welcomed inspectors to the airport each time. But when it came time for special requests and surprise locations, the Iranians always had an excuse. IAEA inspectors were in Iran every three months, and sites that were inexplicably "unavailable" one month would be put on the list to see three months later.

Yitzhak picked up the phone and called a junior officer in Austria.

"Make the calls, Sasha, and get a few major media outlets to carry this one line: *'the IAEA does not look at today's setback in a negative light. Iran continues to be cooperative and we look forward to our visit in three months.'* Do you copy, Sasha?"

"Yes."

"I need it three places."

"Got it."

Reuven looked through a variety of intel reports coming out of Europe, the Middle East and Northern Africa. One headline in particular grabbed his attention: SON OF BIOTECH EXECUTIVE KIDNAPPED IN LYON, FRANCE.

Reuven read deeper. *"Bernard Gaudin (15), son of LyonBio President and CEO, Thierry Gaudin, abducted in broad day light – ransom demands posted on Internet."* Reuven leaned over and clicked on the video link pasted in the classified digital report.

The video was homemade, anything but professional, which made the experience all that more real. The camera pulled back from an image of a black flag with red blood letters that spelled SPEAK. The mask-like face of a small non-human primate seemed to gaze at the letters.

Three adults were standing, two on the left side and one on the far right. They were wearing wool ski masks with cut-outs for eyes, nose and mouth. They were dressed completely in black. In the center of the table was a 15-year-old boy whose mouth was taped shut, and his hands were bound behind his back. Bernard was stripped naked and crammed on one side of an Allentown two-cage metabolic non-human primate cage, 32-inches wide, 29-inches deep and 32-inches high. Feeders and watering units were affixed to the cage. A sliding socialization door separated Bernard from the empty companion cage next to him.

One of the masked men spoke into the camera.

"LyonBio murdered 24 monkeys this week with poisonous gases and mists."

The video cut to a clip of amateur video allegedly taken on someone's iPhone from inside LyonBio's pilot house. Reuven watched four monkeys gasp for their last breaths and die.

"There are 172 more rhesus monkeys that are on death row waiting to be executed later this week. The president and chief executive officer of LyonBio is a

Frenchman by the name of Thierry Gaudin. He and his wife Rochelle have three beautiful children. This is their 15-year-old son, Bernard. Their daughter Marie is just 13 years old, and she has a beautiful voice. We know, because we heard her sing in her choir at Sainte-Luc's. The cage next to Bernard is reserved for Thierry Gaudin's six-year-old son, Philippe. Don't worry, Philippe. When we pick you up, we'll make sure you have a football in your cage because we know you want to win the World Cup for France one day."

Reuven rubbed his eyes in pain. This was not good.

"If LyonBio does not…DOES NOT…stop all animal testing within 24 hours…then we will continue *their* animal tests right here on *Bernard* who has volunteered for duty."

The masked man next to the spokesman pulled out a scalpel and a set of jumper cables and a car battery. He held one end of the jumper cables near the wire Allentown cage while the other was attached to the car battery.

"In the first 24 hours of human experimentation, we will begin with shock therapy to see how electrical charges affect the human brain of a 15 year old."

The loose end of the jumper cables was attached to the metal cage. Sparks flew and Bernard screamed through the tape on his mouth.

"After 48 hours, little Philippe will join his brother as we inject the boys with cleaning chemicals to see if their bodies want to reject those chemicals. Logical, right?"

Reuven closed his eyes in disgust.

"But after 72 hours....well, that's where we get to the good stuff. We will hold a 'live' lab on the Internet where aspiring young biomedical researchers can watch us perform a necropsy on these two brothers. You will be able to see first-hand how bad these tests were on humans. Unlike animals, I'm sure that both Bernard and Philippe will want to tell all of you that these experiments hurt. The animals say the same things, but no one at LyonBio appears to be listening. So SPEAK, A Voice for the Animals, will."

Reuven covered his clenched fist with the relaxed fingers on his left hand.

"If, within 24 hours…Thierry Gaudin announces on television that LyonBio is stopping all…ALL…animal testing…and if we see the GEFCO trucks pull into LyonBio and load all remaining 172 monkeys, then we will not ask little brother Philippe to join his big brother Bernard in the first round of shock testing. If within the first 48 hours, we verify that LyonBio has turned from its evil ways and animal testing has ended at LyonBio, then we will make sure Bernard finds his way back to the café so he can finish his cappuccino. If not, we plan to release our research data in the form of more videos within two days."

The camera zoomed in for a close-up of the spokesman.

"TICK-TOCK, TICK-TOCK."

The picture went dark.

Sainte-Consorce Suburb
Lyon, France

When Lieutenant Colonel Raines, US Navy Captain "Camp" Campbell and retired FBI agent Billy Finn arrived at the Gaudin's house, Marie and Philippe were already in bed and the dining room chairs were filled with Interpol, Europol and Lyon police department officials. Raines had called General Ferguson quickly before she was led out of LyonBio. Ferguson called the SECDEF's office who quickly informed CIA and State. Europol and Interpol were briefed on the international security ramifications of the project, but no specific details were mentioned.

Thierry Gaudin knew what he was manufacturing, but he had no idea who the beneficiary of the vaccines would ultimately be.

Rochelle Gaudin's face was red, and her eyes were swollen. Bernard had only been missing for nine hours, but his mother had endured a lifetime of agony already.

When the Lyon police officers ushered Raines, Camp and Finn into the Gaudin home, Rochelle had no idea who they were, and Thierry only slightly recognized his new client. It was, in fact, "her" project that caused the rhesus monkey deaths. All the money in the world that he might generate for this project was not worth the life of his oldest son Bernard.

"It is finished, Leslie. Done. I want no more part of this project," Thierry said surrendering with his hands and dismissing her arrival. "I know this is a classified project that the Americans want completed, but no more…not with LyonBio, Leslie. Done."

Camp and Finn stood in the back of the dining room as Leslie moved in and sat next to Rochelle.

"Parlez-vous anglais?" Raines asked.

"Yes, I studied two years at Boston College, nice Jesuit school," Rochelle said.

"I'm so sorry about your son. I can only imagine the fear you must be going through."

"What's your name?"

"Leslie…Leslie Raines."

"My name is Rochelle. Do you have children, Leslie?"

Raines paused.

"No…no I don't."

"Then I assure you…you cannot imagine my fear."

"I'm sorry."

"Thierry said this is your project…these were monkeys for *your* experiments…perhaps you can imagine how I must feel about *you* right now."

The Interpol, Europol and Lyon police officers stared at Raines, Camp and Finn with no attempt to hide their disgust.

"Americans!" one of the officers uttered under his breath as the others affirmed the same contempt.

Camp stepped up and over toward Thierry.

"Mr. Gaudin, would it be possible to have a private conversation with you and your wife?"

"I don't even know who you are," Thierry said with

a face full of anguish.

"My name is Camp…I'm a trauma physician…my friend here is Bill, he's an investigator. These police agencies of yours are the best in the business. They have an international reputation, and I'm sure they are working diligently this very minute trying to find your son. Please, sir, may we have five minutes alone with you and Mrs. Gaudin?"

Thierry looked at Rochelle who nodded, so he asked the French officers to step out for a few seconds. They all reached for their cigarette packs and begrudgingly complied.

"I'm going to tell you something that I shouldn't, but I don't think we have any other options at this point," Camp started.

Raines and Finn shot a concerned look over at Camp as Finn started to pace behind the dining room chairs.

"We believe a group wants to launch a biological weapons attack on an entire country. The lives of more than seven million grandparents, children and parents are at stake. Your company was selected to manufacture this vaccine out of thousands of potential companies around the world. You give seven million people their best chance of surviving the unthinkable."

"You want me to trade my son for seven million people?" Rochelle asked as tears welled up in her eyes.

"No, I want you to give us 24 hours to find your son and seven weeks to manufacture this vaccine."

"No. Absolutely not. This program is over," Thierry demanded.

"Then your company is over, Thierry, as well as the future of biomedical research and the hopes of improving human health. It doesn't matter if you use monkeys, beagles, rats, worms or fruit flies, the animal rights extremists will always paint a target on your back. We have to fight extremism wherever it exists. We can fight this, and we can get your son back unharmed. We have a plan."

Thierry was indignant. He didn't want to hear anything Camp had to say.

"How?" Rochelle asked.

Billy Finn stepped in.

"Announce tomorrow morning that you are stopping all research using non-human primates. We have arranged for two GEFCO trucks to return to the loading docks tomorrow morning. The local TV news and newspapers will carry the story immediately."

"I thought you wanted us to continue," Thierry said now thoroughly confused.

"Thierry, I want you to gather up all of the workers who have access to the pilot plant and hold a private meeting with them. Tell them that you must conduct one more test with four more monkeys."

"Four more dead monkeys mean I have a dead son, Mr. Finn," Thierry said as his anger began to boil.

"Leslie will change the test chemical to an anesthesia. The monkeys will fall asleep for a few hours.

They won't be dead."

"What's the point?" Rochelle asked.

"You have employees who have, perhaps unknowingly, caused this to happen."

"That's impossible," Thierry said.

"Thierry…think about it. Someone took video inside the pilot plant on a cell phone camera. No one other than your employees has authorized access. If they took unauthorized video once, then this man or woman will want to take it again, especially if they think you lied on TV."

"So they give the video to these terrorists, and then they kill our son?" Rochelle asked.

"No. We will be monitoring the pilot house to see who your video artist is. They may not know it, but they will lead us to your son," Camp said adding the final components.

"How do you know this will work?" Thierry said as he softened a bit.

"Have *they* offered you a better plan, Mr. Gaudin?" Finn said pointing to the gaggle of Interpol, Europol and Lyon police officers smoking outside on their porch.

"You can do this alone?" Rochelle asked.

"No. I have a friend who runs security for a life sciences company in Switzerland. He's a former MI6 officer with British intelligence. He has more experience with animal rights extremists than anyone else on this planet. This is *his* plan. If you give us the go ahead, he can be here by sunrise," Finn said.

"What about them?" Thierry asked referring to the conclave of investigators in front of his house.

"Let them continue on a parallel path. One of us will find your son," Camp said.

31

LyonBio

Lyon, France

All of the LyonBio employees were gathered in the main lobby of the office complex. A podium was set up outside the glass walls of the executive offices. Media microphones adorned with call flags and logos filled the podium as three TV news crews were positioned with cameras on tripods 30 feet back. Employees gathered on all sides.

Camp and Raines stood in the middle of the throng of onlookers. In the very back of the lobby, Billy Finn was dressed in a janitor's uniform and stood next to another janitor. Marvin Jones had just arrived from Geneva, Switzerland and was quickly outfitted in a LyonBio custodial uniform complete with an ID badge and access cards.

Nobody paid attention to the cleaning crew at

LyonBio. New faces came and went each week depending on which area an employee was working in.

Everybody saw Billy Finn and Marvin Jones, but nobody noticed them.

Thierry Gaudin, the handsome and proud 45-year-old president and chief executive officer of LyonBio exited his office and stepped up to the podium. He clearly had not slept since news of his oldest son's abduction had been given to him the previous afternoon at 4:30pm.

"As you now know, my son Bernard has been abducted. Many of you have seen the video that was posted on the Internet last night. So, it should come as no surprise as I announce that all animal research involving rhesus monkeys has been terminated as of this morning. Two large freight trucks will be arriving at our facilities shortly, and the non-human primates will be removed."

There were gasps in the audience but general approval as well. The employees knew this was a necessary step in order to gain Bernard's release.

Thierry looked into the cameras directly.

"I have done what you've asked…now please do what you have promised. Let my son come home. I would ask all of you to return to your important work and allow the authorities from Interpol, Europol and the Lyon police do their work as well. I will be meeting with each department and the lead scientists throughout the day. We must all continue to work and trust that my son will be released soon and unharmed. Five minutes from now, I would like to meet with all of you who work in the pilot house. Then I will visit the rest of you throughout the morning. Thank you."

Thierry stepped down and slipped back into his office without taking any questions from the media. Through the main entry doors, employees could see two large GEFCO trucks passing the front of the building on the way to the loading docks in the rear.

Billy Finn and Marvin Jones pushed their carts toward the pilot house as Camp followed Raines back to her office where Raines quickly closed the door.

Camp pulled out the two small monitors that Jones had given him at the Lyon Hilton Hotel before they drove in separate cars over to LyonBio.

The video feed from a button camera mounted on Jones' cap was clear and perfect on one TV monitor, and the video feed from the center of Billy Finn's eyeglasses was on the other.

Thierry gathered a small group of 25 employees and cleaning crew in the cramped control room outside the pilot house. Finn and Jones stood on opposite sides and scanned the audience with their bodies, and cameras, as Thierry spoke.

"What I said out front, just a few minutes ago, was not exactly true, and I must apologize to you now. The investigators asked that I say those words hoping to buy more time for my son. I will do anything it takes to bring my boy home, but I will not stop making safe and effective vaccines that keep your children alive and well. If there was a better way than using animals to test for safety and efficacy, I would do it today. But there isn't. This project is too important to stop now. This morning we will have to run one more test on four monkeys, and then we can move this project to manufacturing. I am sorry, but these monkeys will die. I am relying on each of you to be professional. No one must know that we conducted this final test."

Camp and Raines examined the faces of all those gathered. Most seemed to understand Thierry's mission and mandate, but a few looked irritated.

"You *know* what we're doing, Camp," Raines said as she looked at her monitor, "we're profiling."

"Got any better ideas?"

"There…that guy…he looks pissed. Is he pissed at Thierry over the monkeys, or did he break up with his girlfriend last night?" Raines asked.

Finn and Jones worked over the crowd too. Nothing stood out.

"Thank you for your thoughts and concerns. Let's get back to work," Thierry said as he left the pilot house.

The employees went to their workstations as the lead veterinarian asked the animal technicians to bring in four more monkeys. Several employees went to the observation windows, as cages were rolled in and the doors were sealed.

The veterinarian had met with Raines before the mandatory meeting in the lobby. The only thing Raines told him was to change out the lethal project chemical with the aerosolized anesthesia gas. It would look the same, but the monkeys would go down much faster than before when it took a few days before death.

Finn and Jones were positioned on both ends of the observation glass as 16 people gathered to watch the final test that would certainly kill four more monkeys. Raines and Camp watched as well from the monitors in the office behind closed doors.

The gas vapors started to fill the room as the monkeys looked up and started to smell the fumes with abundant curiosity. One sat down, then another, then all four. Within minutes all four were lying down in their cages, apparently dead.

The employees started to peel away as the deed was done. The research had been administered, and the information had been recorded in the tissue samples that would soon be seen under a microscope. A small group of four remained, eyes fixated on the monkeys lying on the bottom of their cages. After one more peeled away, they saw it.

There in the reflection of the observation window glass was an iPhone in the grasp of a young male who was wearing a lab coat. He quickly left the observation area as two others slowly moved away.

Jones carried a broom and walked after the man as Billy Finn went down an opposite hallway. Camp walked quickly out of Raines' office and toward the lobby as Raines stood watching in her doorway.

The young man walked into the main building and over to shipping and receiving, an odd place for a veterinary technician in a lab coat to be. Jones followed the man into the shipping and receiving room and started to gather trash, as Finn swept the floor in the hallway outside the door.

A young woman was filling a vaccine box with bubble wrap and was about to seal the box when the young man in the lab coat walked up to her. He spoke a few words silently then handed her his iPhone. She looked shocked and stunned. The young man left his iPhone with her and exited shipping and receiving as fast as he had arrived. He walked past Jones, who grabbed another trash can to appear busy, and then out into the hallway past Finn and back down to the pilot house.

Jones moved over by the woman who picked up her cell phone and tried to make a discreet call.

"Claude…this is Odette…I have more video…he lied…okay, on my lunch break…give me 30 minutes."

Jones took the trash out into the dumpster that Finn had pushed over and poured it into his can.

"Her name is Odette…she's got the phone… leaving in 30," Jones said as he left Finn and went to the main office.

Thierry's executive secretary was ready and waiting as Jones rushed in with Camp. Thierry stood nearby.

"The girl's name is Odette," Jones said.

"In shipping?" the secretary asked.

"What's her parking badge number, and what does she drive?"

The secretary found Odette's last name and her employee file.

"She's in the Blue lot, farthest away from the building. It's open parking, no assigned spots."

"The car."

"Looking...looking...here it is. Citroen...blue... 2004 model."

Camp and Jones bolted out the front door into Jones' BMW parked in the visitor's section. Finn stayed in the shipping and receiving area and waited for Odette to make her move. Raines identified the male in the lab coat and asked the Interpol officer to detain him.

Odette checked her watch, finished taping one more box, and then walked over to her supervisor.

"Margrit, je vais prendre un dejeuner rapide. Est-ce que ca va?"

"Oui."

Odette walked out the side door and down the sidewalk toward the Blue lot.

"She's out and heading to the parking lot," Finn said quietly in his cell phone.

"Got her," Camp said as he and Jones waited in the back of the Blue lot with the BMW running.

Raines walked back into the main hallway and saw Finn take off his janitor smock and throw it in the trash dumpster. They both ran out the front door and over to Raines' rental car.

Odette pulled out and drove through several streets and into Lyon center as the BMW trailed her from a safe distance. Camp was on the phone with Finn who navigated as Raines drove several miles behind.

Odette stopped her Citroen and parked in a space at the Parc de la Tete d'Or. Golden Head Park was the largest urban park in Lyon and a favorite for locals who loved to stroll around the large lake in the center.

Jones watched from the car as Camp walked in a diagonal direction away from Odette.

Odette pulled out her cell phone and paced back and forth in front of a park bench next to the lake. She closed her phone and sat down.

Jones looked through his binoculars as a young man wearing red glasses, dressed in a black leather jacket walked up and sat down next to Odette. The man consoled her, even put an arm around her, then she reached into her bag and handed him another phone. The man held the iPhone and watched the latest video. Even from 50 yards away, Camp could see the outrage in his body language.

The man with the red glasses and black leather jacket got up abruptly and stormed off as Odette sat on the bench and wiped her eyes with a tissue.

Camp followed him on foot as he left the Golden Head Park and crossed the street to the Lyon Metro, part of the Transports en Commun Lyonnais. The Red Line A train arrived and the man got on. Camp got onto the same car of the train using the Metro tickets he had purchased his first night in Lyon.

Passing the first stop, then the Foch stop, the man exited the Metro at Hotel de Ville and waited for the Orange Line. He was on the northbound side of the platform.

"Jones…we're waiting for the northbound on the Orange Line." Camp closed his phone as Jones pulled out his Metro map. The tires of the BMW lit the pavement as he pressed the speed dial for Finn.

"Start with Cuire, on the Orange, standby from there," Jones said as Raines pulled a u-turn in the middle of the street.

The northbound Orange came, and the man got on. Camp walked on to the next car with a clear view through the glass windows at the man wearing red eyeglasses. The guy was already talking on his phone. Camp hoped that they wouldn't start something stupid with Bernard before he got there.

Three stops up, the man got off the C train at the Henon Metro stop and headed up the stairs to the street.

Camp followed the man as he passed by the De La Croix Rousse Hotel then slid back down a narrow walkway and up the steps to Number 92, Quai Joseph Gillet.

"Ninety-two Quai Joseph Gillet. He just went in." Jones punched the address into his GPS.

"Seven minutes…wait for me."

Jones called Finn with the information as Camp loitered across the street. His mind raced. *What could they possibly do to Bernard in seven minutes,* Camp asked himself. The first three minutes felt like an hour. Camp couldn't wait any longer.

He walked around behind the three-story building. There were three separate sets of stairs leading up to the back door of each apartment. Based on where the red glasses entered, Camp was fairly certain that he needed to be on the second-floor apartment.

Another young man was sitting on the steps at the top of the outside stairs leading to the second-floor apartment and smoking a cigarette. He heard something inside.

"Claude, est-ce vous?"

The man got up, threw his burning cigarette down and went back inside. Camp listened, but never heard the door lock.

Jones pulled up and parked on the street a block down from Number 92 on Quai Joseph Gillen. Finn called Jones and said they were less than two minutes away.

Jones walked up to the front of the building. Camp was nowhere to be seen. Jones knew better than to call Camp on the phone.

"Damn Yank," Jones cursed as he walked up the steps leading to the front door of Number 92.

Camp slid the backdoor open and walked into the kitchen. Dishes were piled high in the sink. The table was covered with cereal boxes and an electric guitar was propped up in one of the chairs.

Camp heard the voices of two men talking in the other room.

He also heard a whimper.

Peering carefully around the edge of the door, he caught a quick glimpse into the main living room. The table had been pushed against the back wall. A black flag with the red letters spelling out SPEAK was pinned to the wall. An Allentown two cage metabolic non-human primate cage, 32-inches wide, 29-inches deep and 32-inches high, sat on the middle of the dining room table.

The cage was empty.

Camp realized that he didn't have a weapon. No weapons on the military transport from Kabul to Tel Aviv with General Ferguson. No weapons on the commercial flight to Lyon when he was exiled to France.

Camp stepped back and looked in the sink. He carefully reached in so as not to disturb the dirty dishes and slowly removed a steak knife and slid it into his back pocket.

The whimpering grew louder.

Looking back into the living room, Camp watched as one of the ski-masked men led Bernard, naked with hands bound behind his back and tape covering his mouth, to the table.

The red glasses man, "Claude" as his cigarette-smoking buddy called him, pressed the record button on the digital camera sitting on the tripod in front of the table and slipped on his ski mask. Claude moved forward and yanked the Allentown cage off the table and threw it onto the floor. Bernard struggled frantically, but the two men placed him onto the table and beneath the flag. A long climbing rope was wound around the table and over Bernard three times, binding his chest and his thighs to the surface.

"You think this is some kind of a joke. We warned you. We told you what the new rules were. Yet, today, today in the video that I'm playing right now, you went ahead and killed four more of our monkey brothers. So…we have no choice…Bernard, your son, will soon be able to tell you how animal research feels."

Claude nodded, and the second man pulled the tape from Bernard's mouth. The boy screamed as a scalpel was raised above his chest.

Jones exploded through the front door with a kick that sent pieces of shattered wood flying into the living room. Camp lunged forward out of the kitchen and was airborne toward the scalpel-wielding terrorist as Jones tackled the man closest to Bernard. Finn ran up and into the apartment as Camp pushed the scalpel out of Claude's hand. Both assailants were easily subdued by a former SEAL, a retired FBI agent and the global head of security for a pharmaceutical company in Switzerland who happened to be former MI6.

"Guys," Raines said with a weak voice as she stood in the doorway to the living room.

The third man had been asleep in his bedroom until

Jones opened the door so rudely with the heel of his boot. By the time the other assailant got his 9mm Glock out of his nightstand, Raines was the only one left he could get to.

The Glock was pressed to the left side of her head, and his other arm was wrapped around the neck of Leslie Raines.

"Se tenir debout," the captor said, motioning for Camp and Jones to stand up and Finn to back away.

Camp let Claude go and stood up slowly. Finn stepped back as Bernard started to cry. Jones slowly rolled off his assailant. He kept his eyes focused on the man holding a gun to the head of Raines. Jones nodded to the man and whispered.

"La police…derriere vous."

The man smiled then an inquisitive look dashed across his unshaved face. Jones pointed and raised an eyebrow again. The silence in the room was deafening.

The man started to turn his head to look for the police behind him.

Jones reached into his jacket and fired his pistol in one sweeping motion hitting the would-be abductor dead center above the eyes. Blood-splatter sprayed over Raines' face as his grip loosened and his crumpled body hit the floor.

Finn tied the assailants up as Raines went to the bedroom to find clothes for Bernard. Camp untied the boy.

"Americans?" Bernard said as he fought back the

tears.

"You're okay now, Bernard." Camp said as Claude and his buddy sat on the floor with ski masks still on and the camera still recording.

"Call your friends from Interpol. The evidence is on the camera," Jones said as he walked toward the front door.

"You're leaving?" Finn asked.

"All that's left is the paperwork. I hate paperwork," Jones said as he bounced down the steps and down one block where his BMW waited for the drive back to Geneva.

32

General Ferguson was plowing through AARs, After-Action Reports, as the two coffee-pouring majors on his staff read through the morning's intelligence briefing.

"Sir, the IAEA got stonewalled this morning in their request to visit Parchin," Major Spann said as Ferguson kept reading reports.

"What else is new?" Ferguson grumbled without looking up. "What's Parchin?"

"Sir, military industrial complex about 30 kilometers southeast of Tehran, part of a test-range for liquid-propellant missile engines."

"That's nice, but doesn't sound nuclear to me. Major, the IAEA operates cameras and conducts regular, and surprise visits, to declared nuclear sites including the

Fordo and Natanz enrichment centers, reactors in Bushehr and Tehran and a uranium metallurgical laboratory in Isfahan. Parshin isn't one of the sites we're interested in."

The two majors were uncomfortable. Spann tried one more time.

"Sir, intelligence suspects they are working on parallel paths, a civilian energy program which they let us monitor, and a parallel military program which is off limits."

"I understand all that, major. I don't require an education."

"Sir, satellite imagery analysis indicates that high-explosive tests were conducted in a specially built chamber at Parchin, a chamber designed to contain components for a nuclear weapon."

Ferguson put his papers down.

"There's more," Major Spann said. "The Iranians are raising the rhetoric bar another notch. They're threatening a first strike against Israel if they feel an Israeli attack is imminent."

"What are the Israelis saying?"

"Nothing today, sir. Oh, and this came in today as well."

Spann handed Ferguson a classified memo from the CIA.

"I'll be damned," Ferguson said as he read the memo. "US Navy Captain Campbell has been officially barred from traveling to Israel on either personal or government business for a period of 180 days…signed by the Director of Central Intelligence."

"Who'd he piss off?" Spann asked.

"Apparently, Special Agent Daniels…Camp got a bit too cozy with the boys from Mossad to suit Mr. Daniels and his lovely sidekick, Fallon Jessup."

Tel Aviv, Israel

Yitzhak handed the phone to Reuven and brought up the field report from Bangkok, Thailand.

"Yes," Reuven said into the phone.

"Looks like the same method as last week in Georgia and India," the female voice on the other side said.

"Iranian hit squad?"

"Yes, sir, not exactly the same, but similar."

"Go on."

"Five bombs in all. We've recovered one that was unexploded. Seems to be a $27 dollar portable radio, easy to buy on the streets. Inside, the radio is packed with tiny ball bearings and six magnets. It sticks easily to the metal on the side of a car."

"Explosive?"

"Looks to be white military-grade explosives with M26 hand-grenade fuse. The assailant pulls the pin from the radio and four and a half seconds later…"

"Smuggled in, or assembled in Bangkok?"

"Probably neither, sir. Our best guess is the diplomatic pouch. Off limits for screening or security."

Reuven hung up the phone, and Yitzhak rolled his chair closer.

"Get on the chain…we want our Ambassador to the UN to complain that Iran is targeting our foreign diplomats."

"Retribution?"

"No, not yet…we need to stall, buy some more time…ask for an international investigation…suggest that Israel will remain committed for months for the international court of public opinion to hold Iran responsible for these acts of unilateral terrorism."

"I'll make the calls," Yitzhak said as he started to roll away.

"Yitzhak…get the sailor routed through to my cell phone."

Qom, Iran

Key members of the Iranian Shura Council had gathered and were sitting on the floor near the marja-i talqid, the one who was chosen for emulation. Senior military officials and members of the intelligence community were seated, as was Ayatollah Yazdi, the spiritual leader in the city of Qom. Yazdi was the one who opposed democratic reforms, the one who was opposed to the people's uprising and the reform movement, and the one who believed that Iran had become too liberal, and too open, since the Revolution in 1979. The Shoeib was seated. He was quiet and introspective. The Supreme Leader was absent, all according to plan. Some from the Assembly of Experts had gathered as well.

Qazvin was present and sitting next to his grandson and famous microbiologist, Kazi.

Omid was sitting among senior military intelligence advisors.

Hot tea was poured, and all shared in subdued fellowship. The talking began to cease though no one had called the meeting to order. The din in the plain white-walled room fell to silence. Yazdi spoke.

"Brothers…the time is upon us…the Age of the Coming is now before our eyes…a well-laid plan must now unfold…may the grace of Allah be revealed in the coming of the Mahdi…the infidels of the Great Satan believe their sanctions can stop what began so long ago with the Prophet's daughter Fatima and Imam Ali… today we have demonstrated that their devices have no power on our Islamic Republic…Iran has, today, cut off oil exports to Britain and France…more nations will be cut off…we do not need Satan's money to do Allah's work…our warships can close the Straits of Hormuz at a moment's notice…our preparations are almost complete…we can soon rain fire down on the Zionist regime according to our will, not theirs…today I announce the date, a date that must not leave this room…the blessed Ali ibn Abi Talib, the cousin and son-in-law of the Prophet, the beloved husband to Fatima, and the first Imam, was born on the 23rd day of October…we shall honor Ali with the revolution…

Brother Markazi, will start the revolution before the appointed day."

The attention in the room shifted to Qazvin who presented his grandson.

"God's peace be upon all of you," Kazi said as choruses of blessings were echoed back to him.

"The wind of torment has been sown and now proven effective in Bourvari, Rasht, the village of Levo, and God willing, in Ajloun before the sun sets tomorrow. On the day that has been appointed, ten days before the Revolution, a festival of Islamic Unity will begin in Beirut, Lebanon. Fifty magnificent hot air balloons will rise into the sky and fly along the coast of the sea to Port Said in Egypt. Television news cameras from all nations will film the festival flight so that our children from all corners of the world will experience our unity. The wind over the Zionist regime pushes in from the sea and over the non-existent land of the Zionists from the north then back south and out to the sea. Like the hands of a clock that starts at 11, the wind pushes to three then back out at seven. The wind of torment shall be released from these 50 balloons at the appropriate time. With international television cameras as our guide and protector, we can come as close to the Zionist coast as we desire. There is no cure for this torment, no protection."

Yazdi nodded to the intelligence commander with MISIRI, the Ministry of Intelligence and Security.

"God's peace be upon you…three days before the

revolution, on the 21st, our Shia brothers in al-Awamiya, a town in the Qatif region of Saudi Arabia, will execute a plan that has been given to them through divine providence. They have unrestricted access to the King. Whether he is killed, injured or escapes, news from around the world will speculate on his fate for nearly two full days. Chaos and confusion will abound in the Saudi kingdom. Rumors and dissension will run through the ranks of the security forces. This will be the moment when our brothers in Yemen begin their push north. They will charge over the border and directly into Mecca where they will reclaim the holy city for the Mahdi."

Yazdi made eye contact with a senior military commander who began to speak.

"God's peace be upon all of you," he said as responses filled the room again. "We will move our Army to the Iraqi border on the 22nd day of October. Early in the morning on the 23rd, God willing, three, perhaps as many as six, nuclear warheads will visit Tel Aviv, Haifa, Beersheba and Ramla. More than 1,000 Shahab missiles will then fly in succession. Beitol Moghadas is a holy city and will be spared from nuclear fire but will receive carefully placed Shahabs. The mighty Iranian Navy will block the Straits of Hormuz. In less than nine minutes, the revolution will be won. The Mahdi's deputy, the Shoeib, will have conquered Israel. May God's name be praised."

Some prayers were offered, and the meeting was

adjourned. Small groups of informal conversation were underway as Yazdi and the Shoeib left the room amidst a large security detail. Omid walked over to Kazi and Qazvin. Qazvin quickly turned his back and walked away.

"This is a very big and important project for you, Kazi," Omid said.

Kazi shook his head as a disgusting scowl smeared across his face.

"But much too big of a project for you, Colonel Farid."

Kazi turned and walked away.

33

Lyon, France

Billy Finn was sound asleep in his double-sized bed at the Lyon Hilton Hotel when his cell phone rang. He let it go to voice mail. The phone quickly started ringing again. He recognized the area code, 212, as New York City.

"Finn," he answered simply and concisely from his grog.

"Billy, did I wake you?"

"No, ah, I mean, yes, who is this?"

"Susan Francis in New York."

"Susan?"

"What! Did you take stupid pills after you retired? Susan Francis, intel, New York field office?"

Finn sat up in bed wide awake.

"Oh my gosh, Susan, I'm sorry. I didn't recognize your voice. It's three in the morning here."

"Sorry, Billy, I was just getting ready to head home myself when I got a strange call. I had your home phone and called your wife. She said you were trolling the hills of Afghanistan as a DOD civilian. She gave me your number."

"Well, actually I'm in Lyon, France right now but probably heading back to Kabul in a couple of weeks. Is everything okay?"

"Fine, but I got this call and needed to tell you about it. I got a call from Pablo."

Finn's mind wandered at full speed. *Who the hell is Pablo?*

"He was patched in from several connections for security purposes – his and ours – we spoke only briefly."

"What did he want?"

"He implied that the two of you recently met. I know that sounds ridiculous, but that's what he said."

Finn paused for what seemed like an eternity. *Pablo!* He wasn't sure how he should answer.

"Finn?"

"Yes, I did meet Pablo. Completely by chance. We even talked about your father and his colon cancer."

Now Susan Francis was silent.

"Were the two of you camping? He said he wanted 'camp' and gave me some numbers for you to call...to get in touch with him. He said it was urgent."

"Give me the numbers, Susan...I think I know what he wants."

Francis gave him three numbers and the associated codes then bid him goodnight.

"Billy, don't get too involved with Pablo. His intelligence door swings both ways, if you know what I mean."

Finn ended the call on his cell and immediately called Camp on the hotel phone.

"What?" came an agitated and sleepy voice on the other end of the line.

"Get your ass down to my room right now. Omid is looking for you."

Tel Aviv, Israel

Reuven walked slowly in the setting sun along the tan sands of the Mediterranean Sea on Metzitzim Beach. He paused and looked out over the sea as the sun seemed to set between Morocco and the Rock of Gibraltar. His heart was heavy. Reuven had two young sons and a lovely wife, but all of his energy, all of his passion, was invested in preserving his country. The entire Middle East seemed to be sitting on a powder keg, ready to explode at any moment.

He had been hopeful that democracy would rise in Iraq and provide stability to the region. But the Americans left hastily with little "shock" and no "awe" while a fledgling Iraq was left to battle pockets of terrorism and internal Shia-Sunni rivalries alone.

At first glance, the Arab Spring uprising in Egypt seemed to be an authentic yearning of the people to have their freedom, but the rise of the Muslim Brotherhood gave Reuven great caution. He knew that Egypt was only tolerating Israel under Mubarak, thanks in no small part to American foreign aid. God only knew what might come up from the south with a new Egyptian government in place or fewer American dollars in the Egyptian treasury.

Muammar Gaddafi's 42-year reign in Libya came to an abrupt end as rebels, with the assistance of NATO airstrikes, tracked Gaddafi's motorcade down, marched him through the streets, and finally administered a judge, trial and jury with a single gunshot to the head inside a drainage pipe. Reuven knew that no matter the political leanings of the rebels that seized control of Libya, they certainly would not attempt to be friends of Israel.

Reuven's head turned and looked to the north as he stood next to the sea. In his mind he could see the flames of war coming from Syria as a resistance movement in the city of Homs endured untold bloodshed while refugees streamed into Turkey and Jordan. Syria was closely aligned with Iran and would do Iran's bidding as proxy soldiers in whatever cause was deemed proper.

Hezbollah, literally the Party of God, stood less than 134 miles away from Reuven as he walked. Armed with as many as 15,000 Katyusha rockets, 1,000 soldiers and tens of thousands of sympathetic volunteers, Hezbollah would march on Israel in a moment's notice.

Is it really worth all of this? Reuven thought as he

walked and waited for his phone to ring. All he wanted was to raise his sons in peace, to love his wife and to provide for his family. *Was that too much to ask?*

"Yes," Reuven said as he answered the incoming call that was patched in from three separate transmitters and relay switches from around the globe.

"Shepherd's Pie for Molly Bloom," Camp said.

"Hello, Shepherd. We need to meet," Reuven asserted.

"Well, that might be difficult. The King of Ireland informs me that I'm not welcome in your pub for at least six months."

"So I hear."

"I want you to meet someone," Camp said.

"That won't be possible for obvious reasons."

"I like impossible. I just spoke with him. We have arranged for a dinner in the booth next to yours. Perhaps we could have three beers? You'll be close enough to look through the glass in your mug. Maybe you'll join us then? "

"Sorry. Not possible."

Camp got angry with Reuven. He was tired of hearing why things would not work, why situations were impossible. Camp was a glass half-full kind of man. Anything was possible. "No, of course not, let's just eat a plate full of the regime's jalapenos and let them burn our mouths."

Reuven was silent. Camp assumed he wasn't accustomed to yielding control.

"I will send you instructions," Reuven finally said.

"No! I will send you the damn menu. Order what you like," Camp said as he slammed his phone shut.

Hilton Hotel
Lyon, France

Billy Finn looked up at Camp who was pacing the balcony at the Hilton Lyon Hotel as Finn took another bite from his bagel with cream cheese.

"That went well."

Camp said nothing. He just paced.

"You didn't even mention that you've spoken with Omid."

"Because I don't have a clue what Omid wants in the first place. Omid and I talked for a few minutes. He said we should meet at the Four Seasons in Amman, Jordan – in the steam sauna no less. Omid said he had something he must tell me. I asked him for a clue, a bone, anything I could hang my hat on and justify the encounter," Camp said as his voice trailed off and lost in his own thoughts.

"What did he say?" Finn asked.

"One word. He said just one word. Armageddon."

Finn got up and pulled a scotch out of the mini-bar, twisted the cap off and poured it down his throat.

"That can't be good," Finn said as he dropped the empty bottle into the tin trash can.

"For all I know, Reuven and his Mossad buddies will gladly kill me *and* Omid if they get a chance," Camp said as he sat on the edge of the bed.

"Or if they need to," Finn added.

"What the hell is that supposed to mean?"

"I'm just saying…sometimes when a guy knows too much…sometimes he just needs to go away…makes life simpler."

"Mossad isn't just going to 'off' a US Navy Captain, Finn, be real."

"Well, maybe that's what Omid intends to do. Maybe he's regretting that he told *you* too much."

Camp stopped dead in his tracks. Omid did call Camp and went to great lengths to find him. Reuven called Camp as well and went all the way around the earth to hide the call.

"Then what do I do?" Camp finally asked.

"Hide…hide out in the open…with both of them."

The Village of Al Wahadinah
Ajloun, Jordan

The men who had sprayed their village for the bugs that were damaging their plants had left nearly four hours earlier. But everyone living near the first three homes sprayed was already sick.

Bacterial infection from the spray had affected adults, children and the elderly rapidly. The infection happened from contact through the skin, mucous membranes, gastrointestinal tracts and inhalation through the lungs. The infection was intracellular, meaning the bacterium multiplied once inside the body. Within hours, the tularemia struck the people of Al Wahadinah in their lymph nodes, lungs, liver, spleen and kidneys. Once inside the mucous membranes or even on the skin, the infection spread faster than they could wash themselves, and long before they could seek help.

The initial tissue reaction to the tularemia was immediate and pronounced. Red spots and open ulcers formed rapidly. A simple lesion quickly became granulomatous, a massive clump of ulcerated and infected cells.

For those victims who inhaled the mist as it was sprayed, their airways were filled with blood-hemorrhaging inflammation. They couldn't get air because their passageways were swollen shut. Fever, sweats, chills, fatigue, body aches and diarrhea were universal symptoms throughout the village.

The young and the elderly couldn't handle the onset of such sudden and dramatic illness. The older children and adults in good health were extremely ill but would survive if they could get medical attention and antibiotics within a reasonable amount of time.

Tularemia, the wind of torment, was more lethal as a weapon of fear than it was as an instrument of death. The reduced probability of lethality was of little comfort to an entire village that believed they were sick to death.

Word spread through surrounding villages and into Ajloun, the capital town in the governorate and throughout the 27 villages and towns in the hilly area, then 47 miles southeast to Amman, Jordan.

Some thought a plague had been unleashed.

Others speculated that the sins of one village had brought God's wrath and judgment as it did in the days of Sodom and Gomorrah.

Health officials and doctors refused to travel to Al Wahadinah. It was, after all, a predominantly Christian village, filled with infidels who consumed contaminated meat and the unclean that drank dirty water. What did filthy people expect?

The Ajloun Castle ruins sat high on the hills overlooking the governorate and all of the villages. The castle stood as testament to the great warrior Saladin who pushed back the Crusaders at Ajloun, just as the Moabite King Eglon defeated the Hebrews on the same holy ground.

Surely God was showing his anger, as only one village – a Christian village – suffered with unimaginable illness, as no one – neither friends, neighbors nor government officials – came to their aid.

34

LyonBio
Lyon, France

Lieutenant Colonel Leslie Raines, US Navy Captain "Camp" Campbell and retired FBI agent Billy Finn were huddled in the executive offices with a much-relieved and revitalized Thierry Gaudin. The Frenchman wasn't nearly as ready to get back to work as the three Americans were. Raines pushed hard for production schedules from manufacturing.

"Thierry, you understood the timeframe when you accepted the project."

"Leslie, I know, but we have had set-backs and too much drama. It can't be done. Five million doses in seven weeks? By October fifth? Impossible. We haven't even done a human clinical trial."

"We've been over this, Thierry," Raines said as she got closer to her threshold of patience. "The human clinical can be waived. This is an emergency situation. We have no choice."

"Not if LyonBio's name is on the product. It must have a clinical trial."

"How many?" Camp asked.

"One trial is sufficient I suppose, given these circumstances.   But finding patients who might randomly be exposed to inhalation tularemia is not something you can just run an advert for on the Internet."

"What about volunteers?   What if we find volunteers who would be willing to take the vaccine and then be exposed to the bacteria?" Camp pressed.

Thierry smiled.

"Sure, do you really think 20 people from Lyon would be willing to take 50 Euros to see whether or not they will get infected by a bio-weapon?"

"What about three people? What if three people would take the vaccine right now and step into the pilot house to see what happens?"

Raines and Finn snapped their heads around to face Camp.

"Ah, I don't know what you're thinking, but change that number to two. This old boy ain't stepping into the rabbit fever chamber," Finn said as he got up and distanced himself from Camp.

"Camp!" Raines said quietly and directly.

"Come on, Les…did you create a vaccine-resistant tularemia or not?"

"I did."

"And did you then create a super vaccine that kicked that bacteria's butt?"

"Yes, but –"

"But nothing. I believed in you from the first day I met you, from the day you rescued my rear end after I borrowed 200 rats from Uncle Sam. Come on, it'll be fun."

"Fun? Have you gone insane?"

"Have you got a better idea?"

Raines was silent.

"Wait, even if the vaccine makes you immune from the tularemia, there's still no way that we can manufacture, package, ship and deliver five million injectibles by early October," Thierry said.

The reality was sinking in. The mission was too big.

"Injectibles...Les, why does it have to be a vaccine injection? Can we make these things sublingual?" Camp said as he found new energy.

"Sub what?" Finn asked.

"Sublingual, tiny droplets under the tongue," Camp explained.

"A solution of the vaccine hits the floor of the mouth as tiny droplets," Raines explained. "The mouth is full of high density blood cells in the mucous membranes there. Immune system cells capture the vaccine and migrate them quickly throughout the body. The impact on the lungs would be immediate. A sublingual *could* disseminate immunity to a broader range of organs in a faster amount of time."

"Did you say time? We need time," Camp said with a school-boy grin.

"It might even be better than a nasal spray. No complications in the central nervous system."

"But would it be efficacious?" Thierry asked. "Will it work?"

"Let me worry about that," Raines said as she stood up. "Can you produce five million sublingual doses by October first?"

Thierry dropped his head.

"There are too many variables…too many unknowns. I cannot guarantee anything."

"But will you try?" Raines pleaded.

"Yes…I'll try."

Raines and Camp headed for the door as Finn followed from a distance.

"Thierry, we will need you to clear out the pilot house for a few hours tomorrow morning. There's not enough time to test a sublingual but we can test an IM, intramuscular injection of the vaccine," Raines said as they left the room.

Camp and Raines walked past the personal protective equipment staging area and over to the vapor-locked door leading into the BSL-3 chamber inside the pilot house as Finn went into the control room. Two LyonBio employees were sitting at their chairs, studying charts and more likely than not talking about Bernard. They didn't realize that the 'janitor' was now in the room. Finn saw all that he needed to know, just as Raines had told him. Because of contamination to their clothing, skin and hair, Camp and Raines couldn't go into the chamber like monkeys. The red lever would activate the misting system that pulled the vaccine resistant strain of the tularemia bacterium out of the holding tank. Six seconds later a fine mist would fill breathing tubes directly into their lungs as they would have to pinch their nostrils to avoid general release of the toxins. Finn's job was easy. He was supposed to release a toxin, a bio-weapon recipe that Raines had cooked up, an enhanced tularemia concoction that had never before existed on the earth naturally. More than an illness producing bacteria, the weapon had lethal potential, especially among the weakest who inhaled the microbes.

Finn could only hope that the vaccine was more powerful than the poison.

Raines and Camp paused at the vapor-lock doors as other employees came and went. She pulled two syringes out of her lab coat and handed one to Camp. She rolled up her sleeve and tore open an alcohol swab and cleaned her arm. Camp paused then carefully stuck the needle into her arm, pushing the plunger in gently as the vaccine worked its way into her system. Camp pulled his sleeve up and dabbed his own skin with another swab. Raines pulled the cap off the needle and injected the vaccine into US Navy Captain "Camp" Campbell.

Finn walked out of the command center and joined them by the door.

"I'm going to head to the lab and get started on the sublingual," Raines said. "I've got to do a lot of research and make several calls. Let's call it as 0930 hours tomorrow morning. I want these vaccines to bake in our bodies for 24-hours."

"Aye, aye ma'am."

"Camp…this is an attenuated vaccine derived from avirulent *Francisella tularensis*. It's not dense, and it's not pathogenic. But it's not Type B either. It's a hybrid. I want you to take these with you."

Camp held out his hand as Raines loaded him up with some tablets.

"If you get sick, feel the least bit odd, take the streptomycin. If you feel real bad, chances are that I will too. Finn get him back here immediately, and we'll hook up two doxycycline IV's and see if we can knock it down."

"Les, why don't we just stay together?" Camp said with a hint of romantic intention.

"I'm racing against the clock, sailor. I need you and your sorry-ass FBI friend to get out of my hair."

Raines winked at Finn as Camp reached out to touch her hand before the two men walked out of the pilot house and into the parking lot for the ride back to the Hilton Lyon Hotel.

General Ferguson got the SIPRNET email Camp sent from his hotel room just as he and the coffee-pouring majors were about to head over to the DFAC for dinner.

"SITREP: *Sir, everything back on track with LyonBio. Human clinical trial underway. Slight change of plans for delivery method. Not enough time for injectibles, so Raines is back in the lab creating a sublingual version. It's within the realm of possible / hopeful. V/R, Camp.*"

LyonBio
Lyon, France

D ressed in her white lab coat, Raines was busy concocting a sublingual version of her tularemia vaccine. Once she had perfected it, Thierry Gaudin knew that she would need to put four more rhesus monkeys back into the pilot house BSL-3 chamber just to make sure under-the-tongue droplets really worked.

Thierry was already working his rosary beads and praying for the health of monkeys.

Camp and Finn arrived at her lab just before 9:00am. They were carrying their backpacks.

"Ready?" Raines asked as she put her work down and checked her watch.

"You're already at it, Raines?" Finn asked.

"What makes you think I ever went back to my apartment last night?" she said. "I can sleep when I'm dead."

She noticed Camp's pack on the floor. "Going somewhere sailor?"

"I had a call last night...from a friend Finn and I

met up in the Hindu Kush…he needs to speak with me, Les. He wouldn't say what, but he's pretty bent out of shape."

"So you're heading back to the Hindu Kush?"

"Not exactly, we're going to hook up in the Middle East."

Raines dropped her face into her hands.

"Oh, good, the Middle East…well that narrows it down for me. Why didn't you just say that in the first place, Camp?"

Raines stormed off and pulled some data up on her computer screen.

"Geez, you're a bit on edge this morning."

"Sorry, just trying to invent a sublingual vaccine to save a few million people. Normal hectic day at the office, sorry, my bad."

"You've got everything under control here, Les. What are we supposed to do? Just stand around and watch you think?"

"Under control? You and I are about to inhale a poisonous toxin. In five hours we might be in the local emergency room. Hell, we could be in the morgue for all I know. And you think you're going to have a little dose of inhalation bio-weapon and just be on your way to the airport!"

"Ah, I'm gonna go grab a mocha, anybody want one?" Finn said as neither Camp nor Raines acknowledged his departure.

"Maybe you've forgotten, but you are on a federal

'do not fly' list into Israel. Have you noticed that most people aren't thrilled with your freelance work? Count me in as one of them."

"I'm not flying to Israel, Leslie."

"Well, that sure narrows down the choices, then."

"Les, I found an Army major with a slug in his brain, stuffed in a frozen shed. He was a gynecologist for God's sake, two kids and a wife…a private practice back in Pennsylvania…it's the least I can do for the guy."

"Camp, you were sent to Lyon…to assist me…need I remind you that you received a direct order?"

"I've been assisting you, Les. Seriously, what more can I do for you? I even let you stick me with the vaccine and became your human guinea pig. If you haven't figured out that I'm crazy about you yet, then you never will."

Camp picked up his backpack and headed to the door. For the first time he second-guessed himself. Maybe he couldn't be the man, let alone the friend, that Lieutenant Colonel Leslie Raines deserved, much less needed.

"Let's get this over with," Camp said as he pulled a water bottle out of his pack. Camp felt foolish and dejected. Raines was out of his league. She had all the intellectual heft and measured her pace with precision. He was just a former SEAL, a knock-the-doors-down sort of a guy, who left piles of debris for others to clean up when the mission was over.

Raines didn't budge. "How crazy?"

Camp turned around and softened a bit. He grasped at any sign of hope.

"Insane crazy, Les…I love you."

Her lower lip started to quiver as she folded her lab coat-covered arms against her chest. Tears dripped down Leslie's cheeks. Camp dropped his bag, moved in close and held her tightly. Tugging her buried face up from his chest Camp kissed her lips as a familiar voice thundered from the corridor and into the lab.

"Three freaking Euros for this little coffee. Damn French," Finn spouted as he walked in, observed the embrace and kiss, then spun a quick u-turn. "Geez! Pick your poison guys, love or rabbit fever? It's 0930, the pilot house is ours. Are we going to do this thing, or not!"

Finn walked out of Leslie's office followed by Camp and Raines as they walked the short corridor to the pilot house. Finn took his place in the control room. Thierry had cleared out all employees and sat next to Finn.

Two transparent and clear vinyl breathing tubes protruded out of the inner chamber of the pilot house and into the personal protective equipment staging area. Camp put the breathing tube in his mouth and pinched his nostrils. Raines closed her eyes, said a quick prayer, and did the same. Both nodded to the control room.

Finn reached for the red lever and gently pulled it down.

35

Bird-in-Hand, Pennsylvania

Seabury and Ruth Campbell were sitting in their living room watching the evening news on CBS. Old Sea Bee was sitting in his well-worn recliner. A 1970s era metal folding TV tray was propped up in front of his chair with a half-eaten bowl of vanilla ice cream starting to melt. Every 30 seconds or so Sea Bee would pick up the crossword puzzle book that Ruth had picked up for him in the checkout line at the Dollar General. He never wrote in the book, but he picked it up frequently. He never saw anything on the pages, but he looked each time. He studied it, always looking for something.

Ruth sat in her velour rocker next to Sea Bee working her long-needled hook crochet project. The ladies' auxiliary at the church had a bazaar the first Saturday of every month to help support the benevolence fund. Hundreds of people in the county were unemployed. Many families were losing their homes to foreclosure. Gasoline prices were rising at the pump. The trucks that hauled milk from the farms to the processors and then out to the stores were paying almost 50-cents more per gallon than the previous year. The cost of milk shot up as did the cost of bread, eggs and flour and just about everything else in the aisles at every supermarket. Now, it seemed like there was no end in sight as to how high fuel prices might climb. The Keystone Pipeline from Canada was stuck on paper thanks to an aquifer in Nebraska. Libyan oil production was uncertain after the execution of one dictator and a revolution by rebels. Another dictator controlled oil production in South America while many there hoped for a new crop of rebels with similar intent. American forces crossed their fingers as military convoys exited Iraq and entered Kuwait, all the while hoping that oil fields would produce rather than burn. American farmers put their corn crops into ethanol production which sent the cost of consumption corn through the roof.

And then there was Iran. They refused to sell anymore oil to the United Kingdom or France in a pre-emptive move as European Union nations prepared to punish Iran with crippling sanctions. Iran tried to sell their over-production to fossil-fuel-hungry India until Turkish refineries stepped in and rejected Iranian crude. Saudi Arabia increased oil production and supply, but

OPEC prices per barrel spiked and jumped on a trajectory that might not level off. The economic boom in China created what most had doubted would ever happen: a burgeoning middle class of more than 300 million Chinese to go along with one billion other peasants and aristocrats. As the middle class expanded, the taste for luxury automobiles, modern appliances and food with animal protein skyrocketed. The entire world coveted energy, massive amounts of energy, and the world was just beginning to realize what the residents from Bird-in-Hand, Pennsylvania already knew. There wasn't enough supply to meet the demand. There weren't enough jobs to pay for that demand and not enough pay to satisfy the bankers who demanded that mortgages be satisfied.

But the world had one commodity that was in abundant supply: uncertainty.

Ruth thought about all of it. The more she thought, the faster her crochet hook moved.

Sea Bee picked up the crossword puzzle book then set it down. He wasn't thinking at all.

"And from Brussels today," the CBS News anchorman reported as Ruth looked up and Sea Bee stared straight ahead, *"the Secretary of Defense is speculating that Israel may launch a pre-emptive first strike on Iran soon. The leak by the Defense Secretary is widely seen as an attempt to publicly pressure Israel to give sanctions and diplomacy more time to work. Israel, on the other hand, may be concluding that the window of first strike opportunity is rapidly closing. Experts*

fear that the Iranians may have stored enough enriched uranium in underground facilities to make as many as six nuclear weapons."

"This is a real mess," Ruth said as she watched the news and talked back to the television.

"Israel, meanwhile, is testing their 'iron dome' anti-ballistic missile defense system over Tel Aviv. With longer range rockets being produced by Iran and supplied to militants in the Gaza Strip, Tel Aviv is now within rocket range. Israeli Defense Forces claim they could have a 75-percent kill rate of incoming Iranian rockets."

"Junior's over there somewhere, you know," Ruth said to Sea Bee who did not respond.

"According to senior Israeli government officials, more than 200,000 rockets and missiles are pointed at Israel by enemy countries every day," the news continued.

"They're gonna just blow that place up, aren't they?" Ruth said.

"While UN sanctions are starting to sting within the increasingly isolated Iranian regime, the Chairman of the Joint Chiefs told a press briefing at the Pentagon today that he believes Iran is still a rational actor and will eventually get in line with the will of the world community."

"Who told him to say that?" Ruth spouted at the TV screen as CBS News went to a commercial break.

Sea Bee picked up the crossword puzzle book, gave it a look, and set it back down, right next to a bowl of ice milk on the metal TV tray.

36

Queen Alia International Airport
Amman, Jordan

The Royal Jordanian jetliner arriving from Lyon, France taxied to the terminal as US Navy Captain "Camp" Campbell and Billy Finn, dressed in 5.11 tactical khakis, desert boots and casual polos, stood in the exit queue on the plane.

The terminal emptied out into the customs bay where Camp and Finn exchanged a wad of Euros for Jordanian Dinars. They presented blue-jacket American tourist passports and told the customs official they were visiting for pleasure, planning a three-day trip to see Petra and other famous sites in Jordan.

They got into the backseat of the taxi for the 18-mile ride to the Four Seasons hotel in Amman, the capital city of Jordan. It was dusk, and campfires were blazing on both sides of the highway as people parked their cars, trucks and camels for evening picnics. Camp looked out the window and saw a blonde woman, maybe 25 years old, dressed in a pink shirt, and riding atop a camel as the owner made a few tourist dollars from a passing taxi.

"Finn, care for a camel ride before we get to the hotel?" Camp asked.

"I'm good," Finn said shaking his head.

The taxi pulled through the wealthy Al Sweifiyah residential neighborhood at the outskirts of the Al Shmeisani financial district and into the Four Seasons pull-through driveway. The hotel was impressive, a crown jewel, sitting atop the hills overlooking Amman.

The bell captain put their two small backpacks on an enormous polished brass luggage cart and took them into the first security checkpoint. The bags were run through a security scanner. A walk-through metal detector greeted Camp and Finn followed by a full body pat down.

The Jordanians had grown intolerant of suicide bombers at the hotels and resorts that attracted international tourists of every language and culture.

With room keys in hand, Camp and Finn found the Square Bar just off the lobby galleria and grabbed two chairs away from other patrons.

Arabs, Americans, Asians, Europeans and Africans were all enjoying cocktails and snacks, in the middle of the bar, in the middle of the capital city, in the middle of a progressive and moderate Islamic country.

"So what's the plan?" Finn asked as his Amstel Light was delivered.

Camp spoke in hushed and subdued tones.

"He said he was coming in from Islamabad through Istanbul."

"Probably on a Pakistani passport," Finn speculated.

"Didn't ask. Wants us to rent a car from the hotel. Doesn't want his credit card used or anything else to track him."

"Is he staying here?"

"Don't know. I assume so. This is where he said we'd meet tonight."

"When?" Finn asked.

"Nine tonight. He said they have a spa, a steam sauna. Guess we're going to strike up a casual conversation while we're naked in the sauna."

"And if you're not alone?"

"Don't know that either."

"What about your Molly Bloom friend?"

"I told him to contact me tonight."

"Does he know where we are?"

"Yes."

LyonBio
Lyon, France

Raines watched the wall clock in her lab move closer to 8:00pm in Lyon. The days on the calendar seemed to be moving faster than the hands on the clock.

Raines thought back to her break-through moment at Fort Detrick. It was the adjuvants. Adjuvants helped her boost the immune response to the tularemia which ultimately prevented the monkeys from dying.

A vaccine adjuvant was a substance added to a vaccine to increase the body's immune response to the toxin. Aluminum gels and aluminum salts were the only approved adjuvants licensed for use in the United States. Small amounts of aluminum helped stimulate a better immune response.

Raines needed to move beyond alum adjuvants and felt constrained by US rules. That's when LyonBio moved to the forefront, as well as an adjuvant called squalene.

In early drug discovery, vaccines contained a weakened, or even dead, pathogen of the same disease the vaccine was supposed to prevent. The pathogen itself forced the body to fight off further infection and therefore became a natural immune booster. Modern vaccines used proteins, or protein fragments from the pathogen, which made them more pure, safer and quicker to produce.

During Raines' first attempts at producing a new tularemia vaccine, the protein fragments she used – instead of weakened or dead complete pathogens – left too many holes missing from the whole bacteria. The missing parts caused an insufficient immune response.

The adjuvants provided the boost she needed. But she didn't use aluminum. Dr. Groenwald recommended she try squalene.

Squalene was a natural organic compound found in both shark liver oil as well as plant-based oils like rice bran, wheat germ and olives. Squalene was one of the key components of the Mediterranean diet and was found naturally in animals, plants and humans. By using the oil-in-water emulsions of squalene, Raines would not only be able to boost the immune response, but she hoped she could produce four-times as many doses from the same amount of protein fragments.

Squalene was the greatest weapon in her biomedical arsenal. She prayed that it would be faster, more effective and much more powerful than bio-weapons, nuclear bombs and intercontinental ballistic missiles, at least in the short-term.

In the temporary French laboratory that belonged to Lieutenant Colonel Leslie Raines, the only thing that stood between the mutual annihilation of two countries was olives, wheat germ and shark liver oil.

As two long-time enemies stared each other down with bio-weapons and the threat of nuclear destruction, one biomedical researcher prepared to out-maneuver them both with shark liver oil. It was all on Leslie Raines' shoulders.

37

Four Seasons Hotel
Amman, Jordan

Camp got his locker key and was issued a large white Turkish towel from the spa attendant and quickly got undressed. The hiss and whoosh sounds of the nearby steam sauna already felt good on Camp's deep tension.

The sounds of another man in the locker room were distinct and clear. He wasn't alone.

For a split second, Camp thought about the defensive moves he'd take if the man was in fact Omid, and if Omid had arranged this elaborate meeting scheme just to eliminate a man who knew too much.

No one emerged from the other aisle of lockers. No knife appeared from around the corner. Camp covered himself with the towel, walked over to the steam sauna and pulled on the glass door.

He stepped up to the tiled upper level of the sauna and moved to the corner of the intersecting walls. He was at the farthest point away from the only door, his only avenue of escape. And he was all alone.

Camp's mind wandered off as tension and fatigue began to melt away. His nostrils and airwaves opened up magically as the eucalyptus penetrated his every pore.

The glass door opened, sucking the humidity and relaxation out before restoring them both on closing.

Camp never opened his eyes. His face was clearly visible. If this was Omid, he would recognize Camp. If it wasn't, he didn't really need to gaze at a naked man covered in a white Turkish towel anyway.

Several minutes passed. Eyes were closed. Hiss. Whoosh. Hiss. Whoosh.

"You shaved your beard."

Camp smiled. It was Omid.

"I wanted to get pretty again."

"Nice hotel, isn't it?" Omid asked.

"It is. Thanks for the recommendation."

"Do you eat breakfast?"

"Occasionally."

The door opened, and two more men walked into the steam sauna. They passed Omid who was sitting next to the door and sat on the upper tiled bench between Camp and the wall. They spoke to each other in German.

"Then you really should try Caffe Mokka on Al-Qahira Street. Incredible patisseries, and they start serving sweet cakes at eight in the morning."

"Thanks for the idea. I may give it a try."

Camp and Omid remained silent for another 20 minutes as the Germans continued to talk and laugh. Camp stepped down off the tile bench first and out through the glass door. He changed in the locker room, returned his key, and rode the elevator up to the ninth floor where he called Billy Finn.

Camp was soon sound asleep when his cell phone rang at nearly three in the morning.

"Yes?"

"Shepherd's Pie?"

Camp sat up fully awake with an instant jolt of electricity.

"Hello Molly Bloom."

"What did you want to order from the menu today?"

"Three orders of Gesher, to go, right about noon."

"Three?"

"I'm hungry."

"That's not possible."

"Oh, that's where you're wrong Molly Bloom. It's very possible. Three orders of Gesher, to go, around noon. I'm very hungry and I'll do anything to have this meal. I said…anything…I'll call the waitress as we're pulling up."

Camp closed his phone and threw a pillow over his head.

Caffe Mokka
Amman, Jordan

Billy Finn drove the car that he and Camp rented from the Four Seasons Hotel. Within 30 minutes, they had navigated morning rush hour traffic and pulled curbside in front of the Caffe Mokka restaurant.

Through the restaurant windows they could see many customers seated and eating. School children passed by on the sidewalks as the elderly and several women in full burka's stopped and chatted with each other.

"So are we going in or what?" Finn asked.

"I don't know…he didn't say…let's wait here a few minutes."

A woman in a black burka, leaning against the wall of the Caffe Mokka, walked toward the car carrying a vegetable bag. She grabbed the backdoor car handle, opened it and got into the backseat behind Finn and Camp.

"Drive," the male voice said from beneath the burka.

Finn put the car in gear and followed the second set of GPS coordinates that Camp had entered at the hotel. Twenty miles past Naour and heading southwest on Highway 40, Finn turned north on Highway 65.

"We're out of the city," Camp said to his backseat passenger.

Omid pulled the burka up and over his head, straightened his hair and put the sunglasses and a New

York Yankees baseball cap on that were inside his vegetable bag.

"You can pull over anywhere along here. We should be good," Omid said.

"We're gonna drive for another hour…just to make sure," Finn said as he looked into the rearview mirror. "Nice to see you again, Omid."

"Good morning, Mr. Finn. I hope you didn't mind that I contacted Susan Francis. I had no other way."

"Susan is the best. She uses the utmost discretion as I'm sure you already know."

"I do. Thank you."

"So what's this all about, Omid? You looking for some more freelance business and thought you'd try your two favorite Americans first?" Camp asked.

Omid laughed.

"Yes, I've really developed my cricket skills as of late and was hoping you could arrange a try-out with the Yankees."

"The Bronx Bombers are always looking for a good second baseman in a pinstriped burka," Finn added.

The three enjoyed some small-talk banter as they drove up Highway 65. They talked about the Hindu Kush, US Army Major Dean Banks and the latest sports news. The northern most end of Highway 65 was coming into view as dirt roads started to split off on each side.

"This is the end of the road, Finn. I've been up here before," Omid said as he examined the countryside outside of his backseat window.

"Officially or unofficially?" Camp asked.

Omid smiled. "Seriously, we need to pull-over and talk. I've got some things I need to talk through with you both."

Finn turned west onto a dirt road as Camp pulled out his phone. A woman answered the call.

"Tell Molly Bloom that we're ready for lunch," Camp said as he closed the phone.

Finn pressed harder on the accelerator.

"There's no restaurants out here, Camp," Omid said with tension rising in his voice.

"Not true," Camp said as Finn's speed increased.

Omid was panicked.

"What the hell are you doing? There's an Israeli check-point in less than a mile."

"Gesher?" Camp asked.

"Yes, Gesher…PULL OVER!"

The car cleared the narrow dirt road and into an open clearing that was blocked by a fully-armed Israeli checkpoint. Omid slid down to the backseat floorboard. Finn slowed the car and cautiously approached the first security officer. The man did not approach the car. He didn't even look inside the vehicle. The first gate was raised. Finn drove slow to the second gate which was raised as well. Finn drove the rental car through a zigzag pattern of cement barriers where two men stood in front of the third and final gate.

Finn stopped the car.

Three black Suburbans were parked just beyond the third gate. Camp opened his car door as did Finn.

"Get up, Omid," Camp said.

Reuven and Yitzhak were expressionless as Finn and Camp approached.

"I thought you had three to-go orders today," Reuven said with a raised eye-brow for Camp.

"I do."

Camp looked back at the rental car as Omid's face finally emerged from the floorboard. Yitzhak pulled his sunglasses off and squinted in disbelief. Reuven looked at the man exiting the car and walking toward him, then back at Camp.

"Now this *is* impossible," Reuven said.

Yitzhak motioned to Finn. "You ride with me and my driver in number one. You two with my colleague here in number two."

Omid had an evil, almost terrifying look on his face. Camp wondered if he felt completely betrayed by himself and Finn, the two men that he thought he could trust. Reuven got into the front passenger side of the number two Suburban. Camp sat behind Reuven; Omid was behind the driver.

"If it's any consolation…the American didn't tell me either," Reuven said as he continued to look straight out the front window.

"You didn't even check me for weapons?" Omid finally said as he gazed out at Israel.

"We may be enemies, but neither of us are fools.

Camp here has given us thorough instructions. We're going for a short ride, then lunch. Hope you're hungry."

"I know it's probably not a good idea to use names so, ah…*Randy,* this is Omid; Omid this is *Randy,*" Camp said as he tried to break the ice and the anxiety.

"So this is the friend you were telling me about, Camp? Is this the famous Omid from the Hindu Kush? Now that I finally get the chance to meet your friend Omid in person, he looks a lot like Colonel Farid Amir, military intelligence, the Iranian Revolutionary Guard. The resemblance is amazing."

Omid closed his eyes in disbelief.

"One would expect that a man such as Reuven Shavit, Director of Mossad's kotsas in the Middle East, would know such things," Omid said as Reuven finally relaxed and smiled, a smile that cut the tension in the Suburban 10-fold as they drove through the Gesher kibbutz near the Beit She'an Valley in northern Israel.

Within minutes the three Suburbans came to a stop on the edge of an outlook. The view was expansive ahead of them as a fertile valley sprawled out for nearly 20 miles.

"This is it, US Navy Captain Campbell. This is where you wanted to eat. We have baskets of food, drinks and sweets in the third car. Shall we? I'm already fully amused with this adventure," Reuven said as he opened his door.

Camp and Omid got out along with Reuven and his driver. Finn and Yitzhak joined them looking out over the valley as the others got the food out of the last car.

"Where we're standing, right now, this ridge...what is it called?" Camp asked.

"In Hebrew, it is *har megiddo*, the Mountain of Megiddo. But as you can see, it's not much of a mountain, more of a vantage point, a rising really. Anglicanized, you know it as Armageddon, and spreading out before us is the Jezreel Valley," Reuven said as baskets of food were placed on the hood of his Suburban. "Shall we eat? I'm sure there's something you want to tell us Camp...now that we're all here."

"Can we walk, down into the valley? Maybe take some food to go?" Camp asked.

"As you wish, this is your order." Reuven and Camp selected some sandwiches, fruit and water and loaded them into the small bags that were inside the basket.

"Go on," Finn said to Omid who was still stunned. "You three go for your walk. Yitzhak and the rest of us will stay up here and eat."

Omid moved slowly to the food, and somewhat begrudgingly filled his bag.

The three men started to walk down slowly into the Jezreel Valley. There was silence. More tension. Reuven and Omid seemed to be waiting for Camp to say something profound.

"This reminds me of a joke," Camp finally said.

"A joke?" Reuven asked.

"I don't remember how it ends, but the beginning is hysterical."

"Then humor us. Let's hear the beginning of your hysterical joke, Captain Campbell."

Camp stopped, turned and faced both Reuven and Omid.

"So…one day a Christian, a Jew and a Muslim were walking through the valley of Armageddon to have a picnic…"

Camp stopped. It was the end of his joke. Reuven looked at Camp, then at Omid. Omid looked back at Reuven, then Camp. At first there was just a smile, then two. The more he thought about it a laugh rumbled out of Reuven's mouth, then Omid. Before they knew it, all three were doubled over in laughter.

They found a nice grassy knoll with rocks, suitable for sitting, eating and enjoying the beauty of Jezreel.

"This place must have incredible history," Camp said as he looked out over the wheat, cotton, sunflowers and corn. "Can you tell me some of it?"

Reuven swallowed some of his sandwich then took a long swig from his bottled water.

"Jezreel means 'God sows.' Since ancient times, this area has been the most fertile agricultural land in all of Palestine. It has always been strategic land. Jezreel and the Esdraelon plain is the only east-west access between the Mediterranean and the Jordan Valley. This was the major north-south trade route between Mesopotamia, or ancient Greece and Egypt. With the desert to the east and both sides of the Jordan River blocked by highlands – and access to the Jordan valley quite minimal thanks to the Dead Sea – most travel ran through the Valley of Jezreel."

"And wars," Omid added.

"Yes, and wars. It became a corridor for invading armies. It was the most level land in the area, perfect for battles."

"From Gideon to World War I," Omid added to the history. "This land was once controlled by the Canaanites who had chariots, mighty chariots. The Canaanites were people from the Gaza Strip, West Bank and Lebanon."

"It was Gideon, the mighty warrior, the destroyer, the judge of the Hebrews, who defeated the Midianites and Amalikites right here," Reuven said.

"But Gideon tested God twice, first with a fleece of wool that was wet, then one that was dry the next morning," Omid said filling in the details.

"Gideon was facing a mighty enemy, but he had 32,000 men among the ranks of his army. God said he had too many men. If Gideon won the battle with an army that large, the men would claim victory because of their sheer numbers and because of their might. So Gideon allowed all those who wanted to go home, the permission to leave. More than 22,000 went home. But God told Gideon that 10,000 soldiers were still too many."

Omid finished the story.

"Gideon took his men down to the water to let them drink. God told him to watch and separate those men who lapped the water with their tongues like dogs, from those who kneeled down to drink. Only 300 men lapped the water to their mouth from their hands. So Gideon marched this army of 300 to the enemy camp. Everyone was given a trumpet and a clay jar with a torch hidden inside. Trumpets blew, and fires raged, as Gideon and his 300 men defeated a far superior army, the Midianites."

All three men fell silent.

"You share a common knowledge of history," Camp said.

"We share much of the same history," Reuven said.

"We shared both sides of many wars," Omid punctuated.

"Too many wars," Reuven concluded. "King Solomon fortified the ancient fortress of Megiddo to guard the pass. It was here that Jehu's army defeated the armies of Jezebel which started bloodshed in the Northern Kingdom that lasted for years. And it was at Megiddo that King Josiah was killed as he tried to block the Egyptians from marching through the pass to save the Assyrians who were, themselves, trapped by the Babylonians."

"Perhaps nowhere else on earth has there been as much bloodshed and violence than right here in this peaceful valley," Omid said. "Megiddo is still the name used...your *har megiddo*, Reuven, and your Armageddon,

Camp…the ultimate symbol for war and conflict."

Camp stood and stepped up on a rock. He held out his arms and embraced the warm breeze as it hit his face.

"Does it really have to be this way?" Camp asked.

"I don't wish for your annihilation, Reuven; most Muslims don't either. The vast majority of Muslims are willing to live in peace. Yes, we'd like a Palestinian state, but we don't need Israel to be destroyed."

"What about the Twelvers?" Reuven asked. "Don't they need Israel to be destroyed, in order to usher in the Twelfth Imam?"

"Their theology is bent; it doesn't feel right. Not all Twelvers believe this, Reuven."

"Most?"

"Yes, most of them do," Omid finally conceded. "But I don't want the blood of Iran, or Israel, to flow through the Valley of Jezreel up to the horse's bridle."

"What about the nuclear program, colonel? What will that mean for Israel?" Reuven asked.

"You have the power to kill me right now, Reuven. Israel has the power to destroy all of Iran and our Persian homeland. America and Russia could destroy both of us if they chose to. If I tell you something…can you assure me that Iran will not be destroyed?"

"I don't have that kind of power, Farid…you know that," Reuven said sincerely.

"If there's any hope, any hope that we can all live as neighbors in this holy and ancient land, I believe there must be an Islamic Reformation, where faithful Muslims can reject radical thought while remaining faithful to Allah. But we need a Palestinian homeland, too."

"Share the plan, Omid. The three of us are standing in Armageddon. Let's not fill this valley up with blood," Camp pleaded as he sat down.

Finn and Yitzhak watched from the ridgeline of Megiddo as Omid spoke for nearly two hours. He shared every detail of the plan he had heard during the meeting in Qoms. He told them about Kazi and the Unity Festival, the MISIRI and their plans for the King of Saudi Arabia, nuclear warheads, a thousand Shahab missiles, a million men on the Iraqi border, and the 8-minute and 53-second clock that would become Armageddon.

The three men, a Christian, a Jew and a Muslim, discussed ways to neutralize the plan, though each knew that even if the plan receded temporarily, the mutual hate would not. The tension might subside, but a new plan would emerge.

The three-Suburban convoy returned to the Gesher gate where border soldiers manned the post and kept a close eye on Finn's rental car. The driver got out as Camp, Omid and Reuven soaked up their meeting in silence.

"There's one more thing that I must mention," Omid said as Reuven turned around to look at him. "Kazi is my cousin…our fathers were brothers. Our fathers rejected my grandfather's thoughts…he was too extreme…his heart was filled with hate…our fathers moved to Pakistan, just to get away from Qazvin, my grandfather…I was only six years old, Kazi was barely a year old…terrorists broke into our house where both of our families lived together under one roof…Kazi's mother and father were killed…I watched as my mother's throat was slit and a single gunshot entered the back of my father's neck. Kazi and I, along with our sisters, were orphans…grandfather Qazvin came to Islamabad and took us back to Markazi Province in Iran…grandfather allowed me to visit every year where he thought my father lived in a home for several months before he finally died…to this day, I have never told Qazvin that my father died way back then…he despised his two sons for not accepting his brand of Islam…there was no reason for him to feel sympathetic when one son was killed and the other son was severely wounded."

"Can you reason with Kazi?" Reuven asked.

"I don't think so. He is very radical. He was Qazvin's favorite. He spent every day in Qazvin's lab at the university. Since he was born in Pakistan he had dual citizenship and was able to study in the states, become a microbiologist and earn his PhD in The Netherlands."

"This is the man who killed our Army doctor?" Camp asked.

"Kazi would never pull a trigger. That's not his style. But the SkitoMister we found…that's Kazi."

"Please, Farid, can you try? For the sake of the children in both countries?" Reuven dismantled his eccentric disposition and spoke with a hint of desperation and humility. "He is your cousin."

"I will try."

The three men got out of the SUV. Camp shook Reuven's hand, said goodbye to Yitzhak and headed over to the rental car where Finn had the engine running.

The Mossad agents looked over at Reuven and Omid. Omid only slightly wondered if this was where his life would finally end. Camp and Finn were not so sure either.

Reuven moved closer as Omid raised his eyes to meet those of the Israeli.

"Ahkh," Reuven said.

"It's the same in Arabic and Farsi...*ahkee*," Omid said.

Camp looked back as Reuven and Omid embraced and bid each other farewell, as brothers.

"Reuven, I'll be in touch with you," Camp yelled from the car.

Reuven waved goodbye and yelled back, "I'm afraid that will not be possible."

38

LyonBio
Lyon, France

Camp and Finn got a good night's rest at the Hilton Lyon Hotel before arriving at LyonBio shortly before noon. Camp's mind was racing with the frenetic exit from Jordan, a quick flight back to France, and the taxi ride back to the hotel.

Raines was sitting in her lab, grinning like a Cheshire cat, with a dozen long-stemmed roses standing in a crystal vase in the middle of her desk when Camp and Finn walked in.

"Hey, its Tom and Jerry…welcome back, boys."

Camp couldn't see past the roses to greet Raines.

"What's this?" Camp said with newfound disdain.

"Guess I have a secret admirer. Not sure if he's here in France or one of my old boyfriends back at Fort Detrick."

Camp walked over to the vase and ripped the card out of the arrangement.

"Help yourself by all means, Captain Campbell," she said as he pulled the card out of the tiny envelope. Camp read the note out loud.

"Congratulations,   Leslie…you   did   it! Manufacturing is underway and five million sublingual doses will be ready to ship on October 5th. Just let us know where they're going. Your friend, Thierry and Rochelle Gaudin."

Camp rolled his eyes and teased Raines.

"Very funny, Les, I hope you got a good laugh at my expense."

"Thank you. I did. But you seem a bit too tense to enjoy it. "

"We've been to Armageddon and back. Literally." Camp explained.

"Twenty-one hours a day in this lab wasn't exactly a trip to Miami Beach either. Lighten up, sailor."

Camp walked over and reluctantly kissed her forehead.

"Congratulations, Les. You're a rock star."

"I've got some good news and bad news, one for each of you. Which do you want first?"

"Bad," Finn said as he took a seat.

"General Ferguson called, and he wants you to return to Kabul, Billy. Your work is done here."

"Thank God," Finn said. "I could use some *bad* news like that. Your sailor is going to get me into trouble if I keep hanging around him."

"The good news is for me?" Camp asked.

"Actually it's good for us. You've been detailed back to Washington, Camp...Walter Reed National Medical Center."

"Are you serious? When?"

"As soon as you can get on an airplane."

"What about you, Les?"

"I'll stay here and babysit the vaccines. They'll ship to Tel Aviv on 1 October. I'll head home when they're out the door."

Raines drove the boys back to their hotel after lunch so they could re-pack their small backpacks and book their travel arrangements. Camp leaned in through the open window of Raines' rental car as Finn went inside the Hilton.

"Got any plans for dinner tonight, sailor?" Raines asked.

"Well, actually I've grown tired of waiting for my lab rat friend to find some social time so, yeah, tonight I think I'm open for dinner."

"I'll pick you up at eight."

Qazvin University of Medical Sciences
Ghods Hospital
Markazi Province, Iran

Omid parked his car in the small parking lot at Ghods Hospital, a lot that had been recently overflowing with tularemia-infected villagers from the

Bourvari District. The hospital and university classrooms were all quite familiar to him. He didn't spend as much time at Ghods as Kazi did, but it was a second home nonetheless.

Omid was six, and Kazi was one when they, along with four sisters between them, came to live with Qazvin after an abrupt and terrifying exit from Pakistan. Their grandfather's house was located in the neighborhood just behind the hospital. At first the boys would join their grandfather in his lab every day after school. Qazvin was a chemist by trade but had added advanced life science degrees to his *curriculum vitae* along the way.

He had picked up a lot of radical thought as well. Qazvin joined a secret society in the 1950's called Hottajieh. He was obsessed with moving Islam in a different direction.

As young boys, Kazi and Omid saw their grandfather grow more extreme. Kazi was young and impressionable. He learned advanced chemistry as a very young boy and Qazvin took Kazi to several of his religious meetings to show him off. Omid was not interested in the lab, or chemistry, or science. His heart was broken over the loss of his parents. He was old enough to remember his own father explaining why the family had left Iran after the Shah was overthrown and why young Omid needed to pretend that his grandfather was dead. Omid turned to writing and literature. He studied world philosophies and the history of war. He knew more about the Middle East and the Persian Empire than any of his counterparts. Omid was a student of Aristotle and examined every detail of Alexander the Great, Darius I the Persian conqueror and Genghis Khan. He understood world religions and was particularly interested in the impact Martin Luther had on the Catholic Church.

Kazi was born and raised for revolution.

Omid was born and raised for reformation.

Qazvin was sitting at his desk, reading some papers, when Omid walked in and tapped on his door.

"Hello, grandfather," Omid said quietly so as not to startle Qazvin.

Qazvin moved his head far enough to look over his reading glasses and see Omid standing at the door, dressed in his military uniform.

He did not answer Omid.

Omid moved in closer and leaned against the wall just a few feet from Qazvin's chair.

"Kazi's portion of the revolution will start very soon. I suppose you are very proud of him."

Qazvin continued to read his papers.

"I have news for you, Qazvin. I just received word from Islamabad. My father – your son – has finally died."

Qazvin put his papers down and removed his glasses.

"Thirty-one long years, grandfather…31 years he suffered in that house, sitting in his wheelchair, waiting to die…that's a long time to wait for death."

Qazvin said nothing.

"I want to talk with Kazi…I want to tell him about my father, his uncle."

Qazvin turned sharply and stared at Omid.

"You will not speak with Kazi…he is the gifted one. That's why you were removed from him 20 years ago. Kazi has been blessed with the power to change the world. You have been cursed with the confusion of too much thought, too many ideas. You are as your father was…worth nothing."

Omid felt the heat of anger flush across his face. He had almost forgotten the yelling and the beatings grandfather Qazvin had given to him when he dared to offer a different opinion, a different thought, or something he learned in a book from history.

"Perhaps you are correct, Qazvin, you are a wise elder. Still, I would like to speak with Kazi…he will want to know that his uncle has finally died."

Qazvin returned to his papers. He had no love or compassion for Omid.

"Kazi has left…the Shoeib and the council have new concern that the Zionists will strike us first…we would have to spend years rebuilding before we returned to this same place…the plan will launch early…before the Zionists can launch their Jerichos."

The air from Omid's lungs was sucked out as Qazvin's words rattled around in his mind. He was numb and powerless. He had to make a call.

"Kazi has gone to Beirut…already?"

"The Unity Festival has been moved up…the wind of torment will blow earlier…all praise to Allah," Qazvin said as he opened a new page on his computer screen.

"Allah? Grandfather, you honestly believe that this is what Allah wants for his children? To kill the innocents, to slaughter the elderly, to bring about war so that the Twelfth Imam, the Mahdi can bring about peace? We are Persians, grandfather. Darius was ruthless when war was the only option, but he built things, he gave us common currencies and trade, magnificent buildings and art, he opened passageways for trade. We are a great people, Qazvin, look what we have built with our own hands. Look at our technology, our science, even the great universities that you and others have built. But you…look at you, grandfather…you have spent your entire life consumed with hate…you have taught Kazi to hate…and now, at the end of your life, you continue to search for ways to kill, while the children of Islam seek ways to live."

Qazvin pulled his reading glasses down and put them on his desk. He pushed his office chair back slightly and then rested his chin on his clasped hands. Omid watched his grandfather's eyes fill with tears.

"You sound like your father, Farid…I remember him saying these words as well…he was so different than me…his brother was so different…they both left Iran… left me…and moved to Pakistan…they dishonored me, Farid…they dishonored Islam…now you dishonor me."

Omid moved in closer.

"Qazvin…baba…I have always loved you…I cherish my grandfather…you know the holy scriptures like no other…I still respect you…I just disagree with you…is that a sin? Am I evil because I hold a different opinion?"

Qazvin started to weep. His chest moved up and down with great emotion as his Pirahan Shalvar filled with moisture from his own tears. Qazvin tucked his fingers into the wide Kamarband belt as he tried to regain his self-control. Omid moved in and embraced his grandfather as he sat in his chair and wept.

"I am an old man now, Farid…I have done many things in my life…some good, some not so good. But I could not let my sons bring dishonor to our family name no matter where they lived…I am so sorry, my grandson. I'm sorry that your father lived so long in agony. He was supposed to die that night…just like his brother."

Rage filled Omid as he held his grandfather. He was in total disbelief.

"You? You killed your own sons?" Omid whispered into Qazvin's ear.

Omid's arms moved slowly from around Qazvin's chest and up toward his head and neck. He tried to fight the urge but he wanted to kill his grandfather.

"Yes," Qazvin whispered as he thrust the tip of his 9-inch Pesh-kabz dagger, housed on the hip inside the Kamarband, deep inside Omid's chest and quickly punctured his lung.

Omid gasped in utter disbelief as he heard Qazvin weep. Sharp pain engulfed his lungs and chest as his mind tried to comprehend what was happening.

With a quick twist, the Pesh-kabz turned clockwise and was pulled out as a mixture of blood, water and air covered Qazvin's clothes. Omid felt life racing out of his body as Qazvin pushed the dagger in a second time, another clockwise spin, then he pulled it out of Omid's belly.

Omid could not believe what was happening. His hands fell down and back to his weeping grandfather's side, then went limp. Omid bent his head down and kissed his grandfather's cheek. The sounds of his grandfather weeping faded slowly as life poured out of Omid and finally into silence.

39

Beirut Luna Park
Beirut, Lebanon

An elderly woman walked through Luna Park in Beirut taking photographs of the 50 hot air balloons and flying teams that had arrived from all over the Middle East. The small, discreet camera was hidden in her hijab and triggered by a clicker in her hand. The woman was a common sight in Luna Park and throughout most of the public areas of Beirut since Mossad placed her in Lebanon 23 years before.

Most of the balloon teams were from Egypt. Three days of carnival rides, music, and food would open the Unity Festival after the Friday holy day. The balloons would race from Beirut, down the Mediterranean coast past Israel and the Gaza Strip before crossing the finish line in Port Said, Egypt. The winning team would receive 100,000 Egyptian pounds, more than $16,000 in US currency.

Organizers had moved the event up by two weeks, claiming that political unrest between Iran and Israel necessitated an earlier festival.

With the start of the festival still seven days away, balloon teams wanted plenty of time to practice, rig their equipment properly and get familiar with the tricky wind conditions that could change at a moment's notice along the sea.

The woman took photos of the posters stapled to trees and taped to sign poles in Luna Park which had created excitement among the locals. She photographed TV news crews from around the Middle East as they were filming and reporting the preparations for the race.

But one thing caught her attention more than anything else. The date of the race had been moved up to October 1st. The woman left the park and headed back to her apartment. She knew this was information that Yitzhak would want to know about immediately.

Tel Aviv

Few things ever surprised Reuven, but the photos Yitzhak showed him and then the Al Jazeera News footage from Beirut left him stunned.

"They changed the dates," Reuven said calmly as Yitzhak began to panic.

"I thought the plan was 10 days before Ali's birthday…the 23rd?" Yitzhak asked.

"Perhaps we have been played. Get Shin Bet and

Aman over here now. Tell them we advise going to 'orange' on the Jericho 3."

Reuven started the call chain to Lyon, France. He needed to speak with Camp.

Lyon, France

Raines uncorked a chilled bottle of Pinot Gris and placed it next to the bathtub in her apartment. The hot water was starting to fill the basin and the aromas of exotic oils and spices began to fill the steamed-up room as she lit four candles.

Most nights since she had been at LyonBio were filled with 20-hour days and a quick nap on her couch covered with Grandma Lydia's hand-knitted Afghan blanket. She was relieved, almost giddy, to have 24 hours of unplugged time just to herself as LyonBio started to manufacture the sublingual vaccine.

Sitting on the ledge of her tub, wearing an open white robe, she picked up her cell phone and made one last call. The call went to voice mail as she knew it would.

"Hey sailor…I know you're probably somewhere over the Atlantic and sound asleep by now…just want you to know that I'm naked, well, almost naked…and ready for a three-hour bath, an entire bottle of wine, and 100 hours of sleep…but guess what…I miss you already. Give me a call when you land so I know you made it home okay…miss you."

Raines ended her call and powered her iPhone to off.

40

ISAF Headquarters
Kabul, Afghanistan

General Ferguson, Billy Finn and two coffee-pouring majors were carrying their food trays and looking for an open table in the DFAC. Finn was positioned right in front of one of the 10 flat-screen TVs that played news, sports and movies – all courtesy of the Armed Forces Network.

The noise in the DFAC prevented anyone from hearing the TVs but they served as conduits of moving wallpaper back to the real world nonetheless.

"Did Camp seem excited about his new assignment at Walter Reed?" Ferguson asked as Finn speared his tossed green salad.

"Seemed to be. Better than coming back to OEF," Finn said.

Finn noticed Major Spann's fixation with the news

report and looked up.

"I'm at a loss about what to do with that man," Ferguson said with his back to the TV. "Maybe getting back in a hospital is the best thing for him."

Finn put his fork down, got up and ran over to the TV so he could hear the report on CNN.

"What is it?" Ferguson said finally turning around.

"The Iranians claim that Israel, through the covert action of Mossad, has assassinated another high level military officer. Colonel Farid Amir was visiting family in Markazi Province when a motorcyclist attached a magnet bomb to his car and drove off as the blast killed the Iranian colonel. No other injuries were reported. Israel denies that it had anything to do with the Iranian officer's death."

Finn ran out the back door of the DFAC and back to the general's office.

Tel Aviv, Israel

Top level officers from Shin Bet, Aman and Mossad were gathered in the conference room closest to Reuven's command center.

Yitzhak turned the TV off.

"Was this the man you met with?" Major General Shalom from Aman asked.

Reuven nodded.

"But this wasn't us," the officer from Shin Bet hoped.

Reuven shook his head.

"Have you heard from the American?" the general

pushed.

Reuven was silent.

"Then we have no choice. There is a firm plan. We know the plan thanks to Iranian military intelligence. We must strike first."

Reuven was powerless to offer a different solution as the general from Aman went to prepare for an all-out military attack as Shin Bet would try to protect the people of Israel.

Yitzhak stayed with Reuven alone in the conference room for a few more minutes then finally left as well. Reuven stared ahead at the wall. His face was void of emotion.

He pulled a piece of paper from his pocket and pulled out his phone. He was tired of the chain. He called the number directly.

Camp answered on the second ring.

"Yes."

"Shepherd's Pie?"

"Molly Bloom! How the hell are you?" Camp said with great enthusiasm.

"Where are you?"

"Just went through customs after a long flight home. Feels good to be home, my friend."

"You've not seen the news?"

Camp stopped in his tracks and put his bag down.

"What news?"

"The festival has been pushed up…by two weeks. Your friend from the Hindu Kush…he's dead."

"Why?" Camp demanded. Reuven could hear the anger in Camp's voice.

"It wasn't us."

"Why does that seem hard to believe right now?"

"If I wanted him dead, he would have never finished his picnic."

Reuven paused and let the silence and realization sink in for Camp.

"So...he tried to stop it, they killed him and they moved the plan up," Camp finally said as the pieces started to come together.

"I must reach your scientist, Shepherd's Pie...we have moved to 'orange'. There is not much time now."

"Okay, Molly, do we need to play all this covert code shit, innuendos and chain calls, or do you want her name and phone number?"

Reuven rubbed his eyes and blew the frustration out of his mouth. There was little time left to maintain controlled conversation security and Reuven had to move quickly.

"I know her name, give me the number...call her first and tell her to expect my call."

LyonBio
Lyon, France

The office phone in Raines' lab was ringing. It was the first time it had rung since she was in France. Raines had forgotten that she even had a desk phone.

"Leslie Raines."

"Les, I've been trying to reach you for almost 18 hours."

"Camp," Raines said with comfort.

"Are you okay?"

"Didn't you play my message? I took a long bath, drank a full bottle of wine and slept for nearly 20 hours straight. I forgot to turn my phone back on. Sorry."

"Les...we have big problems. I have to speak ambiguously, so track with me. Les, the rabbit is coming earlier than we planned."

The rabbit, she asked herself. *Rabbit fever...the tuleremia*. Raines was panicked.

"How much earlier?"

"Two weeks earlier. The rabbit may be visiting our friends as early as a week from today."

"Camp...it won't be ready by then. You know that, right?"

"How much? How much can you have ready?" Camp begged.

"I don't know...some...nowhere close to all of it."

"Les, you're going to get a call from a man. I gave him your number. Don't ask questions just give him answers. Imagine every question he is about to ask you and have the answers ready."

"Good God, Camp...you're scaring me."

"You should be scared, Les. I'm scared."

"What's his name?"

"Doesn't matter. Call him Molly Bloom."

41

Beirut Luna Park
Beirut, Lebanon

The 50 balloon teams met in a classroom at Beirut Arab University. The teams were sponsored by several governments, businesses, news organizations and even airlines. The prize money was put up by QLS, a research organization based out of Islamabad with offices in Iran, the United Arab Emirates and Yemen. Qazvin Life Sciences was highly regarded throughout the Middle East, and Dr. Markazi was their ambassador of goodwill.

"I am Dr. Markazi and on behalf of the many event organizers, I am pleased to welcome you to the first annual Unity Festival. First, I want to thank you for arriving early. The weather forecasts for late October were growing worse by the day. The entire world will be watching, so we wanted to make sure that our skill and expertise were on full display with proper conditions."

The 50 pilots and their teams were excited. The prize money was certainly a good incentive, but the international television news coverage was just plain seductive.   Every balloon was painted with the decorative logos of sponsoring businesses, governments and universities.

"This will be a very challenging race. From Beirut to Port Said is 418 kilometers, or 260 miles. We expect the wind to be blowing from north to south. You may use your own judgment, but we recommend that all pilots stay at 3,000 feet and below," Kazi said.

"What about the Zionists?" one pilot shouted out.

"Obviously, do not stray or even navigate over their non-existent territory. International law indicates that every country's territorial waters extend for 12 nautical miles, or 14 miles by car. But I'm quite certain the Zionists will have international blood on their hands if they shoot down hot air balloons during a Unity Festival race."

The room erupted in laughter and applause

"Come as close to the Zionist's coast line as you feel comfortable doing. But smile for the cameras. Every television news network in the world will have their cameras focused on you as you fly past Tel Aviv. Your skill, proficiency and speed will be on display for the entire world to see. If you are too far out above the Mediterranean, you will not be seen on TV. That is why we are offering a 5,000 Egyptian pound bonus for every team that is filmed on western TV news. Brothers… every team. That's a huge bonus."

The room filled with thunderous applause.

"Each team has different skills. There must be two people in every balloon. To level the competition and make it fair among all teams, each balloon must take a separate vapor tank on board, which is designed to eliminate the advantage that a lightweight team might have over a heavier team. The heaviest team is the benchmark. If the heaviest team weighs 300 pounds, for example, and the lightest team weighs 225 pounds, then the lightest team must carry a 75-pound tank of water. Each balloon will have additional water tanks added to their balloon, depending on the weight deficit between them and the heaviest team."

The pilots were not thrilled with that rule. If every team was even from the start then no team would be a clear winner. Dr. Markazi addressed that.

"As soon as you cross into the Zionist's air space and you can see the hook in the shoreline that is Haifa, you can start to vaporize your water, reduce your weight, and increase your speed. If you start to vaporize your ballast weight before you get to Haifa, then you will be disqualified."

Dr. Markazi lifted up one of the water ballast tanks and the vapor unit that was attached to each.

"I have personally built each one of these systems. Simply turn this knob, when you are over Haifa, and the water ballast in your tank will start to burn off. Any questions?"

The elderly woman, sitting in the middle of the room with various members of Luna Park's employees and event organizers, pressed the clicker in her hands and snapped photos as Kazi demonstrated the vapor unit he had built.

The room full of pilots and teams were more than excited.

"Next Tuesday morning at 8:00am, the Unity Festival race begins from Luna Park. Once your ship has been inspected and your ballast tank has been filled according to your weight, you will receive your ribbon and will be ready to fly."

A young man from the back of the room raised his hand.

"Yes."

"Dr. Markazi, are you a hot air balloon pilot? Are you racing?"

"No, I'm a nitrogas RC pilot, an astrophysicist and a microbiologist. My grandfather is the head of QLS, and he's putting up the prize money. But balloons don't go fast enough to suit me."

The audience of pilots and crew laughed and were probably relieved that Markazi wasn't one of their competitors.

"Now, as a special treat, reporters from three major Arabic networks are about to come in. They want to interview you, learn about your skills and abilities. Talk to them about Islamic unity. Make your countries and your God very proud of you."

A proud round of applause greeted Dr. Markazi as he exited the platform as news crews entered the room on cue. He paused and spoke with one of his assistants.

"Make sure that every ballast tank brings the weight of each team to the maximum."

"I understand, Kazi."

The woman left the room behind Kazi as members of the media and press entered.

42

Lyon, France

Raines was in her rental car driving over to the apartment in the BioPark when an unknown call appeared on her iPhone. She was nervous.

"Hello."

"Were you told to expect my call?"

Raines swallowed and paused.

"Is this Molly Bloom?"

"Please listen carefully…I am bringing a commercial airliner into your city at 2:00am on Sunday morning. I need you to bring all that you have with you, in trucks, so we can load the plane. Is that clear?"

"I understand, but there is not enough time to manufacture the amount you need."

The voice on the other end paused.

"Give me your best guess…how many can you serve in our restaurant by this Sunday at 2:00am?"

Raines had anticipated the question, and she had done her dose calculations. It would not be smooth, and certainly not professional, but it could work.

"I can't serve you the soup in individual bowls in that amount of time," Raines said as she tried to explain the challenges of preparing individual doses. "You will have to ladle it out with your own spoons…one-point-seven, maybe two million can be served, and give them three drops each."

Raines heard Reuven's fingers on a keyboard. She assumed he was doing some quick calculations.

"See you Sunday."

Tel Aviv, Israel

Yitzhak looked at the scratch marks on Reuven's tablet.

"Bring me two of the best meteorologists in Tel Aviv. And get the director to call the Ministry of Health in Jerusalem. We need to meet tomorrow morning."

"Anything else?" Yitzhak asked.

"Yes. Arrange a meeting with the news directors from each TV station in Tel Aviv. Have them attend the meeting with the meteorologists and the Ministry of Health."

Reuven went home, kissed the heads of his sleeping sons and got into bed next to his wife. His eyes stared at the ceiling as the digital clock on his nightstand counted the minutes. He was up in the kitchen pouring his coffee long before his wife or children even stirred.

The Health Minister was not pleased that her morning calendar was cleared by Mossad with just one phone call, but she didn't mind the inconvenience of an exquisite helicopter ride from Jerusalem to Tel Aviv. The news directors played coy and were calculating the angles they could use to beat the other with a scoop on whatever news story was about to break. The two weather forecasters thought they had died and gone to heaven. They were intercepted at their homes by Mossad agents before they could drive to work. Now they were sitting in Reuven's command center, a secret lair in an unmarked building in the middle of Tel Aviv.

Coastal maps of Israel – from Kfar Rosh HaNikra in the farthest point north, to Haifa, Netanya, Tel Aviv, Ashdod, and the Gaza Strip to the south – were all affixed to the walls in Reuven's secret post.

"Our discussions today never happened. Everything said in here today shall be denied…nothing said in here today shall ever be repeated or reported."

Three news directors, two meteorologists and one Minister of Health nodded their agreement.

"Six days from now, we believe our country will be attacked by a bio-weapon. A hybrid tularemia bacterium has been created, a vaccine-resistant tularemia to be precise. But our friends from the west have developed a vaccine that will protect us. We had hoped for a biomedical shield that would protect *all* of Israel. But due to time constraints, we can now only hope for a biomedical wall. I need precise wind forecasts for next

Tuesday morning!" Reuven said as the two weathermen rifled through their charts and laptop programs.

"A storm will pass through on Sunday, but we should be clear on Monday and Tuesday," said the first.

"Winds out of the north and west, 6 to 10 miles per hour. Pushing to the south and then southwest over Egypt. Typical wind patterns for this time of year," said the second.

"If a microscopic particle was floating in the air on the coastline, and the winds you describe pushed it inland, how far might it come?" Reuven asked.

"It might not come inland at all. It could be pushed further south," said the first.

"Worse case?" Reuven pushed.

"Two to three miles…maybe. It's more of a breeze at that strength. Hardly a wind," said the second.

"Madam Minister, from Kfar Rosh HaNikra in the north all the way to the Gaza in the south, how many people live and work within three miles of the sea?"

"I can't answer that right now; I'd need time. I'd need to run some models and create some charts."

"We don't have time, Madam Minister. I need your best estimate."

The Minister of Health looked up at the maps on Reuven's wall and did some quick calculations in her head.

"Tel Aviv would be the largest number, then Haifa down Highway 2. Rishon LeTsiyon is too far inland, but Ashdod could be in trouble."

"How many?" Reuven persisted.

"I'm sorry, Mr. Shavit. I don't know for sure. But I'm afraid...I'm afraid that as many as two million people could be at risk."

The gravity of two million lives weighed heavily on the minds of the three news directors.

"This is another Holocaust," whispered one under his breath.

"No, it won't be. But I need your help. The vaccine is sublingual. Three tiny droplets under the tongue, and you get an immune response that prevents sickness from the tularemia. There is only one thing worse than the tularemia itself...fear and panic. So here's the plan: I need widespread news coverage, calm and matter-of-fact, that flu season is upon us. The health ministry needs to dispatch an army of volunteers from north to south who will start at the coast line and move inland with sublingual vaccines. Set up vaccine tents on the beaches and send others door to door. No mention – anytime or anywhere or under any circumstance – that a bio-weapon has been released. Neither rabbit fever nor tularemia shall ever be mentioned."

"Are you censoring us?" one of the news directors asked.

"No...I'm begging you," Reuven said with great humility.

"What if some people start reporting illnesses?"

"Some will. DO NOT REPORT IT. We will get them antibiotics immediately. No one needs to die from tularemia. They may get sick, but they won't die."

"What if the weather changes, the winds change?" one of the meteorologists asked.

"Let us all pray that the God of Gideon blows back against the winds of torment. We need wall-to-wall news promos on the flu vaccine program beginning on Friday and up until Sunday morning. We start vaccinating along the coast at 9:00am Sunday morning."

"I'm going to need thousands of volunteers," the Minister of Health said.

"We can promote that on TV. Get public service announcements out to radio and ads for the newspapers."

"Money is not an issue," Reuven added. "We have funds for bus posters, outdoor signs...whatever you need. Please be clear on this...put a happy face on everything. No underlying concern. We want to have the most flu-free season in the history of Israel."

43

ISAF Headquarters
Kabul, Afghanistan

General Ferguson had dismissed his coffee-pouring majors as Billy Finn had requested. For 30 minutes, Finn explained the long conversations in the Hindu Kush with Omid, the abduction of Thierry Gaudin's son, the secret calls between Camp and Reuven, the flight into Amman, Jordan, the sauna, the burka, and the Gesher checkpoint into Israel. Finn painted the scene of the Christian, the Jew and the Muslim having a picnic in the Valley of Jezreel beneath the ridge of Megiddo. He explained that while Armageddon was a physical place, the metaphorical meaning transcended all cultures and religions. And Finn laid out the plan that was formulated by the Twelvers in Iran, the 8-minute and 53-second annihilation of Israel and the first retaliation missiles that wouldn't fall in Iran until 10 minutes had ticked off, as one million Iranian soldiers sprinted into Iraq.

Ferguson couldn't decide if he was angry with Billy Finn and US Navy Captain Campbell, or if they were the best diplomats that America had ever produced.

"What do I need to do Billy? Do we need to send Camp back to Israel?"

Finn didn't have a great answer.

"I think it's out of our hands now, general. Raines has created a biomedical shield for Israel. If the tularemia is rendered powerless, if Iran's proxies can't get to the King of Saudi Arabia…then maybe…maybe the plan can be stopped."

"Stopped?" Ferguson asked.

"Delayed…delayed until the next plan is created."

"I need to contact the SECDEF, probably CIA… they need to know."

Billy Finn stood up and leaned over Ferguson's desk and got close to the general's face.

"You know who you need to contact? Sixteen-hundred Pennsylvania Avenue. The next time the people rally in the streets *against* radical thoughts, radical policies and radical military programs designed…DESIGNED… for mutual annihilation, then maybe we need to worry less about sanctions and more about the people. I can assure you, Jim, there are far more Muslims just like Omid, than the few that are like Kazi. I pray to God that Omid did enough…that Raines did enough…that we all did enough. God save us all if we're too late."

Lyon Airport

Lyon, France

One truck filled with 5,000 gallons of sublingual tularemia vaccine was parked on the tarmac of the airport. Airport security had cordoned off the area as 40 officers from Interpol and the Lyon Police Department provided security. Leslie Raines and Thierry Gaudin stood under a single black umbrella as a light rain filtered through the headlights of their car.

The landing lights on the El Al chartered flight were in clear view as the jetliner made its final approach for landing.

The air traffic control tower guided the jet as it taxied over to the maintenance wing where one single truck was parked. The engines shut down as the ground crew pushed a portable staircase up to the front cabin door.

The 747-200F was operated by El Al Cargo. The jet had 10 passenger seats up by the cockpit, and the rest of the airplane was hollowed out for cargo.

The cabin door opened, and two men exited the cabin for the walk down the stairs in the light rain. Flashing yellow security lights lit their faces with sweeps of light. The first man was tall with a very long and narrow face. His hair was combed straight back and small, round, frameless spectacles rested on the bridge of his nose. He wore a full length black overcoat with the collar pulled up high. The second man was shorter, much rounder. His hair was full and flopped from side to side with the wind and the rain. A deep black moustache and goatee covered his face.

The two walked over to Leslie Raines and Thierry Gaudin who stood under the black umbrella, silhouetted against the headlights of the truck in the drizzle of the rain.

It was precisely two o'clock in the morning.

"Molly Bloom?" Raines asked as Reuven stepped closer.

"Lieutenant Colonel Leslie Raines I presume."

Thierry looked over at Raines with a surprised look on his face. He had no idea that she was a high ranking American military officer.

"One truck?" Reuven asked with concern.

"Sir, this is Thierry Gaudin, president and CEO of LyonBio. Without his support and that of his incredible team, not even one truck would be possible tonight."

Reuven looked at them both. His hands were deep in his overcoat pockets.

"On behalf of a grateful nation…thank you. It'll take our crew about 15-minutes, a quick refueling, and then we'll be on our way."

"Sir, this is only 5,000 gallons. Will it be enough?"

"It will have to be. Someone once took three hundred lamps and some trumpets…God made them look, and sound, like an overpowering army. God will have to multiply the effect of this vaccine, too."

"It has a name," Raines said.

"What does, colonel?"

"The vaccine. It was Camp's idea. He told me a little bit about your, um, picnic. The vaccine is called

GideonX."

Reuven smiled as Yitzhak nodded his head with pleasure. Reuven pulled one hand out of his pocket and reached to the inside pocket of his overcoat and pulled out an envelope and handed it to Thierry.

"What's this?" Thierry asked.

"It's 80,000 Euros."

"Sir, we can't take money for this. The Americans have already paid for our services."

Reuven reached out his hand and stopped Thierry from handing the envelope back to him.

"It's not for you. You'll find instructions inside. I recently met an incredible man, a Muslim, a colonel in the Iranian army. His courage may have saved two countries from mutual destruction and prevented a hundred more nations from waging war. He was killed for his courage. Make sure his family is taken care of… that his sons go on to university and study history, become writers, poets, philosophers and great men. Their father was a great man."

Thierry took the envelope and slid it into his pocket as Reuven looked at the skies and the passing storm.

"The storm is moving out of the Mediterranean… for the next three days we are expecting six mile per hour winds out of the north and northwest blowing south and back to the southwest."

"You like to follow the weather, Mr. Molly Bloom?" Raines said with a smirk on her face.

"Today I do. Thank you, colonel…Mr. Gaudin…

good night, and shalom."

Reuven and Yitzhak turned and walked back up the steps to the El Al Cargo 747-200F in a light rain that had all but stopped.

Charles de Gaulle Airport
Paris, France

Kazi's flight from Beirut landed at Charles de Gaulle Airport in France just in time for him to see the lift-off on the flat screen TVs in the terminal. Fourteen international television news crews, most of them broadcasting to the Islamic world, fixed their cameras on 50 colorful hot air balloons as the solitary rider on a white horse rode to the starting line and waved the ceremonial Unity Festival flag to start the race. Unity ribbons from each of the carriages waved back in the slight wind as all balloons lifted up for the race to Port Said, Egypt.

Once he cleared customs, Kazi would be on his way for the second leg of his journey.

44

Tel Aviv Hilton
Tel Aviv, Israel

Reuven and Yitzhak walked down the shore where western camera crews were set up on the beaches by the Mediterranean Sea in front of the Hilton Hotel. The big tents that had served as "Free Flu Vaccination Centers" the previous two days were now filled with producers and on-air talent seeking shade from the sun until the balloon race was within view.

Local universities and high schools had placed hundreds of signs, most of them written in Arabic that simply said "we want unity, too." Three colorful Israeli hot air balloons were tethered on the beaches as well. The words on the balloons said "Let's have this race, not an arms race" in both Hebrew and English for western television audiences.

Yitzhak called his contacts at Palmachim. The Israeli

Defense Forces at Palmachim Air Force Base down the coast were watching the balloons on radar as they passed over Israeli territorial waters and close to Israeli airspace. Unmanned aerial drones detected all 50 balloons starting to release their equalizing ballast through a water vapor system as each balloon neared Haifa.

TV cameras fired up and international news channels cut into regular programming with breaking news as the first Unity Festival hot air balloons were visible from the beaches of Tel Aviv. Most were two to three miles out above the sea at almost 3,000 feet. They were far too close to Israel's shoreline, but the authorities let them race. The colorful balloons against a majestic blue sky and the deep blue sea painted an incredible tapestry of color as six mile per hour winds out of the north gently caressed the faces of thousands of Israelis gathered on the sands to witness Unity.

Millions of homes in the Middle East, Southeast Asia, Europe, Russia, China and North America watched and hoped that Unity would truly come to a very troubled area.

Within minutes all 50 balloons had passed by and were out of sight as they raced toward Port Said. Reuven and Yitzhak watched the balloons disappear from sight, then turned for the quick ride back to their command center.

Casablanca, Morocco

The unexpected and unplanned visit by the King of Saudi Arabia to Morocco for more physical therapy provided a welcomed opportunity for the Shoeib. Sending a Shia assassination force in from al-Awamiya, a town in the Qatif region, was fraught with logistical problems. But an Iranian hit squad in Morocco with access to the Saudi King was a gift from God.

The King had undergone recent surgery in the United States for a debilitating back condition, a herniated disc that required precise surgery, and Morocco was his preferred destination for physical therapy. It was to be his third such visit for physical therapy, rest and recovery.

The King's motorcade drove through the streets of Casablanca, Morocco with a military escort after his private luxury jet landed and parked at the Executive Terminal at Mohammed V International Airport.

The black Mercedes pulled up to the side entrance of Clinique Zerktouni Orthopedics and Rehab center at Rue 9 Avril.

The King got out and waved to those gathered on the streets as six smiling technicians, doctors and physical therapists waited for him under the entrance awning. It was Thursday, and the entire Clinique Zerktouni staff was still buzzing about the international Unity Festival race and the fact that a team from Morocco had won.

The King's contingent of bodyguards engulfed him from the front, sides and rear as they walked briskly from the car toward the entrance way under the green awning. None of them noticed the doctor who reached into his white lab coat or the five others who reached for guns inside their blue surgical scrubs.

Gunfire from three high-powered rifles shattered the morning silence as six members of an Iranian hit squad fell dead from precise two-round volleys before the assassins had a chance to fire a single shot.

The King was pushed inside the hospital by bodyguards as the King's entourage cleared unfired weapons away from the dead "doctors and technicians" lying on the ground by the sidewalk. Saudi bodyguards scanned the adjacent rooftops looking for the shooters just as Reuven's video link went dark.

Reuven turned his TV monitor off, put a piece of chewing gum in his mouth and left the command center as Yitzhak buried his face in his hands.

Qoms, Iran

When word finally reached the gathering in the Shura Council room, the Shoeib threw his cup of hot tea against the wall. The breaking glass and his unrestrained anger captivated the room.

Ayatollah Yazdi asked for the report on the wind of torment. Qazvin reluctantly began to speak.

"The Zionists are lying, using all of their old tricks of deception. There have been some reports that people are very ill in the northern part of the Gaza Strip. But in the non-existent lands of the Zionists…nothing. Not a word has been mentioned. If they are suffering, we do not know….the world does not know."

Yazdi was silent. The room was silent.

"Then it is clear. The Age of the Coming is soon, but it is not yet now. May God's name be praised. We shall continue to wait the return of the Twelfth Imam, the Mahdi, and pray that day will be very soon. But today is not that day."

Tel Aviv, Israel

Yitzhak followed quickly behind Reuven as they left the command center with full knowledge that the Saudi King was safe.

"Full report?" Reuven asked as they walked.

"More than 400 are in hospitals getting antibiotics and treatments. Most of them elderly or children," Yitzhak said as he read the Health Minister's report.

"Fatalities?"

"None…so far," Yitzhak answered.

"News reports?"

"Nothing. Everyone is talking about the Unity Festival and the flu season. Not a word about tularemia. But there is this." Yitzhak handed Reuven a Delta Airlines passenger manifest from Charles de Gaulle airport in Paris.

Reuven looked agitated.

45

Walter Reed National Military Hospital
Bethesda, Maryland

US Navy Captain "Camp" Campbell stopped for an early cup of coffee at his favorite barista in Old Town Alexandria before making the quick drive to Walter Reed in his Defender 90. It was a beautiful Friday morning. He listened to every news story over the previous two days, and there was nothing about an outbreak of illness in Israel. Nothing could have made him happier.

Lieutenant Colonel Leslie Raines was scheduled to arrive at Washington Dulles on Sunday, and Camp was excited to see where his new interest in Raines might go.

The Friday "in briefing" was standard procedure. Camp would get a tour, meet his staff, and get a full briefing on his assignment. The real work would start on Monday.

During the Walter Reed tour, Camp's iPhone started vibrating. The phone indicated "unknown number," so he let it go to voice mail. Within seconds it vibrated again.

"Ma'am, I need to excuse myself and take this call," Camp said without waiting for permission. He stepped outside into the sunshine.

"Yes."

"Shepherd's Pie?"

A warm smile broke over Camp's face.

"Brother Bloom…it's great to hear your voice. I've been watching the news, and I'm very happy for you."

"Maybe that happiness is too soon."

"Okay."

"The evil rabbit hunter."

"I'm tracking…what about him?"

"His name came up on the system. Flew from over here to over there. Got a rental car."

"Where?"

"His alma mater."

"Okay…"

"Shepherd's Pie…tomorrow is what you call… homecoming…alumni day."

Camp ended the call and sprinted toward the parking lot as his tour guide watched helplessly through the window.

Inside the Defender 90, Camp hit Billy Finn's speed-dial number. Finn was sitting in General

Ferguson's office when the call came in.

"What's up, captain? Saving any lives this morning at Walter Reed?"

"Finn...I need your help..." Camp yelled frantically.

"Calm down, what's going on?"

"Just got a call from Molly Bloom...they found Kazi's name on a flight list. He's in the states, Billy."

"That's perfect. We can nail him there."

"Not so fast. Molly said he's got a rental car. This is homecoming weekend for his alma mater...alumni day."

"Whoa...what are you saying, Camp? Are you thinking winds of torment at a college football game?"

"Doesn't sound 'rational,' does it?" Camp asked rhetorically. "You still got Kazi's file?"

Finn ruffled through a stack of folders on Ferguson's desk. The general was perplexed with Billy Finn's burst of energy.

"Here it is. Undergraduate degree? Microbiology, at Auburn."

"Billy, get your Atlanta field office up to speed and give them my number. He had to fly into Atlanta, probably staying at a hotel near Auburn."

"What are you going to do?"

"I'm driving to Auburn, Billy...I don't know what Kazi looks like, but I know what he's capable of."

Jordan-Hare Field
Auburn University
Auburn, Alabama

A crowd of 87,451 cheering fans were packed into Jordan-Hare Stadium, the twelfth largest stadium in the NCAA, for the homecoming football game between the Auburn Tigers and the Aggies of New Mexico State University. A full Friday night of music, parades and the annual float competition had put everyone in a great mood for what was supposed to be an easy win over a non-conference opponent.

Camp made the 750-mile drive from Washington in less than 10 hours. Six members of the FBI's field office, including two snipers, had met with Camp, the Alabama State Troopers and Campus Police from midnight until 2:00am. Three booths at a local Waffle House served as the make-shift command center as each was debriefed on who Kazi was and what tularemia could do. The FBI had ordered two truckloads of the antibiotic ciprofloxacin be delivered to campus medical stations, local hospitals and 24-hour clinics.

Ticket-takers were given a copy of Kazi's college photo, a photo that was taken long before the college student became a man and a wanted international terrorist. The once 19-year-old student from Pakistan had long disheveled hair and a short cropped beard with bare spots. He was wearing an orange and blue Auburn Tigers sweatshirt.

It was anyone's guess what the 32-year-old

microbiologist looked like now. Camp had never seen him.

Two FBI snipers were placed in skyboxes at each 30-yard line on both sides of the field. Spotters with high-powered binoculars scanned the crowds.

Alabama State Troopers had increased their presence and were positioned at 10-yard intervals around the entire field. Normally their job was to prevent inebriated fans from running onto the field of play or preventing rowdy fans from rushing the goalposts after another Auburn victory.

Camp and the director of the FBI's Atlanta field office were in the first-level skyboxes at the 50-yard line. They were looking for one man among 87,451 screaming fans.

The Auburn Marching Tigers Band played and came to a triumphant finish as the vice chancellor walked past Neo, the team's Golden Eagle mascot, and stepped up to the microphone on the 50-yard line that was facing the home team fans.

"Welcome to the Auburn University Homecoming Game!" the vice chancellor said as Camp scoured the faces of those gathered on the field around him through his binoculars.

The crowd erupted. The student section in front of the vice chancellor yelled "War" and the rest of the stadium yelled "Eagle." The first students yelled "War." Then the end zone yelled "Damn," as the rest of the stadium screamed "Eagle." Signs that read WDE started rising from seats everywhere.

"It is my distinct pleasure…to introduce our newest mascot in a great lineage of Golden Eagle's…please welcome…six-year-old Neo."

The crowd went wild as the second year veterinary student from Auburn's College of Veterinary Medicine held Neo up on his gloved arm and forearm. Neo had been hit by a car as a young bird and was nursed back to health with surgeries and rehabilitation by the veterinary students. Neo not only survived but thrived. The majestic bird's long recovery left one unfortunate side effect; the animal had imprinted on people and lost all fear. Though Neo could not be released into the wild, he was transformed from serious injury to fearless mascot. But one behavior of the wild bird did not disappear even with daily interaction from people. Pigeons that made a dash through Neo's flight aviary, or other birds and animals that got too close during training, were often attacked by Neo with violent consequences. Neo was Auburn's War Eagle VIII. Natural survival was as much an instinct for Neo as it was for Auburn's football team.

Camp honed in on the eagle and the handler. Nothing.

"Before we play New Mexico State…we want to honor all of our alums who have come home to Auburn today," the vice chancellor continued.

The fans applauded, and another 10 rounds of "War Damn Eagle" echoed through Jordan-Hare Stadium.

"Today we single out three alums for special recognition. From the Class of 1974, cartoonist and writer, please welcome Jimmy Johnson."

Camp watched as the crowd politely applauded when Johnson stepped up to a white board and quickly drew a character from his "Arlo and Janis" comic strip. The hand-held camera on the field put Johnson's quick drawing on the stadium's JumboTron screens for all to see.

"From the Class of 2002, microbiologist and astrophysicist, Dr. Reza Markazi."

Camp bolted to his feet. "This is our guy!" Camp yelled into his radio and raced out the door of the skybox.

Kazi stepped out wearing an executive two piece navy blue suit with a yellow power tie. Retro-styled plastic framed glasses filled his cleanly shaven face as he put his ARF P-51D Mustang WARBIRD with a 65-inch wingspan down on the stadium turf. The camera moved in as the glow-plug fired up the engine.

Camp ran down eight flights of stairs, two steps at a time, until he reached the field access doors. "That's him, that's him. Shoot him!" Camp screamed as he pushed past security and onto the field.

"What the – we can't shoot the man in the middle of the football field," the director yelled into his headset. "All teams stand by."

The field camera moved in close as Kazi's WARBIRD gathered speed from the 50 to the 40 to the 30 and was airborne by the 20-yard line. Camp dodged through band members and across the field toward Kazi.

As the vet student's eyes scanned the skies above Jordan-Hare Stadium, so did Neo's eyes. The bird was immediately agitated. Natural instincts were kicking in. Neo started straining at his jesses, trying to free himself from the handler's restraints.

A video camera mounted on the top of the P-51 Mustang allowed Kazi to fly FPV with video goggles. First-Person View flight was a type of remote-control flying where a small video camera and analog television transmitter mounted on an RC aircraft allowed the pilot to fly the craft by means of a "live" video down-link, displayed on video goggles or a portable LCD screen.

Kazi pulled his eyes away from his P-51 Mustang long enough to see a man charging toward him, sprinting between band members and whose eyes were fixed on the skies above the field.

Kazi turned and walked off the field toward the visiting team's tunnel, but kept flying the plane through his video screen. The Mustang banked and started to circle the stadium above the heads of 87,451 screaming fans. The words hand-painted on the bottom of the wings whipped the audience into a frenzy: WAR EAGLE. The field camera followed the plane, and the JumboTrons filmed the flight as "War Damn Eagle" echoed through Jordan-Hare Stadium.

Flying FPV, Kazi could see from the aircraft's

perspective, and didn't even have to look at the plane as he ran off the field and stood in the tunnel that led to New Mexico State's locker room.

"Then shoot the damn plane down," Camp yelled over the headsets as he arrived at the place where Kazi had been standing.

"Too many people behind it," the FBI field office director said over the radio.

"The plane…that plane has got to come down. That's our bio-weapon," Camp said frantically as he walked in and out of the dignitaries gathered on the field next to the vice chancellor. "I've lost him. Anybody see where he went?" Camp asked to no one in particular.

Neo, the six-year-old Golden Eagle was restless but still sitting on his perch near the vice chancellor's microphone when one of the Alabama State Troopers started to feel the full panic from the FBI over his radio.

The Trooper edged closer to Neo's handler and shielded his eyes from the sun as he tried to follow the path of the P-51 Mustang now making its second loop around the stadium. The Trooper pulled out his service revolver.

"What's the problem?" the handler asked sensing the Trooper's tension after seeing the unholstered gun.

"FBI says that plane's gotta come down now!"

Camp looked over at the Trooper next to the Golden Eagle and then up at the plane circling above the stadium.

"Untie the damn bird!" Camp yelled. The handler

followed the command and released the jesses.

"And from the Class of 1992," the vice chancellor announced completely oblivious to the hysteria from law enforcement around him, "please welcome NFL football legend and Auburn's 1985 Heisman Trophy winner, Bo Jackson."

The crowd went crazy and Camp watched as Neo drew a bead on the intruding P-51 in his aviary that was banking out of the far end zone and heading the length of the field about 50 rows up.

"In the visitor's tunnel. He's standing in the other team's tunnel," a voice said over the radio. Camp looked toward the opposite end zone where he saw Kazi reaching for the extra lever he had mounted on to his remote control. Kazi started to pull it.

Neo tore violently into the side of the P-51, avoiding the propeller on the front. Clutching the plane in his talons, Neo flew back toward his perch and smashed the plane into the turf right in front of the vice chancellor's feet. The eagle's airspace was once again free from threat.

"WAR DAMN EAGLE, WAR DAMN EAGLE," chants erupted as the camera panned up from the broken fuselage of the P-51 Mustang to the smiling face of Bo Jackson who waved to the fans on the field. Neo returned to his perch, and 87,451 fans cheered the incredible show they thought was fully scripted.

Kazi and Camp watched the death grip talons of a 6-year-old Golden Eagle pluck the WARBIRD out of the air and smash it to the turf. Kazi dropped his remote control, flipped the goggles over his head and sprinted for his rental car in the parking lot.

Camp saw the executive navy blue suit and yellow power tie running like frightened prey. Camp's legs started running before his mind gave him permission to chase.

Camp chased Kazi in and out of rows of parked cars. Kazi reached into his pocket, pulled out the rental car key fob and pushed "unlock" from 20 feet away. Headlights blinked as Kazi pulled the door open.

Camp went airborne over the trunk of an adjacent Mazda. His hands slammed Kazi's head into the doorjamb of the front door as his body pinned Kazi's against the Ford Taurus rental. Camp pulled Kazi out of the car and down to the cement in the parking lot of Jordan-Hare Stadium and started to beat his face with relentless punches. Kazi had no upper body strength and couldn't fight back.

"You piece of shit, you're a disgrace to Islam… you're not half the man of Omid."

Alabama State Troopers caught up and pulled Camp off of Kazi whose face was bloody, battered and swollen. Camp kept swinging as the Troopers restrained him and cuffed Kazi.

"Who are you?" Kazi demanded as blood trickled from his nose and the corner of his lip.

"A friend of Omid."

"I do not know an Omid," Kazi said as the Troopers

started to move him.

"Colonel Farid Amir…Iranian Revolutionary Guard," Camp yelled.

"Farid?"

"He was a great man, Kazi…and you are a piece of shit!"

The Alabama State Troopers started to hand Kazi over to the FBI agents who arrived at the scene.

"Do NOT read him Miranda rights…he has no rights! He's an enemy combatant," Camp screamed.

None of them saw Auburn beat New Mexico State University in the Homecoming game.

46

Washington Dulles International Airport
Virginia

Camp made the 750-mile drive along Interstate 85
and 95 up from Auburn, through Atlanta,
Charlotte, Durham and Richmond and along the 495
to the Dulles toll road exit. He arrived at international
baggage claim just minutes after Leslie Raines cleared
customs.

A long embrace and several tender kisses later,
Raines and Camp were in the Defender 90 heading to
Camp's townhouse in Old Town Alexandria. Raines
took note when Camp decided not to go north on 495
toward her apartment in Frederick, Maryland.

"Did the sailor forget that I live north in
Maryland?"

Camp just smiled and kept driving up Interstate 66
toward Arlington and then cut over on the George

Washington Parkway past Reagan National Airport.

Camp opened two bottles of wine as soon as they got inside his townhouse, a bottle of Pinot Gris for Raines and an old vine red zinfandel for himself. After the long international flight, Raines hopped in Camp's shower and emerged with wet hair and wearing one of his large button-down white dress shirts and nothing else.

"You look tired, Camp."

"I'm fine. Went to see a college football game, and I'm a bit exhausted, but thrilled – no energized – to see you, Les."

Camp pulled her close on the couch and kissed her for what seemed like an eternity. The world seemed less crazy when he held Leslie Raines in his arms.

"Have you called your parents since you've been back?"

Camp sighed and confessed.

"No. Mom and Dad don't know I'm back yet. I'll call them tomorrow morning…when *we* wake up."

Raines set her glass of wine down on the coffee table and excused herself.

"No need to change on my account. I think you're looking pretty hot 'as is' colonel," Camp yelled as Raines went back into Camp's bedroom and rifled through her bag. She pulled out two candles left over from her long bath in Lyon, lit them and placed one on each night table. Then she returned to the couch and handed Camp a DVD.

"You need to watch this," Raines said.

"Now? I'm sitting next to the half-dressed woman of my dreams, getting her loaded and delusional with wine, and now I have to watch a DVD?"

Raines kissed him again and caressed his face.

"Yes…now."

Camp feigned protest for another minute or two, but he knew Raines would have her way. It was no point arguing with this woman. He flipped the TV over to AV-1 and the frozen image of his dad, Seabury Campbell, was fixed on the screen with the word PLAY beneath his image.

"My dad? Is he sitting in the milking barn?"

"Push PLAY, Camp."

Camp's iPhone started vibrating on the couch next to him. He picked it up and took a look. He had received a text message from Eileen at Lightner Farms in Gettysburg.

HEY THERE…ARE YOU STATESIDE?

"It's Eileen," he whispered to Raines, "…let me answer quickly."

JUST GOT BACK ON FRIDAY… EXHAUSTED…WILL COME SEE YOU SOON. LOVE YOU!

"Push PLAY, sailor, or I'm going to clobber you over the head," Raines said. "No more interruptions."

Camp pushed the button and grabbed his wine glass. The DVD began.

"Hello   son…this   is   your   daddy…Seabury

Campbell, Senior…that makes you Junior…well, I'm not sure how to start this so, here goes…I've got some bad news…the doctors say I have Alzheimer's…your mom thinks they're probably right, so does Leslie…by the way, son, between us two men…you're a fool if you let that one get away…mom's already been telling the doctors that Leslie's her daughter-in-law so, don't make her a liar, okay? I'm an old man, Junior…the good news is that this disease hit me late…the bad news…they say it'll take me faster…Leslie wanted me to make this damned video so I said yes…God only knows when you'll get back from Vietnam to see this."

Camp's face fell blank as Raines grabbed his hand.

"I'm a proud old Scotsman, Junior…I don't like to share my emotions with anyone, not even your mother…but Alzheimer's gives you a gift that a sudden heart attack can't give…it gives you a few more moments where you can think straight and say all the things you want said."

Raines reached over and leaned her head on Camp's shoulder. She had seen the DVD a hundred times before.

"I am so proud of you, Junior…I love you with all my heart…I know, I was tough on you, pushing you, and pushing you…Son, I was trying to push you to greatness and you got there…I love you, boy…I love your sisters, and they have fine husbands and have given me wonderful grandchildren…but oh, sweet Mother of God how I love my boy…I've never told you this son, and hopefully you won't see this until I'm dead, gone and fertilizing the beans, but…you're my hero. Every night that you were working those 20-hour shifts, trying to save the lives of young soldiers, I stayed awake with you, too, every minute of the day. Ruth called your XO, that Colonel Ferguson, every other damn day. We knew your hours, we knew what you were doing…I was so proud of you. Do you remember those nights when you thought you couldn't move another inch, when the rockets and mortars came flying in, the IEDs kept blowing your buddies up? That's when I prayed for you the most, boy. That's when God gave you the strength to work another shift, another day, do another surgery. That strength from God was His answer to my prayers. You are my hero, son…I have never met a man with more courage or more strength. I am not worthy to be called your daddy…"

Old Seabury started to cry on the video. Raines looked over as tears gushed out of Camp's eyes too.

"Don't cry for me, son. I have lived a long and wonderful life. Your mother was smokin' hot, so that made it easier to endure! They say I might not even know you when you come back from the war. My mind is foggier than it once was…but my heart is as clear as ever. I love you, Seabury Campbell, Junior…I will always love you…you're my boy…you are my hero."

Camp and Raines watched old Sea Bee get off of his milking stool and move to an extreme close up as he fiddled with the camera's buttons.

"How do you turn this damn thing off?" Sea Bee said as the picture finally went black.

Raines threw both of her arms around Camp as he collapsed in her arms.

"I don't know what to say," Camp whispered as Raines held him tightly.

"I didn't know what to do, Camp," Raines whispered back.

Her arms released him and Camp sat up and looked at her tender eyes.

"You were there for me, Les. You stepped in and took care of my family. I don't know what to say."

Raines wiped the tears from Camp's face and stroked his squared chin.

"Are you mad at me? For not telling you?"

Camp closed his eyes and smiled. "Mad? How could I be mad at a woman as selfless as you? A woman who took care of my parents with such incredible and unselfish love; Leslie, I am beyond grateful. I'm in love with you."

Leslie's lower lip started to quiver. Her smile emerged as her tears welled.

"Look at the two of us. We're a mess," Raines said as she reached for Camp's hand. "Tired?"

Camp nodded. Standing up, she took him by the hand. He grabbed his phone as she led him into the bedroom where two vanilla candles were burning on each night table. Camp sat on the edge of the bed as

Leslie pulled the button-down white dress shirt up and over her head. He removed his NAVY t-shirt as she tugged on the running shorts that quickly landed on the bedroom floor. Leslie pressed her body against his and kissed away the tears that soaked his face as they made love.

Lightner Farms
Gettysburg, Pennsylvania

A car pulled up outside of Lightner Farms Bed and Breakfast. It was almost eight o'clock at night, but the lights were still on even though there were no other cars in the parking lot.

The dome light was turned on and as the address on the envelope was verified: Eileen, Lightner Farms, Baltimore Pike, and Gettysburg, Pennsylvania.

The traveler grabbed a bag from the trunk of the car and stepped up to the door and knocked. An attractive woman in her mid-40s walked through the kitchen and turned the porch light on at the side door by the parking lot.

"Can I help you?" Eileen asked as she opened the door and greeted the stranger.

Eileen's face coiled ever so slightly as she looked into the badly disfigured face of another woman who wore a head scarf and was carrying a bag.

"I'm sorry to bother you so late, but I was hoping to rent a room for the night."

"Actually, it's pretty late and I —"

"I'm from Afghanistan. Captain Campbell said you had a beautiful lodge."

Though polite at first, Eileen demonstrated renewed hospitality and warmth now that Camp's name had been dropped. She welcomed the lady into Lightner and got her new guest settled into room number seven and went back downstairs to put a kettle of water on the stove for hot tea.

The guest sat at the long wooden table while Eileen put the tea bags in the porcelain cups on top of the saucers that had once belonged to her grandmother. She carried the tray full of tea, milk and sugar and put them down on the table. Eileen went back to the kitchen and emptied a box of Girl Scout cookies onto an antique white dish.

"Tell me your name," Eileen asked softly.

"Miriam...I was Captain Campbell's interpreter... before the fire."

Eileen looked at the scars on Miriam's face. She was heartbroken. She had seen many burns as an ICU nurse in Texas, but burns on the face were the most dreadful.

"Oh, you poor thing...my heart breaks for you, Miriam."

"Captain Campbell saved my life."

"That doesn't surprise me...he saved hundreds of lives in Iraq."

Miriam took a bite of a cookie and pulled the tea bag out of her cup and squeezed it out.

"Is that your phone?" Miriam said pointing to

Eileen's iPhone on the table.

"Yes, yes it is. Do you need to call someone?"

"I was wondering if Captain Campbell is home yet. I would like to thank him in person…but I'd like to keep it a surprise."

"Well, let's send him a text message on his phone and see if he responds."

"Don't tell him I'm here…I want to surprise him."

Eileen pulled up Camp's last text message, the one he sent after Jane's funeral and before he deployed to Afghanistan.

HEY THERE…ARE YOU STATESIDE?

Eileen showed the message to Miriam and then pressed send. Within seconds the response was received.

JUST GOT BACK ON FRIDAY… EXHAUSTED…WILL COME SEE YOU SOON. LOVE YOU!

Eileen showed the text response to Miriam, and they both smiled.

"Do you have family, Miriam?"

Miriam's eyes welled with tears. Eileen knew that look and reached out to hold her hand.

"My husband was killed after the fire. I do not know about my son. My sister says he was probably killed as well."

"Terrorists?"

Eileen watched as a flash of fire bolted across Miriam's scarred face.

"Oh, yes…terrorists!"

Eileen and Miriam finished their tea, and Miriam was invited to sit in the oversized leather chairs in front of the Civil War era hearth as Eileen took the dishes to the sink. Miriam opened her bag and pulled it back closer to the fireplace.

"After the fire I was taken to Kabul to recuperate. Once I was good to travel, the State Department put me in the SIV, special immigrant visa program for refugees. I landed in Virginia six weeks ago, and they gave me a one bedroom apartment and said I could live in it for six months. Then I would need to find a job and make money to pay for my rent and buy my food. I don't know anyone."

Eileen sat down in the chair next to Miriam.

"Do you have any idea how hard it is to find a job when your face looks like this, Eileen?"

Eileen cringed and felt sad for the Afghan as Miriam stood up and paced behind Eileen and the leather chairs in front of the large fireplace.

"Everything I had was taken from me in Afghanistan. My husband, my son, my friends, my way of life…even my face. The only thing I knew about America was Eileen, on the Baltimore Pike, and her Lightner Farms Bed and Breakfast."

Eileen was touched to the core by Miriam's story. She grabbed a tissue and the blanket from the ottoman to cover her legs.

"But I will make it…I have a second chance now."

Miriam bent down, removed her hijab, and pulled a

bottle of ether out of her bag. She poured a few ounces into the hijab as Eileen started to detect the odor.

"Is that nail polish?" Eileen asked. Miriam ignored her question.

"God has given me the second chance to make things right...and I want to personally thank Captain Campbell for all he did for me."

Miriam lunged at Eileen and covered her face with the hijab that was drenched in ether. Eileen fought her for a few seconds then her grip slipped and her arms fell limp. Eileen was fading but heard Miriam begin to tape her body to the oversized leather chair. She heard Miriam walk to the kitchen and felt a dish rag go into her mouth before she fell completely asleep.

Miriam ran to the table and picked up Eileen's iPhone. The last text from Captain Campbell was up. She typed in the response.

LOVE YOU TOO...JUST WANTED TO SAY GOOD-BYE...MY LIFE IS NOT WORTH IT ANYMORE...TONIGHT I WILL MEET GOD... PEACE BE WITH YOU.

Miriam hit the send button and sat down on the chair next to Eileen. A minute hadn't passed before Eileen's phone started ringing. Miriam answered but said nothing.

47

Old Town Alexandria, Virginia

Raines had fallen fast asleep on Camp's chest after a series of long flights in from Lyon, France. Camp's 1,500 mile round trip "mission" left him sleep-deprived as well. But all he could think about was his father.

"Alzheimer's," his thoughts kept echoing the words his father had spoken.

The vibration from his iPhone startled him. It was another text message from Eileen.

LOVE YOU TOO…JUST WANTED TO SAY GOOD-BYE…MY LIFE IS NOT WORTH IT ANYMORE…TONIGHT I WILL MEET GOD… PEACE BE WITH YOU.

Camp struggled to open his eyes though his mind was still racing. He read the message a second time. He jumped out of bed jolting Raines awake from her deep slumber. He pressed Eileen's speed dial. Eileen's phone was answered, but no one spoke.

"Eileen? Eileen! This is Camp."

Raines threw her shirt back on and walked out into the kitchen where Camp was frantically redialing the number.

"What's going on?" Raines asked through the groggy fog.

"Eileen…good God, Les, she sent me a text and said she's killing herself."

"What?"

"She won't pick up the phone. I gotta drive out there."

"I'll get dressed," Raines said as she ran back to the bedroom.

Lightner Farms
Gettysburg, Pennsylvania

Miriam hung up as soon as Camp called Eileen's phone.

The phone rang again. Miriam connected the call then hung up when Camp spoke. Eileen's phone rang 20 more times in the next 90 minutes. Each time Miriam let the call go to voice mail.

Eileen started to stir so Miriam gave her another fresh shot of ether.

Miriam pulled out the Smith & Wesson Bodyguard 38, a.38 caliber used hand gun she paid a man to purchase for her at a Pawn Shop in Annandale, Virginia and put the gun in her right hand. The revolver was heavy to hold, and though five rounds were chambered, she had not fired a gun since she lived in Afghanistan. Miriam walked to the side door, opened it slightly, and then turned the button in the handle to the locked position. She looked at the clock on the wall in the dining room above the long wooden table. US Navy Captain Campbell should be there soon, and finally she could thank him for his heroics in person.

Camp's Defender 90 drove down the Baltimore Pike at speeds well over the posted limit and turned on to the gravel road leading up to Lightner Farms with emergency lights flashing. The Defender slid through the loose rocks spraying gravel in all directions before coming to a stop next to a visitor's car.

"Should I come in?" Raines asked with grave concern.

"Hang in the car for now…let me see what's going on first," Camp said as he got out. Raines watched through the windshield as he ran to the side door by Eileen's kitchen.

Miriam heard the gravel and the vehicle as it braked for an urgent stop. She got up quickly from the oversized leather chair next to Eileen, walked to the kitchen then went inside Eileen's walk-in pantry next to the side door.

Camp opened the door and slammed it shut behind him then went running into the lodge.

"Eileen!"

Miriam walked out of the pantry behind Camp and

followed him as he ran over to Eileen who stirred when Camp yelled.

The lodge echoed with the thunder of the first gunshot that hit Camp in the back of his left leg. He fell to the ground writhing in pain. He turned to look at the shooter.

Raines jumped out of the car when she heard the sound of gunfire and over to the side door. It was locked.

Miriam walked closer to Camp as the muzzle of her 5-pound .38 smoked from the first round. Camp squinted through the pain and the discharged smoke in the lodge to see the shooter.

"Miriam?"

"Get up…sit in the chair."

Blood was pouring from Camp's wound, but he pulled himself up into the oversized leather chair and next to Eileen who was now somewhat awake, bound and gagged.

"You took away everything I loved Captain Campbell…my husband…my son…my appointed mission…and now my life."

"Your son is alive, Miriam."

"That's a lie."

Raines ran around to the back of the lodge and looked in through the French doors leading off to the patio from the dining room. The doors were locked. But the images she saw were more terrifying than the sound of the gunshot she had heard.

Eileen was taped and bound to the chair. Another woman was holding a gun pointed at Camp's head in the chair next to Eileen. Raines looked for a rock or something to break the glass. Then she remembered the walk with Camp and General Ferguson after Jane's funeral. She sprinted to the tree line even though her legs felt like they were encased in cement. She pressed the button on her phone for illumination and searched tree-to-tree for the birdhouse.

Think woman, where did he put the Browning?

Raines crossed to the other side of the bark chip path, three trees in she saw the birdhouse. Opening the clasp, her heart stopped beating. Reaching in she felt the cold steel of the Browning 9mm wrapped in cobwebs. The magazine clip was in.

God I pray this thing is loaded.

"You took away the ones I loved…so now I'm going to take away the ones you love."

Camp tried to think quickly. His leg was too badly wounded to jump her.

"How did you find us Miriam? I thought we had hidden ourselves more carefully."

Miriam pulled the envelope from the letter Eileen had mailed to Camp at FOB Lightning.

"Mail call makes things very easy," Miriam said as she tossed the envelope on the ground and took a step back. She raised the gun toward Camp's head as he winced.

"I want you to watch her die first. I want you to

feel the same pain you gave me."

Miriam slowly moved her gun toward Eileen whose eyes opened wide with terror.

Gunfire ripped through the lodge again. The second bullet hit Camp high on the right side of his chest. He screamed in pain as shattering glass bounced on the wood floor.

Miriam looked at Camp with genuine surprise as blood pooled and drenched his shirt. Miriam turned toward the sound of falling glass behind her and squinted.

Raines pulled the Browning's trigger a second time. Miriam clutched her throat as the bullet pierced her neck. Her Smith & Wesson 38 fell to the floor first. Miriam's body fell a second later.

Raines kicked through the glass and unlocked the French doors. She ran first to Eileen's landline phone and dialed 9-1-1.

"Shooting with injuries at Lightner Farms, Baltimore Pike," she screamed laying the phone on its side and rushed to Camp as dispatchers heard the chaos at Lightner Farms.

He was struggling to remain conscious.

"Nice…shooting," he gasped trying to breathe.

Raines put immediate pressure on the chest wound with the ether soaked hijab that was lying next to Eileen and pulled Camp's left arm up to hold it in place.

"Pressure Camp. Keep pressing."

Raines grabbed the sewing scissors on the table

between the two leather chairs and started cutting the tape off of Eileen. She reasoned that it was better to have a half-drugged ICU nurse at her side than to wait for an ambulance all alone.

Eileen and Raines managed to get Camp to the floor next to Miriam. They put a pillow beneath his head and tied his belt around his upper thigh. Raines applied pressure to his chest as Eileen kept pulling him back from the unconsciousness his body was desperately trying to find.

The sounds of approaching sirens grew louder.

"Come on Camp, stay with us, stay with us...help is almost here," Eileen pleaded with him. She got up and ran to the kitchen, opened the door and waved frantically to the EMTs as they ran into the lodge.

His heartbeat was weak and faint from the blood loss. The Lightner Farms parking lot was filling with emergency vehicles and flashing red lights. Two firemen rushed in with a stretcher as an EMT got the IV into Camp's arm, a lead onto his heart and an EKG monitor by his head.

"Come on, baby," Raines tried to urge him through hysteria and tears.

"We're losing him," the EMT yelled as he grabbed the portable defibrillator unit.

Camp's eyes were shut.

"Clear!" Nothing happened.

"Clear!" Camp's heart beat reappeared on the screen. They wheeled him out of the lodge and over to the waiting ambulance. Raines got in the back of the ambulance and held Camp's hand.

"I am not letting go of you Seabury Campbell, Junior…DO NOT LET GO OF ME."

The ambulance door closed and entered the Baltimore Pike with full sirens and lights as it raced to the emergency room at Gettysburg Hospital.

EPILOGUE

Islamabad, Pakistan

Dr. Ja'far drove up and parked outside the departures terminal at Islamabad International Airport as baggage handlers for Pakistan Airlines walked up to the car to help with luggage. Ja'far lowered the window.

"No luggage…just carry-on."

Aara was sitting in the back seat. She wore a beautiful Persian gown with sequins and lace. Her hair was covered with an exquisitely decorated hijab.

"I told you there was no reason to panic. We're here two hours before your flight."

Aara breathed a sigh of relief as Dr. Ja'far got out and opened her door. He lowered his head in respect as Aara carried her small bag and walked into the terminal.

She was second in line at the PIA ticket counter.

"Name?"

"Aara Markazi."

"Looks like we have you on the non-stop flight from Islamabad to London's Heathrow."

Aara smiled and nodded.

"Any bags to check?"

"No…just a carry-on."

"This flight features a Boeing 700-300. We have you in an aisle seat. Is that okay?

"I'd prefer a window seat if you have it."

"Let me check…sure, how about 36A. That's a window on the left side of the plane as you face forward."

Aara nodded. Her hands were trembling.

"First time to fly?" the agent asked.

"Yes. Is it a full flight?"

"Pretty full…312 in economy class…all 49 sleeper seats in business are full."

Aara took her boarding pass and made her way to the security lines. Aara removed her hijab and put it in her bag. Then she spoke to the security agent.

"I need to notify you that I am a diabetic. I have two unused syringes, a jet injector, and three vials of insulin."

The security guard thanked her and notified the screener. She walked through the metal detector and emerged on the other side.

"Baggage check on three."

A woman walked up to Aara's bag and picked it up.

"May I do a second screen on your bag?"

"Yes, of course…is there a problem?" Aara said as

her hands continued to tremble.

"Looks like you have some sharps in your bag. Syringes maybe?"

"Yes, I notified the officer that I am a diabetic."

"No problem…I just need to take a look in your bag."

The female security officer opened Aara's bag and looked through it.

"You're fine. Thanks for your patience. You've also been randomly selected for a private body scan by one of our female officers. They close the drapes so it is very private."

The officer pointed Aara over to where a female officer in a hijab was smiling and waving her over. She stepped into the private screening room, and the woman quickly patted down her entire body.

"Thank you and enjoy your flight."

Aara was served lunch an hour into the nearly seven-hour flight from Islamabad to London's Heathrow. After lunch she leaned her head against the fuselage of the PIA jetliner and fell fast asleep.

The captain's voice over the intercom startled her from her nap.

"We're about 45-minutes out of London. This will be your last chance to use the lavatories before I turn on the seat belt sign in final preparation for landing."

A passenger on the aisle let Aara scoot past the empty middle seat and stood up so she could use the restroom. The back of her seat was against the wall of the restroom. She had heard the sucking "whoosh" sound of the toilet flushing a hundred times during lunch and her nap.

Aara pulled out the disposable insulin vial and the pen-like insulin injector jet. She wound up the spring on the injector jet then rotated the dosing dial to its maximum. She placed the jet into the vial adapter and loaded the injector. Aara flushed the toilet, refreshed her lipstick and dabbed a drop of perfume behind each ear.

The lights of England were well within sight as the seat belt sign illuminated.

Aara said a quick prayer. She asked God to bless her younger brother, Kazi, and her grandfather, Qazvin. She was nervous as to what her new future would hold for her. She looked over and noticed that the man on the aisle had fallen back asleep. She closed her eyes and gently rubbed her breasts.

It had been nearly four weeks since Dr. Ja'far had performed the surgery he had learned from an American Army doctor. Her breasts were indeed larger, and more firm. Aara was pleased with that. She realized how smart Dr. Ja'far really was. He assured her that her breast implants would not be detected as she went through the security screening. He was correct. No one realized that her PIP implants were there, let alone filled with PETN, a military grade explosive. The disposable insulin vials were a convenient way to load the ignition liquid.

"Just wind, dial, fill and inject," were Dr. Ja'far's last words. Nothing could be simpler.

Aara was honored to receive this mission from her grandfather, an important role in the revolution, in The Age of the Coming. She held the injector jet over her chest and pressed the button. A spring-trigger mechanism released the gas charge and set in motion a plunger device that delivered the drug, or in this case the ignition, at a very high speed through the skin and into her breast.

The explosion filled the cabin on the flight that was landing in London.

The End

ACKNOWLEDGEMENTS

I'm neither a scientist nor a soldier but both are my heroes. As such, I depended heavily on each for subject matter expertise. My undergraduate studies focused on world religions and journalism and my graduate studies focused on international relations and political science. This story is a work of fiction but many of the events described are "open source" and, unfortunately, were either planned or occurred.

The research science had to be accurate and plausible to be both believable and powerful. I'm indebted to the contributions of those who have dedicated their careers to biomedical research including Robert Baker, Michael Conn, Stacy LeBlanc, Angela Stoyanovich and Katja Tonsky. I am humbled by both the military and biomedical research experience offered by my friend C.D. Many thanks are in order to both Vickie Collins and Bonnie Sutherland for incredible copy-editing, Lisa Baehr for the book layout, Rebekah Lovorn for subject matter advice, and Joe Pittman for his many editorial critiques. I am fortunate to have a great friend and DPS partner in Kent Politsch who has provided so much wisdom and depth over cigars and ale at Shelly's, our writers' lair in Washington, DC. To Michael Stebbins, Cherie Proctor, Liz Hodge, Nahla al Bassam and Katelyn Arthur, I thank each of you for your passion and dedication to our advocacy work at the Foundation for

Biomedical Research. I am especially grateful to Frankie Trull for her continued courage, resilience and support for the worldwide research community.

To my wife of 30 years, Debra, and our sons Andrew, Ian and Oliver, I thank you for your unwavering love and support as I served as a civilian in distant wars and now continue to play in the creative sandbox of my dreams.

During the first half of 2011, I had the distinct honor and privilege to serve alongside America's finest in Afghanistan at a remote Forward Operating Base in Paktya Province called (you guessed it) FOB Lightning. Special thanks to my team of USAF professionals including Maritza Freeland, Eric Craft and Christopher Hummel as well as Ken Stewart who paved the way for our successful mission. I'd also like to acknowledge several of the life-long friendships that I was blessed to forge through our Friday night FOB Lightning Cigar Club; Mike Stany, Christopher Pearson, Mike Motley, Vince Littrell, Bulldog Kelley, Jason Cole, Gabe Mesa and Chris Frey. Jason, thanks for rescuing me from FOB Shank and getting up at 0300 for the Packers–Steelers Super Bowl.

One of the blessings of serving with America's finest during deployments in both Iraq and Afghanistan is the friendships I made with many Muslim brothers. We danced, drank a lifetime supply of hot tea, played chess, smoked hookah pipes, played ping-pong and talked about our children, families, peace, war, Islam and world religions well into many nights. Thank you for sincerely appreciating the sacrifices that were being made by American men and women in uniform and teaching me about the Twelvers, "rational" agendas and reinforcing the notion that the vast majority of Iraqis and Afghans still desire mutual peace and prosperity…inshallah.

The war in Afghanistan was so much different than Iraq. The people were different, the culture was different and the mission was much more complex and daunting. The way that women and teenage girls were treated in Afghanistan (that I observed) was abysmal at best. That must change! From the new recruits and training Afghan journalists; to training my ANA public affairs students and mentoring the Afghan National Army on FOB Thunder; I am grateful for their friendships and patiently teaching me more about Islamic and Afghan culture. And many thanks to Erin Freitag, who supported my mission in Afghanistan, and to the Civilian Expeditionary Workforce at DOD for sending me.

To my brothers in Iraq – Rafed, Mohanned, and Samir – I continue to pray for your safety and that of your wives and children. I will never forget your courage and genuine gratitude.

When I got back from Iraq I co-founded a military charity called No Greater Sacrifice (nogreatersacrifice.org) which provides college scholarship money to children of fallen and severely wounded American veterans. Please check out the website for more information and do all that you can for those who did so much for us.

According to a Congressional Research Service Report for Congress, from the Revolutionary War through the war in Afghanistan, more than 1,249,329 American men and women have been killed from battle or died from battle-related disease in 12 key wars; Revolution (4,435 war deaths), War of 1812 (2,260 war deaths), Mexican-American War (13,283 war deaths), Civil War (617,528 battle and disease deaths), World War I (116,516 war deaths), World War II (405,399 war deaths), Korean War (36,574 war deaths), Vietnam War (58,209 war deaths), Beirut (266 war deaths), Persian Gulf War (382 war deaths), Iraq (4,484 war deaths) and Afghanistan (1,893 war deaths and counting).

Just in the year 2009 alone, we lost 1,683,571 Americans who fought against eight diseases: heart disease (599,413), cancer (567,628), chronic lower respiratory disease (137,353), stroke (128,842), Alzheimer's (79,003), diabetes (68,705), influenza and pneumonia (53,692), and kidney disease (48,935).

I have been blessed to serve in two wars as a civilian alongside America's finest men and women in uniform as they accept the family sacrifices of multiple deployments and courageously fight for freedom. And I have been privileged to work with animal care technicians, veterinary care technicians, facility managers, veterinarians, investigators, biomedical researchers, scientists, professors and executives who fight every day on the front-lines of disease.

All of you are heroes in my book…

IN MEMORIAM

David Allan Taft, MD
Captain, U.S. Navy
1933-2011

Captain David Taft (U.S. Navy, Retired) died while I was serving in Afghanistan and is among the heroic souls now resting in Arlington National Cemetery. Though we shared the same branch of the family tree as cousins, David was 26 years my elder. As such, I did not have much of an impact on his life. But my mother's nephew's courage and service, especially during the Vietnam War, had a profound impact on me as a child. After volunteering for active duty in Vietnam, David worked for 20 years as a general surgeon in Seattle. In 1989, at the age of 56, he re-entered the Navy. He deployed in August of 1990 as part of Desert Shield / Desert Storm and was attached to the 1st Marine Division entering Kuwait as part of Task Force Ripper. David deployed to Somalia in 1992, again serving with the 1st Marine Division. In 2002, he volunteered to go to Afghanistan but mandatory retirement age rules required him to sit down.

Captain David Taft was awarded the Navy Cross in 1967 for valor. The citation read, in part:

"For extraordinary heroism on 27 August 1967 while serving as a surgeon with the 1st Medical Battalion, 1st Marine Division, FMF near Da Nang, Republic of Vietnam, in direct support of combat operations against communist insurgent (Viet Cong) forces. When a seriously wounded casualty with an "armed" 2.75-inch rocket imbedded in his left leg was brought by helicopter to the 1st Medical Battalion, Lieutenant Commander Taft carefully diagnosed the case, concluding that surgical amputation was imperative and time was of the essence. Anticipating that the rocket might detonate at any moment, he immediately supervised the patient's emergency treatment and transfer to the operating room, setting an outstanding example of calmness and courage. He assisted with the administration of spinal anesthesia which necessitated manipulating and positioning the victim several times. Lieutenant Commander Taft cleared the operating room of all personnel with the exception of the patient, himself and a Navy Hospital Corpsman, and then, with complete disregard for his own safety, coolly and competently performed the necessary surgery…"

Semper Fi, David. Fair Winds and Following Seas.